She held her breath as the inevitable moment drew nearer. Their only chance would be if Rufus didn't step outside of the tunnel, but that would take a miracle. David looked prepared to fight, but from the side of a mountain ledge with a giant of a man? That could end up a bigger disaster.

She pushed a pile of rocks aside with her foot and shuffled as far along the ledge as possible so David could step back and they'd be flush against the wall. When they heard Rufus grumbling, she knew he had to be near the end of the tunnel. Her leg muscles tightened. Elisabeth wanted to run, but there was nowhere to go.

He was so close.

Too close.

She dared not look to see if he had walked onto the ledge. He would only need to step outside to see them.

What was that noise?

Hissing?

Elisabeth felt the color drain from her face, and then turned ever so slightly to look at the ground beside her.

She gasped, and the sound of her heartbeat thrashed in her ears. If anyone thought the situation couldn't get any worse, they'd be wrong. Coiled at her feet, next to the dislodged rock, was a snake, looking as startled as Elisabeth. Her mouth fell open, repulsed, but unable to look away from the creature.

"No…no…no…" she whimpered.

Praise for Tammy Lowe

"Tammy Lowe weaves a delightful historical tale in THE SLEEPING GIANT. The time travel element is exciting and properly twisty. The romance is slow building and swoony. I loved traveling back in time with Elisabeth and look forward to her next adventure!"

~*Katie L. Carroll, award-winning author of Elixir Bound*

The Sleeping Giant

by

Tammy Lowe

The Acadian Secret

The Sleeping Giant

Cover Art by *Jennifer Greeff*

The Wild Rose Press, Inc.
PO Box 708
Adams Basin, NY 14410-0708
Visit us at www.thewildrosepress.com

Publishing History
First Edition, 2022
Trade Paperback ISBN 978-1-5092-4502-4
Digital ISBN 978-1-5092-4503-1

The Acadian Secret
Published in the United States of America

Acknowledgments

I have an enormous thank you for Daniella Hunt of Mirabilia Urbis Tours in Rome, Italy.

Daniella, your enthusiasm is contagious, and your seemingly unending knowledge of the ancient world is incredible. Anyone who spends time with you can't help but fall in love with Ancient Rome. You also have my eternal gratitude for all your additional help with those pesky Latin translations. Thank you a million times.

I'd also like to thank Lucia Tizzano in Pompeii, and archeologist, Marisa Ficorella (Rome with Marisa) for bringing to life the ruins I was walking through. You both helped me "see" what everyday life was like in the first century.

Any historical inaccuracies or artistic license in The Sleeping Giant are no reflection upon these incredibly knowledgeable ladies.

Special thanks to my editor, Lea Schizas, who works tirelessly. What a joy you are. You always manage to make me smile and laugh, rather than pull my hair out. You're the perfect teacher.

And last, but certainly not least, special thanks to my husband, Gord. Thank you for letting me disappear into my own little world to try and get this story out of my head and onto the page. And...for sweeping me off my feet and across the world whenever I ask in order to see all these far-off, magical places. I am truly blessed to have you in my life.

Oh…and Quinton. Thanks for being you—the most awesome son on the planet and my biggest cheerleader. xxoo

Chapter One

"Tell me an if," the voice called on the wind.

The keys tumbled from her fingers and Elisabeth London glanced behind, aware the source of the phantom cry would never be found. She didn't know where the voice came from, but she knew whose it was.

All around, the air surged with energy, like something was about to begin. Déjà vu pulsed through her veins, and her breath quickened.

Was he back?

Trying to suppress a tight-lipped smile, Elisabeth snatched the keys from her feet and hurried into the foyer. On the wall beside her, a clock shaped like an alpine cabin announced her arrival. The gears shifted, and a bird poked its head out, cuckooing three times. She stepped closer to watch a mechanical man and woman come together and begin their dance to a music-box melody. A moment later, the music stopped and the young lovers were separated. The spell was broken. The tiny couple seemed frozen in time, waiting to be reunited in the future so they could continue their waltz once again.

With a shallow sigh, Elisabeth dumped her jacket and backpack at the door and bent down to pat the orange and white tabby cat circling her feet, meowing for attention.

"Aww, have you missed me since yesterday,

Felis?"

Upstairs, a floorboard squeaked as if someone crept along the hallway.

"*Salve,* Mrs. Waters," she yelled up to the second floor.

"*Salve,*" a voice sang out from the living room straight ahead.

A chill ran up her spine while staring at the top of the polished oak staircase.

Sissi Waters lived alone.

Elisabeth took a deep breath and reminded herself that the noises and shadows in the Victorian mansion often had a life of their own. She scurried into the kitchen to start the kettle and emerged a few minutes later, placed a tray with a tea service and small sandwiches atop a table next to the old woman's chair, and turned on an assortment of lamps scattered around the living room.

Perhaps drawing room would have been a better name for the well-appointed space. Fresh pink roses graced the antique tables and scented the air, silk curtains dressed the windows. A pale gold sofa and French armchairs were positioned atop an Oriental rug. You'd almost expect a butler and footman to waltz into the room at any moment. Mrs. Waters claimed to be a retired teacher, but carried herself with such an air of elegance that Elisabeth was half-convinced she was a long-lost royal; maybe a baroness or even a duchess. At eighty-one, with an appearance that remained as radiant as her personality, it seemed impossible she'd ever lose her sparkle.

"*Quomodo…?*" Elisabeth paused to glance up at the chandelier that vibrated for a moment. "*Quomodo te habes?"*

"Oh, *satis bene."* With a bright smile, the old woman prepared herself a cup of tea. *"Grātias."*

Elisabeth cleared her throat and flopped onto the sofa. Despite the wistful feeling inside the house, it was the perfect after-school job. Sissi Waters paid a generous wage in exchange for companionship in the form of tea, a light meal, and a story. However, the one stipulation was she would only speak in Latin. Although overwhelming at first, the old woman was always patient and kind. She seemed to enjoy having a young protégé, and within five years, Elisabeth was fluent in the language. There may be no practical use for Latin nowadays, but Mrs. Waters emphasized the fact that any knowledge one gained in life is never a waste of time.

"Would you like me to read the next chapter to you?" Elisabeth asked, in Latin of course, while holding up a leather-bound book.

"Heaven knows that's a wonderful story, dear..." She leaned forward in the armchair to hand over a different book. "But let's start this one today. It's about Pompeii."

"Pompeii?" Elisabeth's swinging foot went still, and she glanced out into the hallway when the front staircase creaked. "Refresh my memory."

Sissi placed a hand over her heart and gasped. "How can anyone as clever as you forget about Pompeii?" she asked with a playful wink. "Two thousand years ago, a volcano erupted with such force that it buried an entire Roman city, and its citizens, beneath a mountain of ash. Within twenty-four hours not a trace of Pompeii remained."

Elisabeth leaned in closer. Mrs. Waters had the sweetest voice and one could imagine how she must have been as a young teacher, enchanting students with every word she spoke.

"The people believed Mount Vesuvius to be nothing more than a mountain. When it began to erupt, they didn't understand what was happening. Many assumed the gods were angry and didn't even try to flee the city until it was too late."

Elisabeth's mouth fell open. "Seriously?"

"Very." Mrs. Waters took a sip of tea. "For years it was thought the people suffocated from the volcanic ash and toxic gas, but some studies suggest they were cooked with the intense wave of heat."

"That's horrible."

Sissi closed her eyes as if recalling a distant memory. "At least death came in a matter of seconds."

Elisabeth groaned. It might have been fast, but it sounded horrific.

"The volcanic ash that covered the city hardened over time, and the bodies trapped within decomposed, leaving behind what was basically…a mold. After Pompeii was rediscovered, someone had the brilliant idea of filling these molds with plaster. The results were life-like statues of the people who died that day; their agonizing final moments preserved forever."

When Elisabeth let out a spontaneous laugh, Mrs. Waters raised her eyebrows.

"Sorry. I know I shouldn't laugh, but that's totally cool. Gruesome, but cool."

With a nod and a shallow sigh, she continued. "Pompeii became…"

A door closed in the distance.

Elisabeth's hands flew to her chest when Sissi glanced out into the hallway. "You heard that too?"

"It's nothing but the wind, dear. You're awfully jumpy today."

"It's just...it sounded more like the front door."

"Well, I suppose my secret is out now." The old woman chuckled while adjusting the silk scarf around her neck. "That was my young lover sneaking away."

Elisabeth's mouth fell open, and she burst into laughter.

Mrs. Waters' wrinkled eyes twinkled with mischief as she waved a dismissive hand. "Now, as I was saying, Pompeii became a forgotten legend until the 1700s. Men beginning work on a summer palace for the King of Naples rediscovered the city buried twenty feet beneath them." After taking another sip of tea, she leaned back in her chair. "That's what I love about legends, my dear girl. They are often proven to be quite true, at least in part." The old widow fidgeted with her wedding ring as she spoke. "You can start reading. I know you're going to enjoy this story."

Today, like most other days, Mrs. Waters fell asleep with Felis curled on her lap well before the story ended. Elisabeth hurried back down the hallway to the kitchen, tidied up the dishes, and then tiptoed to the foyer. Pulling her jacket on, she glanced to the second-floor landing while clutching her backpack. The ornate console table at the top of the stairs displayed a vase of fresh pink roses. Always pink roses. With nothing appearing to be out of the ordinary, she let herself out of the enormous house.

After tucking cold fingers into her jacket to keep them warm from the chilly air, Elisabeth shuffled her feet to send fallen leaves dancing around her legs. The moon peeping out from behind a cloud cast a pale light over the colorful houses and shops that lined the route home. Her own house sat adjacent to an inlet on Mahone Bay, where the town's white gazebo hugged the water's edge and overlooked the three old churches that stood united along the main road. Right now, the entire area felt dormant. Although the little Nova Scotia town bustled with life during the summer, the rest of the year it slept. Only when the tourists returned in the spring would it explode with life once again.

Elisabeth grinned at the sight of her dad's car parked in the driveway. That meant he was home for dinner tonight and not stuck working late at the hospital. She ran up the steps to the front door, but stopped when something caught her eye. A streetlight across the road flickered, and a man stood beneath it watching her. He tipped his head in acknowledgment and then walked away. As she watched his familiar, melancholy stride, her hand fell from the handle. She sucked in a quick breath.

He was back.

Elisabeth dropped her school bag on the porch, raced down the stairs and to the edge of the sidewalk, tapping her foot while a lone car rattled past. When the road was clear, she sprinted across the street to the gazebo where he waited.

Could it really be him?

With his back to her, for a moment she felt uncertain. The tattered rags were gone, replaced with a sport coat and jeans.

"David? David Perrier?"

He turned around and a single glance revealed an

aching down to the core.

Elisabeth's breath hitched. "Oh my gosh, it's really you. I have so many questions. For five long years, I've wanted answers and you're my only hope."

"Five long years?" He shook his head and the smallest of smiles appeared on his face before disappearing again. "It's been over three hundred and seventy-five years since you and I last spoke." David sat on the bench and patted the space next to him. "Sit."

Elisabeth couldn't take her eyes off him as she sat. His tidy brown hair was darker than she remembered and a five o'clock shadow hid his fair skin, but those electric blue eyes, framed with thick eyebrows, were recognizable anywhere.

"So it is true. You don't age. You look the same as when I last saw you. Not a day over…nineteen? Twenty?"

David stared at his hands. "Something like that."

Elisabeth wanted to drop to her knees and beg for answers, but stayed composed. "When we last spoke, in Scotland, you said you knew me."

"Like the back of my hand." He turned toward her and took a deep breath. "I know you like the back of my hand."

Flustered by the intensity brimming in his eyes, Elisabeth struggled to speak. "But… how?"

Instead of answering, he gazed out at the sea as the waves lapped against the shore. "I'm so sorry, but you have to go back," he said, breaking the silence.

She swallowed the lump in her throat.

"You're seventeen now. The first time we met, we were seventeen. Remember I told you that you saved my life?" David stood and pulled Elisabeth to her feet, holding both her hands to comfort her. "If…" He paused, and the tiny word hung in the air with an unspoken weight. "If you don't…Elisabeth, you're meant to do this. You have to do this."

"No, I don't. I can't. Do you think I'm some brave, adventurous person? I'm not. This happened to the wrong girl."

His expression softened. "No, it didn't."

"What if something goes wrong again? Don't forget, I was almost burned at the stake." She pulled her hands away and lowered her voice to a whisper. "There are risks when you time travel, you know that, and I won't risk losing my family again. I want to stay here, so please don't ask me to go back."

"If you don't go back, this will all be for naught. All of it."

"I'm sorry." She clutched her stomach. "I can't."

"Elisabeth…" He stopped, as if trying to decide if he should say more, and then held her arms in a firm grasp. "For hundreds of years I have lived, but lived in hell." David's voice choked with emotion. "I'm condemned to this prison of my own making until the day I can make everything right again."

She yanked her arms free from his hold. "I'm sorry, but I'm not going back."

Elisabeth didn't understand her emotions. David Perrier was little more than a stranger, so why was her heart torn into a million pieces?

He seemed drained of all life as he ran his hands through his hair while staring at the heavens, searching for strength. He then reached inside his jacket and pulled out a tattered photograph. "This…" David took a deep, pained breath and closed his eyes for a moment.

"This picture was taken six hundred years ago."

She covered her face with both hands and shook her head.

"You need to go back. You've spent years preparing for it."

"Preparing for it? What do you mean?" Elisabeth snatched the picture from his hand and noticed he struggled to hold back tears, causing her own eyes to well up.

He muttered something inaudible and then began to walk away.

"Wait. I...this is going to sound crazy, but I thought I heard you this afternoon."

His posture stiffened, and he turned around.

"It wasn't out loud. It was more...supernatural. I heard you inside my head." Did she really just say that out loud? Elisabeth cleared her throat and shuffled her feet. "I don't remember exactly what you said. It didn't make sense."

"Tell me an if?"

Her head jerked back. "Yes, that's it, but...?"

David squeezed his eyes shut and nodded. Elisabeth saw his hands clench into fists before he turned and walked away. Nothing else was said.

Trembling, she remained in the gazebo and watched him disappear down the street. The ocean waves grew louder, pounding in her ears, until it was the only sound she could hear.

Five years ago, Elisabeth made a promise to herself that she'd never time travel again. Struggling to remain composed, she couldn't understand why these brief encounters with David Perrier always left her on the verge of tears. Not about to let some melodramatic guy she hardly knew change her mind, she perched on the edge of the bench and glanced down at the photograph. Faded beyond recognition, only a small section of it remained discernable, but it spoke volumes. Her chin lowered to her chest, her hand went limp, and the picture fell to the ground.

"God help me."

Elisabeth knew she had to go back.

****

"Dinner's almost ready."

"Okay, thanks, Mom. Are we having lasagna?"

"Yep."

"Smells good," Elisabeth shouted downstairs before reaching into the back of her closet to grab a box concealed under a pile of stuffed animals. Not even Mom and Dad knew her secret. Removing a stack of folded clothing, the treasures tucked beneath brought bittersweet memories flooding to the forefront: a handwritten note, a jewel encrusted box, and a handkerchief. As long as she lived, she'd always remember that summer in Scotland.

Deep down, Elisabeth knew she was in the middle of a chain of events that couldn't be broken, for they had already happened. Time is an odd thing, especially when you have a quartz crystal necklace that enabled you to manipulate the fourth dimension. Scientists say quartz crystal watches keep such accurate time. Ha! If they only knew. Elisabeth had to return to the seventeenth century and her life in the Scottish highlands. She had to help David because somehow their lives were intertwined.

She ran a shaky hand along skirts that had seen both jail time and a battlefield, the period clothing needed to be worn to blend in. Elisabeth's shoulders tensed as she pulled the leine over her head, surprised the white undergarment still fit. With a frown, she tossed the stay aside, refusing to wear anything that resembled a corset. Both the petticoats and skirts barely reached her ankles, but she managed to tie them around her waist, layering one over the other. An apron went on next, followed by a thin brown jacket with cuffs now ending well above her wrists. The neckerchief and vest completed the ill-fitting ensemble, except for the shoes, last worn when she was twelve years old. Any attempt to squeeze into them would be as successful as Cinderella's step-sisters trying to squish their big feet into the tiny glass slipper. A pair of black ballet flats tucked in the closet looked somewhat inconspicuous so she grabbed those instead.

Standing in front of the mirror, she scrunched up the jacket sleeves so they didn't look so short. Elisabeth swallowed a lump in her throat and tried to remain calm, but the fear in her dark eyes reflected back as she tried to push away the memory of her witch trial.

Focus.

No obvious make-up, nail polish, or anything else modern, she brushed her long brown hair back into a ponytail and tied it with a red ribbon. It had been five years, but if everything went according to plan, Elisabeth would end up where she was last; in the year 1652, in Stonehaven, Scotland. As soon as she reached the safety of Castle Ealasaid, her friends would find her something better fitting to wear.

With hesitant steps, she walked to the dresser and fished the necklace out of the jewelry box. Her hands shook when she slipped the simple gold chain over her head. Holding the strawberry-sized quartz crystal pendant, Elisabeth closed her eyes and thought of David. After saving his life, she'd come right back home.

The world around her turned to darkness, and she was falling…falling.

Chapter Two

Elisabeth flinched at the strange noises. Instead of a thousand seagulls squawking and the thunderous waves of the North Sea crashing into the cliffs below the cottage, she was met with the distant screams of grown men and the smell of damp earth and wet stone. Her hands trembled as her eyes adjusted to the darkness. Brick walls were lit with torches and muffled voices could be heard further along a passageway. A mouse scurried across her shoe and Elisabeth stifled a scream while jumping back.

With a shocked look on his face, a dark-haired young man popped his head out from the shadows and clasped his hand over her mouth. "By the gods, out of thin air you appear?" His face turned ashen. "Do not make a sound."

He spoke to her in Latin.

Wide-eyed, Elisabeth nodded, and the man removed his hand from her mouth, pulling her back with him into the shadows, across from a cell where a prisoner paced behind the bars.

"Wait here." He walked a few steps away and Elisabeth noticed he was dressed in a knee-length tunic with sandals.

"Cato? Is that you?" the prisoner whispered, also in Latin.

"Yes, it is me."

"I cannot believe you are here." His voice rose in pitch. "Nor can I believe my bad luck. Death in the arena?" He clutched the metal bars and began to yell. "DEATH IN THE ARENA?"

Elisabeth's nails bit into her palms and she cursed under her breath. If this was Ancient Rome she'd kill David herself.

The inmate pressed his face against the cell door and a sunbeam from a tiny window lit up his features. When he pushed a wave of brown hair off his forehead, Elisabeth's hands flew to her chest. She'd recognize those blue eyes anywhere.

This can't be happening.

She let out a dejected sigh and rushed from the shadows. "David, how do I get you out of there?"

As he stared in confusion, her immersion in Latin now made sense but raised a million other questions. "*You've spent years preparing for it,*" he had said to her in the gazebo.

"David…*quomodo ex illo loco te aufero?*" she asked with a shaky voice.

A slow smile formed on his face when she spoke his language.

Elisabeth stepped closer to the prison cell and then curled both arms over her head as she realized the severity of the situation. "Oh God, tell me you didn't just say death in the arena?"

David's eyes brightened and he reached through the bars, grabbing hold of Elisabeth. "My name is Aquarius, good woman."

She jerked her head back. "Aquarius?"

"I do not know this David of whom you speak, but listen…" He tilted his head toward her and smirked. "If this is a rescue mission, I will repay you handsomely, love."

The other man threw his hands up in the air. "You haven't a bronze *as* to your name."

Elisabeth's heart raced. "Believe me, I am trying to get you out of here…Aquarius." She pulled away from David and ran her hands along the rough stone walls, feeling for anything. "You, what's your name again?"

"Cato."

"Cato, maybe there's a key somewhere. We've got to find a key." She whipped around and glanced at David. "Any chance you know where they're kept?"

He shook his head. "One would assume the guards carry them."

Cato let out a long sigh. "Then, I fear our hopes are in vain."

"I ask you—am I deserving of this?"

"I don't know," Elisabeth snapped while flicking a sticky cobweb off her hand. "What did you do?"

David lowered his chin while raising an eyebrow. "They called me a liar."

"Aquarius, you sold fake jewels."

He crossed his arms and flashed a bemused smile. "Had I known the jewels were fake I would never have sold them for that price."

"You knew they were glass. You crafted them yourself!"

David's mouth dropped. "I assure you, I did not know." He stepped forward and pounded his fists on the bars. "Now get me out of here, friend."

Cato paced back and forth in short spans. "If only I could."

"Then what are you doing here?" David yelled.

"I came…" He cleared his throat. "I came to say goodbye."

Not about to give up, Elisabeth continued to scour the area, looking for anything that might break the lock, until the sound of footsteps scraping over stone startled her.

"I suppose only Jupiter himself can save me now." David's demeanor changed and his voice faltered. "Go. They are coming."

Wide-eyed, Elisabeth turned to look at him.

He stared back with a grave expression. "You do not want to miss the show."

Both hands covered her mouth. "I'm so sorry," she mumbled.

Cato dashed aside and pulled Elisabeth into a dark corner to hide when two burly guards, dressed in red and wearing metal helmets, advanced through the tunnel. She froze, holding her breath while they unlocked the cell door.

"How kind of you to release me. You shall be amply rewarded," David's voice echoed as they frog-marched him down the curved corridor.

"Come," Cato whispered to Elisabeth as he trailed the guards.

Elisabeth watched people lining the passage poke and pull at David as he passed. They stopped where a small crowd waited in front of an iron gate leading to the arena. An old hunchbacked woman, with matted hair and missing teeth, caught David's attention as she ran her boney fingers along his bicep.

"Such a tragedy the beast should devour this arm." With shaky hands, she tucked a red rose through a hole in the fabric of his tunic. "But if the gods smile upon you, you will pass out before the lion devours you."

David looked as if he was about to throw up. "Lion?"

The roar of the crowd filtered down to the tunnel where they waited. Elisabeth brought a trembling hand to her forehead when the gate to the arena opened and the guards stood ready to shove David out into the spotlight. Cato grabbed her arm and ran back through the tunnel and into the spectator stands. Her eyes narrowed while glancing around an amphitheater too small to be the infamous Coliseum. When she caught Cato staring at her strange outfit, he frowned before running up the steps to the top tier. Elisabeth hiked up her skirts and followed, ignoring the glances from people as she raced up the stairs.

They stopped and watched David stumble into the sand. The cheers from the crowd turned to booing, and the back of Elisabeth's throat ached. "Oh dear God, his death sentence is a halftime show?"

"He will put on a good performance. There is none more skilled with a sling than Aquarius."

David found his footing and then raised his arms high above his head in a triumphant stance. He strutted around the arena like a famous gladiator. The spectators jeered and heckled while he paraded in front of them, giving the impression of being unbothered by his fate.

Stopping beneath a section of gilded box seats decorated with colorful frescos, David eyed an important-looking man's daughter for a moment. With a playful grin, he grabbed a braided cord from his belt and held the two ends of it in one hand. He winked at the lady and removed the rose the old woman placed in his tunic, balanced it on a flat pouch in the center of the rope, and whirled it next to him a few times. He then raised his arm over his head and released one end of the cord, which sent the flower floating through the air.

It landed at her feet with exact precision.

The crowd went wild, and David blew the lady a kiss before shooting her father a sly grin. The old man scowled while his daughter hid behind her fan, fluttering it back and forth at great speed.

Elisabeth's heartbeat raced. "What on earth is he doing?"

"Romancing the crowd." With a heavy sigh, Cato shook his head. "Aquarius has never taken himself seriously. I suppose that is what makes him so bloody charming." He crossed his arms over his chest. "But believe me, give him a rock and a sling and he can kill anything."

Elisabeth opened her mouth and then closed it again.

The crowd roared with laughter as David ran a mock victory lap beside the wall, waving his arms in an upward motion to tell the audience to cheer for him. He then flexed his muscles and put on a display of bravado until the growl of a lion echoed through the arena.

A door opened and a large wooden crate was rolled out.

"He may appear unafraid, but I assure you at this very moment Aquarius prays to Jupiter to deliver him from this fate."

David became unsteady on his feet and the crowd grew even wilder. He reached into a leather belt pouch and Elisabeth noticed his shoulders drop.

"No…" Cato turned away and covered his mouth. "Someone at the gate must have emptied his pouch.

Aquarius is unarmed."

A rope pulled the crate door open and David swayed even more. He kicked at the sand in a desperate search for a rock to defend himself with.

Endless seconds seemed to pass while they waited for the lion to emerge and stalk its prey. An eerie silence swept over the arena, and everyone paused in anticipation. Elisabeth buried her face in her hands; not wanting to see or hear any of this. How on earth she supposed to save him? It was far too late for anything to be done.

The entire stadium began laughing again.

Elisabeth gasped and covered her ears. She hated these barbarians. How could they put a man on display to be torn apart by a wild animal?

"By the gods, will you look at that?" Cato reached out to Elisabeth.

She rubbed her arms, struggling to understand what was happening.

A small brown hen poked its head out of the lion crate and then waddled across the sand and over to David— who had fainted. The chicken's head bobbed back and forth, pecking the ground, as he began to regain consciousness.

Elisabeth pressed a hand to her heart and let out a huge sigh.

The man in the gilded box rose, ready to speak. While the people yelled and laughed and booed, David was dragged to his feet by two guards. He shoved them away and stood before the official with his head held high and his legs spread wide.

"You, Gaius Cornelius Aquarius, were convicted of fraud. Your sentence was fair and just for you were deceived, just as you have deceived others. Take this as a lesson. Next time we shall not be so lenient."

The door to the arena opened again. David strutted toward the exit with a thrust-out chest, yet his cheeks burned red while the crowd continued to taunt and throw things at him.

Elisabeth fought back unexpected tears as she turned to glance at Cato. "It's done? Aquarius is safe?"

A slow smile formed on his face as he nodded.

For the first time, she managed to get a good look at Cato. His dark brown hair was cropped short and he had an olive complexion, high cheekbones, and a square jaw. Although muscular and handsome, when he smiled his left canine tooth was chipped, making him look like a big, dumb jock. Almost, but not quite, because the way he crossed his arms over his chest and squinted his eyes suggested the opposite. Elisabeth would bet any money Cato was an intelligent and deep thinker. His appearance and body language contradicted one another. Dental imperfection aside, if you put him in modern clothes, Elisabeth had no doubt her girlfriends at school would go crazy over him.

"Well…uh…I must return to my work. Good day," he said.

"Oh, but…"

With a slight nod, he turned and walked away.

Caught off guard, Elisabeth's muscles tightened. She pushed her sleeves up, determined to find David again. Unsure of what to do next, she followed Cato out of the arena and down a narrow road lined with rows of two-story flats. Fabric awnings blocked out the sun, darkening the street, and the smells of cooking meat and local spices permeated the air. A stray dog wandered ahead, sniffing here and there. Elisabeth fiddled with her skirt while continuing to trail Cato, feeling like a stalker the entire time.

This is crazy. She ran and grabbed hold of his arm. "Wait."

Cato's posture picked up as he turned around.

"Um…I was wondering…" She cleared her throat. "Can you tell me how to find Aquarius?"

With a bark of laughter, he pointed over her shoulder. "He is right behind you."

"Well, look at that." David playfully tugged the ribbon in Elisabeth's hair. "There appears to be a red string tied to her." He then tossed a small rock in the air and caught it again. "I warn you, Cato, do not say a word. Not a word."

Trying to stifle a grin, Cato bobbed his head back and forth and began to do a chicken dance.

David shook his head while dropping the rock into his belt pouch.

"Though you fainted like a little girl, I am relieved you are alive. I can think of no man who'd have been unafraid."

"I was not afraid. I simply blacked out for a moment from lack of food. Do you think they fed me well in there?"

Cato shrugged his shoulders.

"Are you not aware of the hour? Domina will beat you." David stopped and glanced at Elisabeth's strange dress. He leaned in closer with a cheeky smile. "Is that what they are wearing in Rome these days, love?"

Blushing, she nodded. "Yes. It's all the rage." Elisabeth then grinned and lowered her head, knowing how ridiculous she looked in her seventeenth-century skirts.

"I am well aware of the hour," Cato answered as they began walking again. "I am on my way to retrieve my cart."

"You better hurry."

"AQUARIUS!"

Everyone on the crowded street turned to see who the booming voice belonged to.

The color drained from David's face, and he picked up the pace. "It's Rufus."

Elisabeth glanced over her shoulder and saw a giant of a man rushing toward them. His greasy black hair was pulled back in an unkempt manner, and he wore a dark tunic with a rugged brown leather vest laced over top. Standing at least six and a half feet tall, he towered over anyone around him.

"I swear to Jupiter, Aquarius, what did you do this time?" Cato asked while they walked as fast as possible.

"Rufus is sore because I sold him the glass jewels."

"You conned *him*? The slave dealer?" Cato gestured with his head toward the huge man. "Have you gone mad?"

"Possibly. Look, it's not as if I tricked someone who did not deserve it."

"Still, why must you always go looking for trouble?"

"I don't go looking for it." David turned and smiled at Elisabeth. "It usually comes looking for me." He whipped around and, with a dramatic wave of his hand, blew the slave dealer a kiss goodbye before bolting down the street.

Cato extended his arm to stop Elisabeth from

running after him and pointed ahead. Another large man jumped down from an ox-drawn slave wagon and stepped forward, blocking David's path to freedom. Trapped on the narrow street between the giant and his henchman, he had nowhere to run.

Elisabeth gasped when the man unsheathed his sword.

"Do not kill him, Lucius," Rufus screamed as he barreled his way down the street. "I cannot get my money from a corpse."

With a sling in his hand, David took several steps back, reached into his pouch, and then positioned the rock in the middle of his braided cord. He raised his sling to shoulder height, extended one arm, and aimed the rock in front of him. The stance looked similar to how an archer might aim a bow and arrow. "Put down your weapon. I do not wish to hurt you."

Lucius narrowed his eyes.

Elisabeth shook her head in disbelief as she watched David. He might as well have been pointing a shotgun because somehow the effect was just as intimidating.

Lucius gave a nervous laugh, raised his sword, and then charged forward.

In one fluid motion, David extended his arm back and over his shoulder, rotated his sling once, and then released an end of the cord as he lunged forward. A whipping sound resonated in the air and the rock shot out of the sling like a bullet.

Elisabeth's mouth fell open as she watched it knock the sword out of Lucius' hand. The man screamed and grabbed hold of his broken fingers, crying out in pain.

Cato grinned. "Did I not tell you Aquarius is the best slinger? He can hit…" His voice trailed off as they watched Rufus appear from behind and grab David into a chokehold.

"Aquarius, we have a debt to settle." Rufus' wild eyes looked ready to bulge out of their sockets, yet his voice had a calmness to it, which made him even more terrifying.

When he released his grip, David spun around to confront him. "I assure you, Rufus, I will pay you back. I swear to Jupiter, I did not know they weren't real gemstones. On my mother's grave, I will—"

Sucker punched in the stomach, David doubled over, gasping for air as Lucius rushed forward to restrain him.

Elisabeth tensed, and she leaped closer. "Let him go!"

Cato grabbed her arm, yanking her back. "Are you mad? Stay out of it."

Rufus paused to examine Elisabeth. "Your sweetheart defends you, Aquarius."

With a frown, David stared at the ground before he lifted his eyes and scowled at Rufus. "She is not my sweetheart." A slow, adorable grin then spread across his face. "Yet."

Elisabeth's head jerked back, then offered Cato an incredulous look. "Is he *always* like this?" she whispered.

He pressed his lips together to keep from speaking and nodded his head.

The slave dealer cracked his knuckles. "For someone barely a man yet, you seem to have angered so many."

David appeared to brace himself for a beating, but instead was thrown into a wooden cage in the back of the wagon.

"You will work off your debt to me," Rufus said before locking him in and dropping some coins into Lucius' waiting palm.

"Hey! Hey! Let me out of here. I am no slave!" David screamed.

Elisabeth felt lightheaded watching the unfolding scene, trying to figure out her next move.

Chapter Three

Rufus climbed into his wagon and no one in the crowded street paid any care to what had happened. The giant drove past, and his gaze locked onto Elisabeth, sending a shiver up her spine. Her posture slumped while David cursed from his cage before disappearing around a corner. When she turned, Cato was gone. She scoured the crowd and spotted him up the street. With a pounding heart and clenched fists, she ran after him.

"That's it? No reaction? You just…just walk away?" she yelled while following him. "You don't even care that Aquarius was kidnapped?"

"I am powerless to stop Rufus," he said in a too-quiet voice as he continued ahead of her.

"Well, try something, you…you…" Coward is what she wanted to say, but Elisabeth dug her nails into her palms instead. "Don't you care?"

Cato spun around, his face and neck red. "Do I not care?" His raised voice was shaky. "Aquarius was like a brother and the truest friend I had. Though I am a mere slave, he treated me as an equal. Tell me, what chance does a slave have against the slave dealer himself?" His nostrils flared, and he glared at her.

Elisabeth stumbled backward. "I'm sorry, I…I had no idea…"

"Do you not have somewhere to be?" he snapped.

Fighting back tears, she shook her head. Besides

the fact this was Ancient Rome instead of the Scottish Highlands, nothing was turning out as expected. To top it all off, she was dressed for a freaking Renaissance festival.

"Is it your intention to follow me the entire day? Just go. Go now and leave me." He turned and stormed off.

Elisabeth's heart sank as she stood there, alone on the busy street.

About twenty paces ahead, Cato stopped walking. A few moments later, he turned and looked at her through the crowd. As they stared at each other, it was hard to tell who looked more frustrated. Cato shook his head before marching back toward Elisabeth.

"Do you not have somewhere to go?"

"No." Her voice cracked.

"What do they call you?"

"Elisabeth," she whispered. "Elisabeth London."

"Come, Elisabeth London. I must retrieve my cart."

At a loss for words, Elisabeth walked beside Cato as he pulled a wagon filled with water buckets behind him. Row after row of buildings, topped with burnt orange terracotta roof tiles, lined the streets of the bustling town. Shutters thrown wide open from a multitude of shops enticed the crowds of people going about their hectic day to pause and purchase goods from their counter.

Elisabeth's eyes widened in wonder as they passed a small market stand selling beets, figs and truffles. Next door was a butcher shop with dead chickens hanging by their feet from the rafters, followed by a restaurant advertising hot soup and porridge. A huge clay pot arranged with olive branches and adorned with acorns, oak leaves, poppies, and white roses caught Elisabeth's attention. She paused to watch the florist fiddle with a lavish garland lining his counter and took a deep breath to drink in the scent of the fresh flowers. A tavern, a barbershop, a locksmith, someone selling decorative lamps; it was the equivalent of an open-air mall.

An inebriated man staggered out of a doorway and weaved his way toward them, stumbling on the stone curb as he hollered back at his acquaintance. "Next time, the wine is on me, Sennius."

With a bowed head, Cato cleared his throat as he continued to walk straight ahead, pulling his small cart through the mob and toward the drunk. The two seemed to be on a collision course, but before Elisabeth could say anything, Cato crashed into the man and knocked him to the ground. "I am so sorry." He rubbed the back of his neck. "I did not see—"

"Watch where you're going," the drunken stranger grumbled while he shuffled to his feet and straightened his tunic. He swayed for a moment, staring at Elisabeth's outfit while scratching his temple. He then shot her a bewildered glance before continuing on his way.

Elisabeth's mouth fell open when she looked down at the leather coin pouch Cato now held.

"My mistress is stingy with food." With a nervous laugh, he pulled his cart around a corner to count the money. "Wait here." He glanced over his shoulder to see if anyone witnessed the theft, and then ran to a nearby vendor.

"What can I get for you, love," Elisabeth heard the

woman ask him.

"Dates, a wedge of cheese and bread." Cato handed her some coins, grabbed the food, and hurried back to his cart. He stashed a handful of dates away for later and then his eyebrows squished together; staring at Elisabeth while scarfing down his food.

She fidgeted under his watchful eye. "What?"

"Your dress is peculiar."

"Yeah, well, I come a long way from here."

"I know." He leaned in close and whispered, "I know who you are and where you are from."

A jolt pulsed through Elisabeth's body. "You...you do? How?"

"You appeared out of thin air. I am sure of it." Cato looked her up and down and then pointed to the sky. "You are a goddess sent by Jupiter to rescue Aquarius, are you not?"

Elisabeth bit her lip and tried not to laugh. Okay, so he was a little off with his guess. "I swear I'm as human as you."

He stared at her for a few more seconds and then scratched his jaw before grabbing the handle of his cart. "I have to backtrack through the city to collect from the pots I set out this morning. I am behind schedule and must hurry."

"I can help."

Cato shook his head and pointed. "No, the urns outside of that tavern should be full." He walked over and poured the contents into pails in his cart, and placed the pots back against the wall outside the door.

"Halt!" A large soldier marched toward them, frowning while he examined Elisabeth's clothing.

Her leg muscles tightened, ready to run.

"Some more for you," he said before peeing into the urn.

Elisabeth's eyes widened, and she spun around to stare at Cato, using her hand to block the scene.

"*Grātias*." Cato, unfazed, bowed his head and waited for the man to finish urinating.

When the soldier walked away, Cato added it to the rest he had gathered.

"Are you kidding me? You're collecting pee?" Elisabeth asked as the contents of the buckets in his cart slopped back and forth.

"Yes, and Domina will beat me if she discovers I've left the urns outside the taverns."

She shook her head. "Why?"

"Where wine flows the urine is too diluted."

"No, I mean, what do you collect it for in the first place?"

Cato came to a sudden stop. "How else are you supposed to wash clothing?" His brows furrowed and then released as he watched her. "I'll be right back." He pulled his cart of urine through a large open doorway and disappeared inside.

Elisabeth studied the people while waiting for Cato's return. A soldier led a man away by the scruff of his neck, probably for stealing something, and a small group of musicians played instruments for coins. She watched a pregnant woman walk away from a vendor selling honey, and a man with wispy white hair, that stuck out in all directions, walk into a barber shop.

Cato reappeared and waved her inside what seemed to be an ancient type of laundromat with large stone tubs built into the floor. The air smelled of lavender and dirty clothes. As he ushered Elisabeth into a dark alcove in a back corner of the shop, his gaze kept darting toward the exits. "You can sleep in the fullery tonight, but you must be gone by morning. Domina cannot discover you."

They both jumped when a woman's shrill voice rang out. "Cato, in the name of Minerva, what took you so long?"

Cato put an index finger to his lips and then stumbled over his feet as he hurried to his mistress. "I apologize, Domina. I went as fast as I could." He spoke in a carefully controlled tone and stared at his hands to avoid eye contact with his raven-haired owner.

"I went as fast as I could," she repeated, sarcasm dripping from her voice. The petite woman then slapped the side of his head. "You take far too long."

Cato took a slow breath and jabbed his thumbs into his thighs.

"Get back to work, you stupid boy. Where is Avita?" she asked before marching through a large doorway, not waiting for a reply.

With a downward gaze, Cato dumped the urine into one of the square tubs. Once filled, he removed his sandals and climbed in to begin stomping on the clothing. A middle-aged woman joined him. She hiked her dress up, and they stood in the vat of pee, stepping up and down on the clothing, much like the old winemakers did by crushing grapes beneath their feet.

"Here." Cato held out a discreet hand. "These are for you. Take them."

Elisabeth could see the woman's eyes widen and then dart to the doorway.

"Take them. Domina will not know. It's just a handful of dates."

With a nervous smile, she accepted his offering and ate them as fast as possible, hiding the pits in a fold of her smock. She then reached over and squeezed Cato's hand in thanks.

While Elisabeth crouched against the wall and watched them pull the fabric out and drag it to a clean tub of water, Domina marched back into the room.

"Cato, come," she called out as if speaking to an animal.

Standing in the doorway, towering over the woman, was Rufus. Elisabeth did a double-take and adrenaline pumped through her body. David must be nearby.

Cato glanced around uneasily before he climbed out of the large tub and proceeded toward them.

"This is the one I wish to sell."

The slave woman gasped. "Not Cato! Domina, I beg you. This fullery is all he knows."

"Hold your tongue, Avita."

Cato's eyes bulged as he stared at Avita, a look of terror on both their faces.

Rufus grunted and stepped closer, grabbing Cato's cheeks in his beefy hands. "I saw this one earlier."

"What do you mean?" Domina asked, her voice flat.

"With Aquarius." He forced Cato's mouth open to look at his teeth.

"With Aquarius?" She crossed her arms and cursed under her breath.

The slave dealer inspected Cato's trembling hands, and pulled his eyelids up to see the whites of his eyes. He touched his dark hair and inspected his scalp. Elisabeth cringed while Rufus scrutinized every body part.

"I will give you seventy-five *denarii* for him."

"Seventy-five *denarii*? Are you mad? I can sell cattle for at least one hundred a head. He is worth at least the price of a cow."

Elisabeth clasped both hands over her mouth.

Rufus gave a half-hearted shrug. "Look at him. He is too thin."

"He is not too thin. Look at his muscles. Those are the arms of a hard worker. I will not take less than three hundred *denarii*."

"One hundred. I will need to fatten him up before he can be resold." The slave dealer slapped Cato's arm for emphasis.

"Do not attempt that ploy with me, Rufus Leptis. You can clearly see he is in good health and built like a Greek god. If you do not want to give me an honest price, fine. I shall sell him elsewhere. Someone is always in want of an obedient and well-trained slave."

Rufus stared at Cato, trying to decide how to pay the lowest price. "Two hundred, but not a *denarius* more."

Domina seemed to be thinking the offer over. "Fine."

"Come," Rufus demanded after paying for the slave.

Domina made an unhurried exit through the back of the shop. "Get back to work," she warned Avita on her way out.

Cato's chest hitched. "May I retrieve my sandals?" he whispered.

Rufus gave a curt nod.

Wringing her hands quickly, Avita jumped out of

the water. Shaking her head in denial, she ran to Cato and threw her arms around him.

The slave dealer's face was devoid of emotion, yet he stared at the floor and allowed them a brief goodbye.

"Be…" Cato gulped at the air. "Be strong, Mother."

Elisabeth's head jerked back.

With a quivering smile, his mom caressed his face. "My baby. My boy. Be brave and never forget that I will always.…" Avita choked on her words. "I will always…"

Cato kept blinking his eyes to hold back tears. "I love you, Mother…" He paused, struggling to compose himself. "Always."

Elisabeth took deep breaths to try and calm herself.

With slow, deliberate steps toward Cato, Rufus dragged him by the arm, pulling him outside and to the waiting slave wagon.

David began screaming again. "Let me out of here, Rufus! Let me out of here. I am no slave! I swear to Jupiter, if I…"

With the coast clear, Elisabeth ran outside. Her arms dropped to her sides as Rufus drove away with David and Cato, both locked in the cage.

She bent forward, hands on her knees, and closed her eyes. "What am I supposed to do?" she mumbled until the sound of a quiet moan jolted her back to reality. Elisabeth ran to the doorway and over to Avita. "Do you know where Rufus is taking them?" She choked on tears of her own.

"Rome." The slave's shoulders curled over her chest. "He is likely to sell them in Rome."

"Which way are they heading?"

Cato's mother walked as fast as she could onto the street and pointed a thin finger in the direction she wanted Elisabeth to go. "If you make haste, you may arrive at the main road before they do. The slave trader must pass through the city gates." She then looked down at her feet. "Are you going to buy him?"

Elisabeth did a double-take. Too rattled by the question to answer, she turned and rushed down the street, dodging people and carts and fighting her way through the crowds. She passed several wagons, but didn't see the one that carried David and Cato. Arriving at the pedestrian gate in a matter of minutes, she clasped her hands under her chin, hoping she'd made excellent time.

Outside of the city, rolling green hills stretched toward the horizon and dark foliage dotted the landscape. Elisabeth ran a short distance along a road paved with large stones, checking to see if the slave wagon was ahead of her. On the left loomed the edge of a forest. While slowing to catch her breath, she fiddled with her necklace and tucked it beneath her dress to ensure it remained safe. A few more wagons appeared, but none carrying David and Cato. She decided to stay and stake out the area, convinced she had beaten them out of the city.

Turning toward an ominous sound, Elisabeth saw an army of about one hundred soldiers, bright red capes billowing behind them as they marched. A drum issued a melancholy beat and the blasts of a bugle urged them onward. She stepped back from the road and hid amongst the trees, wringing her hands while trying to figure out what to do. She needed to come up with a plan. Fast.

"The fortunes smile upon me today," a deep voice whispered in her ear.

Elisabeth held her breath while taking a step away. Forget finding Rufus; he had just found her.

"You hide from the centurion as well?" he asked.

After spotting the wagon hidden behind a tall, overgrown shrub, she glanced around, unsure of what to do.

"Release them. At once." Elisabeth wished her voice hadn't sounded so squeaky in front of the giant man.

Rufus let out a belly laugh while reaching out to touch her hair.

She slapped his hand away and took a step back.

"The manner in which you dress tells me you are not a Roman. You travel alone?"

"Of course not." Elisabeth took another step back.

"Where is your family?" He leaned on his heels, confident and in control while waving his hand toward the city.

Elisabeth trembled as she took another step back.

"Are they nearby?" Rufus took a relaxed step closer.

"Yes. They are at…at the…"

"The answer is obvious." A twisted smile formed on Rufus' face. "Did no one ever teach you it is unwise for a young woman to travel unaccompanied?"

Without warning, he grabbed her arms, pinning them behind her back. Elisabeth struggled but was no match for him. When she tried to scream his filthy hand covered half her face. She kicked and thrashed her legs, trying in vain to free herself.

Rufus let out a deep, gratifying sigh. "You're a

spirited one."

He carried Elisabeth like a ragdoll, to the wagon where the two oxen hitched to it stood waiting. Rufus unlocked the cage and pushed her in. After locking it again, he waited until the centurion had marched his men over the hill before heading back toward the road. The cart shook and Elisabeth lost her balance, falling over in an ungraceful heap at David's feet. She pounded her fist on the floor of the wagon and let out a dramatic groan.

"Are you ever going to introduce me to your new friend, Cato?" David shot her a sideways glance and sat down. "It appears she has fallen for me."

Elisabeth sneered at him while brushing herself off. This whole mess was his fault.

A slow smile formed on Cato's face and he dropped to his knees. "Her name is Elisabeth. I believe she is a goddess here to rescue us."

"What?" Her mouth fell open. "Wait…no…Cato, I already told you—"

"She protests, yet I know what I saw. This morning, in the arena, she was not there…and then she was."

David raised an eyebrow.

"I swear to Jupiter, Aquarius, she appeared out of thin air. I am sure of it."

"You suffer from delirium."

"I know what I saw." Cato turned to Elisabeth. "Tell me the truth. Are you a goddess from the heavens come to rescue us?"

David rolled his eyes. "Under the present circumstances, she appears to be as mortal as you and I."

"You prayed to Jupiter to lead you out of the arena, did you not?" Cato asked David.

"Perhaps."

"Do you think she's a nymph?"

With a huff, Elisabeth threw her hands up in the air. "I give up."

David slouched against the bars of their cage and paused to examine her. He then bit down on a smile and looked away at the setting sun.

Chapter Four

Elisabeth jolted awake when the wagon hit a bump. An enormous full moon lit up the night sky and a cool breeze blew through their cage. "Was I sleeping long?"

David shook his head.

Her stomach growled, and she massaged her jawbone. She'd been grinding her teeth all day.

"Rufus," David yelled out. "We're not worth a single *denarius* to you if we starve to death."

A short while later, Rufus led his oxen to the side of the road, outside what looked to be an inn or a tavern. He disappeared into the dilapidated building for a few moments before returning.

"Manducare." He unlocked and opened the door to the cage and tossed in some bread and cheese, gave them a bowl of olives, and handed a jug to Cato. "Drink."

"I'm sorry, but this looks disgusting. You call this a meal?" Elisabeth asked in a scathing tone, shocked at her own rudeness.

Startled for a moment, Rufus squinted at her without saying a word before locking the cage and returning to the tavern.

Wide-eyed, David and Cato stared at each other and then burst into laughter.

Elisabeth swiped at tears, trying to hide them. How on earth could they find anything funny while locked in the back of a slave wagon?

"She looks unwell," David said. "Give her something to drink."

Elisabeth took the jug Cato handed her, forced down a big gulp of water, and then bit into the stale bread.

"So, you are Elisabetta, sent from the heavens by Jupiter to rescue us." David folded his arms over his stomach and stared at her. His intense gaze had a way of holding on and not letting go.

Elisabeth forced herself to look away and inspect the lock on the cage door. "Unfortunately, it's nothing like that. Any idea how we can escape from here?"

"Well…" He raised an eyebrow. "Can you control thunderbolts, love?"

"Do I *look* like I can control thunderbolts?"

"Not at all."

"Well, there's your answer."

Cato let out a heavy sigh. "Perhaps she is not a goddess. We are naught but slaves after all."

David raised his voice. "I will never be a slave."

"You were once," Cato mumbled.

"What did you just say to me?"

"You heard me."

"Be careful," Elisabeth warned. "Good friends make even better enemies."

"When I want your opinion, I will ask for it," Cato snapped.

"Don't take your anger out on her."

With an exasperated moan, Elisabeth watched the open door of the inn and noticed the people inside getting drunker and rowdier. At one point, Rufus stumbled over the threshold with a curvaceous woman.

He whispered in her ear while running a clumsy finger along the neckline of her dress, and then she took his hand and led him back into the building.

It appeared they were staying put for the night.

The young men spread out and made themselves comfortable on the wooden planks. Cato was snoring in a matter of minutes and Elisabeth tried to follow suit, but tossed and turned instead. When she pulled her knees up and leaned back against the bars of the cage, David opened his eyes and the two stared at each other for a long time, holding some unspoken conversation. Elisabeth then looked out into the night, hoping she could get him out of this mess as soon as possible.

An hour or more must have passed. David woke and rubbed his hands over his face before glancing at Elisabeth with a pained expression. "You haven't moved." He shuffled over until he was beside her. "You should sleep."

"I can't." Her voice choked with tears as she leaned over and fell against him. "You don't understand, but I need to get you out of here."

Elisabeth could feel his muscles stiffen. He jerked his head back and gave her a disbelieving look. "It is of no use to think that way." He cleared his throat. "To think of escaping."

"Aquarius, how can you say that?"

"It is life," he said before gazing off into the distance. "It is the law."

"That doesn't make it right."

David let out a deep breath and stared at his hands. They sat in silence. Elisabeth leaned her head back against the bars and closed her eyes. She must have dozed off because the sound of the cage door being rattled awoke her as Rufus fumbled with the keys. She looked at David and her cheeks flushed red when realizing she'd fallen asleep with her head on his shoulder.

"Come with me." The slave dealer slurred his words as he spoke to Elisabeth. "Marcus Cordius wants to look at you."

Her heart raced, and she scurried further back into the cage.

"Rufus, you're a drunken fool." David's posture became rigid and he pushed Elisabeth to safety behind him. "You do not want to sell the girl here. She will make you far more money in Rome."

Rufus opened the door, shoving David aside. He grabbed Elisabeth's ankle, dragging her across the cage.

Eyes bulging with fear, Elisabeth clawed at the floor of the wagon, trying to stop Rufus from pulling her out. There was no set plan, only that she couldn't be separated from David here. She'd never find him again.

David shook his head while rubbing a hand over his heart. He then grimaced and grabbed hold of her wrist. "I've got you!"

As they pulled Elisabeth in opposite directions, her muscles tightened and she arched her back in pain. Rufus cursed under his breath, his huge hands gripping either side of her waist.

"Don't just sit there, Cato!" David roared. "For once in your life, help me."

Wide-eyed, Cato shook his head. He clutched David's arm and tried to pull him to the back of their prison cell. "What are you doing, Aquarius? Stay out of it."

Rufus' body shifted back and forth as he tried to

balance himself and, with one final heave, yanked Elisabeth out of the cage. With a loud grunt, she hit the ground, landing on her tailbone. The giant placed his heavy foot on her stomach, pinning her down while fumbling with the keys to lock the door again. Elisabeth's eyes watered. She dug her nails into the dirt. When the smooth surface of a rock brushed against one palm, she clenched it tight.

The keys stopped jingling. Rufus stepped off of Elisabeth, pulled her up, and shoved her against the bars of the wagon. With a frown, he lurched over, trying to smooth her hair and straighten her skirts. As the slave dealer attempted to make his merchandise more appealing, Elisabeth slipped one hand behind her back and dropped the rock into the cage, hoping David would see it.

"Now…" With a slow motion wave, Rufus gestured toward the inn. "Marcus Cordius wants to look at you."

David let out a heavy sigh as they walked away. "Like I said, you're a drunken fool, Rufus Leptis."

The giant stopped and pinched his lips together.

"I thought you were a better businessman than that, but…apparently not."

Rufus turned around, his head jerking back when he saw David standing in his archer's stance.

Elisabeth held her breath.

The slave dealer let out a booming laugh. "You will never be able…"

With precise movements, David extended his arm back and over his shoulder and then released one end of the cord as he lunged forward. The rock shot out between the bars of the cage and hit Rufus right between the eyes.

Rufus collapsed in a heap on the ground.

Elisabeth scrambled for his keys. "Is he dead?"

"I hope not." David rushed to the front of the cage. "But his head is going to hurt."

She unlocked the door and grabbed David's arm. "Quick, we have to get out of here."

Cato froze. "We'll be fugitives…outlaws…the punishment alone…?"

"Come on," David said in a sharp tone. "What have we got to lose?" He pulled Elisabeth to a run.

Cato took a deep breath. "You've gone too far this time, Aquarius." He then threw his hands up in surrender. "And by the gods, I know I am going to regret this."

They ran over the hills and as far away as possible. When Elisabeth turned around to see if they were being chased, she saw the silhouette of Rufus stumble around the wagon. An angry roar pierced the night air, and a dog started barking.

"Shut up!" someone yelled.

"My slaves have escaped!"

David and Elisabeth tried to catch up to Cato, who had ended up a fair distance ahead of them. They kept running, grateful the full moon was bright enough to light the way. Although they could no longer hear the commotion behind them, torches flickered in the distance now.

"Are you all right?" David asked when Elisabeth slowed down.

"I'm fine." Her voice was quiet as she flinched at every noise.

"We cannot stop," he said with a soothing tone,

guiding her along at a slower pace across the shadowy countryside.

Cato's dark form reappeared and motioned them in another direction. "This way." He stood with his hands on his knees, trying to catch his breath after their bolt for freedom. "We have to keep moving. Rufus will not give up until he finds us."

They marched for hours over the hills, beneath the moonlit sky. Elisabeth grew tired, and David said little.

"I can't believe you knocked that giant out cold with a little rock. You suit your name, David." The moment the words left her lips, she realized her mistake.

"I am Aquarius." He turned around to face her, his voice filled with wonder. "And that is not the first time you have called me that."

"I meant to say, you reminded me of David, like from David and Goliath."

"I am not familiar…"

"You've never heard of David and Goliath?" Elisabeth slowed down to re-tie her ponytail with the red ribbon. "It's a really famous story."

He gave her a half-hearted shrug. "No, but I do agree David would be an improvement upon my given name."

"What's wrong with your name? Aquarius seems like a fine Roman name."

He grabbed her hand, forcing her to quicken the pace. "Tell me your David story."

"Well, a long time ago there was this huge soldier called Goliath. He was basically untouchable. Goliath would yell to the armies of Israel that if someone won a fight with him, he'd let their whole army win. However, everyone was afraid to fight him. Finally, this young shepherd named David comes by. He goes down to the river, picks up a bunch of rocks, and starts walking toward Goliath saying he will fight him. The giant laughs, but David takes aim and throws his rock—"

"Let me guess." He tilted his body closer and whispered. "David hit the giant right between the eyes."

"Yes." Elisabeth nodded for emphasis. "He killed the giant."

David smiled while staring at her in the darkness. "How can you know nothing of slingers?"

Elisabeth's eyebrows squished together. "Huh?"

"Most shepherds are skilled with the sling."

"Really?"

"What better weapon to fight off wild animals, as well as direct a straying sheep?"

Elisabeth shrugged.

He let out a deep, gratifying sigh. "With my slings, I can wound, not just an opponent's head, but any feature on his ugly face. I can also outrange any archer with just as much accuracy."

"You're telling me that a rock and that rope you use are just as effective as a bow and arrow?"

David chuckled. "Yes, that's what I am telling you. Perhaps your young shepherd was more skilled than you give him credit for," he said while looking over his shoulder.

Elisabeth looked behind to see if Rufus was catching up, but the torches seemed to be getting further and further away. As they continued in silence, she pondered the entire situation. Mrs. Waters had spent five years insisting she learn Latin. That wasn't a coincidence.

"If I ask you a question, will you answer me truthfully?" David asked, interrupting her thoughts.

She cleared her throat. "As truthfully as I can."

"Tell me, are you a goddess from the heavens? Cato said he saw you appear out of thin air. As mad as that sounds, I believe him to be of sound mind. And, of course, there is the manner in which you dress."

"I promise, I'm as human as you."

"I hear water ahead," Cato called back with excitement as he led the way into a forest.

Pressing a hand to her stomach, she took a deep breath. Cato's timing couldn't have been more perfect.

****

By the time they reached the river, they found a small clearing in the woods. The morning sun began to rise and Elisabeth collapsed on the shore. "I'm exhausted."

Cato pointed up to a walled city in the distance that could be seen between the trunks of the trees. "We should head there after we rest. We need supplies before we continue."

"I will be back," David called over his shoulder as he marched away.

Cato took a long drink from the river with his cupped hands and sprawled out, face down, on the ground.

When David didn't return after a few minutes, Elisabeth's body tensed. "Aquarius?" she called into the trees as she walked to the edge of the clearing.

No answer, except the tapping of a woodpecker.

Until then, she'd assumed David was having a quick bathroom break.

"He went to that city without us, didn't he?" She

paced back and forth. "I should have gone with him."

"Will you stop pacing?" Cato ordered. "You are distracting me. I need my beauty sleep."

She rubbed the back of her neck. "Aren't you worried?"

"Not in the slightest. Aquarius can take care of himself." He rolled onto his back and put an arm over his eyes to block out the sun.

****

It seemed like hours as Elisabeth awaited David's return. Her arms were clutched around her chest while worst-case scenarios played out in her imagination. She watched and listened, wishing he would come strolling through the trees once again. What could be taking him so long? Would heading to the city herself to look for him help? How would she even know if Rufus had recaptured him?

"Cato, seriously. I'm really worried. He's been gone so long."

"He will be back." Cato tried to sound reassuring, but Elisabeth noticed him squint and watch through the trees as well. "We will not panic…yet."

She stood up and paced. "When should we panic?" She then sat again.

Cato rubbed his face. "All right, if he has not returned by—"

Elisabeth jumped to her feet, exhaling a deep breath. "Oh, thank God. Aquarius is back." She nudged Cato with her foot and ran toward David, trying to stop her hands from trembling. "Don't *ever* do that again."

David's mouth fell open. "Do what?"

"Rufus is hunting for us and you disappear for hours? Thank God you're back. I was worried sick about you. The three of us need to stick to—"

He did a double-take. "You were worried about me?"

"Well of course I was," she said with a dramatic sweep of her arms.

David gave her an incredulous look, fiddled with the sack slung over his broad shoulder, and then tried to suppress an obvious grin.

How had she not realized how attractive he was before? His blue eyes were his distinguishing feature, but Elisabeth was finding his smile to be even more disarming.

He leaned in closer and raised a playful eyebrow. "You do not need to worry about me, love."

"Yeah, I do," Elisabeth muttered, avoiding eye contact as she walked away.

He grabbed her hand to pull her back and held it longer than necessary. "Here." David placed the sack on the ground and took out a canteen. "You must drink something."

"Thank you." Elisabeth snatched the canteen from his hand and, although parched, took a small drink before giving it back to him.

He shook his head while attaching a dagger to his belt. "More."

"I don't want to take it all."

"You need more than that small sip." He stole a glance at her and then tossed a loaf of bread onto Cato's lap. "We must make haste. I've spotted Rufus."

Elisabeth stomped her foot. "That was exactly my point." She took a big gulp of water and handed the canteen back to him.

"All right." David's tone was soft, and he nodded

at Elisabeth while speaking. "I see your point. For now, the three of us stick together at all times."

Cato tore off some bread. "Where did you see Rufus?"

"Heading to the gate." David gestured toward the city. "Here." He handed Elisabeth a bundle of cloth and a pair of sandals and then sat down beside Cato.

With a slow smile, Elisabeth held a long, beige tunic against her, judging its size.

Cato took a drink from the canteen. "Tell me, Aquarius, how did you afford all of this?"

"Consider it borrowed."

"Borrowed?" Cato chuckled. "As always, I envy your nerve. Only you could walk away with an entire sack of things. I'm more…sleight of hand."

Elisabeth turned and gave David an incredulous look. "You stole it?"

He wiped at his mouth, trying not to laugh, and angled his body toward her. "I assure you, it was for a good cause. You need to blend in, and you do not appear very Roman dressed in *that*. It's for your protection, so… you're welcome."

With a small smile, Elisabeth shook her head and rubbed a hand over the rough fabric. "Thank you…I think." She tried not to giggle before disappearing behind a large tree.

Peeling off the layers of her Scottish clothing, she slipped the plain dress over the white leine. The sleeveless tunic fell to the floor, and she tied the belt around her waist, adjusting the length. Tucking the crystal necklace out of sight, Elisabeth gathered her old clothing under one arm and returned to where David and Cato ate their breakfast.

"Much improved," Cato said when she reappeared. "You do not look so peculiar now."

David gazed up at her, cleared his throat, and then looked down at his hands. "Much better."

"Thank you, Aquarius. I feel I can blend in now."

"Good. Now, we head to Rome."

"Isn't Rufus heading to Rome?" Elisabeth asked while putting on the sandals.

"Not without us. He is not likely to arrive in Rome empty-handed. His only purpose to travel there is to bring the goods to market."

Elisabeth rubbed her forehead. "The goods?"

"Us," Cato said as he and David both stood up. "We are the goods."

Elisabeth bared her teeth, a low growl coming from her throat.

"We must get to Ostia." David picked up the sack and started to walk away. "It will take several days, but from there we will cross the Adriatic and then disappear somewhere along the Peninsula of Haemus."

"Aquarius, wait. I think we should stay here until tomorrow morning," she suggested.

David turned around and rolled his eyes.

"No, really. Listen to me for a minute. If Rufus is searching for us in the city, we should let him keep looking and, hopefully, he'll be the one putting the distance between us. He's expecting us to run. Why don't we just hide until he's gone?"

"Perhaps we should stay here," Cato said. "Elisabeth looks exhausted and we have a good camp hidden in these trees."

"I'm not exhausted," she lied, determined to keep up with them. "I just think my idea is..." Elisabeth pursed her lips, trying hard not to smile.

David's eyes widened. "Better?"

She made a funny face. "I didn't say that."

He gave her a knowing look. "But you were going to. You think your idea is better."

Cato nodded in agreement with Elisabeth.

David crossed his arms in front of his chest. "You, my so-called friend, are agreeing with her?"

"Aquarius…" Cato couldn't stop smirking.

"I see I am outnumbered." He pinched the bridge of his nose and squeezed his eyes shut. "Fine. I don't suppose it is the worst idea I have ever heard."

Elisabeth gave David a cheeky grin and then with a dramatic wave of her hand, blew him a kiss goodbye like he'd done to Rufus.

When his mouth fell open, she laughed, turned, and bounced toward the trees, heading further downriver. "I'm going for a short walk to check out the area. I'll be back," Elisabeth hollered over her shoulder.

David yelled after her. "Did we not just agree that the three of us remain together?"

"I'm not disappearing for hours in some city. I'm taking a walk through a few trees. It's completely different."

"I am coming with you," David called out. "It is unsafe."

"I'll be fine."

Cato snorted.

"By the gods, they are fickle creatures, are they not?" she heard David say.

"I heard that, Aquarius," Elisabeth yelled.

"Well, you are," he shouted back.

She walked along the river bank, certain she was

alone. Adjusting her extra clothes under one arm and holding the crystal in her fingers, she closed her eyes and thought of home.

Chapter Five

Elisabeth opened her eyes and heard her mother calling.

"Dinner's ready!"

Crap.

In her own room again, the only thing she wanted to do was sleep.

"Coming."

She threw the old Scottish clothing into her closet, took off the long tunic and sandals, and grabbed a pair of jeans and a t-shirt from the dresser before heading downstairs for lasagna.

The fact that time stood still in one century while she was in another was fascinating. Elisabeth didn't understand how the crystal worked, only that you could jump between timelines. She re-entered at the exact moment in time and space she left. However, there must be starting and ending points because she appeared out of thin air in front of Cato.

"Oh! I can't believe I almost forgot to tell you the most incredible thing happened today." Her dad's eyes sparkled as he took a seat at the dinner table. "The hospital just received several hundred million dollars from an anonymous donor. Some philanthropist wants the entire hospital completely revamped with state-of-the-art equipment, a new wing, the whole nine yards."

Mom's mouth fell open. "You're kidding me."

"I know. It's incredible."

"Why here and not in some big city? That's seems a bit odd."

Dad shrugged his shoulders and took a bite of lasagna. "I don't know, but I'm not complaining."

"Hey." Elisabeth turned her head away to gather her thoughts and then looked back at her father. "Sorry to change the subject, but I was wondering...how did you first meet Mrs. Waters? She used to be a patient of yours, right?"

"No, but she did stop by my office one day to talk. I'll never forget it. As soon as she sat down and looked at me, she burst into tears. Her husband had died, her children were grown, and she had just moved here and was very lonely. Somehow, you came up in conversation."

"Really?"

"Yes. She wondered if you might like an afterschool job. You'd earn money, and she'd have company. It was a win-win situation."

Elisabeth's heartbeat slowed at the thought of Mrs. Waters being all alone in the world like that. "It's impossible not to love her, isn't it?"

Mom nodded. "She is such an elegant and sweet woman. Every time I see her she looks like a million bucks. I swear, that woman has more charm in her baby finger than most people could dream of."

"Oh my gosh, Mom, half the time I can't help but imagine she's some foreign Queen here in hiding."

Her dad laughed and pushed his glasses up. "I can totally picture it. You obviously still like working for her?"

"Oh yeah, yeah, totally. But, you have to admit, the

whole Latin thing is…never mind. Forget I said anything." Elisabeth shrugged and twirled her fork.

Dad's eyebrows drew together. "Are you feeling okay? You look exhausted."

"Yeah, I'm okay. Just really tired. I've got a big history assignment I'm working on." It was sort of true.

"What's it about?" her mother asked.

"Ancient Rome. You guys honeymooned there, didn't you? I mean, in Italy, not in ancient Rome." Elisabeth chuckled at her own joke.

"Yep," her father said. "We went to Venice, Rome and then… "A slight smile formed on his face. "Abby, remember that drive down to the Amalfi coast?"

"How could I ever forget." Elisabeth's mother cocked her head to one side and then started laughing. "Do you remember the crazy traffic in Naples and we couldn't get the rental car to the other side of the road?"

Dad started howling. "We couldn't turn left because the median was in the way, and we couldn't figure out how the heck to end up on the opposite side of the street, no matter where we turned—"

"So you ended up stopping all the traffic and driving right over the median!"

With a smile, Elisabeth shook her head and then excused herself from the dinner table.

****

Although exhausted, sleep wouldn't come. Elisabeth's mind raced, and there was a strange, fluttery feeling in her stomach. She groaned, punched the pillow, and then hopped in the shower to freshen up. She brushed her teeth, tied her hair back with the red ribbon, and put the long tunic back on. A good night's sleep at home would be the smart thing to do, but

Elisabeth was eager to go back.

She held her crystal, thought of him, and everything turned to darkness.

****

Standing beside the riverbank once again, Elisabeth turned around and saw David step behind a tree. She couldn't help but smile. "Aquarius, I see you."

He cleared his throat and walked toward her. "One never knows what lurks in the forest."

"Besides you?"

He lowered his eyes and chuckled before looking up at her with a grin. "Oh, you mock me, do you? I wanted to be assured of your safety." A moment later, he froze, watching something on the ground behind a tree. He then grabbed a sling from his belt, a rock from his pouch, and shot whatever he was looking at.

She held her arms tight to her body. "Oh God, what did you just kill?"

"You don't want…" David stopped mid-sentence and gave her a bewildered stare. He turned to look behind and then marched right up to her. "You were just holding your old clothing."

"No, I wasn't." Elisabeth shook her head, knowing full well the clothes were in her bedroom at home now. "No, they're at the camp still."

"I swear to Jupiter…" With a smirk, David walked around her slowly. "Are you telling me they did not vanish before my eyes?" He cocked his head and raised an eyebrow.

Elisabeth bit her lip and flopped down on the ground, trying to think of something to say. "A little cool out tonight, isn't it?"

With a wide stance, he crossed his arms in front of

57

his chest. "Changing the subject, are you?"

"Yes."

"In that case…" He took off his sandals. "There is a storm brewing."

"There's not a cloud in sight." Elisabeth pointed to the heavens.

"Trust me. It will storm tomorrow. Now, close your eyes." He gave her a mischievous grin. "Or… not."

"What? Why?" she asked while covering her face with both hands.

A moment later, there was a splash and Elisabeth looked up to find David in the river, his tunic at the water's edge.

Her cheeks flushed red as she laughed. "What's the water like?"

"Freezing. I'm coming out," he warned as Elisabeth turned around to give him privacy.

Clean and dressed, he sat beside her and dropped a handful of rocks that he'd gathered from the edge of the river into his leather pouch.

Elisabeth stood up. "I guess we should go back now. Cato will wonder where we are."

"Not yet." David reached up and pulled her back down beside him.

Elisabeth held her breath.

He shifted back and forth, looking uncomfortable about something. "Tell me an if?"

Her posture perked up and she leaned in closer. "Tell you an if? I don't understand…"

"A secret. Something in confidence. An if."

"A secret? What do you want to know?"

He gave her an easy nod. The answer was obvious.

Elisabeth shook her head. She couldn't tell him the truth. Not yet. "I have no secrets to tell."

His shoulders slumped and he looked away. "I see."

She sat beside him, fidgeting with a twig. "Well, what about you? Why don't you tell me an if?"

David let out a deep breath and then cracked his knuckles. "If I told you I used to be a slave..." He glanced at her, as if to gauge her reaction, before continuing. "Last evening, you asked about my name."

She nodded.

"It was a cruel joke by my mistress."

"What do you mean?"

"Aquarius means water gatherer. I gathered the urine for—"

"Like Cato?"

"Exactly like Cato. We were owned by the same fuller. Raised together close as brothers."

"You were owned by Domina?" Elisabeth gasped and grabbed his arm. "Why is Cato a slave and you're not?"

"My mother died giving birth to me and my father...my father was the fuller."

Her eyes widened, and she touched her throat. "Your mother's master got her pregnant?"

David nodded. "She was a particular favorite of his, resulting in my birth. As you can imagine, Domina, who is barren, took a particular dislike to me."

"Was your father at least kind to you?"

"No, but I have no tale of woe, for when he died a few years ago, he freed me in his will."

"Aquarius...?" With no mother to care for him and no fatherly affection shown to him, she wanted to ask if anyone had *ever* loved him. "Never mind."

He became quiet and lowered his head, but kept his gaze on her. "You're not a slave, are you?"

Elisabeth shook her head.

David sighed and stretched out on the ground, putting his hands behind his head. "Not like me."

"Aquarius, you're not a slave either. Not anymore."

"I half wish I was."

Her mouth fell open. "Why would you say that?"

"I have known no other life. If not a slave, where do I fit in?" His eyes searched hers for an answer.

She stared at him, at a loss for words.

David sat up and leaned in close. "How do you do that?"

"Do what?"

"Drag out these deep, dark ifs."

Butterflies began doing loopy-loops in her stomach. "Aquarius, I don't mean to."

"I cannot explain it, but…" David's tone was uncertain. "I feel as if I have always known you."

Elisabeth slowly nodded her head. She'd felt the same connection the moment she first met him—in Scotland. However, she couldn't tell him that.

He reached out and grabbed her hand. "And look at you—you fit in as much as I do. You are either a witch….or…or a goddess from the heavens." A cocky smile formed on his lips. "And I do not believe you to be a witch," he muttered under his breath as he stared at her.

She snatched her hand back. "You're mistaken."

"Am I?" He leaned in closer, plucked the red ribbon from her ponytail, and raised an eyebrow.

"So…you are a witch?"

"Aquarius…" She tried not to smile.

"I knew you would do me good the first time I saw you. My luck has changed ever since you appeared, out of thin air, beside Cato."

Elisabeth put her hand on his chest and pushed him back. "No, I was lost. You're mistaken."

David shook his head and leaned in even closer, his voice a whisper. "It was very dark, but I saw you from my cell. You appeared out of thin air. I thought I was going mad until Cato said the same thing."

"You are both completely mad." Elisabeth stood up and brushed her dress off. "Now, can I please have my hair ribbon back?"

"You mean this red string?"

"It's not string. It's a ribbon and you can give it back now."

"No." With a smirk, he stuffed it into his belt pouch.

Her face heated, and she marched away. "We need to check on Cato," she called back over her shoulder.

David scrambled to his feet, his eyes gleaming when he caught up to her. "Allow me to lead the way."

Elisabeth's posture relaxed now that he'd stopped asking questions. She smiled back at him. The less people that knew she could time travel, the better, and he had no reason to know yet.

"You have returned." Cato forced a smile as he struggled to ignite a small fire with two sticks.

David flashed a confident grin. "Why don't you ask a certain someone to light that with her mighty powers?"

"Fine." Elisabeth gave a crisp nod and sat down.

"Bring me my thunderbolt."

Of course she had to tell him her secret, her *if* as he called it, but not yet. She sat and watched him run his hands through his hair. "How old are you, Aquarius?"

"Septendecim," he replied. "But soon to be eighteen."

Oh yeah. He already told her that in the gazebo. "Me too. What about you, Cato?"

"I am a year older," he said as a small puff of smoke appeared from his little pile of dried leaves.

Elisabeth felt weighed down while sitting quietly, hands clasped in her lap. Question after question buzzed through her mind. David must think she was cold and heartless for not sharing her secret with him, but what was she supposed to tell him? That she's a time-traveler? What about the fact he somehow becomes immortal and is the one who sent her to the past? Should she mention that he's wandered the earth in torment, condemned to some personal hell for centuries? As she watched him staring down at his hands, he seemed deep in thought.

A cold chill ran up her spine. *Dear God, what on earth happened to you?*

At that moment, as if she had spoken those words aloud, David's eyes looked up and met hers. A million questions of his own were asked in that single glance. Elisabeth swallowed the lump in her throat and looked away, turning her attention to Cato, who was blowing on the smoke and arranging small sticks around a tiny flame. She then curled up on the ground and struggled to keep her eyes open.

****

When Elisabeth awoke, she lay still, listening to

the embers crackle and to Cato speaking in a hushed tone. She took deep breaths, enjoying the musky scent of the campfire. Several hours must have passed, for the sun had set and through the clearing, the night sky lit with countless stars. The wind rustled through the leaves and an owl hooted.

"It is a young man's duty to see the world," a strange voice said. "One learns much when traveling abroad."

Elisabeth rose in surprise and looked across the fire.

A thin old man with a white beard and a dark olive complexion sat cross-legged on the ground. Dressed in light brown robes, he wore a piece of woolen fabric on his head, which draped behind his neck and shoulders, held in place with a cord.

"Ahh, she rises," the stranger called out to Elisabeth in the most exuberant voice.

His bushy eyebrows were darker than his snowy beard and the deep laugh lines etched around his eyes gave his face a unique charm.

"You must be starving," Cato said while taking a bite of something. "Aquarius has caught us a fine meal."

Elisabeth felt a slight chill in the night air and walked around the fire to where David sat eating. He made a spot for her and she took a seat beside him. Trying to be discreet, she leaned over and whispered, "If this man found us, do you think Rufus might too?"

David gave her a reassuring smile and held out a small piece of barbequed meat. He moved closer to answer and, as she tilted her head to hear him better, his lips accidentally brushed the tip of her earlobe, causing goose-bumps to form on the back of her neck. "No, the old man didn't find us. I found him."

Elisabeth looked at him wide-eyed before taking the food he offered and then averted her gaze; aware she was blushing. "This is good," she said while eating the barbequed meat and reaching for more. "What is it? Chicken?"

"Rat." David licked his fingers and reached for another piece.

Wait.

What?

With her mouth full of meat, she froze and felt the color drain from her face.

Did he just say rat?

She jumped to her feet, ran behind a tree, and spit out the meat. Elisabeth then scrambled for the canteen and took huge gulps while they laughed at her distress.

"I just ate a rat?" she shrieked, holding her stomach as she walked back over.

"How can anyone not like rat?" David had a bemused smile. He rubbed her back when she planted herself next to him again. "You said yourself it was good."

Elisabeth wrinkled up her nose in disgust. "You hunted rats?"

He nodded, leaned in close, and then popped another piece of rat meat into his mouth.

"Ugh." She recoiled and groaned. "I don't think I like you anymore," she said with a laugh while swatting at him.

David couldn't stop chuckling as he tried to shield himself from Elisabeth's playful jabs.

"Balinus, are you sure you won't have some?"

Cato asked.

"Thank you, no. I don't partake in eating the flesh of animals." The old man turned to Elisabeth. "I am Balinus." With a giggle, he clasped his hands in front of his chest and then shouted, "How-are-you-this-evening?"

Elisabeth's head jerked back and she grinned. "I'm fine, thank you."

"Fine?"

"I'm good."

"Oh, just good? Not great? Fantastic? Wonderful?"

She shook her head and laughed. "I just ate a rat, remember?"

"Ah, yes." He winked at her.

"I'm Elisabeth." Without thinking, she leaned into David, who immediately put his arm around her shoulders.

"Ee-liz-a-beth." Balinus seemed to be pondering the pronunciation. "I've always thought that to be a pretty name," he decided.

Across the fire, Cato smirked and gave a slow shake of his head at the old man's antics.

Elisabeth nudged David, and he turned to look at her, a relaxed smile on his face as he pulled her in for a hug, kissing the top of her head. Her heartbeat raced, and for a fleeting moment forgot they were runaway slaves.

"That crystal around your neck is quite unique," Balinus said.

Elisabeth tucked the necklace beneath her dress, not realizing she had left it out for others to see. "It's nothing special," she said, hoping he'd change the subject.

Balinus sat forward. "Your friends are almost convinced you are a goddess from the heavens."

"Well, my friends are mistaken," she said with unusual tartness, uncomfortable as the three of them stared at her.

David's arm was still around her, offering a comforting squeeze on her shoulder.

"Perhaps," Balinus cupped his elbow with one hand and tapped his chin with the other. "Yet that crystal gives me reason to pause and wonder if they are not correct. It appears…Atlantean?"

She raised her eyebrows. "Atlantean?" The topic made Elisabeth curious, but nervous. "The lost continent of Atlantis is fiction." She glanced at David, who seemed to hang on her every word.

"Not-according-to-Plato," Balinus said with a sing-song voice while breaking bread and handing her a piece. "Yes, it may be a legend now, but there is an odd thing about legends."

"What is that, old man?" Cato asked.

Elisabeth looked at David again as she answered. "Legends often turn out to be based in truth."

"Exactly right," Balinus said with a bubbly voice. "Do you not love how there is always some form of truth in legends? In fact, in all stories? That is why we love them so much."

"What is this Atlantis you speak of?" Cato asked while reaching for the canteen.

"A large and mighty island nation called Atlantis once flourished on the planet. One day it was there, and then…"—Balinus paused and flicked his hands for dramatic effect—"Poof! The next day it was gone. It vanished into the sea."

Elisabeth's pulse increased when she thought about the story she'd read to Mrs. Waters about the lost city of Pompeii. One day Pompeii was there, the next it lay hidden beneath volcanic ash until it was rediscovered centuries later. She made a mental note to figure out what year she had ended up in. Had Mount Vesuvius erupted yet?

"Did you know the gods once lived in Atlantis?" As Balinus spoke, his voice possessed childlike wonder.

Cato leaned in closer. "The gods lived in Atlantis?"

The old man's joyful attitude was like an infectious virus and his smile was just as contagious.

Elisabeth could feel David's posture perk up.

Balinus nodded and, despite his advanced age, he bounced to his feet, gesturing with his arms as he spoke. "Yes, the gods were able to do great things. Things we could never even dream of. They could send the human voice over great distances. Light and heat could be directed into different buildings by an unseen force.

"By Jupiter, I cannot begin to imagine the powers these gods must have possessed," Cato said with a wide grin.

Elisabeth's jaw dropped as she listened to Balinus explain the technology that the Atlanteans possessed. What he was explaining was not a mystery to her.

"These gods were able to harness the power of the crystal. That is how they powered their vehicles, which traveled by land, flew in the sky and sailed across the sea at remarkable speeds and…."

Balinus was describing things like telephones,

electricity, cars, and airplanes. The advanced technology the Atlanteans were supposed to have possessed were modern conveniences that Elisabeth was quite accustomed to. How could someone like Plato write about these things thousands of years ago?

Balinus' voice weakened when he saw the look on Elisabeth's face. "Oh…do forgive an old man for rambling on."

David caught Balinus' expression change and turned to glance at Elisabeth himself. She pulled away slightly, her heart racing.

"Are you all right?" David asked.

Elisabeth put out her hand to hush him. "No, I mean yes. I'm fine."

"Don't stop," Cato pleaded with Balinus.

The old man stared down at the ground before looking up again. "A wise sage once said; 'He who knows, does not speak. He who speaks, does not know.' I am afraid I speak too much."

"Yet you say nothing," David whispered to Elisabeth.

With a pained expression, she turned to look at him and then lowered her gaze.

"Well…I shall bid you all a good night," Balinus said with a graceful bow.

Cato movcd to a spot he reasoned was comfortable looking and was snoring in seconds. Elisabeth didn't know how they could sleep so well on the cold, hard ground.

"You will be warmer here by the fire," David said as he lay down. She agreed and stretched out on the other side.

The temperature continued to drop. Elisabeth

couldn't go back and get a blanket or a sweater from home. Instead, she closed her eyes and curled up in a ball, shivering.

"You are going to catch your death," she heard David whisper a short while later. "Get in this. It will keep you warmer."

Elisabeth opened her eyes and watched in confusion as he began to tuck her feet into the empty sack. "Aquarius, what on Earth are you doing?"

"I am trying to get you into the sack."

She sat up and gave him an incredulous stare. "Excuse me?"

"You are cold. Get in."

"Oh…" She squeezed her eyes shut; trying desperately not to laugh as she climbed into the empty sack and pulled it up around herself like a sleeping bag.

"It will have to do," he said with a frown while standing over her. "Is that satisfactory?"

She grinned and mimicked him. "Yes, it is satisfactory."

David smirked and shook his head.

Elisabeth curled up again, happy the sack kept her a bit warmer. "Thank you," she whispered, not realizing she'd placed her hand over her heart, and sighed when he bent down and tucked the makeshift blanket around her.

"Good night, *cor*…" He stopped, cleared his throat, and walked back to his spot on the other side of the fire.

She lay in the dark, shaking her head in disbelief, and then a slow smile started to build. Well, he'd just succeeded at getting her into the sack. Elisabeth tried so hard not to laugh that she snorted, which made her break into a fit of giggles.

David poked his head up from the other side of the campfire. "Something amuses you?"

"No," she said in a high-pitched voice, then pursed her lips, still trying not to laugh. "Good night."

Chapter Six

The warmth from the rising sun on Elisabeth's face woke her the next morning. Too tired to move, she lay staring at the smoldering remains of their campfire, hoping to have a few more minutes before marching off. The notion of trudging along all day, yet again, did not appeal to her. She'd love nothing more than to head up the hill to the walled city, eat proper food, sleep in a proper bed and have a peaceful day before heading south to Rome. Surely Rufus was searching elsewhere by now. If only she had money, Roman currency, they'd be able to hide within the city walls in comfort, instead of outside in the cold.

While listening to the river splash over rocks, an idea popped into her mind and it filled her with excitement.

David and Cato deserved a fun day and she had the power to make that happen.

Elisabeth yawned and stretched, attempting to wake the others as she crawled out of the sack, literally.

David opened one eye and stared at her, not saying a word.

"I'm sorry. Did I wake you?" She flashed a mischievous grin.

Cato let out a loud groan and turned over.

"I'll be back in a minute. I need to go to the bathroom, so don't follow me this time."

"Do not go beyond that tree," David ordered.

"Well, yes, sir." Elisabeth gave him a melodramatic salute and then walked over and stood behind the tree. She reached for the crystal and thought of home.

****

In her closet, Elisabeth found the item she was looking for. Pulling out the jewel-encrusted box, she inspected the stones, deciding which gem to take. While tracing her finger along the name engraved on the top, *Elisabeth,* her heart skipped a beat as she recalled the night it was discovered in Scotland. Hidden beneath the floor of the old church, David had placed it there for her to find.

David.

Choosing a ruby, she pried it off and held it in her fist. Grabbing the crystal necklace with her other hand, she closed her eyes. The world turned to darkness and she was falling…falling.

****

Looking down at her palm, the ruby sparkled in the sunlight. Elisabeth gave it a thankful squeeze and tucked the crystal necklace into her dress again.

Counting to ten, she took a deep breath before returning to her sleepy friends.

"Aquarius," Elisabeth said with a bark of laughter. "Look what I just found!"

"What is it?" David propped his head up on one hand.

She walked over, sat down beside him, and opened her palm to show off the breathtaking stone.

He raised an eyebrow. "You expect me to believe you just found that?"

Elisabeth nodded.

David squished his brows together and then wiggled them as he gazed at the ruby. With a suppressed grin, he tried to sneak a peek at her from the corner of his eye.

"Will you please stop making those stupidly adorable faces?" she said while trying not to laugh.

A cocky smile spread across his face. "Is it real?"

"What did she find?" Cato called over.

"Of course it's real."

"Is it real?" David asked again, with a firmer voice. "I can see you are up to something." He sat up and tickled her. "There is wickedness in those dark eyes of yours."

She laughed and pushed his hands away. "Come on. Get up, you guys. Let's go eat a good meal and buy some proper supplies."

"What are you going on about?" Cato asked, standing up and yawning.

Elisabeth walked over to show him the gem. He held it in his fingers and scratched his chest while examining it. "Is this one of your glass jewels, Aquarius?"

David reclined against a tree trunk and stretched his legs out in front of him. "No, it's not."

Cato shook his head and handed the ruby back before walking behind a bush to relieve himself. "You mean to tell me you just found it?" he shouted over.

With a snort, David shot Elisabeth a knowing look. "So she claims." His fingers formed a steeple under his chin and he studied her with a smug smile. "Come here."

She pranced back and stood over him, bouncing

from one foot to the other. "Yessss?"

He chuckled and grabbed Elisabeth's hand, pulling her down onto his lap. Her stomach fluttered as his hand rested on the small of her back.

"What?" she said with a soft voice.

David pushed a wayward strand of Elisabeth's hair behind one ear and stared at her, shaking his head in confusion. His voice was quiet when he spoke, intending to keep their conversation private. "What am I supposed to make of you? You say you are as human as Cato and I, yet…I just want to know the truth about you. If only you would tell me."

"I've never lied to you," she whispered. "I'm not a goddess. I am not from the heavens. What does any of that matter, anyway? Who cares? We have a ruby now and shall want for nothing."

"Tell me the truth. Is it real?" he asked again, while running his fingers up and down her back, causing Elisabeth's heart to race.

She looked at him in earnest and nodded. "I brought it from my home. It's real."

David's mouth fell open and he wrapped his arms around her waist like it was the most natural thing to do. "Do you not see what this means?"

"Yes. It means you can eat something other than dry bread and rats, buy some proper supplies…"

He lowered his eyes and chuckled to himself before looking up at her again. "Elisabeth, you are not thinking big enough."

"What?" Her head flinched back. "What do you mean?"

"Don't you see it?"

She glanced elsewhere, as if looking for an answer,

then gasped and flung her arms around David's neck. "Oh my gosh, Aquarius, I've been an idiot."

He sat with his eyes squeezed shut, shaking his head in disbelief.

Cato sauntered over. "What is going on?"

Elisabeth let go of David and turned toward Cato. "This ruby is real. It's mine from home and it will buy your freedom; for both you and Aquarius."

"It's real?" He shuffled back two steps, not saying another word.

David pulled her close again and she could see his eyes were tearing up. "Ignore what I previously said about being a slave," he whispered. "Things have changed. You…you would do that for us?"

Elisabeth stared down at her fingers, which were now somehow intertwined with his. "In a heartbeat."

"There is…" Cato cleared his throat. "There is one problem. I'm not convinced Rufus will believe it is real. Don't forget, Aquarius, your glass jewels got you into this mess."

Oh crap. He was right.

Elisabeth stood up. "It's all right. I've got a plan."

David's eyes narrowed. "Oh, you do, do you?"

"No," she said with a heavy sigh, while pacing back and forth. "But let me think."

After a few minutes, she bit her lip as an idea took shape. She walked over to Balinus and could sense David's eyes were glued to her.

"Balinus? Are you awake?"

He stirred and then sat up, a bright smile somehow still plastered across his face. "Good-morning-to-you." He made it sound like one extra-long word. "How-are-you-today?"

Elisabeth laughed. "Almost as good as you, Balinus. Can I ask you a favor?"

"I do not know. Can you?"

"I have a favor to ask you," she said, rephrasing her question.

"But of course," he replied with a high-pitched voice.

She held out the ruby for him to see.

He clapped his hands together in glee. "Very, very nice."

Elisabeth chuckled and shook her head. "Before you leave, will you take me up to the city and help me exchange this for coins?"

"I would be very, very happy to."

"Wait, no, stop," David hollered over. "You do not go anywhere without either Cato or me."

"Aquarius! Rufus is going to be looking for the three of us. I think I should go to the city with Balinus. He isn't going to be looking for a young lady traveling with her…" She turned and looked at Balinus. "Grandfather?"

The old man tilted his head back and forth a few times as if pondering the idea and then nodded. "Oh, well, alrighty then…granddaughter."

"I will go with Balinus, sell the ruby, and make sure that Rufus is nowhere in sight. If anyone asks, I'm his granddaughter. Once we have the actual coins there will be no dispute about whether the ruby is real or not. If we are captured again, the coins will buy our freedom…a ransom, if you will."

David's nostrils flared. "Elisabeth…"

She planted her feet in a wide stance. "Aquarius, I am leaving with Balinus right now to do that. When

I've decided it's safe, I will come back and get the two of you." She nodded for emphasis to show she was serious.

David jumped to his feet. "You have got to be kidding me!"

Cato started laughing. "Well, she has a good point."

"Be quiet, Cato," he snapped as he stormed over to Elisabeth. "No. I absolutely forbid it."

Her mouth fell open. "Forbid it? Where I come from," she pointed up to the sky, "you don't get to tell me what to do." Ugh—she hadn't meant to play the goddess card.

David was wringing his hands and pacing.

"Look, I'll be fine," she said, her tone more gentle.

He grabbed her arms and pulled her close, whispering frantically, "How do you know we can trust the old man? What if he kills you...or worse?"

"Kills me? He's like what...? Ninety years old?" She raised her eyebrows and tried not to laugh.

"Oh, I am *so* glad to see my distress amuses you." He threw his hands up in defeat. "Fine. Go. I haven't the power to stop you."

Balinus walked over and squeezed David's shoulder. "If you want to worry, that is fine. I would not take that experience from you. A wise sage once said, 'If you try to change it, you will ruin it. Try to hold it, and you will lose it.'"

"What, in the name of Jupiter, does that even mean?" David stormed off and flopped down at the base of a tree, crossing his arms as he cursed under his breath.

Balinus extended his elbow and gave Elisabeth a

wide-eyed look. "Ninety years old?" he whispered, causing her to dissolve into a fit of giggles.

"Sorry," she said while linking an arm with his. "It's the white beard and robes. Do you realize you've got an entire wizard vibe going on?"

He tilted his head to the side. "Wizard?"

"Yes, like a mystical wise man."

"Oh," he said with an uncertain tone as he looked down at his clothing. He then turned away, but she could see he was trying to keep a straight face. "Ninety," he muttered under his breath and then looked back at her. "I'll have you know I am not a day over sixty-four."

****

"The birds are very talkative today," Balinus said as they climbed the steep road to the city. "Silly, I know, but I understand the language of the birds." He offered a knowing grin.

Elisabeth shook her head. "Oh, you do, do you?"

"I understand all languages."

"Well, what are the birds saying?"

"There is a storm coming."

Elisabeth looked up at the cloudless blue sky. "Aquarius said the same thing yesterday. How do the birds know this?"

"Because the scorpions are out." He giggled and pointed to one on the stone wall beside the road, being devoured by a bird.

Elisabeth put her hands up and backed away with a shudder. "Ugh…gross!"

"So, Aquarius encountered a scorpion, did he?"

"I suppose that's what he killed."

"I know this city well. Follow me," the old man

said as they approached the city gate.

"Balinus, why do you help us when you know we are being hunted by a slave dealer?"

"I must go where my inner wisdom leads me," he said as he led her through the city square. "It is my *unfashionable* opinion that all men are born free."

"Me too," Elisabeth said with a heavy sigh. "Me too."

They walked past unadorned brick walls and stopped before an enormous wooden door. Without saying a word, Balinus pointed at a bench to the left of them, indicating Elisabeth should take a seat. He then pounded on the door three times. A moment later, it opened, and he spoke to a man.

"Strabo will be able to give you coins for the ruby," Balinus said when he sat beside Elisabeth.

"What's going on?" she asked as she dropped the gemstone into Balinus' waiting hand.

"Strabo is a good friend. We studied together. When Nero vowed to rid Rome of all philosophers, I went to Alexandria and Strabo came here."

"What? You're a philosopher?"

Balinus shrugged his shoulders and chuckled.

She couldn't help but laugh in return.

"I've advised a few of the Emperors. Nero…well, Nero was just…" He made circles with his finger beside his head indicating that Nero was crazy. Balinus laughed again and patted Elisabeth's knee playfully. "Vespasian though, I do enjoy his company. I am on my way to Rome to see him for our—"

"I apologize you were kept waiting, old friend," a well-dressed, bald man called over from the doorway.

"Ah, wonderful to see you, Strabo," Balinus said as

he walked toward the door with his arms outstretched.

Elisabeth watched them greet each other with a traditional handshake. Strabo then pulled Balinus in closer and gave him a warm hug.

"I didn't know you were traveling this way."

"Nor did I," Balinus said as he followed Strabo through the door. "Nor did I."

****

Elisabeth tapped her foot, waiting for the old men to finish their business. She watched the door and fidgeted while looking around to see if Rufus was nearby. When Balinus did not return for at least forty-five minutes, she began to pace in front of the bench. Finally, after about an hour, he exited the house clutching a wrapped package and a leather pouch.

Elisabeth's posture perked up. "Did he exchange the ruby for you?"

"Yes," Balinus said, but his perma-grin was gone. "I apologize for taking so long. Something quite…unexpected came up."

She leaned in closer. "Is everything all right?"

Balinus nodded and stared down at the package in his arms with a dazed look on his face. "Oh my, I almost forgot…" He dropped the pouch into her hand. "Here are your coins. Strabo gave you a fair price."

"I can't thank you enough. You must take some for yourself, as payment."

"No need," he said, shaking his head.

"No, really, please take some. Save them for a rainy day."

"Well, if you insist." He reached in and took some coins, and then winked at her. "For a rainy day. Come, walk with me. I shall return you to Cato and Aquarius in good time."

She smiled and linked her arm through his. "Thank you again for your help."

"Anytime, my *granddaughter*." He lovingly tapped her hand. "But first, we must talk." He stopped walking and looked at her. "Do you like games?"

"Sure," Elisabeth said, shrugging her shoulders.

"Wonderful!" They started walking again. "Let us play one, shall we? I am going to guess where you are from. All right?"

"Where I am from? Umm…" She let go of his arm and stammered, not sure how to answer.

His eyes smiled as he looked at her. "Your friends half believe you to be a goddess, perhaps sent by Jupiter." He pondered this scenario, not seeming to expect an answer. "But, for some reason, I do not think that is correct." He laughed and then shook his head. "I believe the gods were bigger." He held his arm up high to indicate a taller person.

"I'm just a normal girl," Elisabeth insisted. "I—"

"Yet, you have an Atlantean crystal. I am sure of it. And you seemed to know what I spoke of when I spoke of the technology the gods possessed."

Elisabeth twisted the fabric of her dress as she listened.

"I can't help but think…" He tilted his body closer to her. "Perhaps you are from a faraway land where your people have caught up to the technology of the gods? I've heard it said there is a place like this hidden in the mountains between Serica and Jambudvipa, but I do not believe you come from that part of the world." He touched her arm and smiled. "You are like everyone else, yet at the same time, you are so different."

Elisabeth listened; her posture rigid.

"I have traveled this world far and wide. Many say I am the most traveled man of our time. Perhaps you…perhaps you are simply from…another time? A time more advanced than I can even imagine. So the question becomes not *where* you are from, but *when* you are from, does it not?" His nose wrinkled as he paused to examine her.

Elisabeth's hand flew up to touch her parted lips.

Balinus then nodded his head. "Yes. I thought so. Fear not, for I shall keep your secret. Tell me, Elisabeth, do you believe in coincidences?"

"Um, I'm not sure. Why?" she asked with a shaky voice.

"There is no such thing as a coincidence." He made strong eye contact and spoke in a steady, lower-pitched voice. "Repeat that to me so I know you will never forget it."

"There is no such thing as a coincidence."

"Again."

"There is no such thing as a coincidence." Elisabeth became still. It turned out this cheerful little man was so much more than he appeared to be.

"What century are you from?"

"The twenty-first."

"How exciting!" He squealed with delight, and Elisabeth couldn't help but crack a smile.

"Balinus, what year is it now?"

"The year of the Consulship of Augustus and Vespasianus."

A sudden coldness hit right down to her core. Did they not record the date using numbers yet?

She grabbed onto his arm for support and stared at

him with bulging eyes. "You say there's no such thing as a coincidence, right? What do you know about the city of Pompeii?"

"What is wrong?"

"Balinus, please tell me we're not anywhere near Pompeii?"

"No, no. That is far south of here."

"And it's springtime right now?" She looked around, trying to guess the month.

He nodded.

"Promise me you won't go anywhere near Pompeii this summer," she insisted.

"Oh, I already know. I can read your mind."

Elisabeth rolled her eyes. "I'm serious. Promise me."

"Come, I shall return you to the boys now. Aquarius will be sure I've killed you."

"Or worse," she said with a slight smile.

"Or worse." Balinus chuckled and clasped the package Strabo had given him tight to his chest as he picked up the pace.

****

When they neared the city gate, David burst out of the shadows of a doorway with a theatrical groan. "There you are." He looked at Elisabeth and let out a heavy sigh as Cato fell in line beside him. "It's about time."

Elisabeth crossed both arms over her chest. "What are you doing here? I told you I'd come get you if and when it was safe."

David shook his head. "Do you honestly think I would let—?"

"Aquarius followed the two of you from the

moment you left," Cato interrupted.

Elisabeth raised her voice slightly. "You've been here the whole time? Aquarius, I said—"

Balinus turned to Cato. "Since these two lovebirds are safe in your hands once again, I shall bid you good day."

Cato chuckled and nodded.

Elisabeth looked at Balinus and shook her head. "I assure you, Aquarius and I are just friends, nothing more."

The old man pointed at her while giggling. "If you insist." He patted her arm. "I am sure our paths will cross again, so until then, may the gods be with you." He then turned and headed toward the city gate.

"Balinus, wait." Elisabeth ran after him and gave him a hug goodbye. "I hope our paths do cross again."

"They will." He tapped his finger on the package in his arms. "I am most certain of it."

Chapter Seven

Elisabeth ran back to David and Cato and remembered the leather pouch in her hands. "Look." She held it open so they could see the coins inside it. All the frustration melted away as they stared at the gold and silver pieces.

Cato stood speechless, and David gave a slow shake of his head.

"Here, you hold it, Aquarius." With a grin, she tied the bag shut and tossed it to him.

The blue skies clouded over as they wandered the streets of the city. Elisabeth couldn't help but stare at David. His chin held high with pride, she decided he had the perfect profile.

He turned and caught Elisabeth watching him and shook his head in disbelief at the fortunate turn of events. Hopeful that Rufus was long gone from the area, they had a pouch full of coins and a hilltop town to explore. Things were looking up.

They strolled along the crowded stone sidewalks, past food stalls and merchants selling their wares. Carts and wagons congested the streets, and the bustle of everyday life went on all around them. Elisabeth stopped and watched people order food from an open serving window. It appeared to be a restaurant specializing in sausage.

"Is anyone else hungry?" Cato asked.

Elisabeth nodded as heavy raindrops began to fall. "I am."

A clap of thunder shook the ground, and David leaned his body closer to her. "Did I not tell you there was a storm brewing?"

"It was a scorpion you killed yesterday, wasn't it?"

"Of course not," he said with a wink, and then directed her toward the doorway of the busy tavern to get out of the rain.

A serving counter ran along one side of the room, and rustic tables and stools were scattered throughout the eatery. Elisabeth looked up at the large wagon wheel hanging from the center of the ceiling with six oil lanterns positioned around it, illuminating the dark space like a pre-historic chandelier.

David and Elisabeth followed Cato to a small table, and they all sat down. A few minutes later, an attractive young woman appeared. Curly black hair was piled high atop her head and a leather belt cinched her long green tunic at the waist. Placing her hands on David's shoulders, she leaned into their table.

"What can I get for you?" she asked with a honeyed voice as gold earrings dangled playfully from her earlobes.

"We are starving. How about some bread and…?" David was all smiles as the barmaid stepped beside him, running a finger along his jawline rather suggestively.

Elisabeth crossed both arms in front of her chest while David leaned back with a wide grin.

"Can I bring you boys wine?"

He took a deep breath, savoring the moment, and then stretched his arms out wide. "Why not."

"Anything else?" she purred.

He raised an eyebrow. "What about the sausage?"

"What about it?" The woman leaned forward, flaunting ample cleavage, and gave him a slow smile. "It rivals anything from Lucania," she said before waltzing away.

"Wait!" David shouted.

At that moment, he attempted to sneak a glance at Elisabeth, but she caught his gaze and rolled her eyes.

The barmaid sauntered back over, and David pulled the woman onto his lap.

"What's your name, love?" he asked.

Elisabeth's nails bit into her palms while clenching her fists.

"Severina." She gave him a playful swat before standing back up again.

"Have you a room upstairs we can rent for the night?" he asked while holding onto her hand.

Severina pulled her fingers away and tapped his nose. With a grin, she pointed to a middle-aged cook hard at work behind the bar. "He would *never* approve."

They watched the man chop a piece of wood with an axe and throw the pieces into a fire beneath a large brick oven.

David gave Severina an innocent look. "It is for my friends and I. Tell your father we are passing through and need a place to stay."

She let out a throaty laugh. "Well…for you, sweetheart, anything. I'll show you upstairs as soon as you are ready."

He chuckled under his breath when Severina whispered something in his ear before leaving to get their food.

Elisabeth's jaw dropped. She refused to look at David, who started tapping his feet on the floor. "I see we've just met the village tramp," she mumbled.

Cato couldn't wipe the smirk off his face. "Well now, I quite fancy her. The friendly sort, is she not, Aquarius?"

David plucked at his clothes as if cooling down. "Indeed, she is, Cato."

Elisabeth let out a dramatic groan. What a stupid idea to come into this stupid restaurant. It wasn't even raining anymore. She turned to David and held out her hand. "Give me back the coins. I want to hold them."

He felt the pouch on his belt, and his eyes twinkled with mischief. "They are safer with me."

"No. Give them to me. I need them."

While attempting to suppress an obvious grin, David used his foot to slide her stool further away from him.

"Aquarius…" Elisabeth tried to sound firm, but only managed to cross her arms as her face flushed.

Severina returned with two jugs and three cups and put them on the table. She then gave a little smile over her shoulder before sashaying back to the kitchen.

Without saying a word, David reached for a cup, poured water into it, and then hooked his foot around Elisabeth's stool.

Her mouth fell open, and she stared at him, while Cato chuckled, shaking his head.

David leaned forward, wiggled his eyebrows, and pulled Elisabeth back beside him, placing the cup in front of her.

*"Severina," he muttered to himself. With a long,

low whistle, he then grabbed the jug of wine.

Elisabeth flashed him a fake smile and took a sip of water. She no longer had an appetite.

****

"Follow me," Severina said when they finished their meal, leading the three of them up a wooden staircase and then down a short dark hallway with three doors. She opened the last one to show them a small but quaint room. The walls were a pretty shade of pale red, almost pink, with an ornate blue border painted over top. A wooden-framed bed was pushed against one wall and a small bench against another. Elisabeth would be able to get a good night's sleep here.

"This will be fine," David said. "How much do we owe you?"

After they settled the bill with Severina, she smiled at David. "Let me know if you need *anything*. Toilets are outside, to the right," she added as an afterthought before heading down the stairs.

David walked back into the room to look around again, nodding his head. "Elisabeth can have the bed, and there is enough space on the floor for Cato and I."

Cato nodded in agreement. "I want to go to the bath," he announced. "Are you coming with me, Aquarius?"

Elisabeth looked up in surprise before realizing they were speaking of the infamous Roman baths.

"What about Elisabeth?" David said. "We cannot leave her by herself."

"You two go. I don't mind waiting here for you. I'm tired and would rather sleep anyhow." The truth was, she wanted to go home.

David started to protest.

Cato laughed and pushed him aside. "Elisabeth, lock the door. You are not to let anyone in under *any* circumstance. Understand?"

She nodded.

"She will be fine, Aquarius," he said, before winking at Elisabeth. "Severina will protect her."

Severina.

Severina.

Severina.

She'd scream if someone said that stupid name one more time. With a sullen expression, Elisabeth began to close the door. "I'll be fine," she whispered.

Cato pulled David away and Elisabeth stood silently in the doorway, watching them walk toward the staircase.

"So, Aquarius is in love at last," she heard Cato tease.

David gave him a playful shove into the wall. "Is it that obvious?"

"Yes!" he said with a hearty laugh as they started down the stairs.

Elisabeth's arms dropped to her side, chin trembling.

Severina.

She shut the door, locking it. There was a burning sensation in her chest while looking around the sparse, dark area. There was no desire to be here in this ugly room with its ghastly red and blue walls, its uncomfortable wooden bench, and its horrible bed. Stretching out on the thin, pathetic mattress, Elisabeth held her crystal while thinking of home.

****

Her tense muscles relaxed as she soaked in her own

tub, trying to figure out why she felt angry at David for liking Severina. Who wouldn't? She was pretty, flirty, and perfect if you like older, trampy, loose, unscrupulous, untrustworthy, in-your-face type of women. Elisabeth was obviously not his type since she was none of those things. She wasn't jealous. How could she be? David was her friend, nothing more.

Oh God, I'm falling for him.

She sank low in the tub, slipping beneath the water. Her chest ached so much.

Coming up for air, she wondered if it was better to hide her true feelings, rather than risk losing a friendship. David had somehow become her favorite person in the world. At least now she had part of him, although it wasn't his heart. With a heavy sigh, she thought back to the arena. Even when faced with death, he took the time to flirt with a pretty girl. He was nothing but a typical player. She needed to remember why she was there in the first place; to save his life. The sooner she did that and returned to her reality, the better. No matter how much she enjoyed being in his company, nothing good could come out of an emotional attachment to him, especially when the feelings were one-sided.

She grabbed a towel, climbed out of the bath, and brushed her teeth. After combing her long dark hair, she chose to leave it down for a change. She curled her eyelashes, put on some lip gloss, and slipped into her Roman gown once again.

A thought popped into Elisabeth's mind. Although it was pure evil, she couldn't help but grin at the idea. Throwing a housecoat over her dress, she tiptoed downstairs to the basement to search through the box of

Halloween supplies.

She found dad's old grim reaper costume and carried it back up to her room. Elisabeth ditched the bathrobe before slipping the long black cloak over her tunic. The costume puddled on the ground and when she pulled the hood up, her face was hidden from view. Nobody would know it was her.

She held the crystal and closed her eyes. The world turned to darkness, and she was falling…

****

Back in the rented room, Elisabeth dragged the small bench into the hallway to the top of the crude staircase, pushing it into the corner. As the tavern downstairs tended to a steady stream of customers, she took a seat and leaned back against the wall, closing her eyes while waiting for David and Cato to return.

She hadn't meant to doze off and jumped when she heard their voices. Elisabeth adjusted her costume, double-checking that the hood covered her face while David and Cato climbed the stairs.

"Fortune? I will tell you your fortune," she said in a creaky, disguised voice.

David pushed past her. "We are fine, old woman."

Oh crap.

She stuck her leg out, blocking Cato's path. "What about you?" With a cackling voice, she lifted her hood to reveal her true identity to him.

Cato's mouth dropped. With a huge grin, he nodded at her. "Aquarius, come back here." When he sat down, Elisabeth concealed herself once again. "I have a feeling this fortune teller is worth listening to."

David walked back over, leaned against the wall, and fidgeted with a large blue cloth he was holding.

"Your hand," Elisabeth said to Cato while extending hers.

She stared at his palm, studying it.

"You are a very good friend to one," she said. "Close as brothers."

Cato nodded and looked up at David. "Impressive."

"You run from something."

He nodded again. "The old woman is spot on, is she not, Aquarius?"

No response.

"Be warned that good friends often become great enemies. Never forget your friendship and your brotherly bond. It means much to both of you. More than words can say."

"Thank you, old woman," Cato said as he stood up. "I shall heed your wise words."

"You are next." She motioned toward David without turning her head.

"Go check on Elisabeth. I will be there momentarily," he said as he sat down.

Elisabeth lowered her head, making sure her face was completely hidden, waiting as Cato opened the door to their room, glanced inside, and then closed it again.

Cato cleared his throat. "It seems Elisabeth is sleeping. I will wait downstairs so she is not disturbed." He smirked as he walked past them and climbed back down the narrow staircase.

She held David's hand in hers, palm up, running a finger along what she assumed was his lifeline. Her heartbeat quickened, and she took a calming breath before disguising her voice. "I see a *very* long life ahead of you." She paused, pretending to be entranced by the lines. "You…you have a new friend. This…Elisabeth?"

"Indeed, I do," he said. "And I am quite bewitched by her."

Elisabeth wiggled in her seat, trying to contain the grin that threatened to take over her face. "You ask her too many questions. She doesn't like that. Don't ask her so many questions. All will be revealed to you in time."

David nodded and leaned in closer while Elisabeth stared at his palm.

"This…friend, she is a nice girl, no?"

David shrugged his shoulders and leaned back again. "You tell me. You're the fortune teller."

"True, true." His hand felt so natural in hers as one finger traced along another line.

"Old woman, I have a question for you."

"Hmmm?"

"What does this lady friend think of me? Can you see that? She keeps everything inside and tells me nothing about herself."

Elisabeth squeezed her eyes shut, and with a deep breath, let the words tumble out of her squeaky voice. "You are becoming her favorite person in the world. You….you like this girl?"

"She's all right. She's no Severina though."

Elisabeth didn't mean to squeeze David's hand so hard when he said that. "Yes, yes, Severina." She cringed saying the name. "Oh, I see this…Severina. She is no good for you. No good I tell you."

Elisabeth glanced up ever so slightly to try and catch David's expression. The huge grin plastered across his face spoke volumes.

She hadn't fooled him at all.

"Ugh!" Elisabeth groaned, slapped his hand away and then burst into giggles.

David couldn't stop laughing as he reached over to pull her hood off. "What in the name of Jupiter…"

Although smiling, she tugged the hood back down over her face to hide her flushed cheeks. "Why'd you let me go on if you knew it was me?"

"What?" David slapped his knee as he stood up, still holding the blue fabric in his hand. "And put an end to that performance? Never."

Elisabeth pulled the hood off again and, for the first time, noticed he was dressed in a new tunic. "You look very nice, by the way." She attempted to sound nonchalant while her heart continued to skip beats.

David pulled her up while shaking his head and grinning. "What were you thinking? Wait…" He was moving around, unable to keep still. "You were trying to discover if I have feelings for you." He smirked and raised an eyebrow. "Admit it, love."

"Oh, you flatter yourself too much." She yanked the costume off while walking toward the room, somehow finding the strength to speak without betraying her emotions. "Are you going back downstairs to be with her now?"

David gave her a dazed look. "Her?"

"Severina."

His mouth fell open. "Severina?"

"I know you're…"—Elisabeth paused and rolled her eyes theatrically—"in love with her."

David's head jerked back.

"I heard you and Cato on the way out earlier. Go and have fun. You deserve it. I don't want to cramp your style or anything so just pretend I'm not here."

Elisabeth tried not to let her shoulders droop as she turned to open the door.

David grabbed her arm and pulled her closer. "What is it exactly that you heard?"

"Nothing, forget it," she said, avoiding his gaze.

He stood taller. "We have become good friends, you and I, have we not?"

Elisabeth looked up at him and held her breath, nodding.

David lowered his voice. "Elisabeth, do you *really* think people can fall in love so fast?"

"Who? You and Severina?"

He pursed his lips. "Yes, of course."

"I wouldn't know," she said with a shrug.

David gave her an incredulous look, but then his tone became soothing as he reached over to stroke her cheek. "Is that a tear?"

"No." She shook her head while wiping the stray tear away.

He grabbed her hand. "Let us go for a walk. Much needs to be said."

Elisabeth closed her eyes and took a deep breath. Although craving his very touch, she pulled her hand away before walking into the room. She folded the grim reaper costume into a tiny square, put it on the bed, and paced the floor. "You should probably go downstairs and check on Cato." Her voice choked with emotion and she needed to sit down. Exhaustion was getting the better of her at the moment. She felt like a fool.

"I am quite certain Severina keeps Cato entertained in the tavern."

"Well, at least she moves fast," Elisabeth mumbled dryly while perched on the edge of the bed.

David stepped into the room after her, both hands clasped behind his back. "Why, Elisabeth, you almost sound jealous."

"Jealous?" She forced a laugh and then sniffled, needing a Kleenex. Of course she was jealous. She wanted to be the only one he flirted with. "Don't be ridiculous. I'm not jealous. Why would I be jealous?"

"You and I are going for a walk and I will not take no for an answer." David pulled a handkerchief from his waistband and walked over, handing it to her. "Now stand up. I have a *palla* for you." He unfolded the deep blue cloth he had been holding.

"A what?" she asked while wiping her nose with the hanky.

David's posture stiffened as if surprised by her comment. "A *palla*."

"Oh." She still didn't know what it was, but stood up in front of him.

He sucked in a quick breath. "I do not believe it. You have no idea what I speak of, do you?"

With a vacant stare, she shook her head and stuffed the hanky into her belt, sure he wouldn't want it back now.

He stepped closer and draped one end of the blue fabric over her left shoulder. His eyes never left hers as he wrapped the cloth around her, causing shivers when his hands brushed her back. Flustered by his intense gaze, Elisabeth's heart pounded with such force that she was certain he could hear it as he brought the fabric under her right arm, across her chest, and over her left shoulder again. By the time David reached over and untucked her long hair from beneath the fabric of the *palla,* she was trembling.

He held her arms in a firm grasp. "There. Now you shall never spend a night shivering cold again."

Elisabeth swallowed the lump in her throat and looked down, immediately recognizing the traditional Roman garment. It was a cross between a shawl, a cloak, and a blanket. When she looked up and gave him a shy smile, his gaze was still locked on her.

He didn't move or say a word.

He didn't crack a smile.

He simply stared at her.

"What's the matter?" She looked down again to see what was wrong.

David drew Elisabeth against him and raised her chin. "I cannot take my eyes off you." He moved his face closer and his gaze wandered to her lips, lingering there for a moment.

Her heart thumped as she pushed his hands away, taking several steps back before he could kiss her. He seemed sincere, but it had to be a well-rehearsed line. "Please, don't say things like that to me." She didn't mean for her voice to sound so tearful.

He squeezed his eyes shut. "What a fool I have been. I never meant for you to believe…"

Covering her face with both hands, Elisabeth took a deep breath, struggling to compose herself before looking at him again. "I don't know what's gotten into me. I'm not usually this emotional." She felt like an idiot.

With an understanding nod, he stepped closer and pulled her to his shoulder in a side hug. "Let us go for that walk."

"Aquarius, no. I'm exhausted. I don't feel like walking anywhere."

"Then I shall carry you." With a boyish grin, he scooped her off her feet and headed toward the door.

Caught off guard, she couldn't help but laugh. "Fine. I'll walk. Just put me down."

He lowered her feet to the ground and then grabbed her hand. "There is something I wish to show you."

She angled her body away from him and squinted. "What-do-you-want-to-show-me?"

With a bemused smile, he leaned closer. "Ev…" He paused. "You shall see."

Wide-eyed, Elisabeth cleared her throat and reached for the costume folded on the bed. She pulled at her ear and followed him out of the room and down the stairs. Why did David always leave her with such conflicted emotions? Taking a deep breath, the time had come to tell him where she was from. It was unfair to both of them to keep the truth a secret any longer.

He led her down the stairs, where Cato sat at one of the tavern tables with a jug and a cup in front of him.

David's brow wrinkled and he walked over. "Is everything all right?"

Cato looked up; his eyes glowing as he grabbed the back of David's neck to pull him closer. "I am in love!"

"Again?" With a laugh, David freed himself from Cato's firm grip.

"I cannot believe it, Aquarius. Severina is my one true love."

"Severina?" David grinned and shot Elisabeth an incredulous look. "She *does* move fast."

"It's a shame she's another man's wife, is it not?"

Elisabeth quietly exhaled. "She…she's married?"

Cato nodded and leaned back with his hands behind his head. "I feel sorry for the guy because I intend to make her mine."

David burst into laughter. "Last time it was Lusta, and before her it was Octavia. Take it easy, friend. It is the wine that gives you a fool's courage."

Elisabeth giggled. "Lusta?"

"His last one true love," David said with a smirk as he led her out of the tavern and onto the sidewalk.

"So tell me, Aquarius…" Elisabeth nudged him with her shoulder while they walked. "Are you upset that Severina is paying attention to Cato now?"

"I am devastated. Can you not tell?"

Her cheeks flamed. "I mean, not that I care or anything, after all, we're just good friends."

"By the gods, Elisabeth, I am certain no friend will drive me as mad as you do." He pulled her close and kissed her forehead. His eyes seemed to dance when he looked at her. "When you pretended to be the fortune teller—"

She grimaced and covered her face with both hands. "I am so embarrassed."

"Don't be. I confess I was thoroughly entertained."

"When did you know it was me?"

With a satisfied smile, he reached for her fingers. "From the very instant you held my hand in yours." He paused to watch her reaction.

Elisabeth's mouth fell open.

His grin seemed to contain secret knowledge. "It appears I know these little fingers, for it took but a moment."

Elisabeth's body temperature rose. The new *palla* certainly kept her warmer.

Not letting go of her hand, he whistled a merry tune and led the way through the hilltop city, past rows of two-storey brick apartments. David seemed oblivious to the world around them, but Elisabeth couldn't help looking over her shoulder for the slave dealer who hunted them.

"Where are we going?" she asked when they climbed a steep alleyway nestled between the walls of two buildings.

"You shall see." He stepped behind her, covering her eyes with his hands, and led the rest of the way. David was so close; she could feel the rise and fall of each breath he took. "All right, you can look now," he said with a content sigh as he stepped beside her. "Cato and I took a wrong turn earlier and found this garden."

It seemed they were in a small park; an oasis overlooking the entire green and golden countryside spread out below them. A river twisted its way toward the horizon, where lush forests replaced the endless rolling hills.

"It's so peaceful up here," she said, trying to imprint the image into her mind forever. "It is so different from where I live."

"And where is it that you live?"

"In a historic sea-side village in Nova Sco…" She froze and glanced at the ground before swallowing the lump in her throat. "Nova Scotia," she whispered.

Sensing her unease, David changed the subject. "I have never seen anything like this in my life. To be able to look down on the earth from this height is…" His voice trailed off and they stood together in silence, lost in the moment.

Elisabeth cleared her throat and reached for his fingers. "I'm ready to tell you an if."

David let out a huge breath and turned toward her.

"Finally." He squeezed her hand and his smile was genuine, lighting up his entire face. "I know you hide something from me, but I swear to Jupiter, you can tell me anything."

"I was waiting for the right time, but I just don't…?" Heart pounding, she wondered if the decision was right.

Aquarius was not yet the immortal David Perrier who seemed to know her so well. She wasn't sure how he'd react to the news she was a time traveler. Heck, Elisabeth wasn't sure how *she* would react to meeting someone from the future. It boggled her mind, and she knew it would be no different for him.

"You can trust me." He led her to a secluded stone bench nestled amongst pink rose bushes in full bloom. The spot was pure eye candy: the marble seat, the abundant flowers, the hilltop view.

"Pink roses." Elisabeth took a deep breath, drinking in their fragrance. "They're my favorite."

David picked a flower and handed it to her. "Then we agree you shall always have pink roses." With a playful grin, he sat down on the bench and patted the space next to him. "Sit."

Elisabeth sat and tried to think of the best way to tell him. Her hands shook. "I'm…um…" Her gaze darted around the empty park. "Aquarius…I'm…" The flower tumbled and she leaned over to pick it back up and began twirling the stem in her fingers. "I'm…"

David stared down at his hands. "You make me fear what you have to say." He squeezed his eyes shut and took a deep breath. "Please, tell me your if."

She bounced her knee. All her muscles seemed to be twitching. "If I was…a…"

He edged closer.

Elisabeth reached out to touch his hand and tucked the folded costume under her arm. "I think…I think the best way is to show you." She slid away from him on the bench, scooped the crystal out of her dress, thoughts of home on her mind.

Home.

****

Standing in her room, she wasn't sure what to do. Still twirling the stem of the rose, Elisabeth tried to think. Her rumbling tummy sparked an idea.

Leaving the *palla* on the bed, along with the costume and flower, she threw a bathrobe on and went downstairs. Her father sat reading in the den as she walked toward the kitchen.

"I'm still hungry," she said, realizing that to him, they ate dinner about an hour ago. "Where's mom?"

"Working on her new painting," he answered without looking up. "Make sure you clean up your mess when you're done."

"I will."

Deciding Aquarius should have a nice dinner, Elisabeth took out a plate and scooped her mother's lasagna onto it and warmed it in the microwave. She tossed a small salad to go with it and then grabbed a large tray and arranged everything on it, adding two forks, two napkins, two glasses, and a bottle of her dad's fancy sparkling water. Noticing some fresh baked chocolate chip cookies, she grabbed a few of those. Everything looked perfect as Elisabeth added a small vase, picked up the tray, and tried to shield the amount of food from her dad while walking past him.

"Elisabeth…?"

"Don't worry, daddy, I'll bring the dishes down when I'm done." She climbed the stairs as quickly as possible.

"If your mother catches you with food in your room, I saw nothing."

"Okay."

Elisabeth placed the tray on her desk and wrapped the palla around herself before taking a quick glance in the mirror to make sure she looked presentable. Adding the pink rose to the vase, she grabbed the tray and sat on her bed, balancing everything on her lap. With the crystal in her fingers, she closed her eyes and thought of David. The world around her turned to darkness and she was falling…falling.

****

"Oh no…grab that!" She let go of her necklace and almost dropped the heavy tray from her lap.

David jumped up, and the color drained from his face when he grabbed it from her. He put the tray down as fast as he could and then covered his mouth with his hand. To him, Elisabeth had made a tray full of food materialize out of thin air.

He paced back and forth in front of the bench and then leaned over with both hands on his knees, shaking his head vigorously. "Cato was correct? You are a goddess from the heavens? I swear, deep down I did not really believe it could be true." He gave her a pained stare. "I did not want it to be true."

Elisabeth trembled. "Aquarius…" Had she misjudged everything? "No, it's not what you think."

Not listening, he pointed to her necklace. "That crystal." David took a step backward. "That is how you get your powers, is it not?"

Elisabeth nodded and wished she knew how to comfort him as he continued to put space between the two of them. "It's not what you think. I'm not a goddess. I'm just from a different...time."

He jerked his head back. "A different time?"

"She looked around to double-check they were alone. "Aquarius, I live two thousand years in the future."

He shook his head while rubbing the back of his neck.

She watched David's face. His eyes widened and then he looked up at the sky. "You live in the future?" he muttered, almost to himself.

"Yes. Somehow I can travel back and forth between time. I'm just as human as you."

"You are not a goddess?" His eyes squeezed shut, but he let out a deep breath.

Was that a sigh of relief?

"No, I'm not. I've never lied to you." Elisabeth watched every gesture he made, trying to read his body language and hoping she hadn't ruined their friendship. "I'm just like you, but I can somehow travel through time. I don't know how it works. It's...it's magic. I don't understand it myself."

The silence was deafening.

"Please say something," she begged, wringing her hands.

He paced back and forth, lost in his thoughts.

Elisabeth tugged at her long hair and groaned. "I bought this stupid necklace when I was twelve years old from an antique shop. I had no idea what it was capable of. This isn't normal, not even for my time, Aquarius. I don't think there's a single person in the entire world who knows what this quartz crystal can do. Nobody even knows I'm here."

Except for you, she wanted to add.

Elisabeth buried her face in her hands. "I'm only here because of you."

"Because of me?" His voice was disbelieving. "What do you mean?"

"Nothing. Never mind." She slumped over in defeat. "Who am I kidding? Nobody believes in magic."

"I do," David whispered and stepped closer, his posture stiff. "Magic is everywhere. Just look at nature. Does the caterpillar not turn into a majestic butterfly? Do grapes not turn into intoxicating wine, and then into vinegar?"

"Yes, but…"

"None of that matters, though." He gave her a side-long glance. "It is too late," he said before swearing under his breath.

Elisabeth's bottom lip trembled, and she turned away. "Then please go because I don't know what I'm doing here." Her voice choked on tears, and she wiped her nose with the handkerchief. "Please…just go."

David's head jerked back. "Go?" He sat beside her on the bench, close enough that their legs were touching. With his attention focused only on her, his hand touched the back of her head, curling his fingers through her hair, and turned her to face him. "I said it's too late. I am a part of this now and I refuse to go anywhere."

Elisabeth held her breath.

"Tell me, does this change anything?" He spoke with a soothing voice.

With a glassy stare, she shook her head. "I'm still me. Nothing has changed. Nothing at all." She let out a whimper and fell against him. "I need a hug."

With a small, shaky laugh, David drew her closer. Her arms wrapped around his waist. She cuddled into his chest, pulse and heartbeat calming down.

"I am relieved you are not a goddess." He rested his chin on the top of her head.

She looked up at him, her eyes wet. "You're quickly becoming my favorite person in the entire world."

He released an appreciative sigh and smiled at her. "It is a shock, to be sure."

"I guarantee it was a bigger shock for me to end up here."

David took a deep, pained breath and squeezed his eyes shut. "I didn't even stop to think that you…" He hugged her tighter. "Well, you shall tell me all about—"

"Yes, I'll tell you all about it, but first we need to eat." She pulled away.

He raised an eyebrow.

"I brought us a really nice meal because we're not eating rat again." With her chin held high, Elisabeth placed the tray between them, picked up a fork, and scooped a piece of lasagna onto it. "Try some."

David glanced down at the tray, picked up the other fork, and inspected it. He then helped himself to a big piece of pasta.

"Good, isn't it? My mother is a great cook."

David nodded. "What is it like? In the future?" he asked while helping himself to another forkful.

Elisabeth didn't know where to start. How do you

explain the twenty-first century to someone in Ancient Rome? "Do you remember what Balinus said about Atlantis?"

His eyes widened.

She gave a half-hearted shrug. "That's how it is. It's not perfect, but it's nice. We have light at the flick of a switch and heat at the push of a button. We can travel great distances very quickly, even across the sky. But here…here it is so…" She searched for the right words. "It's barbaric and dangerous. Slavery is perfectly acceptable. Most of the food sucks." She took another bite of pasta. "To be honest, I pretty much hate everything about being here."

David's muscles stiffened.

"I don't mean…" She cleared her throat. "I don't mean *you*." With a bemused smile, Elisabeth shook her head and gave him a playful shove. "I like *you*."

A lot.

He quietly exhaled and reached for some more lasagna. "Do you use the power of the crystal?"

"No, we use other things, but life is similar to what Balinus described."

David scratched his cheek and looked at Elisabeth. "So, you are Atlantean?"

"No. I'm Canadian. There's no such thing as Atlantis. Well, that I know of. We don't believe it existed. We think of it only as a legend."

His eyes narrowed. "A legend? Yet you possess the same tools the gods did. Why do you believe it is only a legend?"

Elisabeth looked down at the ground and tugged at her bottom lip, pondering his question. "I don't know why I believe that. It's what we've always been taught so I never questioned it."

"Well, they say the gods of old came from the heavens. Perhaps they were wrong. Perhaps they came from another time," David said.

Her imagination wandered off as she thought about it. "Who knows?" She shrugged while opening the bottle of sparkling water. "It's an interesting idea, anyhow." Elisabeth poured the water into a glass and offered it to him, eager to see David's reaction to the bubbles.

He held the delicate glass in his hands and stared in awe at the tiny bubbles dancing within it. "What is it?"

"This is fancy, expensive water." Elisabeth's eyes widened and she smiled as a thought entered her mind. "Aquarius, from this day forward your name has a new meaning."

His eyebrows squished together as he stared at her.

"Well, I hate that your name was a cruel joke. A name should come from a place of love." Her cheeks flushed and she tucked a strand of hair behind one ear. "It's just...I think this water is like you. It's effervescent. It's fun, energetic, and full of life. This is who you are when someone calls your name." She shrugged her shoulders and spoke in a too-quiet voice. "These are the qualities I think of. Not what Domina intended it to mean."

David openly stared at her, seeming to be at a loss for words.

Elisabeth swallowed the lump in her throat, clinked his glass, and then took a sip, loving the way the bubbles tickled her nose.

A slow smile formed on David's face, and he glanced away for a moment.

She picked up one of her mother's cookies and sucked in a quick breath realizing that his entire chosen name came from her. *David Perrier.* Elisabeth leaned across the tray, a knowing grin on her face. "Wait until you try chocolate. It's the greatest thing in the world."

When they finished their meal, Elisabeth returned home and tidied up the kitchen. She placed the vase with the pink rose on her desk before returning once again to David. To him, the tray simply vanished from sight, with Elisabeth never having left his side.

David crossed his arms while observing her. "Why are you here?"

Her chin dipped down. "What do you mean?"

"What I mean to say is, what is the purpose of you being in my time?"

She glanced at the ground, avoiding eye contact. "I don't know." She didn't want to tell him it was because he sent her to save his life.

David moved in closer. "Can you do this traveling without your crystal?"

"No." Her shoulders tightened, and she instinctively reached for the necklace to assure it was still there, safe. "If anything happens to it, I'm trapped here. It's happened before. When I last traveled to another time, I was arrested and almost put to death. People thought I was a witch." She lowered her voice to a whisper. "Aquarius, I am terrified of being trapped here. Nobody even knows I'm here. Nobody knows I can time travel."

A familiar song could be heard from the branch of a nearby tree, and David reached over to touch her cheek. "You suddenly seem like a fragile little bird to me. Why do you stay?"

She fidgeted with her *palla,* and cleared her throat. "Because of you."

His eyes bulged. "Me?"

Elisabeth gave him a shy nod and then stilled, listening to the bird's simple song. "Is that…is that a cuckoo bird?"

"Yes. When the hawk turns back into a cuckoo, you know that spring has arrived and—"

"Wait. What?"

"The cuckoo bird turns into a hawk in the winter."

She shook her head and covered her mouth, trying not to laugh.

David reached over and gave her a light-hearted pinch. "I seem to amuse you."

Elisabeth couldn't stop smiling. "That is so adorable; I hate to tell you the truth."

"But everyone knows…" He lowered his head and raised an eyebrow. "All right, then explain to me why there are no cuckoos in the winter, love?"

"Because…" Elisabeth clamped her lips together. "Because they fly south when it gets cold."

"Really?" David pulled in a deep breath and secmed to ponder the idea before he changed the subject. "The sun is going to set." He pointed to the glowing sky and then led her back toward the scenic lookout.

As they stood side by side, watching the sun disappear below the horizon, Elisabeth brushed David's hand with her fingertips. His response was immediate, and he grabbed her hand, holding it firm and safe within his own.

"Everything looks so peaceful from up here." Elisabeth's gaze wandered across the crimson sky and then back down to the river that now sparkled in a dazzling shade of auburn. "It's so beautiful. It doesn't seem real, does it? It looks like it's painted on and is nothing but an illusion."

"You are right." David let out a sigh. "It seems too beautiful to be real."

She turned and smiled at him, relieved he adjusted to her news. "Do you want to check on Cato?"

"No." His brows pulled in. "But I suppose we should. I have a feeling it was unwise of me to leave him in the condition we found him."

Chapter Eight

Inside the doorway of Severina's tavern, David came to a sudden stop. His posture became rigid. Before Elisabeth knew what was happening, he'd pushed her to safety behind him as people cheered at a brawl taking place in the middle of the crowded pub.

"You are not to move from this spot, Elisabeth," David yelled. "Do you understand?"

Trembling and wide-eyed, she nodded.

"And for once, do as I tell you," he hollered before running toward the chaos.

Craning her neck around a ginger-haired man to get a better look, she saw the rotund cook holding Cato in a headlock. He ran around in circles, his puffy face red with anger as they groaned and crashed into tables.

David pushed through the onlookers and pried the attacker off of Cato.

"I am going to kill you!" the man screamed as he yanked his axe out of the top of a nearby table.

"Let me guess," David said while dodging the man's flying hatchet. "Severina's husband?"

"Who knew he'd be so cross?" Cato shrugged his shoulders before hurling himself into the man's back, knocking him off his feet.

At that moment, a huge hand gripped Elisabeth's arm and slapped a shackle onto her wrist.

"The fortunes smile upon me." Rufus' eyes

113

narrowed and, in mere seconds, Elisabeth's hands were chained together in front of her.

Strained breath battered out of her while she struggled to break free from the slave dealer. People around her cowered and made space for the giant man.

Across the room, to the right, David lifted his eyes, then jerked his head back and gasped. Cato stood up, wiping sweat off his brow, while Severina's husband lay panting on the floor, out of breath.

With quick movements, David raised his hands to hold Rufus off. "Unchain the girl. Listen to me, we have enough coins to pay for her. We can buy our freedom."

The slave dealer cocked his head. "An escaped slave thinks he can buy a fugitive?"

"Here." David threw the leather pouch across the room and it landed on a table in an empty corner to her left. "You are a business man and I am paying for our freedom, now let her go."

"I cannot. She is a fugitive who stole my property."

Elisabeth's pulse raced as the giant dragged her by the arm, his grasp so tight it was cutting off the circulation. They stumbled around Severina as she tended to her husband, who had somehow crawled across the floor to the other side of the room unnoticed.

Rufus leaned over to grab the pouch from the table and balanced it in the palm of his free hand to determine the weight of the coins inside. "Not enough," he said while shaking his head and breathing noisily.

David's jaw clenched. "Take a closer look. You will find there is more than enough."

Rufus shook his head and glanced at the growing crowd gathered at the front of the tavern. "Not after what I've been through to track you three down."

Severina stepped back, trying to distance herself from the unfolding drama, while her husband rolled off the floor and abandoned his axe in the process.

Elisabeth's mouth was dry. "Take me and take the coins and let them go," she said with a shaky voice. "I can read, write, and am well educated."

Rufus let out an arrogant laugh. "She makes a passionate plea, Aquarius."

"Stop talking, Elisabeth," David said through gritted teeth. "Let her go, Rufus. It is Cato and I you want."

"Please, Aquarius…" Her bottom lip trembled. "It's useless. Don't come any closer." She could see no other way out for him. Elisabeth would not allow him to be recaptured and sold into slavery.

David let out a long sigh and then held his fists straight out in front of him to surrender. "It seems you've bested us, Rufus."

Elisabeth's mouth fell open. "Aquarius…no!" Her body tensed.

"Come on, Cato," David said. "It is of no use to continue running."

With a satisfied huff, Rufus pulled another pair of shackles from his belt. "Chains will bind you this time, Aquarius."

Elisabeth tilted her head back in frustration. The large wagon wheel chandelier hanging from the ceiling caught her attention. She paused to examine it and noticed it hung from a chain and pulley system that attached to the wall behind her.

Of course! It had to be lowered in order to light the oil lamps and then raised back up again.

More and more spectators amassed in the doorway to watch the small slave revolt taking place at the back of the restaurant like it was quality entertainment. Even if the three of them managed to get past Rufus, the shouting mob blocked the exit. It seemed hopeless until Elisabeth heard several people cheering and wagering on their escape.

"You will wait here and not move a muscle," the slave dealer whispered through clenched teeth, and then started across the room.

Opportunity appeared when she glanced down at the abandoned axe near her feet and then turned to look at David. Catching his attention, he wiggled his brows at her.

She gave him a glassy stare and then raised her head to point out the light fixture Rufus would be standing under at any second.

David did a double-take and then a slow smile spread across his face.

The giant froze. He sensed something. "Aquarius, I swear to the gods…"

David rolled his eyes and kept his arms straight out in front of him in an attempt to reassure Rufus of his surrender.

The slave dealer took cautious steps forward once again.

Adrenaline rushed through Elisabeth's body. She lugged the heavy axe off the floor, held it in her shackled hands, and charged toward the chain that held the chandelier up. With a guttural roar, she raised the axe over her shoulder and used all her might to send it chopping into the links. When the heavy wooden wheel and oil lamps came crashing down on Rufus, he screamed and the crowd went wild.

In a matter of seconds, the entire mob began brawling amongst each other.

The man with ginger hair rushed toward Elisabeth and she swung the hatchet with manic energy. The axe was heavy and difficult to wield, even more so with hands chained together. She kept swinging, hoping to keep Big Ginger away, only to end up pinned against the wall with nowhere to turn.

When the man wrenched the handle away from her with ease, Elisabeth heard the whipping noise of a sling and her attacker groaned, dropping the axe to the floor. He then unsheathed a dagger from his waist and swirled around.

David bolted across the room toward her. He planted his legs in a fighting stance and raised his bent arms to chin height; his weapon nothing but a sling draped between two clenched fists.

Elisabeth gave him a blank look. How the heck did he plan to defeat a knife-wielding man using a piece of rope?

With the dagger in his hand, Big Ginger threw the first jab.

As David stepped aside to block the knife, he wrapped the rope over the man's extended wrist, flipped around, and pulled Big Ginger's arm back with him, dropping him to his knees in the process. David then wrapped the rope around the man's neck, which pulled his tied hand and the knife along with it and rendered Big Ginger useless. With a final tug, David had him supine on the floor.

"Aquarius?" Elisabeth stared at him in amazement.

David cursed under his breath. "I liked that sling."

He then shot Elisabeth a devilish grin. "Are you all right, love?"

She trembled all over but nodded.

"You know, I'd probably have dropped the lanterns on Rufus like this…"

Elisabeth winced when she noticed the entire pulley system was held on a simple hook.

With a flick of his wrist, David sent the remaining chain links flying to the floor. "But I do appreciate a rescue with dramatic flair," he said with a suppressed smile while holding a hand over his heart.

Elisabeth's cheeks flushed. "Yeah, well…at least I didn't surrender."

"I had a plan." He dangled the bag of gold and silver pieces in front of her. "Now, what do you say we get out of here?" He tossed the coins up into the air to send the money scattering to every corner of the tavern. "Come on, Cato!" he screamed.

The frenzied crowd scrambled to pick up the coins as Rufus roared with anger, crawling across the floor and trying to collect as many as he could. With an amused snort, David grabbed Elisabeth's arm and bolted out the door.

They ran along the streets and out of the city as fast as possible. Not stopping at their former camp, they maneuvered their way through the dark countryside for what felt like an hour, until Elisabeth collapsed on the ground, unable to take another step. With the heavy iron chains locked around her wrists, it was impossible to continue at their pace.

David dropped down beside her. "Are you hurt?"

"I'm fine," she said, struggling to catch her breath. "But I think my heart is going to burst through my chest. And these…" Her voice choked with tears, holding up her shackled wrists. "These hurt so much." The chains clinked as she put her hands back down again.

"I'll find a way to remove them as soon as possible."

Cato pointed into the distance with a shaking hand. "Come on. We must continue to put some more miles between Rufus and ourselves."

"Give her time to rest," David snapped as he held a canteen out to Elisabeth. "Here, take a drink."

Cato paced back and forth. "If we are captured again because some girl can't—"

David lifted his head and glared at him. "Some girl?" His tone deepened. "You'd not have even dreamt of freedom had it not been for her. At least she wasn't cowering in a corner like you were."

Cato scrubbed a hand over his face. "I didn't mean what I said. I'm sorry. I am so sorry. I'm an idiot."

David drew in a slow, steady breath. Elisabeth lowered her head and swallowed hard before forcing herself onto her feet again. The three friends trekked onward, trying to follow the foot path through the night. After several hours of hiking along the shoreline, they could see a small campfire glowing ahead of them.

"There's safety in numbers, right?" Elisabeth walked with them toward the fire, trying to stop her chains from clanking with every step.

They crept closer, noticing the lone figure asleep begin to stir, before sitting up, surprised by their arrival.

"Ahhh, it is you again. I thought I heard someone coming," a cheerful voice rang out.

Cato gasped. "Balinus? Is that you, old man? We

have caught up to you?"

"Why yes, it appears you have. Come, rest by the fire, my friends. I shall sleep more peacefully with you here."

"Many thanks, Balinus." Cato flopped down on the ground near a tree and stretched out.

"You did not spend the night in the city?"

"We decided it wiser to continue our journey," David said.

"Ahhh, I see." Balinus pulled his cloak around himself tighter and put his head back down. "I am glad you got away. Sleep well. Aurora will soon rise."

"Over here," David whispered to Elisabeth as he found a spot beside the fire.

They sat cross-legged, facing each other with their knees touching.

"Let me look at those shackles."

She held her wrists out for him to inspect the lock. He glanced around Balinus' little campsite.

"If only I had something to pick the lock."

"Hang on…" Elisabeth reached for the crystal necklace.

****

"What about this?" She offered him a bobby pin that had been sitting on her dresser.

David tilted his head and smirked. "Let's give it a try, shall we, love?"

He fiddled with the hair pin for a few minutes, bending it this way and that until it resembled a pair of tweezers. Then, he pulled her hands onto his lap, inserted it into the lock, and removed the shackles in seconds.

She let out a small yelp. "Oh my gosh, you're

amazing."

"It was nothing." David chuckled and leaned in closer. "It's all in the hands. I'm sure a snake could have done that with as much ease." He flicked the broken bobby pin into the fire.

"Um, last time I checked, snakes don't have hands."

"Are you sure? I mean, kiss me if I am incorrect but…"

Elisabeth groaned and gave him a playful shove. "No, no…on second thought, you're definitely correct." With a grin, she wrapped the new *palla* around herself like a blanket and then curled up on the ground.

David confined his laugh to a snort while making a spot for himself nearby. "Hopefully we can get a few hours of rest."

Although exhausted, sleep wouldn't come. The smell of rotting leaves filled the air, while dark shadows lurked behind every tree. A wolf howled in the distance. Elisabeth kept reliving the events at the tavern with the slave dealer. She clutched both arms to her stomach as worse-case scenarios played out in her imagination. Their last encounter with Rufus had been too close.

With no desire to stay here in Ancient Rome, Elisabeth knew she'd have to go back to her reality— without the runaway slave she found impossible not to fall for. She gulped at the air and struggled not to cry, but a quiet sob escaped.

David must have heard for he scooted closer, pulling her into his arms.

"Oh God, Aquarius," her voice quaked. "I was so scared."

"You are the bravest person I know," he whispered.

"But I'm not. You have no idea how frightened I am."

"And that is what makes you so brave. You do what you believe needs to be done, even though you are frightened." He hugged her tighter. "That is my definition of bravery." He then let out a deep sigh and buried his face in her hair.

Too exhausted to reply, Elisabeth turned her head into David's chest and closed her eyes. Tomorrow they would continue, but for now, she would try to sleep.

****

The morning light filtering through the trees woke Elisabeth. Already awake, Cato sat cross-legged pulling fibers off a tree bark while David twisted it into rope.

"Do you think we should move on now?" she asked.

David nodded. "As soon as I have a new sling. It won't take much longer."

Elisabeth adjusted the *palla* over her tunic while waiting. Other than a knife and a canteen, they were in desperate need of supplies.

"We should tell Balinus we're going," Elisabeth said when David stood and tucked the rope into his belt with the other slings.

David pointed at the old man. "But, he sleeps so peacefully."

"Balinus," Cato called out. "We are leaving now."

The old man sprang to his feet within seconds, grinning from ear to ear as he rolled his blanket up before attaching it to the wooden frame he carried his provisions on. "As luck would have it, I am also

122

leaving." He heaved his pack onto his back and walked off toward a trail.

David and Cato looked at each other and then burst into laughter.

"Do you mind if I accompany you? I too am heading south," Balinus called back over his shoulder. "To Rome."

"Not at all," Cato said, taking several long strides to catch up with him.

Song birds serenaded them as they followed a narrow trail for several hours. Through olive groves and open fields, they each seemed lost in their own thoughts until Balinus handed out bread and olives.

"We will repay you," David said as he accepted the meal.

"Not necessary. I do not have a lot, but what I have, I am happy to share with you, my friends." He then pointed behind them. "Take a look at that."

Elisabeth whipped around, staring at the meadow dotted with spring flowers. The wind rustled through the tall grass and a sweet, familiar scent filled the air. "Yet another…field? What am I looking at?" she asked, oblivious to what Balinus saw.

"Elisabeth!" David gave a slow shake of his head. "How can you be so blind to what is right in front of you?"

Cato chuckled and exchanged a knowing look with Balinus. "That can be taken one of two ways," he whispered. He then grabbed a long stick and poked at the grass.

"Ca-to," David warned as he strolled away from the path and bent down to pick wild strawberries hidden beneath the leaves. "A field full of them." He took a deep, satisfied breath before popping them into his mouth.

"Oh my gosh," Elisabeth squealed. "I love strawberries." She ran into the field and then stopped abruptly. "What are you doing, Cato?"

"He's checking for snakes," David said as he walked toward her. "They like the berries too."

She flinched. "Are you serious?" Elisabeth turned around and started to tiptoe back toward the path. "Never mind," she whispered.

With a laugh, David reached for her arm, pulling her closer. "It's fine. There are no snakes right here," he said, handing her several tiny berries.

Grown wild beneath the Umbrian sun, they were the sweetest and juiciest strawberries she'd ever tasted. Elisabeth used her skirt as a makeshift basket to gather a handful.

Cato pointed to a hilltop town in the distance. "We can get supplies there."

"Are all your towns built on hills?" Elisabeth asked as she stared up at it.

Cato gave her a confused glance.

"Never mind," she said.

David grabbed Cato to pull him back, out of Balinus' earshot. "We cannot buy supplies. Rufus has all our money," he whispered.

Cato nodded in understanding. "All right, when we get there, you create a diversion and I'll pull my old sleight of hand…"

"Wait." Elisabeth popped another strawberry into her mouth. "You're not planning to steal again, are you?"

"Just for necessities," David said, trying to reassure

her. "And we won't choose anyone who looks like they need—"

"No. Don't do it. I, um…I…remember that ruby I brought from home? I didn't mention it before, but funny thing is…" She gave a nervous laugh, dumped the strawberries into David's hands, and reached for her crystal.

****

Her big, comfy bed looked tempting. Determined to stay focused, Elisabeth reached into her closet and pulled out the jewel-encrusted box. Searching for something small, she chose a tiny emerald and pried it off. While admiring the intense green stone, it suddenly dawned on her why David had left it for her in Scotland. Precious gems could be exchanged for any currency, in any era.

Like being taught Latin, it seemed to be part of a preparation she knew nothing about.

She squeezed the emerald in her fist and returned to ancient Rome.

****

"Here," she said, holding the gemstone up.

Cato gave her a strange look. "What is going on?"

Elisabeth knew he didn't believe her. "Nothing."

To tell Cato the truth meant explaining where she was from, and that was not an option. David knew because he was part of this, and Balinus figured it out himself. But Cato? The fewer that knew her secret, the better.

David tried to look nonchalant, but couldn't keep the grin off his face as he finished the strawberries. "Surely you are not complaining, Cato. It appears you were right all along. Elisabeth is a goddess sent by

Jupiter to rescue us."

"Aquarius, did you hear me complain? I did not complain. I merely…"

David laughed and grabbed Elisabeth's hand. "Let's go," he called out as they continued along the path toward the hilltop town.

"Allow me," David said after they'd wandered the busy streets and found themselves standing outside of a jewelry shop. He tilted his head and smirked. "I have experience selling gems."

"Yes, we are quite aware." Cato waved his hand dismissively as he followed him to the counter.

Elisabeth noticed that, except for some restaurants and taverns, you didn't walk inside a store. Business was conducted from the sidewalk and you could watch the craftsman working at the back of the shop.

Balinus pointed up to the second floor when he spotted Elisabeth observing her surroundings. "Most craftsmen live right above their business." He then clasped his hands together when something from a bakery caught his eye. "Oh, those look wonderful. I won't be but a moment." He crossed to the other side of the street.

Trusting Cato and David to take care of business, Elisabeth strolled further along the sidewalk and studied the people and the shops. Had anyone else ever been able to stand back and watch history this way? Scanning through the fascinating crowd, she leaped back when she recognized the giant of a man walking up the street.

Rufus was, by far, taller than anyone else around him. Elisabeth's breath quickened as he headed in her direction. Had he seen her? Trembling, she turned and hurried back to the jeweler to warn David and Cato. He must be stopping at the towns en route to Rome, and like little pawns, they kept falling right into his path.

Forced to a sudden stop, a middle-aged man dressed in pale green blocked her path. "I do not believe we have met," he said, while stroking his throat.

"No, I don't suppose we have. Excuse me." Elisabeth tried to walk around him.

"Why the hurry?" He squeezed her arm.

"Take your hand off of me," she said through clenched teeth.

"Come now." His tongue darted out to lick his lips while pulling her closer. "You *must* know who I am?"

From the corner of her eye, Elisabeth could see David and Cato running toward her.

"Unhand her at once!" David yelled.

Desperate to get out of here before Rufus saw them, Elisabeth kneed the stranger in the groin as hard as she could. His eyes bulged, and he released his grip, and then hunched over in shock. As Elisabeth raced toward David, she heard the man let out a long and quiet groan.

Cato couldn't stop laughing. "Remind me never to anger her, Aquarius."

David's hands clenched and unclenched while charging straight toward the man, threatening him with certain death.

"I just saw Rufus. We need to get out of here." She grabbed David and Cato by the arms and pulled them up to a shop counter where the smell of dead fish filled the air.

In a state of frenzy, Cato searched the street. "We cannot leave without basic supplies. Where is he?"

"Right there." As Elisabeth made a discreet signal, the slave trader crossed the road and ventured into a tavern.

While standing at the fish counter, a bald man with numerous chins stepped forward. Wearing a bloodstained apron and gesturing with a large cleaver as he spoke, he didn't make Elisabeth feel much safer.

"*Salve*. What can I get for you?"

"*Salve*….sir. Would you be so kind as to tell us where we can purchase basic provisions and supplies?" David asked.

"Cloaks? Blankets? That sort of thing?"

Cato answered with a curt nod.

The fishmonger frowned and used his bloody knife to point down the street.

"Thank you," Elisabeth called out as they left. "Where's Balinus?" She glanced around.

"We cannot worry about him right now." David ushered them quickly to another shop. "You two keep watch while I make the purchases." As fast as possible, he paid for three blankets, three dark cloaks, two satchels, and two wooden frames like the one Balinus used.

"Aquarius, we still need food before we go any further." Cato tied the blanket to the frame and hauled it onto his shoulders like a primitive backpack. "Put the cloaks on." He draped one around himself and pulled the hood up.

David nodded and gave a handful of coins to Cato. "We have to split up. I need you to find lead sling-bolts and canteens. I will get several days rations. Meet outside of the city as soon as possible."

"What do you want me to get?" Elisabeth asked.

"You are staying with me." David put his cloak on and pulled the hood over his head.

"No, I'm helping. What do you want me to get?" She adjusted her hood.

"No. Elisabeth, do not even think about—"

"Can you two argue later?" Cato said. "If Rufus is in that tavern, this might be our only chance. I'll see you in a few minutes. What about the old man?"

David shook his head. "Just get some sling-bolts and canteens and get out. We cannot stop to find Balinus."

Cato nodded and then turned, keeping his head bowed as he walked down the street, eventually sliding up to a storefront.

David pulled Elisabeth beside him. "There was a food market near the gate. We will head straight there."

To reach the main gate, they had to first make it past the tavern Rufus had entered. Elisabeth's pulse raced as they walked by it. With her face hidden beneath the hood, she turned the slightest bit and saw him standing at the long bar talking to someone. Her posture sagged in relief. A moment later she spotted Balinus, heading toward a bookshop.

Elisabeth tried to catch the old man's attention as they marched past him.

"Oh there you are," Balinus called out. "I won't be but a moment. There is a little place here filled to the ceiling with rare scrolls that…"

David shook his head and kept walking. Elisabeth turned and gestured for him to follow.

Balinus nodded in understanding as he joined them.

Reaching the food market, they quickly filled their

new satchels with a few days' rations and then made their getaway. Outside of the city walls, at the bottom of the hill, they found a secluded spot and paced back and forth, willing Cato to return.

"This can't be good, Aquarius. He's taking far too long." Elisabeth took off her heavy cloak and began to twist her hair.

With a wrinkled brow, David nodded and tied both their cloaks to the new backpack.

Balinus was unnaturally still. "Do not worry so. He will be here."

"I hope you are right, old man. I hope you are right." David rubbed his face and stared up at the city gate.

Chapter Nine

After what seemed an eternity, Cato came running down the hill.

"We need to get out of here. Rufus is describing us to anyone willing to listen. I had to detour around the city to get out." Cato heaved his pack up higher on his back. "I thought he would give up by now, but he has a serious grudge against us. Aquarius, here..." He held out his hand. "Your lead sling-bolts."

"Thanks." David dropped what looked like almond-shaped bullets into his belt pouch.

"I know the way," Balinus said, and started toward a wide trail.

"How do you always know which way to go?" Cato asked.

"Do you remember what I told you before? I believe it is a young man's duty to see the world." He waved his arms in the air, gesturing to the land all around him. "I know this area especially well. As I told Elisabeth, some say I am the most traveled man of our time."

"I confess, it's reassuring someone knows where we are going." David helped Elisabeth over a tree trunk that had fallen across the path.

Cato tilted his head to the side. "Why do you believe it a man's duty to see the world?"

"A *young* man's duty," Balinus answered in his

exuberant voice. "A wise sage once said, 'The further one goes, the less one knows.'"

Cato laughed and then fell in line beside the old man. "We plan to sail across the Adriatic from Ostia."

"Ostia?" Balinus chuckled. "If you plan to cross the Adriatic, heading to Ostia from here would be unwise, unless, of course, you prefer traveling a rather circuitous route."

Elisabeth stared at David, wide-eyed. "We're going the wrong way?" Her posture slumped. "Oh my gosh, Aquarius…we're going the wrong way?" She exchanged an incredulous look with him and then they both laughed.

Cato crossed his arms and let out an exaggerated sigh. "I am so glad the two of you find everything so amusing." His lips pinched together. "This is terrible."

David managed to confine his laugh to a snort. "Oh come on, Cato. Try to see the humor in a situation for once? It cannot be that bad."

"No, no, Aquarius is correct. It is, in fact, not terrible," Balinus said. "You still need to continue south, but may I suggest after we reach Marmore, you head east, toward the port of Theate."

David quietly exhaled. "Thank you, old man."

****

Before long, the landscape became more and more rugged and the rolling hills disappeared, making way for lush green forests that stretched as far as the eye could see.

"Sons of death! You stupid donkey, come on," screamed a frustrated man standing in the middle of the footpath, trying to pull his animal forward.

"Salve." Balinus' singsong voice greeted the

stranger when they approached. "And-how-are-you-this-fine-day?"

The man grunted his response. Although he tugged and tugged, the donkey didn't budge, instead choosing to hold its ground and give the occasional flick of its tail. The man tried pushing it from behind, but remaining unfazed, it turned its head to eat some leaves from a nearby shrub.

"Do you need some help?" David called back, long after they'd walked past.

The man threw his hands up in the air. "Please, at this point I will try anything," he yelled back.

"No, Aquarius. I mean it." Cato shook his head in disapproval. "You will only be drawing attention to us. We need to be forgettable."

David laughed and clapped Cato on the back. "I do realize how truly unforgettable I am, but—"

Elisabeth let out a spontaneous laugh. "Aquarius!"

"I'm joking," he said with a bemused smile. "But what harm can come from helping the poor man?" He took out his sling and placed a rock in it.

"Wait." Elisabeth grabbed his arm and raised her voice. "Don't you dare hurt the animal."

His eyes twinkled with mischief. "I will not touch it. The donkey just needs a little scare."

She gave him a warning glance.

"Trust me." He held his rope out, aiming the rock.

Elisabeth stepped back and watched him whirl the sling over his head several times. As if pitching a baseball, he rotated his arm and released one end of the cord. The rock whipped out of the sling and smashed to the ground behind the animal. Startled, the donkey brayed, stamped its foot, and started moving again.

With a satisfied smile, David held his arms out wide. He then pointed his thumbs at himself and did a ridiculous victory dance.

Elisabeth covered her mouth, trying not to laugh.

"Well done, Aquarius." Balinus' upper body shook with his infectious laugh. "Well done."

"*Gratias*." The man's grin lit up his entire face. "How far until the next town?" he asked before continuing in the opposite direction.

"Two hours at a steady pace," David called out.

Elisabeth stepped beside him and her hand lingered on his arm. "That was great."

"Yes, that was great, Aquarius." Cato's tone was sharp, and he frowned. "As always, you are the best. You just float through life with never a care. Everyone always loves you even though you are really quite…" He opened his mouth to criticize and then stopped short.

"Quite what?" David asked with a playful grin. "Don't stop there."

"Arrogant."

His eyes widened. "You think I'm arrogant?" David smirked and then looked at Elisabeth. "He thinks I'm arrogant."

"No…" She turned to Cato, who kept silent, staring at the ground. "I think you're mistaking his confidence for arrogance."

David tilted his face toward her. "Thank you," he said with a wink. "You see, Elisabeth does not believe me to be arrogant."

She pressed her lips together to keep from smiling. "Most of the time."

With a groan, he put his arm around her shoulders,

pulling her closer as they walked along the footpath.

"I do know him better than any of you." Cato laughed too loudly. "You are an arrogant show-off, Gaius Cornelius Aquarius. Don't you think so, Balinus?"

The old man offered Cato a questioning gaze. "A wise sage once said, 'When you are content to be simply yourself and don't compare or compete, everyone will respect you.'"

"Ha! So you agree that Aquarius…"

With strong eye contact and a weak smile, Balinus leaned in but said nothing.

Cato's head flinched back and he rubbed his forehead. "You think I'm envious of Aquarius, don't you?"

"Oh, alrighty then." Balinus shrugged his shoulders. "If you say so."

"Is that not what you implied?" He whipped around and glared at David. "I am not envious of you," he yelled. "Balinus…wait, what are you trying to say?" Cato jogged to catch up to the old man.

David swallowed an obvious lump in his throat and detached a sling from his belt to fiddle with.

"A bit of an over-reaction, wasn't it?" Elisabeth whispered, attempting to keep her voice light.

"No. Not for Cato."

****

As the road wound its way through a dense forest, a continuous thundering sound filled the air and Elisabeth's posture perked up. While trailing Balinus and Cato, she and David gazed all around, searching for the source of the noise.

"Wow, will you look at that…"

135

They stared in awe at an enormous waterfall nestled deep within the woods.

David's mouth went slack and then shook his head in disbelief. "That is incredible." He began to whirl his sling beside him, seeming to do it out of habit.

From their vantage point, they were almost level with the top of the falls, standing to the right of it. The rushing water poured over the edge in a giant freefall, creating a mist in the trees. From there, it widened and flowed over the next drop, which was about half the height of the first one. It then bubbled and danced over jagged rocks and continued toward its third and final fall, eventually turning into a rushing river that disappeared into the forest.

David continued to fiddle with his rope as they hiked along the twisting lane now meandering downhill, winding its way near the rushing flow of the water. When they reached a spot where the path leveled out, Elisabeth stopped and pretended to be fascinated with a smaller cascade beside her. In truth, she wanted to rest but knew they must keep putting distance between themselves and Rufus. While no Olympian, she did consider herself to be in good physical shape. However, it came as no surprise she didn't have the stamina of David and Cato; they were young virile Romans in the prime of their lives. How do you explain Balinus, though? How on earth was the old man able to keep their pace? He was already a fair distance ahead with Cato and the two seemed…

"Whoa, be careful. Not so close to the edge, love."

A split second later, Elisabeth felt a rope drop down around her shoulders. She turned and gave David an incredulous look when she realized he'd tied his slings together and used them as a lasso on her.

With an impish grin, David gently tugged the rope, causing it to tighten around her arms. "You wouldn't want to get…swept off your feet." He smirked and drew Elisabeth back toward him and away from the raging river.

She pinched her lips together to keep from smiling and bounced on her toes. "I'll have you know my feet are planted firmly on the ground. I'm not about to let myself get…swept away."

He clutched his chest and groaned. "Your words are a dagger to the heart."

Elisabeth giggled. "We are talking about the waterfall, are we not?"

David raised an eyebrow as he untied the rope. "Why? What are *you* talking about?"

She felt her ears burning. "Nothing."

He burst into laughter. "We'll rest here." He dropped his shoulder pack to the ground, blew a loud wolf-whistle with his fingers, and waved Cato and Balinus back.

Elisabeth bit down on a grin and shook her head, glad to take a break. Feeling warm in the afternoon sunshine, she took off the *palla* and spread it on the ground like a picnic blanket and then stretched out on her side. "I am sooo tired."

David gave an understanding nod as he planted himself beside her. "I know, my…"—he paused and cleared his throat when Balinus and Cato drew nearer—"I know."

"Let's eat," Cato said as he flopped down.

The four friends sprawled out and ate a small dinner, mesmerized by their surroundings.

"It is an amazing view," David said as he shared a handful of grapes with Elisabeth.

"Check out that rainbow in the mist." She rolled over onto her stomach and propped herself up on both elbows. "It's breathtaking."

Balinus nodded. "According to legend, that waterfall was created when a beautiful nymph named Nera…"

"What's a nymph?" Elisabeth whispered to David as he stretched out beside her in the same position.

"A nature spirit."

"Do you mean a fairy? Are they the size of my thumb with wings?" she asked while leaning against him.

David shook his head and made a funny face. "A nymph is the size of a human and has no wings."

Cato narrowed his eyes. "Oh come now, why do you, of all people, pretend to not know what a nymph is." He looked straight ahead. "For all I know, you could be one yourself."

"Cato, I already told you, I'm—"

"A nymph is a minor goddess of nature," Balinus interrupted. "In the days when the gods still walked the earth, humans and those from above intermingled. For better or for worse, the gods ruled over everything. Acting as guardians, they ruled our planet and everything on it."

Elisabeth tilted her head to the side, not wanting to miss a single word spoken.

"One day, a handsome young shepherd named Velino was tending to his flock of sheep when he noticed Nera dancing in the forest. Captivated by Nera's beauty, he hid amongst the trees to watch her.

But…as if sensing his presence, she looked up and saw him." Balinus paused for dramatic effect. "The moment he gazed into her eyes, Velino realized she was not a human, but a nymph. However, in that single glance, the two fell madly in love."

Elisabeth's lips pressed together.

"The next day, Velino returned to the same spot to try and find his beloved once again. Nera loved the shepherd and had been waiting in the forest for him. Once reunited, they pledged their undying love and he gave her a ring as a symbol of his devotion. Velino left, vowing to return the next day. They were prepared to do anything to be together. She'd leave the world of the gods if she must, for she could not live without him any more than he could live without her."

Elisabeth swallowed the lump in her throat and glanced at David. His eyes were wide as he listened.

"But…" Balinus' voice became louder and he held up his index finger. "News traveled to Juno that Nera was in love with a mortal."

"Who's Juno?" Elisabeth whispered to David again.

"The wife of Jupiter. She is a rather important goddess."

"Got it." Elisabeth nodded and turned her attention back to Balinus.

"Although not uncommon for the male gods to mate with human women, Juno was furious the nymph had fallen in love. Perhaps it was jealousy, but as punishment, she turned Nera into a river." With dramatic flair, Balinus gestured toward the rushing water. "Behold, the River Nera."

Everyone paused to stare at the surroundings once

again.

Balinus rubbed his hands together. "The next morning, Velino returned, but he could not find Nera anywhere. He searched the forest and then climbed to the top of the mountain to see if he could see her in the river below. From high above, he thought he saw her drowning. Afraid she would die, Velino jumped from the cliffs into the water below to save her life. Venus saw what the shepherd did…"

David leaned in and lowered his voice. "Venus is the goddess of love."

"I actually knew that one," she said, smiling back at him.

"Venus saw Velino jump, and taking pity on the young shepherd, she turned him into the waterfall so that he could be with Nera for all time. And to this day, the River Velino flows into the River Nera."

Elisabeth shook her head. "Why do star-crossed lovers never have happy endings?" she asked in a gentle tone.

Balinus shrugged his shoulders. "Some say the ring he gave her lies at the bottom of the falls, right where the rainbow comes in."

Cato leaned in closer. "Well, what happened to—?"

Elisabeth stared at him. "You don't actually believe it happened like that, do you?"

Cato opened his mouth to say something but closed it again when Balinus exchanged a knowing look with Elisabeth.

"While I confess, I do prefer the legend; the truth is far less romantic," the old man said. "The waterfall is man-made."

Cato began to voice his denial, insisting it to be true.

"Man-made, as in…made by a man's jump?" Elisabeth asked.

Balinus laughed. "No, I do mean man-made. It was built three hundred years ago to force stagnant waters over the cliff."

Elisabeth gasped, realizing the beautiful waterfall was made in about 300 B.C. "I can't believe it!" She rolled over onto her side and propped her head up with her hand. "That huge waterfall is man-made? Seriously? I never in a million years would have guessed. Now to me, the truth is far more amazing."

Balinus gave her a wink. "I am very, very delighted that impresses you."

"But why do people bother with the romantic tale? Why not just tell it like it is. The fact it's man-made is just as fascinating."

His voice, as always, remained bubbly and light. "Remember what we spoke of earlier, Elisabeth. There is a measure of truth in all legends and stories. That is why they resonate with us and why we love them so."

"Yes, but they are so far-fetched, Balinus. I mean, turning nymphs into rivers?"

He clasped his hands to his chest. "Do you not notice how the gods possessed such human emotions?"

Elisabeth's eyes narrowed as she sat up. "No. What are you saying?"

"Nera was in love. Juno was jealous and angry. Venus showed sympathy. It is well known that the male gods lusted after our women."

Elisabeth glanced at David and then back at Balinus. "I don't understand."

"During the Zep Tepi..." Balinus' voice was steady and lower-pitched.

"The what?" David sat up beside Elisabeth.

"Zep Tepi is the time when the gods lived here on earth, long before the great flood. Zep Tepi is the time of Atlantis."

"Okay, wait a minute," Elisabeth interrupted. "You guys really believe the gods lived here in the ancient past and walked around, in the flesh, ruling over everything and generally acting like they owned the place?"

Cato, David, and Balinus all looked at each other and nodded.

"Well, where are they now?"

"They left," Cato said matter-of-factly.

She cocked her head. "Take away all the fancy stuff, turning people into rivers and waterfalls, but you're telling me that eons ago, some beings came here, from...above." She made air quotes with her fingers. "They had advanced technology and very, very real human emotions, and they..." Her voice trailed off as she stared at David with a puzzled look on her face.

She had always thought of the mythological gods as fantasy, but the more she heard about them, the more they sounded like advanced and manipulative humans. She ran two fingers along the chain of the necklace while her thoughts drifted, not realizing she was still staring at David.

Elisabeth knew if she came here, to the ancient world, and brought modern technology with her, it would be easy to pretend to be some sort of goddess and position herself to be worshipped. That kind of power, in the hands of the wrong people...

David poked Elisabeth to get her attention and leaned in close. "You have not taken your eyes off me," he whispered. He then grinned and wiggled his eyebrows.

"Oh…" Her cheeks flamed.

David chuckled and pulled her into a playful hug. "I'm teasing. You looked far too serious."

Balinus cleared his throat and then pointed to a large entrance in the side of the mountain that was impossible to miss. "Do you see that cave over there? It leads to quite an impressive view."

"Really?" Elisabeth said.

Balinus nodded, his cheeks ruddy as he smiled at her.

Elisabeth nudged David with her shoulder. "Come on. Let's check it out." She stood and straightened her tunic before dragging him to his feet.

"I do not appear to have a choice in the matter, do I? I thought you were tired?"

"I feel better now." She bounced on her tiptoes. "I've never been in a cave before. Are you coming, Cato?"

"I will be there shortly."

"Cato, take your time, my friend." David smirked at Elisabeth as he raised her hand and kissed it. "Take your time."

Elisabeth's mouth dropped and she turned to look at the others before bursting into laughter.

"Oh, I see how it is." With a smile, Cato put his hands behind his head and stretched out on the grass. "Well then, on second thought, finish the story you were telling me earlier, old man. I know when I'm not wanted."

Chapter Ten

David and Elisabeth walked a few hundred yards to the mouth of the cave that looked like two large doorways carved out of the bottom corner of a mountain. There was no way anyone walking along the path would miss it.

Elisabeth flung her arms out wide. "This is awesome," she shouted and then bounced up the rocks toward the entrance. "Come on, Aquarius."

David whistled a tune while following close behind. Water dripped from a crack in the ceiling and trickled down the wall, plunking as it splashed into a puddle on the ground. They rounded a small bend and found themselves inside a dark tunnel; the only light from another exit at the far end.

Elisabeth searched for David's hand in the dark. "You go first." With a nervous laugh, she nudged him in front, grabbing his arm when she heard a squeaking noise. "Oh my gosh, that better not be a bat." Her senses seemed heightened, but she enjoyed the adrenaline rush while breathing in the water-saturated air.

Halfway through, he stopped. She stood behind him in the dark, listening to the mighty roar of the waterfall ahead of them. In the pitch black, the only other sound was their own breathing. David turned around.

"What? What's the matter?" She hugged him tight and let out a nervous giggle.

"Shhh."

"Oh my God, what do you hear?"

"Only you, *cor meum*," he said with a laugh as he gave her a playful pinch. "You are such a wicked little thing."

"Wicked? Why am I wicked?"

"You…" If David wanted to say more, he didn't. Instead, he took her hand, leading the way down the bumpy passageway toward the light at the end of the tunnel.

Elisabeth pointed to the exit ahead of them while walking into a cool mist. "It's raining outside now."

"No, it's not rain. Will you look at that?"

With a dramatic squeal, Elisabeth stepped out of the tunnel and onto a generous sized ledge that overlooked the white rapids. A naturally formed balcony was partly covered with a grassy roof from the surrounding forest. It smelled like moss and rich earth. The sun streaming through the trees cast an emerald light that gave the entire area an ethereal feel, like something out of a fairy-tale.

High above them, to their right, the top of the first cascade of the waterfall could be seen through the thick foliage. At first glance, the mist it created looked like heavy rain. Elisabeth's hand covered her mouth as she peered straight down in front of her, watching the frothy river crash into large boulders before it disappeared over the second drop of the waterfall to their left. The setting both thrilled and terrified her.

David grinned, watching her reaction.

She stilled. "This place is so romantic."

"Well, of course it is. Why do you think I brought you here?" With a bemused smile, he tilted his head closer to her and chuckled. "Am I not the most romantic person you know?"

Elisabeth rolled her eyes, trying not to laugh. "You are such a player. I can only imagine how sorry you are to be here with me, instead of Severina or—"

David curled his arms over his head and gave her an incredulous look. "By the gods, Elisabeth, you will be the death of me." He reached for both of her hands, lacing his fingers through hers. "How can you not see the truth? I am so in love with you."

Elisabeth's mouth fell open, and she shuffled back a step.

"It is you. It has only ever been you. When you overheard us in the hallway, we were not speaking of Severina. We spoke of you. I am so sorry," he said, shaking his head. "I never meant for you to think…"

Elisabeth struggled to compose herself. "Why?"

He pulled her into his arms now damp from the mist. "Why what?"

"Why all the…" She let out a heavy sigh. "Severina?"

David winced and squeezed his eyes shut for a moment. "To make you jealous."

"That was a stupid thing to do."

"I can see that now." He had a pained expression and his voice was shaky. "I wanted to know if you might be falling for me…"

Her pulse raced.

"Even half as much as I have fallen for you." David's gaze never drifted from her face and he seemed restless as he held her even tighter. "Tell me an if?"

Elisabeth's heart pounded. "If... " The tiny word hung in the air, but this time she understood why. "If only you knew how crazy in love with you I am." A flush crept across her cheeks.

He let out a huge breath. "In my entire life, nobody has ever said..." His voice choked with tears, but he relaxed and loosened his arms.

"You are my if," Elisabeth whispered.

David's relief was obvious as he let go and took a small step back. He held his chin high, a boyish grin plastered across his face. "She loves me."

Elisabeth lowered her head. Her knees were wobbly, but she wore a smile that could not be contained.

With a gleam in his eye, he guided her chin upward with his hand, yet without touching this time. To anyone watching, it would have appeared to be choreographed steps between two dance partners. The space between them felt electric. He slipped a hand around her waist, slowly pulling her close.

"Don't ever try to make me jealous again."

"I wouldn't dream of it." He moved his face closer and his gaze wandered from her lips to her eyes and back to her lips again.

Elisabeth took a deep breath. "Do-you-know-what-my-mother-says?" she blurted out before he could kiss her.

David's chin dropped to his chest and he laughed, shaking his head. "No, *cor meum,* what does your mother say?"

"The right boy will not make you jealous of other girls, but will make other girls jealous of you."

"Your mother is wise." He lifted his head and his

tone was warm and caring.

She swallowed the lump in her throat. "I think that—"

"Elisabeth?" David moved one of his hands to the back of her neck, his thumb resting near her ear, and pulled her toward him. "Stop talking," he whispered before his lips moved over hers.

She closed her eyes, trying to calm the butterflies in her stomach.

His gentle kiss was somehow familiar. In an instant, a thousand fears were washed away. When the kiss ended, another began with more intensity and longing than the first. They'd waited centuries for this single moment. Her closed eyes prickled with tears from a wave of a déjà vu. Wrapped in his embrace, she recognized everything: his earthy scent, the grape-flavored taste of his kiss, the feel of his unshaven face brushing against her. They'd been here together before, in that space between dreams and reality.

When David pulled back, Elisabeth took a deep, savoring breath while trying to suppress a silly grin.

He cupped her face in his hands. "I swear, from the moment I first saw you, I knew you with all of my heart."

Beaming, Elisabeth reached up and held his wrists. "I don't think there was ever a time when you and I have been strangers."

He moved his hands to her waist, pulling her closer. "I cannot explain it, but when you—"

"Are you still alive?" Cato shouted through the darkness of the cave. "What is over there?"

David kissed Elisabeth's forehead. "Come see for yourself," he called out.

Elisabeth, breathless with a pounding heart, turned to look down the tunnel. She leaned into David while her mind wandered to thoughts of love, of Balinus' story of Velino and Nera. Did a shepherd and a nymph really believe they could be together? Did they not see they were star-crossed lovers from two different realities?

A chill coursed through her.

Did a time traveler and a Roman slave really believe they could be together? Pushing back welling tears, Elisabeth already knew David's bleak, endless future and personal hell. She'd seen the torment etched into his ageless eyes.

No happily-ever-after awaited them.

"How can we ever be together?" Her voice broke. "I am a time-traveler, and you…"

He rested his cheek on the top of her head. "For whatever reason, you are here now, *cor meum*. You are here now."

She knew the reason she was here now. To save David's life.

Wait…

Elisabeth's breath hitched.

Whatever stops him from aging hasn't happened yet. If she was here to change one event, couldn't other things be changed as well? A little tweak here? A little adjustment there? Surely to God, time-travel must have some perks? Elisabeth exhaled before looking up at him, heart aflutter. "You…you are going to grow old."

"Of course I am. You and I, we are going to grow old together." He smirked and wiggled his eyebrows.

Elisabeth laughed and swatted him. "I can't think when you do that with your brows."

"What are you thinking?"

That she'd risk angering the gods if it meant altering his tormented future. With a devilish grin, she shook her head, but said nothing. Depressing thoughts pushed aside, her eyes narrowed while staring into the dark cave. "Why can't I see Cato in there?"

"We're looking into the darkness now. It will be more difficult leaving since we were heading toward the light on our way in, but do not worry for we can feel our way along the walls."

"We have to touch those slimy walls? There are probably spiders, earwigs, and God knows what else." Elisabeth wrinkled her nose. "If I faint, will you carry me out?"

David laughed. "Undoubtedly."

With a satisfied smile, she hugged him.

"Aquarius," Cato shouted as he drew nearer.

"Yes?" David's gaze remained on Elisabeth.

"Have you mentioned you are in love with her yet, because I swear to—"

"Ca-to," he warned.

Elisabeth's mouth fell open. She exchanged a wide-eyed look with David before they burst into laughter.

"About bloody time." Cato's silhouette appeared when he neared the end of the tunnel. "I swear to Jupiter, Aquarius, if you had not yet confessed how you felt, I was going to tell her myself." He shook his head while looking at Elisabeth. "By the gods, has he ever fallen for you. Have you ever asked him why he keeps that red hair ribbon of yours? Aquarius thinks I do not remember why, but…" Cato's eyes widened. "I remember why," he said with a dramatic nod of his head.

A flush crept across David's cheeks. "Yes, well…" He cleared his throat. "Perhaps some other time."

Cato sucked in a quick breath as he took in their surroundings. "Wow."

"Impressive, isn't it? When Aquarius and I…"

David put his hand on Elisabeth's arm to hush her before glancing at Cato. Catching his attention, he put a finger to his lips. They moved out of the light, back into the cave, listening to a voice at the other end.

"It's Balinus," Elisabeth said after recognizing his bubbly voice, but then a torch appeared. It seemed to be heading through the tunnel, toward them. She held her stomach.

"Are your slaves in there?" Balinus yelled out.

"He warns us," Cato whispered as his shoulders curled forward.

"That is what I attempt to find out, old man," Rufus roared back while waving the flame in the darkness. "My slaves are close. They were spotted north of here helping a man with his donkey, or some such nonsense. I know it was them. I am sure of it."

Elisabeth realized they were trapped. She followed Cato and David as they crept back out onto the balcony, sliding up against the cliff wall. Cato hid to the right of the doorway beside a thick branch that grew down through the forest brush. David went to the left, positioning Elisabeth behind him.

"Aquarius…shoot him," Cato whispered through clenched teeth. "What are you waiting for? Take a shot."

David's posture stiffened. He shook his head.

"Gaius Cornelius Aquarius, if you are here, I

suggest you announce yourself immediately," Rufus called out, his voice getting closer.

Elisabeth's breath hitched, and she grabbed onto David. He pulled her against the rock wall of the mountain before unsheathing his dagger.

"They are obviously not in here," Balinus called out in a flat tone. "There is just a ledge at the other end."

Rufus let out an exaggerated sigh.

The thundering sounds all around them seemed to fade into the distance as Elisabeth stood pinned against the side of the cliff. Her gaze darted up to the grassy overhang. There were only two ways off this ledge; the tunnel or the rushing river that would sweep them over the falls within seconds. About to hyperventilate, Elisabeth buried her face in David's back. Every millisecond moved at an unbearable speed. She held her breath as the inevitable moment drew nearer. Their only chance would be if Rufus didn't step outside of the tunnel, but that would take a miracle. David looked prepared to fight, but from the side of a mountain ledge with a giant of a man? That could end up a bigger disaster.

She pushed a pile of rocks aside with her foot and shuffled as far along the ledge as possible so David could step back and they'd be flush against the wall. When they heard Rufus grumbling, she knew he had to be near the end of the tunnel. Her leg muscles tightened. Elisabeth wanted to run, but there was nowhere to go.

He was so close.

Too close.

She dared not look to see if he had walked onto the

ledge. He would only need to step outside to see them.

What was that noise?

Hissing?

Elisabeth felt the color drain from her face, and then turned ever so slightly to look at the ground beside her.

She gasped, and the sound of her heartbeat thrashed in her ears. If anyone thought the situation couldn't get any worse, they'd be wrong. Coiled at her feet, next to the dislodged rock, was a snake, looking as startled as Elisabeth. Her mouth fell open, repulsed, but unable to look away from the creature.

"No...no...no..." she whimpered.

David's focus remained on the entrance to the tunnel, but he squeezed Elisabeth's hand in reassurance, oblivious to the snake on the opposite side of her. When it twisted its gray and black body and raised its triangular-shaped head, she covered her mouth, attempting to take a slow step away. At that moment, it lunged, moving fast and sinking its fangs deep into her ankle. It bit her not once, but twice, before slithering in the tunnel's direction. The sharp sting was instant, feeling as if the snake had injected red hot lava into her leg.

In shock, Elisabeth's fingers reached up and touched her already numbing lips. David and Cato faded away; Rufus and even the snake were no longer a concern. The only thing on her mind was the crippling pain. It felt like someone was tearing apart the flesh from her ankle with a red hot poker. A high-pitched scream bounced off the cliff walls. Had it come from her? The blood dribbled from the puncture wounds and the area seemed to swell.

She couldn't think straight. What was she supposed to do?

"A viper!" David yelled, snapping Elisabeth out of her daze. He spun around and pulled her to safety against him, not realizing she'd already been bitten.

Disoriented, she stared at the river below, teeth clenched as the agony from the bites increased tenfold. Her face started to tingle.

The serpent coiled itself, looking ready to attack again. Cato jumped back, unsure what to do. At that moment, Rufus stepped outside and almost stumbled over it.

The slave dealer screamed when the snake tried to strike at him. He rammed his flaming torch into it, struggling to keep the snake away.

"Hold off, man!" David yelled. He made one single rotation of his sling and sent a rock smashing into the head of the snake, killing it instantly.

Out of breath, Rufus wiped sweat from his brow. He then turned his head and stared at David, who stood with his feet planted wide apart, dagger drawn, ready to take on the giant.

Before anyone made a move, Elisabeth fell hard to the ground, too weak to stand as the burning sensation spread throughout her leg. Writhing in agony, she squeezed her eyes shut and nausea washed over her.

David gasped, dropped the knife from his hand, and fell to his knees at her side. "Try to remain still so the poison does not spread."

"Aquarius, she's been bitten," Cato screamed. "Her ankle, look at it."

"I can see that," he snapped. The veins in his neck bulged. He turned, glaring at the dead snake on the ground next to him. David picked the carcass up in his hands. With a guttural roar, he hurled it over the edge before gathering Elisabeth into his arms. She stared at him with an incredulous look and he shook his head in denial; his voice choked with emotion. "No…"

Trying to breathe through the crushing pain, she felt so cold and couldn't stop shivering. She could feel the venom circulating through her body, numbing her cheeks and fingertips.

David was hunched over, rocking her, when Cato swooped down, grabbed the dagger that had dropped, and held it up to Rufus' throat. "She will likely be dead by tomorrow." His posture then slumped.

Elisabeth gasped. Cato couldn't be talking about her.

"Viper asp," Rufus said with an understanding nod.

She stared at David, waiting for him to say they were mistaken.

"Stay calm," he whispered to her. His hand shook as he touched her face. "Stay calm and try not to move."

Cato lowered his voice. "Give me your word you will not stop Aquarius from being with her tonight, and you have our word we will go with you when she is gone."

A cold gust of fear swept through Elisabeth. She shook her head before looking at Cato, then back at David, convinced she'd heard wrong, on both accounts. "No….no…"

Rufus grunted and nodded his head again. "I am not a heartless man."

Cato handed the dagger back to David, who quickly sheathed it.

Elisabeth shivered, eyes rimmed with tears. "Cato didn't mean…?" She closed her eyes, stomach churned in knots. The pain increased with every passing second.

"Hush, *cor meum,* do not listen to Cato. He speaks nonsense. You are going to be fine." David's voice cracked as he lifted her off the ground. "You are trembling."

"Take off her sandal." Balinus stepped forward. "Her leg will continue to swell."

With quick but delicate hands, Cato removed both of her shoes.

Elisabeth twisted in agony and let out an ear-piercing scream, begging for mercy as the torment became unbearable.

"Balinus…" David choked back tears. "What can we do?"

Rufus' voice rose in pitch. "Come. I have an onion for the asp bite. That might help ease the pain." He held up his torch. "Stay behind me. I'll light the way."

Carried by David through the tunnel, Elisabeth shivered, squeezing her eyes shut. "Cold…I'm so cold." Her leg felt like it was being sliced by a thousand razor-sharp knives.

"Shhh, *cor meum,* I will get you as many blankets as you wish. Remember, I promised you would never be cold again." David's voice was emotional. "Just stay with me."

"Watch your step right here, Aquarius. The ground is uneven," Cato warned.

She couldn't make her hand move to reach the crystal.

****

Elisabeth winced in agony before struggling to

open her eyes. Why was she outside and not in her room? A small crowd gathered around—some faces unrecognizable.

Half sitting, half lying down, with her head cradled in the crook of David's arm, he nervously rocked back and forth. "Please don't die. Please don't die," he whispered repeatedly in her ear.

"Kuzey, fetch bucket for girl," a gray-haired stranger with a sonorous voice called out.

Kuzey, a strapping man in his mid-twenties, with dirty blonde hair, whipped around. "What for?"

"Girl will be sick."

With a confused look, Kuzey gestured toward the grass, indicating she could throw up anywhere.

The man with the slow, deep voice smacked him on the back of the head. "Get bucket for girl." He then put his hand on David's shoulder. "I am Hayri. We camp nearby and hear screams." When Hayri spoke, his jaw seemed to remain clenched, which caused a slight muffled effect whenever he said anything. You couldn't help but stop and listen, hoping he might say more. His voice was velvet. "If any way we can be assistance..."

Not looking up, David shook his head in reply.

With a sympathetic nod, Hayri strolled toward a man with jet-black hair and deep olive skin. "Temel, is food cooked?"

Temel nodded.

Kuzey reappeared and dropped a pail on the ground next to Balinus, before joining Hayri and Temel.

As the three men stood around, Elisabeth noticed they all wore pants, rather than tunics. She turned to bury her face in David's arm. Her stomach cramped and she was sure her leg was on fire. How can you experience this much pain while still conscious? The burning sensation was overwhelming.

"Aquarius…?" She froze at the sight of her leg stretched out in front of her. It didn't look real. The left one was swollen to almost twice its normal size, but even worse than that; the skin had turned a deep shade of eggplant purple from the knee down. Elisabeth's breath became raspy. She knew remaining in this time meant death within hours. Even if she returned home and made it to a hospital, her leg looked like it would have to be amputated.

Cato attempted to give Elisabeth a drink of water, but she turned away from the canteen when the rise of bile lodged in her throat. On cue, David lifted her to the side, holding her hair back while Balinus positioned the bucket to vomit in. Humiliated, tears streamed down her cheeks. She gritted her teeth, trying to endure the agony. She didn't want to die here. Not like this.

David lowered her back down in his arms before brushing the hair off her face.

Balinus looked troubled but gave Elisabeth a loving smile while arranging blankets and cloaks on top of her.

"For girl." When Hayri handed Balinus a blanket, Elisabeth noticed that his dark eyes were void of any warmth. "When she…gone…you welcome share our fire." He then pointed a dirty finger at the muscular blond. "That Kuzey."

Kuzey gave a curt nod.

"My son dumb-looking one called Temel."

With a nervous smile, Temel ran a hand through his curly black hair.

"Many thanks." Balinus' voice was quiet.

"We give privacy for say goodbyes." Hayri walked toward the tree line, followed by Kuzey and Temel.

"She will not stop shaking." David looked up, his eyes turning cold and hard. "Where is Rufus with the damn onion?"

Onion?

"Anti-venom... I need...my dad," Elisabeth mumbled in English while trying to reach for the crystal necklace. I need...to...go home." It took all the energy she had to speak as her body contorted with pain. "Hospital..."

"She suffers from delirium," Cato said in a quiet voice. "What is she saying?"

With a quick movement, David reached for her hand and pulled it away from the crystal. "No, *cor meum*, do not use that. You need to stay here."

"Aquarius?" Balinus jerked his head back. "You know where she is from?"

Elisabeth struggled to keep her vision focused.

David's mouth fell open and he raised his head, whispering to Balinus, "I was not aware *you* knew."

"Do you not think it would be best to let her return?"

David shook all over. "I don't know."

"If she stays here, Aquarius, I am certain she will die. I would like to believe they have a cure for this in the future, my friend."

Although he whispered, David's voice seemed to be on the verge of hysteria and his hold on her tightened. "Nobody knows Elisabeth is here. She may not be found in time."

"Oh, I see, I see." Balinus shook his head. "We

have a dilemma. One cannot cure the dead."

Cato narrowed his eyes. "What are you two speaking of? In the name of…she is not really a goddess…she cannot be…"

"Not now, Cato," Balinus said.

"You *must* tell me."

"Not now, Cato!" David yelled.

Everything around Elisabeth seemed to take on a yellow tinge as her eyes clouded over and tears rolled down her cheeks.

David's shoulders began to quake. With frantic hands, he searched for the hanky tucked into her belt and then dabbed her tears away.

"I found the onion." Rufus appeared and shuffled back a step with an incredulous look on his face. "Her eyes are bleeding? It is only a matter of time and then…"

David glared at him. "Speak another word and I will cut out your tongue." He then whispered to Elisabeth, "Shhh, everything is going to be fine. You are going to be fine."

Elisabeth cringed at the sight of the bloody tear-stained hanky in his hand. She looked away, but ended up seeing her leg instead. How could it swell that much? Can a leg explode? Was it actually a possibility?

"Should we cut her leg to let the poison bleed out?" Cato whispered.

"She is bleeding enough." When David looked up at Rufus, his tone deepened again. "Give the onion to Cato, sit over there, and stay out of our way. We will let you know if we need anything else."

For some strange reason, Rufus obeyed. He walked to his wagon and began winding up, organizing huge lengths of rope, trying to keep himself busy.

Cato pressed a slice of the onion against the puncture wounds on Elisabeth's poisoned leg. "What were you two speaking of? Will somebody please tell me what is going on?"

David brought a shaky hand to his forehead. "Not now, Cato. Just keep the onion on the bites to draw out the venom." He shook his head as he looked at Balinus. "Maybe she should return home. I don't know." He held Elisabeth tighter, as if afraid to ever let her go. "Tell me, old man, what do we do? We cannot let her die." David turned his head away from the others. As Elisabeth attempted to extend her hand, he reached for it and kissed her fingers before wrapping them around the crystal for her. "If your people can save you, go home, *cor meum*. Go home. But please…come back to me…" His voice lost all its power. "Come back to me."

She stared at David as he scrubbed a hand over his face.

I love you, Aquarius.

She hadn't the strength to speak the words out loud. The blood rushed from her head, down through her body. Her muscles became rigid, her eyes seemed to want to roll backward, and then everything turned to darkness.

****

Elisabeth felt clammy and gross as she grimaced in pain.

Someone was stroking the hair off her forehead, over and over again in a soothing manner. It felt nice. Calming.

She struggled to open her eyes.

David.

"Pray she does not have another fit," Balinus said.

A fit? She had no recollection of having a seizure.

Elisabeth's eyes widened. She was going to be sick again. Balinus grabbed the bucket while David held her up. Afterward, her entire body lay limp and lifeless when her head was lowered back down onto his lap.

"She will not survive," Balinus mumbled before he stood up, beginning to pace back and forth.

David crumpled over top of her. "*Cor meum,*" he whispered, while stroking her damp hair.

Her eyes clouded over with bloody tears. She tried to focus her thoughts, but her mind seemed groggy. Why was she still here? Why hadn't the crystal brought her home?

David sat up again. "Cato, she is burning up."

Cato walked closer, put his hand on David's shoulder, and said quietly, "Aquarius, say your goodbye, my friend, while she can still hear you."

Elisabeth knew her body was dying, limb by limb, organ by organ.

Her heartbeat quickened when she stared up at David. She adored him and wished her parents could have met him. Elisabeth let out a gut-wrenching moan, realizing she'd never see her mom and dad again or get to say I love you one last time.

Oh God, this can't be happening.

Cradled in David's arms, she felt him shove Cato away in anger. "She is not going to die."

Balinus sat beside her and spoke in a serious tone. "My dear girl, I have something that will help you. I am going to put it under your tongue. I want you to let it dissolve there. Do you understand?"

Elisabeth didn't have the strength to respond, let

alone open her mouth. Cloudy thoughts entered her mind before floating back out again.

What good would anything he gave her do?

An onion had been their biggest hope for pain relief.

People still die from venomous snakebites in the twenty-first century.

She had no chance of survival here in the first century.

Gently forcing her mouth open, Balinus placed a tiny amount of powder under her tongue. "The taste is reminiscent of honey," he said with a nervous grin. He then reached over and patted David's back. "Aquarius, get some rest, my friend. She will live."

"Look at her...she is..." He paused and pressed the heel of his hand to his eyes, trying to compose himself. "How can she possibly?"

"Twice bitten by a viper asp," Cato muttered under his breath. "It does not get much worse than that, old man."

"Come. It is getting dark," Balinus insisted. "We will join our new friends around their fire tonight."

Cato snorted. "I don't trust them as far as I can spit. They wear trousers."

The old man gave him an incredulous look.

"Seriously? Everyone knows only barbarians wear trousers."

"If you say so." Balinus picked up his things and walked into the trees, leaving the others, including Rufus, to trail behind him. "Let us join the barbarians around their fire."

"This changes nothing," Rufus growled as he led his oxen behind Cato and Balinus into the forest. "Once she dies, you and Aquarius are coming with me."

David cradled Elisabeth in his arms and buried his face in her hair. He then raised his head and cried out into the night with such distress that the others must have thought him deranged with grief.

Elisabeth's hand rolled off her lap and flopped onto the grass, as if she was already a corpse.

Chapter Eleven

Crickets chirping through the night, seeming to call out to one another, awoke Elisabeth. She lay still and listened to the hypnotic sounds of the river rushing beyond the waterfall. The campfire crackled nearby, and she enjoyed its warmth on her face while everyone slept. Everyone except for David, who held her fingers in his and caressed the back of her hand with his thumb, over and over again.

He sat cross-legged beside her, holding vigil. His puffy eyes looked off into the night with an empty stare. Raising her opposite hand, she reached for the crystal and then realized she felt (dare one even think it?) better.

David gasped at the movement. "Elisabeth?" He let out an uncontrollable sob.

Her smile couldn't be contained. What the heck had Balinus given her? Elisabeth let go of her necklace, wondering how to explain a venomous snake bite to her parents when she was supposedly studying at home. She stared at David and watched the glow from the dancing flames light up his face. If the old man could cure her, Elisabeth would stay right here for now.

"I think whatever Balinus gave me is working."

He let out a huge sigh and lifted his eyes toward the heavens.

"Have I been sleeping long?"

"Hours." His voice choked with tears. "You have had several doses of Balinus' medicine."

"Can I please have something to drink?"

"Of course." He scrambled for the canteen before lifting her head so she could take a sip.

Elisabeth drank and then gave a small yelp. "Look." She pointed to hundreds of fireflies twinkling in the trees behind him and tried to sit up more. "I've never seen so many."

David propped a cloak beneath her head so she could watch them. "You mustn't get too excited." He lay down next to Elisabeth, on top of the blankets that covered her, and rested his head on his folded arm.

Her breathing was labored. "Aquarius?"

He reached for her hand.

With a sigh and a slight smile, she watched the fireflies dance amongst the trees, looking like hundreds of enchanted fairies. "When I was little, my parents took me camping. One night, I wandered off and ended up befriending a mysterious man at a nearby campsite. I can still picture him sitting in that circular clearing, staring into the fire with his back to the trees. He was nothing more than a shadow in the darkness." She stopped to take a breath.

"Take your time, *cor meum*," David whispered. "Take your time."

Elisabeth paused and closed her eyes for a moment to recall more clearly the events of long ago. "The stranger called out to me by name. Curious, I crept forward and asked him how he knew me."

"What did he say?"

"He told me he was magic and said we *all* have magical powers, but we've forgotten. He told me never to forget that."

Elisabeth started shivering and David sat up, tucking the blankets around her tighter.

"I stayed, talking to him for hours. I didn't even know my parents were searching for me until they found me later in the evening. They were frantic. The man invited my mom and dad to join him around the fire. Soon they too were mesmerized by his stories."

Elisabeth paused to rest, watching the twinkling lights dance upon the branches.

"He gave me a jar to catch fireflies. I ran around the campsite, filling the glass until I had lots of them. Then I returned, planting myself at his feet. Opening the jar, the man removed a firefly, squished the beetle in his fingers, and then peeled the glowing light off of the bug."

David nodded in understanding. "It is a powder."

"Yes," Elisabeth said, her eyes lighting up at the memory. "The man rubbed the powder on my face in a war paint pattern. It continued to glow and flicker on my nose, on my cheeks, blinking on and off as I danced around the fire."

"With twinkling firefly butts smeared all over you," he said with a smile.

Elisabeth grinned while nodding her head. "That's exactly what he said." She reached for his hand again, looking at him in earnest. "Aquarius, I've never understood why, but I've always felt there was something magical about that night. As long as I live, I will never forget it. I think…I think that man was you."

David jerked his head back and had a dazed look on his face. Then, with a weak smile, he leaned closer. "It could not have been me, *cor meum*," he said in a soothing tone.

She rubbed her forehead as exhaustion set in. "Your name is David Perrier. I know you in the future."

His eyes narrowed in concentration.

"I don't know why, but you don't age."

With a sad smile, he stroked the hair off her forehead. "I assure you I do." David removed the cloak that propped her up to make her lay back down again. "I will be right back, but then you need to rest."

Elisabeth let out a heavy sigh while closing her eyes. "Aye-aye, Captain."

A few minutes later, she heard a gasp and turned to see a little boy, no more than eight years old, trembling beside her. Eyes as blue as the t-shirt he was wearing peeked out from beneath a mop of brown hair. His mouth fell open as they stared at each other; his jeans and sneakers looking out of place. Elisabeth squeezed her eyes shut, but when opening them again to comfort the small child, found he was gone. The pain in her leg started pulsing. Was this a hallucination? Where was David? She wanted him. Needed him. The powerful venom was playing tricks with her mind now.

"Have another drink of water," David whispered when he returned a few minutes later. He put the canteen into her hand while kneeling beside her.

She lifted it to her lips, taking a sip as he slipped an arm beneath her head. When Elisabeth looked up at him, she spewed water everywhere and started laughing.

"What?" He leaned closer, with blinking firefly lights smeared across the bridge of his nose.

"Oh…don't make me laugh, it hurts." Giggling, Elisabeth wiped her mouth with the back of her hand.

"You've got something on your face," she said with a huge smile.

He cocked his head while grinning. "I do?" David rubbed some of the glowing powder off with his finger and inspected it before dabbing it on her forehead. "Sleep well." He then whispered, "You need rest to build your strength back up so we can escape from Rufus as soon as possible. Cato and I are working on a plan with Balinus' help."

When he began to move away, Elisabeth shook her head and reached for his arm. "Stay beside me," she whispered. "I don't trust that Hayri guy. His eyes are cold."

David glanced across the fire. "Did you notice how many men there were?"

Elisabeth turned her head, expecting to see three extra people.

"Nine." He swallowed a lump in his throat. "When we arrived at their camp, there were six others already here. That will make our escape from Rufus more difficult."

Her breath hitched.

"Hopefully they will leave first thing in the morning, but I do not intend to let you out of my sight. We'll try to buy more time here and then escape as soon as you are able to walk."

"I'm sure everything will be fine." She fidgeted with the stack of blankets and then chuckled when looking at him again. "I love that your nose is still blinking."

"So is your forehead."

"Tell me an if," she whispered.

"All right." David lowered his voice and leaned

closer. "If you knew how much I tried to make you smile when we first met, you'd think me mad."

"What?" she said with a light giggle. "Why?"

"I thought the way to your heart was to make you smile. The problem was, the more you smiled, the more I fell."

She pulled the blanket over her mouth, hiding her grin.

"See." He shook his head, but his eyes twinkled with mischief. "You're smiling and there I go again, falling."

"Oh, puh-lease." Elisabeth gave him a playful shove. "You are too stinking cute. I bet you've used that line a million times."

David's mouth fell open and then he clamped his lips together, determined not to laugh. "Never. You need to rest now." He tucked the blankets around her before kissing the top of her head. "Goodnight, *cor meum.*"

Chapter Twelve

The sound of music filled the air—if you could call it that. After sitting up too fast, causing lightheadedness, Elisabeth groaned and lay back down again.

"By Jupiter!" Cato hurried to sit at Elisabeth's feet. "Aquarius, wake up."

"Do let the poor boy sleep," Balinus said as he walked over.

In a daze, David bolted upright, shaking the grogginess away. "Tell me what I can do?" he asked while adjusting the cloak beneath Elisabeth's head.

She reached for his hand. "Nothing."

David let out a sigh of relief.

"What's the escape plan?" she whispered.

"Tonight, if you are able to walk, we disappear into the night while Rufus sleeps."

Her mouth fell open. "That's the plan?"

David frowned before looking away. He then wiggled his brows, stealing a glance at Elisabeth from the corner of his eye. "I never said it was brilliant."

She couldn't help but grin. The faces he made when frustrated were hilarious yet adorable.

David then looked at the slave dealer, who seemed to pay them no attention. "Rufus knows we will not run away without you, but he does not know you have improved so quickly. He must believe it is best to let you recover here, so we will use his overconfidence to our advantage. When he sleeps tonight, we will make our getaway. The old man is helping us."

Balinus nodded. "We shall follow the river east for one hour until we reach *Lacus Velinus*. Near the lake is a villa. Aurelius, the owner, is a good friend." He paused to look at Elisabeth. "With the medicine I've been administering, you should be strong enough to walk there."

"Of course, I will help you," David said, squeezing her fingers.

"Do not let Rufus or the others know you are almost healed," Balinus said. "You must use that to your advantage."

"But what about my leg? Do you think…" Elisabeth stopped and lowered her head. "Mr. Velvet is coming," she whispered.

Cato snickered at the nickname.

Hayri meandered over from the opposite side of the camp to where they sat. "You must be luckiest girl." Everything about the man seemed unrushed, from the way he walked to the way he talked. "I never imagine you survive."

"Hayri, you in this round?" Kuzey called out. "Rufus is joining."

"Yes. I come." He then shouted over at his black-haired son, who appeared to be the source of the music. "Temel, play something not so sad on *aulos*." He shook his head and mumbled, "Athena herself want *aulos* back just to hear him no more."

"Yes, *Baba*." Temel blew into an instrument resembling two small flutes, although the shrill sound was more like a bagpipe. If you closed your eyes, you could almost imagine being in Scotland.

Elisabeth watched Hayri stroll back to Rufus, Kuzey, and the other barbaric-looking men. They shouted and cursed while gathered around what she guessed to be a dice game. "What are they playing?"

"We call it knucklebones," Cato answered. "It is a game played for fun." He enunciated each word as if she was from another planet and had never seen men playing a game before. "It is played using the dried ankle bones of a sheep and is…"

With a heavy sigh, Elisabeth turned to look at David. "You told him, didn't you?"

Smirking, he laid a hand over his heart and shook his head. "I swear, it was not me." He then reached over and smacked the back of Cato's head. "What are you doing? Talk to her like you normally do. Idiot."

Cato's ears turned red. "What? She didn't know what it was. Clearly, they do not play knucklebones in the future."

She stared at Balinus as he sat down beside her. "You told him?"

"What-if-I-said-he-guessed?" he asked in his sing-song voice while tapping his fingers.

Elisabeth pursed her lips.

"Well…alrighty then." Balinus leaned forward and said, "I told him, but only because he was aware something was not right."

"And I will try not to take it personally that you told everyone except me. Am I not also your friend?" Cato threw some kindling into the campfire.

"Of course you are." She lowered her gaze. "It's just…"

He rubbed his forearms and it looked like he

wanted to say something. "Elisabeth…?" He cleared his throat and twisted his wrist. "I just want you to know that your secret is safe with me. I mean it." He then turned to look at David with a huge grin plastered across his face. "And what a secret it is."

Elisabeth couldn't help but chuckle. "Well, thanks for being there for me yesterday."

He shrugged his shoulders and took a drink from his canteen.

Judging by the light filtering between the moss-covered trees, it was early afternoon. Sunbeams peeking through the leaves cast an eerie green light all around their campsite, making the area feel somewhat supernatural. Why were Hayri and his men still here?

"How do you feel?" Balinus leaned closer and lowered his voice again. "You slept through the night and all of the morning."

"Weak, but the pain is almost gone. Do you really think I'll be able to walk for an hour?"

"Have you seen your leg?"

Elisabeth cringed at the thought of her leg, now a dead purple stump. How was she going to explain this whole mess to her father? She'd never told her parents about the quartz crystal because they'd never believe her, and if they did, they'd never in a million years allow it to be used. She wouldn't have cared before; she'd vowed never to use it again, but things have changed. It was overwhelming to even think about the future right now.

With a gleam in his eyes, Balinus nodded. "Go on, look at your leg."

With David's help, she sat up. Fearful, she pulled the blanket aside, lifting her tunic to the knee. Elisabeth cried out in relief and covered her mouth. "Oh my gosh, it's...I thought for sure it was going to have to be ampu..." She teared up. Her leg was once again flesh coloured and almost back to its normal size. She waved her hands in front of her face, trying hard not to cry. "What the heck did you give me, Balinus?"

Cato let out a long, low whistle, and David hugged her as she shook her head and squeezed her eyes shut.

Balinus looked over his shoulder at Rufus and the others before leaning closer, whispering, "I am going to give you some more of the elixir I gave you yesterday. Just the tiniest amount as it is very powerful, as you can see. Too much and your body could go into shock."

Elisabeth nodded and then covered her legs with the blankets once again. "Thank you. From the bottom of my heart, thank you."

Balinus reached into his robes, pulling out a glass vial that was a bit larger than his middle finger. He removed a cork stopper and placed a minuscule amount of dark red powder onto the tip of his thumb. "This is all you need." He dropped it beneath her tongue. "Let it dissolve there."

"What is it?" Elisabeth asked.

Balinus put the stopper back in the vial and tucked it into the folds of his robes. "It is just a stone."

"That is not a stone." Cato stood up and poked at the campfire. "It is powder."

Balinus laughed. "You are very observant. It is oft called the stone that is not a stone."

"Whatever it is, it saved my life." Elisabeth pressed her fingers to her smiling lips. "Thank you. Thank you for that...miracle medicine. I know I wouldn't have gotten better this fast at home." She could already feel something powerful surging through her body, giving her strength. "What is it?"

"It is naught but an age-old remedy." Balinus was less animated than normal. He reached for his satchel, fidgeting through it, before putting it back down again. His eyes darted from Elisabeth, to Cato, to…

David's posture perked up. "What troubles you, Balinus? I can see something weighs heavy on your mind."

The old man's smile wavered. "As a matter of fact…"

Cato sat back down, put his hands behind his head, and stretched out. "Go ahead, get it off your chest."

Balinus spoke in a quiet voice. "Elisabeth, why are you, for lack of a better word, here?"

She wasn't about to admit that an immortal David Perrier sent her here; that their lives were somehow intertwined throughout time. Flustered, Elisabeth shrugged, fidgeted with her dress, then looked at David. A flush crept across her cheeks as she vaguely recalled telling him that he didn't age. Oh gosh, what was said last night?

Balinus pursed his lips. "I don't believe you are here to simply…fall in love."

Elisabeth cleared her throat. "Well, no…of course not. I, uh…" She was here to save David's life.

"I believe you are here for a reason still unknown to you."

"You do?" Her voice filled with wonder.

"I am not sure where to begin."

"How about at the beginning?" Cato suggested as he sat up.

"I suppose that is as good a place as any." Balinus

made himself comfortable and crossed his legs. "Do you remember when I told you about the time of Zep Tepi, when the gods still walked the earth?"

Elisabeth nodded.

"Zep Tepi is the Egyptian name for this period, long before the great flood. It was the time of Atlantis." He held his hands up to the sky. "Zep Tepi was when the gods came down from the heavens and lived in harmony with man and nature."

While Balinus spoke, Elisabeth cuddled against David.

"Before the gods left, they shared their knowledge with mankind."

"How?" Cato asked.

"They wrote it down on a stone tablet, for those wise enough to understand it."

Elisabeth's heart beat faster. "Are you talking about the Emerald Tablet?"

This was almost identical to the story she'd been told in Scotland. If she changed the word *gods* to *fairies*, it appeared to be the same tale of beings that came to earth at a time long before the great flood, before recorded history as we know it. These two legends must be the same.

"The Emerald Tablet." Balinus smiled and nodded his head. "My intuition was correct again. You do know about that of which I speak."

She gave a slow, disbelieving shake of her head. "I guarantee you know more than I do."

Elisabeth tried to stay focused, but her mind wandered. Was Celtic fairy lore a mutated version of the stories of the mythological gods, altered by storytellers over time?

David wrapped his arms around her, pulling a blanket to warm them both.

Balinus continued. "The Emerald Tablet was written by the Egyptian god, Thoth."

"Thoth?" Cato asked. "The Greeks call him Hermes. Is that not right, old man?"

"Yes, Thoth, Hermes, Mercury to the Romans; they are the same."

"Son of Jupiter," Cato added as he glanced over his shoulder at the others, who still seemed to be enjoying their game of knucklebones.

"Thoth was an Atlantean." Balinus paused to take a drink of water. "The gods left before the days of the great flood and Thoth hid the tablet in a pillar for mankind to find someday."

"How long ago did this happen?" David asked.

Balinus looked deep in thought as he rested his index finger on his lips. "More than ten thousand years ago."

Cato let out another long, low whistle.

"Legend has it the tablet was one day discovered by an Egyptian Pharaoh named Akhenaten. Akhenaten happened to be married to the most beautiful woman in the world at the time, Queen Nefertiti."

"Really?" Elisabeth said. "I've heard of both of them."

"Later, when Alexander the Great conquered Egypt, he discovered the Emerald Tablet amongst all the riches and treasures."

Elisabeth looked him directly in the eye. "This is the part I know. Alexander the Great put the Emerald Tablet on display at his library in Alexandria."

"Close." Balinus sat up taller. "For a period of

time, he decided to share the teachings with the world. He did put it on display, but this was at the Temple in Heliopolis. People flocked to see it, to try and interpret it."

"Then they had to hide the tablet again, to keep it safe," Elisabeth said.

David leaned closer to Balinus. "Why would they need to do that?"

Balinus' face lit up. "Because the Emerald Tablet is too powerful and important to lose. It belongs to all of mankind, not a select few. It contains only thirteen lines and is a formula or...recipe. When translated, studied, and understood, it is an information guide to the entire universe and how it works."

David glanced at Cato, and the two exchanged wide-eyed looks.

"The knowledge it contains is so powerful that men have tried to suppress it since the dawn of time."

"Why?" Cato edged closer.

Elisabeth swallowed the lump in her throat and answered for the old man. "To keep the knowledge for themselves. Long before it could be destroyed, the Emerald Tablet disappeared again, in order to keep it safe."

"There have always been powerful people trying to suppress knowledge." Balinus' smile wavered. "And here is the dilemma. Is it suppressing knowledge when you are keeping it safe? Until the day it can be shared? I believe the Emerald Tablet belongs to all of mankind, yet I also believe it should remain hidden for the time being. The secrets it contains, if in the hands of the wrong people..."

Elisabeth gave a half-hearted shrug. "What does it

matter anyhow? It's not like we're ever going to see it. I don't think many people in my time have even heard of the Emerald Tablet. It's become one of those forgotten legends."

Balinus wrinkled his nose. "My dear girl, if you came here and brought your knowledge and tools with you, what would happen? What almost happened?"

"My technology would be mistaken for magic. People would think I was a god. I'd have a sort of power over them, I suppose."

Balinus nodded. "Because you have knowledge of things we know nothing about, you have power. Knowledge is power. Repeat that back to me so I know you will never forget it."

Elisabeth grinned. "Knowledge is power."

The old man shook his head to show how serious he was and wagged his finger. His voice was firm. "Knowledge is power, and if you control the knowledge and the way people think, you control the people." He paused to let his words sink in. "Elisabeth? Curiosity begs me to ask you; would such an item, an item that belongs to all of mankind, be safer in your time?"

She bit the inside of her cheek while pondering the question for a moment, recalling a news article her parents had discussed once that stood out in her mind. During the 2011 Arab Spring uprising in Tahrir Square in Egypt, the locals formed a human chain to protect the antiquities inside Cairo's famous museum, home to King Tut's treasures, among so many other artifacts. "*Antiquities like that belong, not just to the Egyptians, but to all of mankind,*" her mom had said.

Elisabeth nodded. "Yes, I think so. I mean, the world is certainly not perfect, but…"

"Tell me, is there such a thing as a coincidence?" Balinus asked.

"A wise man once told me there is no such thing as a coincidence."

"Brilliant man," he said with a smile. "The day after I met you, we traveled to see Strabo to exchange your gemstone for coins."

Elisabeth nodded.

"Go on…" Cato moved closer.

Balinus reached into his satchel and pulled out the wrapped package Strabo had given him.

Elisabeth held her breath. "I remember that. You looked shaken up when you came outside. You were holding it in your arms and I asked if everything was all right."

He nodded. "Aquarius, Cato, you are perhaps old enough to recollect events of nine years ago when Titus led an attack on Jerusalem. The temple was destroyed and all the treasures within were brought back to Rome."

Cato's mouth fell open. "Go on…"

"Careful. Mr. Velvet is watching us," Elisabeth said while looking at her hands, trying to appear inconspicuous.

Balinus rubbed his forehead and then glanced over his shoulder for a moment to assess the situation.

Hayri stared at them, until someone called his attention back to the game. She didn't know why, but the way he watched them unnerved her.

Balinus patted the package on his lap and lowered his voice. "This was part of the looted treasure from the temple. It somehow ended up in King Herod's possession, probably through his Egyptian territories and…"

"Get to the point, old man," Cato said as his hand covered his mouth.

"Well, what I am trying to say is that I've been entrusted with the task of…of making sure this remains safe."

Elisabeth moved back slightly. "What is it?"

Balinus took a long pause before responding. "It is the Emerald Tablet."

"You son of a donkey!" Cato let out a dramatic squeal. "You have got to be kidding me."

David's posture stiffened and Elisabeth's hand reached up to her mouth as she stared at it.

"What's going on over there?" Rufus yelled.

"Nothing," she hollered back. "Mind your own business," she added under her breath.

From a distance, she noticed Hayri frown and run a hand through his gray hair. His gaze darted back and forth between Elisabeth and Rufus, the slave dealer.

"I think the reason you are here," Balinus said, whispering quickly, "is to make sure this stays safe. I think that is why our paths have crossed."

Elisabeth shook her head in denial. "What am I supposed to do with it? This can't have anything to do with me. Follow the pattern: An Atlantean god, an Egyptian pharaoh, Alexander the Great. I am not the next logical person on the list."

Balinus gave her a warm smile. "You yourself said nobody else can do this *time traveling* and nobody knows you are here."

"I'm here because…never mind. I'm here…I don't know why I'm here, but it's not because of that. I can't take that…that…*thing*. That's like saying, 'Here, do you mind bringing the Ark of the Covenant home and stashing it under your bed?'"

Balinus shrugged his shoulders. "Well, alrighty then."

"Oh, of course I'll take it. It's just...come on, it's strange."

"If you say so, but look at it this way. You appear from the future. I meet you and the following day I come into possession of the tablet upon which is written the knowledge of the gods. Is it not logical to think that you are the next person meant to keep this safe? In your care, it is guaranteed to be safe for the next..."

"Two thousand years," David said with a shaky voice.

"Okay, give me the..." She couldn't bring herself to say Emerald Tablet. It felt surreal. "Give me the stone."

Balinus let out a deep breath as he placed it on her lap. "The stone of the philosophers."

Elisabeth gasped and then jerked her head back. "What did you call it?"

"The stone of the philosophers." He tilted his body closer to Elisabeth. "Since before the reign of Alexander the Great, wise men...philosophers like myself...have been trying to decipher it, but you already know that."

"Yes, but you called it..." Elisabeth trembled as she carefully unwrapped the stone, needing to see it for herself. It appeared to be green granite, rather than emerald, and was smaller and lighter than she'd imagined. The thirteen lines on it were raised and written in another language.

"It is written in Sumerian," Balinus said as if

reading her mind.

"That elixir you gave me has to do with this, doesn't it?"

"Oh, you are very clever," he said with a secretive grin.

Breathless, Elisabeth's heart pounded.

It all made sense now.

The Emerald Tablet is the Philosopher's Stone.

"Oh my gosh." Her hand covered her mouth.

The Emerald Tablet is the Philosopher's Stone. Balinus' red powdered medicine was the elixir of life, which grants the recipient…immortality.

Elisabeth leaned closer and whispered. "You know how to make the elixir of life?"

"The what?" Cato asked.

Balinus shook his head. "No, no. I am not that wise. It was given to me. Truth be told, I've yet to meet anyone who has been able to." His eyes twinkled. "But, I believe we are in the presence of a sleeping giant."

The hair lifted on the back of Elisabeth's neck as she stared at David. "Yes, I think we are."

Chapter Thirteen

Elisabeth ran her fingers along the tablet, admiring the work of art. The words were bas-relief carved, rather than engraved. "It's not made of emerald," she pointed out.

Balinus shook his head. "Originally, emerald only meant green stone. Any kind of green stone."

She sucked in a quick breath and gave David an incredulous look. "This is probably the most sought after treasure in the history of mankind."

"I guess we now know why you are here," he said with a slow shake of his head.

Elisabeth swallowed the lump in her throat. "Well, I wasn't expecting this, that's for sure."

If one understood what the stone said, the result was the ability, not just to make the elixir of life, but to turn lead into gold.

"Lead into gold," she muttered to herself.

With a cautionary look, Balinus cleared his throat as Cato gave her a sidelong glance.

She now understood why the Emerald Tablet had to be kept out of the hands of the wrong people. The Philosopher's Stone was the recipe for both immortality and unlimited wealth. You'd be able to play the role of god or goddess to perfection, even in modern times, with the knowledge it contained. One could rule the world, if ruthless enough.

Elisabeth's shoulders drooped while thinking of other ways this knowledge could impact a life. She then stared at David. His beautiful eyes were still full of mischief and wonder; not a trace of the tormented, ageless windows they become. With a wrinkled brow, she turned to Balinus. "How can this ever be used for good? For unselfish reasons?"

He laid his hand upon his heart and then gestured toward Elisabeth. "Well done, my dear girl. You ask the right questions."

She smoothed out her tunic, as if subconsciously trying to appear worthy.

"The tablet itself is neither good nor bad; it is but a stone. The words written upon it are neither good nor bad; they are but words speaking of the laws of nature. It is the individual who assigns the meaning. It is easy to see what a selfish person would do with the knowledge, but what of an honorable person? Think of all the good that it could bring to humanity. It could heal the sick and feed the poor. Remember, all things in moderation."

Her smile wavered, but she nodded in agreement.

"Was the stone not put to good use saving your life?"

"Yes, but you're different. I imagine most would take this to the other extreme." She paused before continuing. "Can you read it, Balinus?"

"Reading it and understanding it are two entirely different things." He moved closer and ran his hand along the words, reciting them as if by heart. "*A fundamental truth, that cannot be doubted*, is what the first line says." He moved his fingers to the second line. "*As above, so below. The work of wonders is from one.*"

Elisabeth's eyes widened. She looked up at Balinus. "*As above, so below*? I've heard that before, but never realized the origin." She paused as Hayri began walking toward them. Without missing a beat, David wrapped his arms and blanket around her protectively, hiding the Emerald Tablet on her lap.

Cato shot his friends a wide-eyed look, stood up, then rolled his shoulders. "Above, below, blah...blah...blah, this is too complicated for a simpleton like me. Come on, old man. How about a game of knucklebones instead?"

Balinus tilted his head back and forth, weighing the decision. "Alrighty then," he said with a quick, fake smile before following Cato to the other side of the camp. "How-are-you-today?" he belted out as he walked past Mr. Velvet.

Hayri nodded and then sat down in Balinus' former spot. He lurched forward. "How you feel? Good?"

Elisabeth shrugged her shoulders.

David lowered his head to study the man. "The gods allowed her to live, but she must continue to rest."

Hayri narrowed his eyes. "What you hide on lap?" he asked in a slow, sharp tone.

Beneath the blankets, Elisabeth slid the tablet behind her. "I have nothing on my lap."

"Come now. You tell Hayri." With a toothy grin, he inched forward even more. His icy gaze bounced from Elisabeth to David. "I watch. I see old man give something to girl."

David's nostrils flared. He shrugged the blankets off his shoulders and rose to his feet. "She told you it was nothing."

Hayri gave a dismissive snort, then stood up.

187

"Whoa. What I do to make mad?" He turned to look at his men for support before looking back at David. "Perhaps you hide something valuable?"

With a wide stance, David sniffed, clenching his fists at his side as he stepped forward. "I suggest you walk away now. Do not speak to us again, for I do not trust you."

"Is there a problem?" Kuzey called out as he crossed the camp in several long strides.

Hayri stepped back, staring at Elisabeth while speaking to the blond. "Something not right."

Trembling all over, Elisabeth pulled the blankets around her once again to conceal the tablet while fishing the crystal out of her dress at the same time.

When Kuzey turned toward her, David reached for one of his slings.

At that moment, Rufus' booming voice caused everyone to stop and look his way. "Leave my slaves alone," he screamed while storming toward them. "Do you know how much I paid for them? If you so much as lay a finger to damage my property…"

Another scuffle broke out where Cato had been playing knucklebones.

"Sons of death!" Rufus screamed. "I told you they are my proper…" His voice trailed off when Temel drew his sword, pressing the blade to Rufus' chest. The slave dealer held steady hands up and lowered his voice. "Come now, Temel. You and I can do business if you wish. After all, I did not…"

Elisabeth's heartbeat raced. She caught Balinus' intense stare, his eyes begging for the Emerald Tablet to be brought to safety. She nodded, pulled it back onto her lap, but then froze when the rest of Hayri's men surrounded Cato. He was lying on his back at the wrong end of six swords.

David shoved his sling back into his belt, drew his dagger, and pushed Hayri out of the way. He began running to Cato's defense when Kuzey charged at him; the small hunting knife was no match for the blond man's *gladius*. It took but a moment before he had it at David's throat.

Hayri walked toward Elisabeth. With a quick, disgusted look, yelled, "Kill them all. Take what they have."

"STOP!" Elisabeth screamed as loud as possible. "Don't you know who I am?" she said to Mr. Velvet, who stood close by.

Hayri blew a piercing whistle with his fingers before holding up a hand to stop his men. With a slow shake of his head, he turned to Elisabeth. "No. Tell me."

Trying to act as natural as possible, she pulled the blanket tighter while clasping the crystal in her fingers and thinking of home.

****

Still wrapped in the blanket, Elisabeth stashed the Emerald Tablet under her bed, then forced herself to stand up.

"Oh crap, oh crap, oh crap."

She paced the room, rubbing the back of her neck while trying to figure out what to do next. Besides being outnumbered, they were also out-armed. Both Cato and David were seconds away from being killed. She was going to have to think and talk her way out of this mess or they'd all end up dead.

The jewel-encrusted box caught her eye. Sure, a

few gemstones were missing, but countless more remained, embedded in the gold. Everything about the object resembled a priceless treasure. With a deep breath, she reached for it, hiding it on her lap before returning. Since time travel always returned Elisabeth to the exact moment in time and space she'd left, Hayri would never even know she'd left. Nobody would.

****

Elisabeth placed the gilded box next to her, tucked the necklace away, then ascended to her feet.

Dropping the blankets from around her shoulders to the ground, they served their purpose of hiding the jewels for the time being. Catching Balinus' gaze, she nodded to let him know the tablet was safe.

Hayri jerked his head back with a shocked look on his face that Elisabeth could stand with ease.

"Let my men go. All of them," she ordered, surprised at how firm her voice sounded.

Hayri rubbed his chin and laughed.

"I am…" she paused, trying to think of an important sounding Roman name. "I am Julius Elisabeth."

He rocked on his heels, studying her. "From house of Julii?"

"Of course." With a slight nod, she tossed her hair over one shoulder, trying to come across as pompous as possible while glaring at Mr. Velvet. "Do you not realize what—"

"You dare threaten Julia Elisabeth, a descendant of Caesar himself?" David pushed Kuzey's sword away and walked toward Elisabeth. "Are you all right?" he whispered while looking her over.

She nodded.

Still pinned to the ground, Cato shook his head, forcing a nervous smile. "Glad I'm not you, now that you've angered the gods." He slipped away and hurried to Elisabeth's side. "Like Caesar himself, she is a descendant of Venus."

One man snorted.

David whipped around, his eyes hard as he stared at the culprit. "Then explain how she survived the night after being twice bitten by a viper asp?"

With perfect posture, her shoulders back, neck held high, she spoke directly to Hayri. "Now, I order you to release my men and I at once."

"Lies," Kuzey called out. "They travel in a slave wagon."

Elisabeth swallowed the lump in her throat before waving a dismissive hand at him. "Our disguise, of course, so savages like yourselves would not accost us."

Hayri's lips pressed together in a slight frown. His men stood ready to act should he command them to do so.

Balinus crept to her side, followed by Rufus. The slave dealer's face appeared ashen. "I am her bodyguard," he muttered.

Elisabeth did a double-take as Rufus stared at his feet.

Hayri crossed his arms. "Prove it. Prove you a Julii."

Forcing an arrogant laugh, she bent down to retrieve the jewel-encrusted box hidden beneath the blankets. "Would a slave own this?"

Hayri shuffled back a step. He then waved Kuzey and Temel over to discuss the situation. She'd never seen Mr. Velvet so animated.

"I will let you take this and you will let us go," she said in a steady, slow-pitched voice.

"If girl really a Julii, she worth fortune."

Elisabeth whispered in David's ear, "Did I just tell them I was related to Julius Caesar?"

His mouth went slack, and he nodded.

"Oh my God." She looked straight ahead in a daze.

David gave her a pained stare. He then turned, grabbing hold of her arms. "What in the name of Jupiter are you doing?"

"What was I supposed to do, Aquarius? They had a sword to your throat," she said in a frantic whisper.

"Why must you always try to protect me? That is not your job. It is my job to protect you."

Her eyes rimmed with tears. She stole a glance at Hayri, who was still deep in conversation with his men, before looking back at David. "I have to do what I came here to do."

He gave a hard, obvious swallow. "And that is?"

"Save your life."

"The tablet?"

She shook her head. "You."

Hayri let out a deep, gratifying sigh before clearing his throat to get her attention. "We want ransom. Twenty talents of silver."

What the heck is a talent?

Elisabeth pulled away from David and forced another laugh. "You idiots. I'm worth far more than that."

Kuzey's mouth fell open. She heard Cato gasp.

David's chin dropped to his chest. He shook his head. "Elisabeth…stop…talking," he warned in a carefully controlled tone.

While walking toward Hayri, David grabbed hold of her arm, but she yanked herself free and continued.

"Listen." She tried to ignore the pain from the snake bites, realizing overexertion was causing it to flare up. "You need to free all of my men if you want to collect the ransom. Well...except for my bodyguard." Elisabeth paused to stare at Rufus. "I couldn't possibly be without him amongst you barbarians," she said while waving her hand in a melodramatic fashion.

Rufus' shoulders slumped.

She turned behind to glance at David. Her chest tightened as he paced back and forth, dragging his fingers down his cheeks. Her breath hitched, but she looked away, forcing herself to continue. "In order to secure my ransom, send my gilded jewelry box with Aquarius, Cato, and Balinus, for they will need proof of my captivity. My men will tell them you, my kidnappers, demand fifty talents of silver for my release. Do you hear me? Not twenty. Fifty."

Hayri's velvet voice rose in pitch. "Fifty?"

Elisabeth rolled her eyes. "Asking for anything less than that is just an insult."

He stared at her with an incredulous look.

"Think of it." Her speech remained slow and articulate. "Fifty talents of silver."

A huge smile formed on Hayri's face and he nodded. "I believe girl." He held his hands up in front of his face. "She have balls size of Caesar's."

"Send the three of them to collect it," Elisabeth ordered. "Immediately."

Hayri shook his head. "Not three. Just one." He pointed at David. "That one."

Cato cleared his throat and pulled Balinus to his

side. "No, you must send us as well. Aquarius cannot bring back fifty talents of silver himself. That's the weight of fifty men."

The weight of fifty men? Doing the math mentally, a cold chill rushed up her spine, realizing she'd just promised them about five thousand pounds of silver.

"I will stay with her," Balinus said. "Let the young men go and collect the ransom."

Elisabeth glared at him. "Balinus, no. I order you…"

Hayri nodded. "Girl and bodyguard stay. Three collect ransom."

David's nostrils flared and his face reddened as he grabbed Elisabeth. "I am not leaving you here."

"Oh…yes…you…are," she said with a raised voice, before whispering again. "If you stay here, they'll kill us all."

"I give time for goodbyes. They have five days for gather silver and return, but no more or girl gets…" Hayri dragged his finger across his throat.

David turned away from Elisabeth and curled his arms over his head.

"Five days? Then they must each have a horse," Elisabeth called out as she eyed several tethered amongst the trees. "I will not have them walking the entire—"

"Temel," Mr. Velvet called out as he strolled away. "Bring three horse."

The rest of his men went back to their game of knucklebones like nothing out of the ordinary had taken place, but they watched Elisabeth as much as the sheep bones they played with. If she stepped a foot outside of their camp boundaries, there was no doubt they'd react

194

in a second.

David brought a shaky hand to his forehead while drawing in slow, steady breaths. When he turned to look at her, his eyes were watery. She could see the muscles and veins straining beneath his skin. "Elisabeth...what in the name of...what have you done?"

"Go. Take Cato. Set up a new life somewhere and grow old. Take this..." Her voice faltered as she thrust the jeweled box into his hands. "Send for Cato's mother. You will have freedom and more riches than you've ever dreamt of."

David threw the box to the ground. "I don't want any of that!" He then yanked Elisabeth into his arms. "I only want you," he whispered.

Her stomach was in knots. Cato stood awkwardly back, glancing elsewhere while listening. Balinus motioned at Rufus to move toward the campfire with him.

She had saved David's life and had hidden the Emerald Tablet. She was done here. While her brain said that everything was now as it should be, her heart was filled with uncertainty. Elisabeth's breath caught in her chest as she pulled away. "I am not staying here. As soon as you walk away from this camp, you will be a free, wealthy man—and I'm returning home. For good."

His face reddened as he glared at her. "What about us?"

"There is no us. My plans for the future never included you." Elisabeth's hands fell to her side. She immediately regretted what she'd said.

David looked like he'd been punched in the gut.

His eyes filled with rage. He pressed his fist to his lips while pacing back and forth. Elisabeth took a deep breath, reached for his arm, hoping he'd calm down.

"Aquarius, it would never work between us. Both of us know why."

His neck corded as he looked past her, unable to make eye contact.

"Promise…" Elisabeth choked on her words. "Promise you will leave here and you won't come back to look for me."

David's jaw clenched. "No." He shook his head and stared at her.

"Don't you get it? I never wanted to come here in the first place." Elisabeth's shoulders caved in. "You must forget me. Do not return to try and rescue me because I won't be here." She looked over and gave Cato a pained stare. "Make him go. I beg you."

With a slack expression, Cato rubbed the heel of his palm on his chest and nodded. He walked over, and grabbed David's arm. Elisabeth struggled to catch her breath while heading back toward the blankets.

"Aquarius," Cato said in a soft tone, "we'll think of something."

David shoved him away while screaming. "How can we leave her here with these savages?" His eyes bulged and he pressed his fists to the sides of his head. "Have you all gone mad?"

Elisabeth began a desperate search for the blue *palla* he'd given her, then dropped to her knees, clutching it tight once she'd found it.

With an animalistic growl in his throat, David drew his dagger. "HAYRI!"

Her hands flew to her mouth. Elisabeth gasped for

air when David barreled toward Mr. Velvet.

Cato struggled to hold him back.

"I swear to the gods, I will kill you and then every single one of your—"

"Aquarius, my friend!" Balinus's voice sounded emotional as he rushed toward David, helping Cato restrain him. "Put the *pugio* away."

Hayri planted his feet in a wide stance, drawing his own dagger. "I give my word; you go now, no harm come to girl. But…" He paused to clean dirt beneath his fingernails with the point of the blade before nodding at his men. "You stay, girl dies first. While you watch."

David's body tensed, on the verge of springing, but Cato and Balinus both had a firm grip on his arms.

"Five days." Hayri sheathed his blade once more. "I treat girl like own daughter. You bring silver." He donned his fake grin. "Then we part good friends."

"Your word," David said with an intense, fevered stare. "No harm will come to her."

Hayri pounded his fist on his chest. "My word."

David wrestled free from Cato and Balinus, sheathing his knife before stumbling toward Elisabeth.

Still kneeling, with the *palla* clutched in her arms, she looked up at him as he drew nearer. "Aquarius, I'm so sorry," Elisabeth whispered. "I thought I was helping." She reached out to touch him but pulled back as if no longer worthy.

David hunched over, falling to his knees before her.

"Aquarius, I'm so sorry, but why can't you see that you must go? You have to understand that I am trying to—"

"Elisabeth, stop talking," David said in a raised

voice while staring at the ground. He then pulled her tight to his chest, whispering in her ear, "Get it through that thick skull of yours—you are the only thing in the world that matters to me now. You can go home if you must, but I will return to see if you are here. I will kill Hayri and all his men when I return, whether you have chosen to stay or to leave."

"Aquarius, please, that's crazy talk. You must listen to me—"

"No. For once, you will listen to me, girl."

She swallowed the lump rising in her throat.

"I will be back in approximately five hours." He spoke in a steady, slow-pitched whisper. "When I return, it will be with a small army of men."

Cheeks wet with tears, she felt the color drain from her face.

"Here." David removed the dagger from his belt to attach it to hers. "If anyone comes near you, use this, no hesitation. Are you cold?" He took the *palla* out of Elisabeth's hands, wrapped it around her, then kissed her forehead. "I will be back after dark," he whispered.

A small frown etched her lips as she stared at him. His mind was made up.

David reached over to touch her fingers. "Will you still be here?"

Her shoulders quaked. "Do you want to know an *if*?"

He pulled back slightly and rubbed the back of his neck. "Yes."

"If you're stupid enough to return…" She paused, convinced she was making the wrong decision. "…then I will be here."

He let out a shaky laugh when Elisabeth threw her

198

arms around his neck. "Please, please be careful." She pulled him closer. "Against my better judgment, I will wait here for you. Why couldn't you just leave well enough—?"

"The same reason you couldn't," he whispered. "You said there is no us, but I know there is."

"I was trying to protect you." Her voice broke. "I didn't mean what I said."

He wiped a tear from her cheek. "I know."

"Ready?" Cato called over as he grabbed the jeweled box and packed it away with his provisions, along with their blankets and cloaks.

Elisabeth let go and stood.

David scrambled to his feet and pulled the canteen strap over his head. "Ready as I will ever be." He then wrapped his arm around Elisabeth's waist and pulled her to him. "I will be back, *cor meum,* with a small army of men. Nothing will keep me—"

She interrupted him with a long, inaudible sigh before leaning in to kiss him goodbye. "I wish you'd go away forever."

"No, you don't," he whispered in her ear before walking over to Cato and Balinus. "Rufus," he called out, "as the personal bodyguard of Julia Elisabeth, if you allow anyone...*anyone*...to lay a finger on her in my absence, I will kill you when I return."

Rufus nodded and then tiptoed toward them. Elisabeth held her stomach while they prepared for their journey.

"Never trust men wearing trousers," Cato muttered under his breath. "I mean it. When we get to the lake—"

With a warning glance, David cut him off. "Grab

all the rope you can find. I saw plenty in Rufus' wagon."

Cato grimaced. "What do we need rope for?"

"For carrying a treasure on," he said with a strained smile.

A feeling of dread washed over her. Elisabeth couldn't bear to watch them ride off, so she walked away to curl up on the blankets. Five minutes had passed, although it felt like an hour, when a gentle hand touched her shoulder. Elisabeth's tummy fluttered, imagining for a moment that David had returned.

Rufus sat down beside her. "They are gone," he said with a heavy sigh.

Elisabeth glanced over her shoulder, squeezing her eyes shut, holding back tears.

After a long silence, the slave dealer cleared his throat. "I'm quite certain Cato has never been on a horse before today."

She sniffled. "Why do you say that?"

"He almost mounted it backward."

Elisabeth chuckled while wiping her nose with the back of her hand. "I can totally picture it."

The shrill noise of the *aulos* rang out. Elisabeth clamped her hands over her ears, wanting to be alone, in peace to gather her thoughts. Instead, she found herself in the middle of an Italian forest, with a kidnapper, his thugs, a slave trader, and some idiot playing a horrible instrument that sounded more like the squeals of a tortured pig than anything musical.

She couldn't stop herself. In a fit of rage, Elisabeth jumped up, stomping her feet. "Temel, shut up!"

The music came to an abrupt stop. He gave her an incredulous stare before turning to Kuzey. "Does she not realize she is the captive?"

The blond snorted and shook his head.

Elisabeth's cheeks flushed as every head turned to look at her. She swallowed the lump in her throat. All of Hayri's men burst into laughter.

"I'm sorry, but I would like to have a nap now and I can't sleep with you playing that thing." She threw herself onto the ground, pulling the *palla* up to her chin.

"Let girl rest. Put *aulos* away, Temel."

"But, *Baba*..."

Hayri shook his head.

"I take it you are not fond of that instrument," Rufus said.

"Is anyone?"

He scratched his cheek. "Do you know what an onion has in common with an *aulos*?"

"What?"

"They both make me cry."

Elisabeth rolled her eyes and then sat up. "How do you sleep at night?" she asked with a shaky voice.

Rufus jerked his head back. "Give me one reason why I should not?"

"You sell people, human beings...as if they are nothing but livestock. What you do is wrong on so many levels."

He crossed his arms over his chest, and his brow pulled down in concentration. "I do nothing wrong. Out of Aquarius, Cato, and myself, it is I who obeys the law. Think about that."

Elisabeth gasped.

"I am a businessman."

"A businessman?"

"It's not personal." He shrugged and then forced a

laugh. "They are the fugitives. They are the outlaws. Not me."

"Just because it's the law…can you not think with your own brain and see that it's not right?"

"Not right?" He shook his head. "What do you mean it is not right? Aquarius and Cato are lucky. As slaves, they have not a single thing to worry about. Shelter, food, security…it is all provided for them. This…" He gestured toward their kidnappers. "This is what happens when a slave is left to his own devices. Mayhem."

Elisabeth turned away, wishing she was anywhere but here.

"Look, it is part of the natural order. It has always…*always*…existed. Slaves cannot take care of themselves. Without masters, they'd die off. Can you imagine if there was no slavery? Society would plunge into anarchy. A world without slavery does not exist, nor will it ever exist. Wake up. When you are older you will understand. This is the real world."

Elisabeth glared at him. "I am no slave."

"Well, at the time, I thought…" Rufus paused and his hands locked together on his lap. "Perhaps, I might have kept you for myself. My intuition was correct because you've proven to be a very determined and intelligent young lady. Over time, you'd have become the perfect helpmate to run my business." He began to study a twig beside him with great interest. "Who would stop me from taking you as a wife?"

"Your wife! The wife of a slave trader? Oh, so you just thought you could…" With a huff, Elisabeth grabbed her sandals. "Never in a million years could I ever love someone like you."

"Love! By the gods, girl, who said anything about love? I am talking about marriage." Rufus cocked his head. "You are not a Julii, are you?"

"Of course not," she snapped.

He let out a sigh of relief.

Unable to listen to his drivel a minute longer, she tied her shoes and paced back and forth, ignoring the pain in her leg as her mind wandered.

"If I may be blunt, I am surprised Aquarius has deserted you."

Elisabeth let out a dramatic groan. What was she supposed to do now? Was she finished here?

How strange to think that, in reality, only a few hours had passed since her encounter with David in the gazebo on her way home from Mrs. Waters' house.

"Oh my gosh." Elisabeth froze. She'd forgotten about Mrs. Waters. The old woman had to know more than she let on. "Is there such a thing as a coincidence, Rufus?"

He gave her a blank look.

"The correct answer is no. There is no such thing as a coincidence." Elisabeth turned around and fished the crystal out of her dress. She needed to talk to the old woman right away.

Why had she spent five years teaching her Latin?

****

"I left something at Mrs. Waters' house," Elisabeth shouted while running out of her room and down the stairs. She grabbed her key ring and bolted out the front door, not sure mom and dad even heard.

Elisabeth pulled the *palla* over her head, wrapping it tightly to keep warm. The leaves crunched beneath her sandals while sprinting down the street, vision blurred with tears. The trip seemed to take twice as long as normal, and her leg throbbed with every step. She should have taken her mom's car.

Gasping to catch her breath, Elisabeth pounded on the door of the Victorian mansion before fumbling with the key and bursting into the foyer. "Mrs. Waters," she screamed out in panic. "Mrs. Waters!"

The old woman stood in the doorway to the living room with Felis purring around her legs. "I'm right here, dear." While staring at Elisabeth's filthy tunic, her dark eyes filled with tears. She then scrubbed both hands over her face and walked closer.

"Why did you teach me Latin?" Elisabeth sagged against the wall. "I need to know why. What do you know?"

Mrs. Waters didn't answer. Instead, she cocked her head to one side and reached out to touch the blue *palla*.

"Please, you must tell me what you know. I'm looking for someone named Aquarius." She shook her head and corrected herself. "I mean David. David Perrier. I need to find him. Please, I am begging you."

The gears of the cuckoo clock shifted; the bird poked its head out once. They both glanced over to see the time; seven-thirty. Upstairs, something dropped, sounding like it shattered into a million pieces.

Adrenaline surged through Elisabeth's body. Her posture became rigid while watching for Mrs. Waters' reaction to the noise.

The old woman gave a slow, understanding nod.

Elisabeth whipped around to race up the staircase, past the console table that displayed its predictable bouquet of fresh pink roses, and into the shadows that had unnerved her for so long. In all her years of visiting this grand old house, she'd never ventured upstairs to the second floor. It felt off-limits like she'd be stepping into some forbidden wing.

Throwing open the first door she came to, Elisabeth froze in the entryway, unsure if her eyes deceived her. She gasped, covering her mouth with both hands.

David grabbed onto the fireplace mantle for support. "Elisabeth…" His shaky voice trailed off while he struggled to compose himself.

Elisabeth's lip trembled. She bolted across the room to throw herself into his arms.

"*Cor meum*," he cried out in relief before burying his face in her long hair, no longer able to contain the centuries of emotions he'd held in.

Chapter Fourteen

The room looked like an English gentleman's study, with leather-bound books overflowing from floor to ceiling shelves. A rolling library ladder hung from a metal rail, tempting you to climb to the rafters on a quest to seek a tale of adventure and romance from some forgotten novel. Once discovered, a leather sofa and two chairs were positioned on an area rug in front of a dark paneled fireplace where one could read in comfort, the pages illuminated by brass light fixtures scattered throughout the space. A pale pink rose in a vase on a cluttered desk stood out, breathing life into a room filled with texts written a long age ago.

The study had a melancholy air about it, not unlike that feeling you get in a used bookstore. Elisabeth sucked in a quick breath, and with it the distinct scent of old books, of dust and vanilla. There wasn't enough time in the world for someone to read all the books here.

Her limbs felt heavy when she realized David had time to read them all.

She couldn't stop trembling and looked up at him with feverish eyes. "I've messed everything up. I think I've finished what I was meant to do, but…"

"Shhh." His voice was soft. "You haven't messed anything up."

"I hate it there." Elisabeth clutched at his arms.

"The only reason I stay is because of you. Tell me if I'm supposed to go back. Am I supposed to wait for you to return, because I don't know anymore?"

"Wait for me to return?" His breath hitched. "What do you mean? How can you possibly go back?" David, with rapt attention still on her, reached for a nearby throw. "You're shaking like a leaf." He wrapped the blanket around her shoulders.

Elisabeth took a step to the side, wincing in pain.

"What's wrong?"

"I was bitten by the viper asp yesterday, or the day before. I'm not sure."

David's eyes bulged. "The snake bite? That was yesterday to you?" He led her to the sofa. "I hate to tell you..."

Elisabeth sucked in a quick breath as she sat. "What?"

He knelt at her feet, removing the sandal from her swollen leg. "You still need to go back. I didn't realize..."

"I thought you said..."

David opened his mouth to say something, but then lowered his head to inspect the puncture wounds.

"I'm not done? It's not over?"

"I'm sorry. I know how..." He fumbled over his words. "I know how much you hate it there, but..." David shook his head. "It's far from over."

Elisabeth's eyes widened, noticing his brown hair was a touch shorter. Dressed in jeans with a black t-shirt, he'd easily pass for a university student. When David glanced up at her, those electric blue eyes still had their power over her to grab hold and not let go.

All these centuries had passed, yet he remained

unchanged, except for a hint of sadness from deep within his core. Elisabeth clutched her arms to her chest as a horrible thought occurred. Did David even love her anymore? He cared for her, that was obvious, but he couldn't have the same feelings of love for her today that he'd had all those…

"You stare at me, Miss. London."

A flush crept across her cheeks. "I'm trying really hard not to, but it's just…" she reached over, touching his cheek, studying all his features.

David nodded in understanding. "Believe me, I know. When I saw you earlier today, now dressed like this…" He shook his head in disbelief. "…you're almost like a ghost to me."

"I assure you," she whispered, "I am quite real." She ran fingers along his jawline. "But you haven't aged." Her chest hitched while holding back tears. "Why does that make me feel so sad?"

"Because…" His voice choked before reaching up to take hold of her fingers from his face. "Because I promised that…"

"All right, my dears, where's the broken glass?" Mrs. Waters' sweet voice sang out as she shuffled through the doorway, holding a broom and dustpan.

David pulled his hand away, gave a nervous sniffle, and then made a quick gesture toward a shattered picture frame on the floor next to the fireplace. "I accidentally dropped it. The glass broke, but I'll clean it up." He stood, rubbing the back of his neck while pacing. "I completely forgot about it."

"No need. I'm here now." Before sweeping up the shards of glass, Mrs. Waters bent down to retrieve the frame. "Well now, this has always been a favorite picture of mine." With a sigh, she ran frail fingers along it. "Don't feel bad." She then put it on the fireplace mantle, leaning it against the wall, and swept up the glass before leaving the room to dispose of the garbage.

Elisabeth watched as David continued to pace across the floor while running his fingers through his hair. "Why do you take the elixir, Aquarius? Why don't you let yourself age?"

He rubbed the back of his neck.

"You told me you're in a prison of your own making until the day you can make everything right again, but what is it you're trying to fix?" She leaned forward, shoulders curled over her chest. "Please tell me what's going on?"

He swallowed a lump in his throat before sitting down beside her on the couch, shifting his body so he faced her.

"How do you know Mrs. Waters? Why did she teach me Latin?" Elisabeth shook her head in disbelief. "How much does she know?"

"Everything." David reached over, holding both her hands in his. "She knows everything."

"My ears are ringing." Mrs. Waters walked back into the room. "You two must be talking about me," she said, while rummaging through a desk drawer.

Elisabeth let out a theatrical groan and squeezed David's fingers. "Will one of you please tell me how you two know each other?"

His glance darted to the old woman.

Her hands suddenly felt awkward in his. Elisabeth pulled them away to put her shoe back on.

"We go way back." Mrs. Waters shut the drawer before looking at David. "I do realize you've been waiting a while for this day to arrive, but I really think she—"

"Oh…?" A small smile formed on his face. "I've been waiting a while?"

"Okay, a very long while."

He snorted and looked away.

"I really think I should speak to her privately. I do know her better than you do," Mrs. Waters insisted.

David raised an eyebrow. "That's debatable."

She smirked while rolling her eyes.

Elisabeth tensed, reaching for David's arm, not wanting him to go anywhere.

"Just ignore the crazy old woman, *cor meum*," he said with a slight grin. "I'm not going anywhere."

Sissi chuckled. "Fine, have it your way." She moved in front of the fireplace.

"Look, if she's going to hear it from anyone, it's going to be from me. And can I just point out it's really awkward with both of you here together?"

Elisabeth stood up, crossing her arms as she confronted Mrs. Waters. This was the time for answers, not games. "The past five years, you were preparing me for all of this, weren't you?"

Sissi rubbed a hand against her chest and nodded.

"How did you know I could time travel?"

The old woman let out a shallow sigh. "Because I have been orchestrating this from day one."

With a gasp, Elisabeth's fingers flew to her lips. "You? But I don't get it. How could you have possibly…?" She stopped midsentence and stared at the picture in the broken frame behind Mrs. Waters, struggling to understand what she was looking at.

"Let's just say I have a vested interest in the two of

you." With a smiling face, Sissi turned to David. "She's noticed the picture."

He mumbled something inaudible and wiped shaky hands down his pant legs.

The old woman whispered soothing words back to him and then walked out of the room, leaving the two of them in privacy.

David stood and paced the floor.

Mrs. Waters' words pounced around in Elisabeth's brain while trying to come to terms with what she was looking at. A 5x7 photograph sat in a larger matted frame, the glass part of it now broken. "It's the same picture you showed me in the gazebo." Her mouth went slack while picking it up. "This is me, isn't it?"

David pulled at his collar and nodded before taking it away from her.

"Just a sec." Still wanting to look, Elisabeth snatched it back and took a seat again.

She could now see the entire, clear picture, which was a carefree, almost candid shot of the two of them and appeared as if David had swept Elisabeth off her feet the moment before it was snapped. Dressed in bright medieval clothing, he smiled at her rather than the camera, with a look of complete adoration on his face. Elisabeth wore a flowing blush-colored dress and had one arm around his neck and the other stretched playfully to the side in a moment of excitement. With her head tilted up, she appeared to be in the midst of laughter.

"This is beautiful," she said while staring at the glow on her cheeks that was a perfect match to the crown of pale pink garden roses in her dark hair. Sucking in a quick breath, she looked up at David. "I'm older in this picture."

He cleared his throat and glanced around the room, avoiding eye contact. "A bit."

She scrubbed a hand over her face, feeling like a complete idiot. Why had she run here and into his arms tonight? Whatever happened between them was ancient history for him. Literally. "David…" She paused. It felt weird calling him that now. "Look, I'm not stupid. I can tell I'm making you uncomfortable just by being here. You're all…" She made a dramatic gesture with her hand. "You're all fidgety and you can't stop pacing. I get it, really I do, and I think I've figured out what's going on."

His head flinched back. "You have?"

"Well, sort of." She glanced at the picture again. "You've learned how to make the Philosopher's Stone yourself. That is obvious. Maybe you needed my help or you needed the Emerald Tablet. You found Mrs. Waters and you two probably had an arrangement to teach me Latin. I'd be able to go back into the past, save your life, and you'd be able to go on and have a limitless supply of gold and God only knows what else." While staring at the floor, her voice became quiet. "Which is really sad because the Aquarius I know would never have…" She looked up at David to gauge his reaction.

He squinted in amusement before closing his eyes, shaking his head as a slow smile started to build. "That doesn't even make sense."

"Well, obviously, I'm still working out the details." With a huff, she turned away to gather her thoughts. "I have to remember that I've just come from being with you as…as Aquarius. I'm in love with a young runaway slave, but now you're…" Elisabeth wiped a stray tear from her cheek before giving him a dismissive wave. "You're David Perrier, going around, being all mysterious and broody." She stared at her trembling hands, fighting hard to keep the tears from flowing. "And you've since lived a thousand lifetimes without me." She let out a dejected sigh and looked up at him with a trembling chin. "It's probably a miracle you even remember me, if you really stop to think about it. How could someone remember a—"

"Stop talking, Elisabeth." He stared at her with a pained expression. His jaw clenched tight, on the verge of tears himself. "God, I've missed your non-stop banter so much, but…" With an incredulous stare, he pulled her to her feet. "It's a miracle I even remember you?" His eyes were over-bright as he held her close. "Never doubt that everything I'm doing, that I've ever done, has been for you."

Elisabeth stiffened in his arms. The picture slipped from her fingers. "What do you mean?"

With a wrinkled brow, he stepped away from her, picked up the picture from the floor, and carried it to the desk.

"Aquarius, please. Tell me."

David stared straight ahead, appearing to be deep in thought as his breath burst in and out.

"Tell me an if?" she whispered.

When he finally spoke, his voice was quiet. "If I live a thousand lifetimes, I can grow old with you once."

Elisabeth's eyes widened, and she looked up at him. "What?"

He let out a huge breath, turning toward her. "I live

213

a thousand lifetimes so that I can grow old with you once." David's arms hung limp at his sides.

Elisabeth's pulse raced. She turned away, shaking her head. "Oh, God, no. You can't have done this for me. I'd never…I would never have asked this of you." Her hands flew to her throat.

"You never did." He spoke in a soothing tone. "I am waiting for the day when I can make everything right again."

"Aquarius, what have you done? I've been determined to make sure you grow old. Now you tell me I'm the cause of all your torment?" Her knees wobbled beneath her. "I see centuries of torment when I look into your eyes."

David rushed over, pulling her into his arms. "Elisabeth…"

She looked up at him with a glassy stare. "This debt…how can it ever be repaid?"

"There is no debt."

"Yes, there is." Her voice choked with tears. She looked away. "Oh my God, you're killing me, Aquarius. How can I ever live up to this? How could anyone? What kind of man would live a thousand lifetimes for another person?"

He lifted her chin so she was looking at him. "You're not asking the right question."

"What is the right question?"

"What kind of person would a man live a thousand lifetimes for?"

She let out an uncontrollable sob, rushing away from him and over to the desk, standing behind it to give herself distance and time to think. "I can't…this is too much to deal with right now. You're…" Her voice trailed off when looking up to see Mrs. Waters standing outside the door in the hallway; her eyes red while dabbing her nose with a tissue.

David sat on the edge of the sofa, holding his head in his hands.

Several quiet minutes passed. Elisabeth stared down at the desk, the photograph catching her attention once more. "We look so happy," she said with a quaking voice.

David raised his head. "We look so happy?"

"In this picture."

He looked down again and fidgeted with his fingers. "We were."

As Mrs. Waters walked across the room to sit beside David, Elisabeth's eyes skimmed the surface of the crowded desk. Her head flinched back, noticing the familiar letterhead. "This is the hospital my dad works at." She picked up the letter, but didn't read any of it; it was the name at the top that caught her eye.

Dr. David Waters.

Her hand drifted to her mouth, realizing what it meant. A sudden coldness hit Elisabeth right to the core. Her muscles tightened. No wonder he became uncomfortable every time Mrs. Waters walked into the room when she was there. He had lived a thousand lifetimes, and Sissi Waters was one of those lifetimes.

"You two are married." She could feel her cheeks flush red.

David let out a deep sigh. "Elisabeth." His voice cracked. "Yes, but it's not what you think. I'm so sorry, but—"

"No, no, don't be sorry. It's all right." Her mouth went dry. "Believe me, Aquarius…" Taking a deep breath while struggling to compose herself, she nodded to pretend the news hadn't shocked her. "I can easily see how you would have fallen…" Elisabeth's voice choked with tears. "Fallen in love with her." Her shoulders slumped while staring at the old woman.

He was married to her.

To Sissi Waters.

To elegant Sissi Waters.

To Sissi, I'm eighty-one but still prettier than you, Waters.

Elisabeth swallowed a painful lump in her throat. "Since I was twelve years old, I've been a part of her everyday life. I've adored her from day one."

The old woman lowered her head, muttering tearfully to herself.

"She's elegant, charming, intelligent, and anyone can see she was beautiful in her youth…as I assume you know firsthand."

David stared at her with a pale, haunted look. "You don't understand."

"Yes, I do. She's pretty much perfect in every way." Elisabeth's head pounded. She wanted to be alone. "I'm such an idiot. You have to pretend to be a widow, don't you? How else would you be able to explain having a husband that never ages?"

David's tone deepened as he spoke to his wife. "Why aren't you telling her?"

Sissi let out a heavy sigh while staring up at the ceiling. "Because, as you and I both know, she's a very smart girl. She'll figure it out."

Elisabeth fell into the chair behind the desk, gripping the sides of her head to cover her ears. She felt like a fool for being jealous of an eighty-year-old. "I am trying to understand. I mean…Aquarius has lived for centuries. So much has happened that I know nothing about." Eyes clouded with tears, she reached for the crystal.

"*Cor meum,* wait…" David stood up, rushing toward her. "Don't run away. You're not listening. You…"

"Let her go."

"But she's going to go back thinking—"

"She's only running to you."

Elisabeth closed her eyes.

"Believe it or not, that went according to plan," Sissi whispered to David.

"Elisabeth, you will be the death of me," she heard him say before the world turned to darkness.

Chapter Fifteen

"Excuse me, Rufus, I have a headache." Elisabeth tucked the crystal away before grabbing her cloak and canteen. With uncertain steps, she staggered toward the edge of the clearing, flopped down on the ground, and curled against a tree trunk, needing to be by herself.

Kuzey whistled to get Hayri's attention.

Mr. Velvet turned around. After studying Elisabeth for a moment, he gave a curt nod, allowing her to sit there.

She lowered her head while cursing at him under her breath.

A small part of her wished life would go back to the way it was before the encounter with David, before ending up here in Ancient Rome. This entire mess was Mrs. Waters' doing. Now everything had become so complicated. How could someone play with a life like that? How could such a sweet old woman be so cruel? Something didn't add up. If they were married, and she believed they were speaking the truth, then why didn't he stop taking the elixir? Why wouldn't he grow old with Sissi? It didn't make sense. Perhaps it was a marriage of convenience. Elisabeth let out a shallow sigh. What does that even mean, anyhow?

She sniffed, then wiped her nose, aware the bigger part of her wouldn't change a single thing when it came to Aquarius. The boy with a knack for chasing trouble and making stupidly adorable faces had stolen her heart. If only David…Aquarius…would hurry and return safe and unharmed. It seemed Elisabeth's intention was to run straight to him, just as Mrs. Waters had said. There was no denying the old woman knew her well. Time crawled by, but the only thing to do now was wait for his return. At least here in the ancient world, he was still hers, and hers alone.

"Girl. Come eat food," Hayri called over, interrupting her thoughts.

Elisabeth looked up. "I'm not hungry."

He shrugged his shoulders and bit into a piece of meat. "Fine. Suit self."

So far, David, Cato, and Balinus had been gone for about an hour. They must be riding to the closest town or village, rounding up a small army of mercenaries and using the jewels to pay for their services. They'd return once night fell and ambush the camp. Elisabeth bit her nails, chest heavy as various scenarios of her imminent rescue played out in her imagination.

How many men would there be?

Would they storm the camp while brandishing swords?

She knew for certain her priority was to get out of here and as far away as possible. This may be violent ancient Rome, but David was delusional if he thought she'd let him stick around with a bunch of bloodthirsty men while they tried to kill Hayri and his gang.

Her head jerked back when a pebble hit the ground close to her. Elisabeth sat up taller, watching as a second pebble landed, and then a third. With a racing heart, she leaned against the tree trunk. "What the heck are you up to?" she whispered, knowing this was

David's way of telling her that he was nearby.

Elisabeth smoothed her tunic, wanting nothing more than to run to him, wherever he was. She pulled the canteen strap over her head before putting on her cloak. Hayri and his men sat around the fire drinking, while Rufus lay sprawled out, looking quite bored.

A loud cracking noise was followed by a short scream. One of Hayri's men dropped to the ground.

Surprised, the barbarians scrambled to their feet, drawing their weapons.

"He's been shot by a sling-bolt," Kuzey shouted.

As Mr. Velvet hid behind his men for protection and surveyed the area with slow, cautious movements, Elisabeth jumped up, shuffling back a step, unsure of what to do.

Hayri spun around, glaring at her. "Get girl!" he yelled.

Instinct kicked in. With her injured leg, she'd never outrun them, but Elisabeth turned, dashing through the trees, straight into the brush behind her, anyway. Twigs snagged at her long dress as she scrambled over the uneven terrain.

Where the heck did David go?

Her chest ached. She couldn't stop herself from looking back to see how many of the barbarians were chasing her. Elisabeth's eyes bulged. Kuzey was getting closer. Her heartbeat thrashed in her ears. She jumped over a fallen tree while struggling to fish out the necklace. Before she could get the crystal, Kuzey lunged, knocking her to the ground. With a scream, she landed face down on the dead leaves and sticks that littered the forest floor.

"Don't move," he hissed while flipping Elisabeth

onto her back, straddling her. "I've got the girl!" he yelled to the others.

She swore at him, continuing to struggle and break free.

"I said don't move." He raised his fist.

She froze, squeezing her eyes shut and turning her head. Just then, the whipping noise of David's sling rang out.

Kuzey slumped on top of her.

Whimpering, she pushed his body off while scrambling to her feet, then spun around in a frantic search for David.

Hayri appeared and clutched her arm to the point of bruising it. "When I find boy…" His voice trailed off, nostrils flaring as he dragged Elisabeth back to the camp.

When they returned to the clearing, Temel pointed into the forest. "*Baba*, several of her men are running. I hear them."

Mr. Velvet slammed Elisabeth against a tree. "Tie her," he ordered Temel while holding her in place. He then drew his sword to lead the rest of his gang into the woods, toward the source of the noise. "Do not let girl out of sight," he called back.

Her pulse quickened. There was no way David and Cato could have returned with help this soon. Something was wrong. Unable to move, she gave Temel an intense, fevered stare.

A slow smile formed as he moved closer, pressing his body against hers. He jutted his chin out, lowering his voice. "Not so high and mighty now, are you?"

She turned her head away from his horrible breath, fighting back angry tears while his hands wandered over her dress.

"Get your filthy paws off me or—"

"Or what?" With a snort, he began to lift her long tunic.

A rock smashed into the ground behind Temel, causing him to jerk his head back and whip around. It reminded her of the way David had startled the stubborn donkey they'd encountered.

Temel drew his sword. "You missed."

David's eyes were cold and hard as he advanced toward him. "Did I?" He picked up a long and heavy branch from the ground.

"He never misses." Elisabeth sagged against the tree. "That's how Aquarius moves an *ass* out of the way," she said through gritted teeth.

With a smirk, David lowered his head and raised an eyebrow. "She's right, you know." He then pushed his shoulders back and charged at Temel, holding the long stick out like a spear.

Temel lunged with his sword.

"Oh God, be careful, Aquarius."

David switched the branch in his hands so he held it vertically before retreating into the defensive, blocking the attack. "I am always careful, my love," he said while struggling to fend off the heavy blows.

When he had enough space between them, he positioned the stick like a spear, trying to punch Temel with the end.

With uncontrollable trembling, she watched their violent dance. How could anyone defeat a sword using a tree branch?

David then retreated into the defensive, holding the thick branch straight up in front of him, blocking the blows from the *gladius* repeatedly, before treating it like a spear once again and thrusting it at Temel.

"I won't be but a moment," David said as he jumped back.

Temel, expecting him to return to their established routine, lunged forward and was caught off guard when David changed his grip on the huge stick. Instead of retreating into the defensive, he flipped it around, pounding it into Temel's chest like a battering ram. With the wind knocked out of him, he lost his balance and stumbled backward.

David lifted the makeshift weapon high over his head to bring the final blow crashing down on Temel's skull. He then tossed the heavy stick aside. Rushing to Elisabeth, his gaze darted up and down in a frantic search to find any wounds. "Are you all right?"

"Aquarius…" Her voice choked with tears.

"Shhh, don't worry. I'm here." He unfastened the rope, freeing her.

Temel was still out cold when Rufus poked his head out from behind a bush, gave them an incredulous stare, and then ran toward the wagon, attempting his own escape.

David placed a stone in his sling, aiming it up through the trees. "We need to hurry. It won't take them long to figure out they chase rocks and their own horses."

Elisabeth was puzzled. "What do you mean?"

"I untethered their remaining horses and scared them off." David swung his arm back over his head, releasing the stone with such power that Elisabeth flinched at the loud whipping noise. It soared up over the treetops, toward the spot Hayri was searching. "That should allow us a few more minutes. You don't have to go far on that leg."

"Where are we going?"

"To the cave."

"Aquarius, no. That's a terrible idea."

"Are you able to run there?"

She nodded, knowing it was close.

"Don't worry. I have a plan," he said as they sprinted, hand in hand.

"I thought you were coming back with a bunch of men?"

"Just trust me, will you?"

Elisabeth swallowed the lump in her throat.

A huge bundle of rope had been placed on the ground outside of the cave. David picked it up, pulling it over his head and under his arm so it lay diagonally across his chest. He then helped Elisabeth over the rocks to the entrance.

She jumped at every noise. "What if there are more snakes?"

"Nothing will harm you, *cor meum*. I promise."

"I'm going to hold you to that promise."

"You can hold me later," he said with a wink. "Right now, we have to get you away from Hayri."

Elisabeth shook her head. "What's with the rope? Where are Cato and Balinus? Aquarius, this is a terrible plan."

"You don't even know what the plan is."

"Well, I don't like it so far." Squeezing his fingers, she let out an appreciative sigh as he led her through the dark tunnel. "You never left me with Hayri and his gang, did you?"

"Did you honestly think I would leave you with

those barbarians? Even for a minute?"

"Then why'd you tell me you were going to get a bunch of men to kill Mr. Velvet?"

"Because you're not going to like my real plan. Watch your step…"

In the pitch black, she stumbled over something. "But you said it's a great plan."

David grabbed Elisabeth's arm and helped steady her. "Oh, it is…but you're not going to like it."

Her shoulders tightened. "I'm scared to ask. What is…?"

In one sweeping movement, David pulled Elisabeth to the side of the tunnel, pressed her back up against the wall, and covered her mouth with his hand as she was about to let out an involuntary scream.

"Shhh, they're here," he whispered.

Wide-eyed, her posture tensed.

He positioned himself beside her. She breathed heavily with fright, squeezing her eyes shut while they listened to noises at the entrance of the cave.

"Hayri," a voice called out. "We should check in here."

She flinched before grabbing onto David. They were going to die. Mr. Velvet was going to recapture and kill them, as promised. With her stomach in knots, Elisabeth realized she couldn't continue like this any longer. She didn't belong here in ancient Rome and she didn't belong here with him. What a fool to have believed anything different.

"Girl knows tunnel goes nowhere," Hayri said. "We continue search forest. Come."

In the darkness, Elisabeth sagged against David as the men made their way back out of the cave. Her shoulders curled, and she choked on tears. "Aquarius, I can't do this anymore."

David reached for her as she began to crumple onto the floor. "Everything is going to be fine, *cor meum.*" His voice was soothing. He dropped the rope wrapped around him to the ground, then pulled her to his chest. "They are gone now."

"I'm sorry, but I'll never be brave and adventurous like you. I shouldn't have come here in the first place. I can't do this anymore."

"Elisabeth." The way he said her name set her aquiver. "Trust me."

"I do, but…I need to go home." Her trembling fingertips reached up to touch her lips. "At first it was exciting, but now I'm just scared and tired. I never asked to be a time-traveler. I didn't start this."

David lightly rubbed her arms but kept silent.

"I have a calculus test next Tuesday that I haven't studied for yet." Her voice lost all its power. "Can't you see I don't belong here with you?"

"You do belong here with me," David said with a steady, lower-pitched voice. "My entire life, I have always felt there was a missing piece that belonged right here." He felt for her hand, placing it on his chest, over his heart. "It's you. You're the missing piece. And look how well you fit." He pulled Elisabeth against him, wrapped his arms around her, and rested his chin on the top of her head. "You fit into the space here perfectly. You belong with me."

She remained quiet, snuggling into his embrace.

"You know it too," he whispered.

Blind in the darkness, Elisabeth closed her eyes, listening to his beating heart. It did feel like she belonged there. Chin trembling, she answered with a small nod.

"I promise to have you on horseback and away from here in a matter of minutes. We are so close, *cor meum*. It is but an hour to the lake where Balinus' friend will give us shelter, where you can heal from the snake bite. After that, we can go anywhere. Rufus is gone. We will begin a new life." He remained calm and focused. "And it can be as dull and boring as you wish." David's thumb brushed her cheek. "My Elisabeth." His voice was barely a whisper. "Nothing will be the same if you go."

She let out a long, low sigh. "I'm nothing but putty in your hands and you know it."

He cleared his throat and slung the rope back over his shoulder.

"You're smirking, aren't you?"

"I never smirk." He chuckled, grabbed her hand, and led her through the dark tunnel.

"You're smirking," she mumbled. "And I guarantee your left eyebrow is raised. You talk with your eyebrows the way some people talk with their hands, and every time you smirk your left eyebrow goes up."

"Nonsense," he said with a snort.

"Oh, it's true. You and your…" A chill ran up her spine as a steady but quiet squeaking noise surrounded them.

Bats.

"Tell me, why did your parents choose the name Elisabeth for you?" David asked as they made their way toward the light.

"You're trying to distract me, aren't you?"

"Perhaps."

Elisabeth wrapped both hands around David's arm, pulling herself closer to him. "I was named after a beautiful Bavarian princess who once lived in the palace where my parents first met." She swallowed the lump in her throat. "My mother was working as an English tour guide and…"

"English?"

"That's the language I speak at home." She flinched when something fluttered above her head. "Oh God." She violently rolled her shoulders. "My father ended up in one of her tour groups. He always says he was more interested in my mother than the palace."

"You were named after a beautiful princess?"

"Yes."

David turned and smiled at her. "You suit your name," he said as they stepped outside onto the ledge and into the late afternoon sunshine. "You made it, *cor meum.*" His voice was soft. "Now, do you see Cato or Balinus over there?" he asked while searching amongst the trees.

A whistle sounded.

"There's Balinus." David pointed to the other side of the raging river.

Elisabeth felt weak in the knees. "We're not crossing…?" Her voice trailed off while following the flow of the river, all the way to where it disappeared over the second drop of the falls to their left.

"Actually, we are."

Her breath hitched. "How? Aquarius, there's a freaking waterfall right there."

David hurried to a thick branch that grew down through the forest brush and knotted one end of the rope to the limb. Working fast, he grabbed the other end of the rope and wrapped it around his palm several times. He continued to fiddle with it, eventually ending up with a little pouch. He then grabbed a rock and slipped it into the pouch he'd just made.

"Aquarius…?" She wanted to cry.

David placed the rock at his feet, reached for Elisabeth, and cupped her face in his hands. "*Cor meum*, look at me."

Her eyes were damp.

"Everything is going to be all right," he whispered. "I will not let anything happen to you. This is good, strong rope and we have the perfect incline. The only thing you need to do is hold on to me. Remember, I promised nothing will harm you and you said you were holding me to that promise."

She shook her head. "I never meant the holding part literally."

He led her by the shoulders to a specific spot. "Stand here."

"Why?" she whimpered.

"I need space to do this." He then let out a wolf whistle to let Cato know he was ready.

Elisabeth clutched at her throat.

David held the end of the rope with the rock a few centimeters off the ground and began to move his arm back and forth, creating a pendulum swing at his side. When he was ready, he aimed and released, sending the rope soaring straight across to the other side of the river. He turned and gave her a satisfied smile while wiggling his eyebrows.

Elisabeth's hand covered her mouth as she watched Cato and Balinus scramble for the rope and wrap it around the trunk of a tree. "You made that look so easy."

"Hayri," a voice echoed through the tunnel. "They are in the cave. I hear them at the other end."

"Bring me girl," Mr. Velvet hissed.

"*Cor meum*, come here." David strung two of his slings over the rope and gave a tug, testing its strength one final time.

She froze.

He reached over and pulled Elisabeth next to him. "Get on my back."

"Kill him and bring girl!"

Elisabeth's pulse raced, and she jumped onto David's back. Holding on for dear life, she peered over his shoulder to watch the mighty river below them crash into boulders as it rushed toward the waterfall.

"Ready?"

She glanced up at his muscular arms as his hands wrapped tight around the slings. She nodded, swallowing the lump in her throat. "Yes."

"Hang on, love. It'll be just like flying," David said, attempting to keep his voice light.

He then stepped off the ledge.

Her heart pounded as they soared across the river on a makeshift zip line toward Cato and Balinus on the other side. It did feel like they were flying. Below them, the river spilled over the rocky cliff and she stared in awe at the surrounding scenery. To the right, they cleared the trees. The powerful waterfall from the first cascade appeared in all its magnificence, and instead of being frightened, she whooped loudly as they zipped through the iridescent mist. The rope continued into the forest a bit, where she could now see it tied around a tree trunk with Cato and Balinus holding it tight.

"Don't let go, old man," Cato yelled out as he ran toward them, wrapping his arms around their bodies to slow them down. "Ready?"

"Now!" David yelled.

Cato let go, and David started peddling his legs to soften their landing. He let go of the slings and they tumbled to the ground in a heap, pausing as they lay still for a moment to catch their breath. David then jumped to his feet, and with a booming laugh, lifted Elisabeth in his arms and spun her around.

"You did it," he shouted.

She couldn't help but laugh.

Cato worked fast to undo the pouch in the rope and remove the rock. Just as he sent the end of the rope drifting away in the river, Hayri and his men stepped out onto the balcony. "By the gods, only you could have made that shot, Aquarius."

David put Elisabeth down. "I'll take this back now," he said with a wide grin as he placed his hands on her waist, pulled her closer, and removed the sheathed dagger from her belt.

She released an appreciative sigh while staring at him. "Gaius Cornelius Aquarius?"

He playfully raised an eyebrow. "Yes?"

Elisabeth bit down on a smile. "You're my hero."

He gave her a wide-eyed look and then they both burst into laughter.

"I was wrong, my friend." Cato handed David his slings. "I said you'd never get her to cross, but you did it. Mind you, that just proves the two of you are absolutely mad."

"Not only did Elisabeth cross…" David stopped

and chuckled as he attached the slings to his belt. "I think she enjoyed it." He looked at her with a bemused smile. "Admit it."

Elisabeth glanced down to hide her grin. She'd never admit it.

With a deep, gratifying sigh, David put his arm around her shoulders and kissed the top of her head. "She is the bravest person I know."

"Not in a million years would you get me to do that," Cato said with a laugh.

Balinus chuckled. "A wise sage once said 'loving someone deeply gives you courage, while being loved deeply gives you strength.'"

Cato rolled his eyes. "Did the wise sage mention the part about love making you absolutely mad?" He clapped David on the back. "To the horses, shall we?"

Chapter Sixteen

Balinus led the way along a deer path through the forest. As they rode, the thunderous sound of the waterfall faded off into the distance. Grateful to travel on horseback with David instead of hiking across the rugged terrain, Elisabeth glanced over one shoulder and smiled at Cato, who followed close behind. He sat taller in the saddle, squared his shoulders, but then looked away, avoiding eye contact.

"Aquarius..." Elisabeth wrapped her arms around his waist tighter. "...Cato looks terrified on the horse."

"Really?" David turned his head to check on him. "You're a natural up there, brother," he called back before breaking into song to distract Cato.

Elisabeth couldn't stop giggling as he sang.

David reached back and gave her a playful pinch. "It appears my singing offends for you haven't stopped laughing."

"Not at all." She took a slow, easy breath and leaned forward, resting against his back. "Quite the opposite."

When the path widened, they were able to let the horses pick up the pace. Riding alongside the River Velino, at the foot of a lush mountain, Elisabeth's gaze wandered to the beautiful peaks that now surrounded them. They were traveling from the sky to the sea. With a deep breath, she drank in the crisp air and enjoyed the warmth of the sun.

Balinus stopped and waited near the water's edge for the others to join him. "We need to ford the river here. The lake is that way."

Cato cleared his throat. "How far to your friend's villa?"

"Just beyond this mountain."

"Thank Jupiter." Cato raked a hand through his hair.

"Tell me," Balinus asked while wagging his finger at Cato. "What is the opposite of love?"

"Hate."

The old man shook his head. "Fear. The opposite of love is fear." With a grin, he pointed to Cato's horse. "A wise sage once said, 'Courage is knowing what *not* to fear.'"

"I think Balinus is saying that the poor horse only wants your love." David couldn't stop chuckling. "So love the horse, Cato. Love it with all of your heart."

"Aquarius…" Cato yelled back with a challenging tone. "It is much safer to be feared than it is to be loved."

Balinus let out a heavy sigh and then led the way into the water.

"Well, I disagree," David shouted. "Ready?" he whispered to Elisabeth as their horse trotted down the bank.

"Ready." She curled both legs up to keep them dry until they came up on the other side.

The river forked in two directions and Balinus kept to the left-hand side, following a dirt road. When they rounded the next corner, Elisabeth's mouth fell open. Before them, a picturesque lake, with a shoreline that twisted and turned in a carefree manner, lay nestled at the foot of the mountains. Like a giant mirror, the peaks, the blue sky, and even the clouds overhead were reflected on the surface of the water. The way the blues and greens fused together with the white from the clouds reminded Elisabeth of her mother's painting palette, the small wooden board on which paints were arranged and mixed. A dragonfly bombinated nearby, while a man in a small wooden rowboat slipped his oars in and out of the water.

"Aquarius, it's so peaceful here."

He gave her arms, which were wrapped around his waist, an affectionate tap. "I didn't realize it was this close. I hope Rufus paid no attention to Cato when…"

Elisabeth's shoulders dropped. "When what?"

"Nothing." David shook his head. "I should not have said anything to worry you."

Her hold on him tightened as the horse trotted on. "Tell me."

"Did you not hear Cato mention going to the lake in front of Rufus?"

"When?"

"Before we left to get your supposed ransom."

Elisabeth glanced behind, noticing a young boy fishing at the water's edge. "No."

"Then we can only hope he too paid no attention."

She let out an exasperated sigh. "Surely to God, Rufus can't still be—"

"*Cor meum,* look up," David said as they rounded a bend in the road.

Above them, a massive villa sat perched on the hillside. The two-story home overlooked the lake and had a porch running the length of it that was also two stories. A terracotta tiled roof covered the upper balcony and the entire façade was lined with white and burgundy columns.

David gave a disbelieving shake of his head. "Balinus! Balinus, old man! I see we've reached your friend's humble home," he yelled out and then laughed.

"Indeed, we have."

Elisabeth jerked her head back. "Did he just say what I think he said?"

"By the gods, I believe he did." David continued to follow Balinus up a narrow side road and toward the entrance. "His friend lives here?"

Elisabeth's mouth dropped when they arrived at the front of the compound. It didn't look like a house. It didn't look like any country villa she'd ever imagined. It looked more like a two-story luxury hotel.

Balinus began to alight from his horse. Cato let out a long, low whistle and followed suit.

David dismounted and then turned around to reach up for Elisabeth. "*Cor meum*, we're home," he said with a wink as he held her by the waist.

With a beaming face, she fell into his arms. "Rufus will never believe we're in there," she whispered. "I can't think of a safer place to hide out for a few days. Balinus is a genius."

David's grin couldn't be contained, no matter how hard he tried. "You may be right," he said as he put her down.

Balinus handed Cato the reigns. As he stepped onto the marble front porch, the enormous door flew open. An out-of-breath man stood before him, draped in silky fabrics of brown and burnt orange. He appeared to be in his sixties, with a rosy but weathered complexion, a bulbous nose, and thinning gray hair. His mouth was downturned, his droopy eyes hinted at sadness, yet there was something playful written on his face at the same time.

Struggling to catch his breath, he nodded rather than speaking. Then, with closed eyes, he leaned over, resting his hands on his knees.

Elisabeth's posture picked up. She walked closer to see if he was going to be all right. When Balinus burst into laughter, she exchanged a confused look with David.

The man stopped panting and stood tall. It had all been some inside joke. "I heard your name being called." Although his face remained expressionless, he spoke in a warm tone. "Can you imagine my shock when I heard your familiar voice answer?" He pressed his lips together to keep from smiling and pulled Balinus into a hug. "You've stayed away far too long, old friend."

"Aurelius," Balinus said with his exuberant voice. "I hoped you'd be here."

"Yes, well…" He let out a heavy sigh. "Nicea," he called to an elderly man that stood nearby. "Take Balinus' slaves so they can—"

"No, no-no," Balinus interrupted. "I remain steadfast in my beliefs. Forgive our attire, but these are my travel companions." He held his chin high and waved them over. "My friends."

Aurelius gave them a sheepish look. "Do accept my humblest apologies. I…how rude of me."

When another slave appeared to take their horses, Elisabeth stepped onto the porch. David and Cato awkwardly followed, standing on either side of her.

"This is Aquarius," Balinus said.

David thrust his chest out while shaking Aurelius' hand.

"And Cato."

Cato cleared his throat and gave a polite nod.

"And this is our lovely Elisabeth, and to be honest, the reason we are here. She requires rest after being bitten by a viper asp on our journey."

Aurelius gasped. "A viper asp?"

"Twice." Elisabeth extended her ankle to show him. "Balinus practically brought me back from the dead."

"By the gods….Nicea, come here." Aurelius motioned the elderly slave over. He whispered instructions and sent him running off on some errand. He then turned back to Elisabeth. "An asp?" His hand lifted toward her and then lowered again. "How are you even walking?" Aurelius then scooped her into his arms.

Elisabeth yelped. A flush crept across her cheeks as he carried her through the entranceway into a large atrium. Two stories high, it was painted in shades of cream, white, red and black. The space was stunning.

"I am quite able to walk," she said before shooting the others an incredulous look.

"She is recovering well." Balinus chuckled, offering David a reassuring pat on the arm as they followed.

With a slow, steady gait, Aurelius carried Elisabeth, yet his eyes drifted up, giving the impression that his mind had wandered off.

The ornate tiled floor caught her attention first, for it was a work of art. Noting the four doorways to her left, four to her right, she guessed them to be bedrooms. The centerpiece of the atrium was a small recessed pool. Surrounded with bronze statues on pedestals, it was filled with rainwater from an open skylight in the coffered ceiling.

Elisabeth's lips parted while looking through the open doors straight ahead into a magnificent courtyard. It beckoned to her. "You can put me down, really. I can walk."

Aurelius had a sleepy look. "It's fine." He gave a half-hearted shrug. "I carry all my guests."

Elisabeth burst into laughter. "Why do I not believe you?"

He put her down, trying to suppress a smile. "Are you certain?"

She nodded and sucked in a quick breath while gazing straight outside toward the courtyard again. Nicea hurried toward them, carrying a large silver goblet, and presented it to his master before seeming to make himself invisible.

"Here. Drink this." Aurelius handed Elisabeth the cup. "It is an antidote for poison and will rid your body of the venom."

She lifted the goblet to her lips and took a small sip. The so-called medicine tasted like citrus, grapes, and honey. Thirsty, she took a large gulp of the fruit punch, knowing it would do nothing to help.

"How did it happen?" he asked with a sidelong glance.

"We were in a cave by a waterfall. I kicked some rocks out of the way and…"

Aurelius covered his mouth and cursed into his hand, attempting to muffle a swear word.

Elisabeth gave him a mischievous grin. "That's exactly what I said." She then took another long drink.

"You were at Marmore?" His body seemed to tense and he glanced over at Balinus. "I've heard reports of pirates…"

Her free hand flew to her chest. "Pirates? But we're nowhere near the sea."

"Well…" Aurelius paused. "If they are forced further inland, I suppose that means Pliny has been doing his job well."

Elisabeth became still and stared at Balinus. "Do you think…Hayri…?" She took another drink, enjoying the taste of the fruit punch.

He tilted his head back, to weigh the possibility, before nodding.

Elisabeth's eyes bulged and she grabbed onto Aurelius' arm. "I think we were kidnapped by them. By the pirates."

His voice rose in pitch. "When?"

"After I was bitten by the snake."

He did a double-take and couldn't suppress his grin this time.

"Do pirates wear trousers?" Her voice was filled with wonder.

Aurelius laughed and turned to look at Balinus. "Where did you find this delightful creature, and why on earth did you let her fall into the hands of pirates?"

"An unfortunate event, yes, but Elisabeth has learned a great lesson," Balinus said with a gleam in his eye.

Her head jerked back. "I did?" She took a final drink of the so-called medicine, emptying the large cup.

He nodded. "You did. A wise sage once said, 'He

who controls others may be powerful, but he who has mastered himself is mightier still.'"

Aurelius leaned close. "He himself is a wise sage."

"But I don't even know what he means," she whispered with a grin. "By the way, you have a beautiful home."

"Well, you are my guests now and I am luckier because of it. Come. Drink, rest, and then you must share your tales of adventure with me." He began walking again.

"How is little Aurelia?" Balinus asked as he fell in line beside his friend.

"Aurelia is not so little anymore. She is wed to Polybius' son…"

Elisabeth stepped back to walk with David and Cato. "Can you believe this place?" Feeling a bit unsteady, she stopped by the entrance of the courtyard to lean against the door frame, attempting to savor the décor.

Flanked by six bronze statues of maidens, and surrounded by low shrubbery, the sun glistened on a shallow reflecting pool that ran down the center of the space. The water feature was the focal point of the courtyard, which appeared to be the heart of the villa. Beginning to feel rather warm, Elisabeth took her cloak off, tucking it beneath her arm. With a sigh, she then hunched forward.

Paths, benches, and trees dotted the garden, while the house itself wrapped around the entire courtyard. Rooms opened up off a covered walkway lined with white columns. Every nook and cranny was bright, airy, beckoning one to stay to enjoy the spot. She tried to take another drink from the goblet, but only a tiny drop trickled out.

Waving her arm in slow motion, Elisabeth pretended to be a tour guide. "And thish courtyard is what the ancient Romans called a *peristyle*," she mumbled before starting to giggle. "Aquarius…?"

David turned while Cato continued with the old men.

"Wait for me." Elisabeth shuffled toward him. "I feel…I feel fuzzy," she said, while dragging her cloak along the floor.

As David marched back, his shoulders tightened and he grabbed her arms. "Something is wrong."

She tilted her head to look up at him. "Did I ever tell you how my parents met? My mom was a tour guide at a palace and…"

"And your father ended up on one of her tours. Yes, you told me," he said with an obvious attempt to keep his voice light. His hands trembled as he took the empty goblet from her. "What was in this?" he whispered frantically.

Her eyes bulged while snatching the goblet back. "Oh my gosh, Aquarius…I think…I think I've been poisoned." Elisabeth let the cloak slip from her fingers to the floor.

He lowered his head to study her before glancing behind at the others, still deep in conversation as they strolled along the colonnade. With a wrinkled brow, David grabbed the sides of Elisabeth's face in his hands and kissed her on the mouth.

Her knees buckled.

David let out a huge sigh of relief.

"I will kiss thy lips. Haply some poison yet doth hang on them," she recited with closed eyes. Elisabeth

then swatted his chest. "I'm juss messing with you. It was nothing but a grape punch I drunk." She made a funny face. "Drank."

"And you have finished it already'?"

Her eyes glowed while nodding. "Aquari..." Elisabeth paused to giggle. "Aquari. I'm gonna call you that."

He swallowed his laughter and shook his head. "Please don't."

She snorted. "Do you want to know an if?"

"Yes," David murmured as he took the goblet once again.

"If..." She squinted. "If..." With a theatrical groan, her hands flew up in the air. "It doesn't work as an if. Never mind."

Elisabeth took a step, intending to catch up to the others, but David reached for her arm to hold her back.

"Tell me your secret anyway," he whispered with a bemused smile.

"It's just that I kinda love how you worry about me." She tried to whisper, but it came out too loud. Elisabeth licked her lips while shrugging. "But all the drink was...it was some sort of grape punch with lemon and honey. I don't know." Her voice deepened and the giggling started again. "But it was gooood."

David tried to hide his grin. "*Cor meum...*" He tilted his head forward. "Your lips tasted of wine."

"My lips tasted of wine?" She gave him a dazed look. "Are you sure?" A huge smile spread across her face. "I think you should check again." Tilting her chin up, she closed her eyes while puckering her lips, waiting for another kiss.

David leaned forward. "You are drunk," he

243

whispered.

Elisabeth gasped and her hands flew to her chest. "I am not…I am not dur-runk." She stared down at the empty goblet in his hand and then looked up into his blue eyes. "I'm just happy."

David chuckled and picked up the cloak. He then put his arm around her waist to help her walk. "Balinus," he called out. "I am afraid Elisabeth is not at all accustomed to wine."

Aurelius walked over and laughed as he took the empty goblet. "It is my fault. I should have told her to sip it." He pressed a fist to his lips and exchanged a smile with David. "It was simply the juice from a citron mixed with wine and honey to sweeten."

Balinus nodded in understanding and looked at Elisabeth. "It is an effective remedy for poison. Unfortunately, you've been near death, are exhausted, and have not eaten a proper meal, so the wine has gone straight to your head."

"Elisabeth can sleep off the effects of the wine and rejoin us afterward." Aurelius motioned the slave over. "Nicea, have Eumelia tend to her."

"I will tend to her," David insisted.

With a polite nod, the slave led David and Elisabeth back toward the atrium, through one of the doors, and into a small bedroom.

"Ha! I knew these were bedrooms, Aquari." She poked David's chest with her finger.

"Us."

"Huh?"

"Aquarius," he whispered in a carefully controlled tone.

Elisabeth smirked and raised a brow.

Nicea tried to hide his grin.

Elisabeth lurched over and stared at the slave. "Thank you, Nicea. I want you to know that where I come from—"

"Elisabeth…" David warned.

"Oh, right." She nodded and tried to wink before turning back to the slave. "Never mind where I come from, but let me tell you something. Where I live, we do not—"

"Stop talking, Elisabeth." David bit down on a smile and cleared his throat. "Thank you, Nicea. That will be all."

On the walls of the tiny, but well-appointed bedroom, a garden scene was painted in shades of blue, green and brown, resembling expensive wallpaper. Jewel-toned curtains danced on the spring breeze as David helped Elisabeth to a narrow bed topped with silky blankets.

"I'm being sent to my room, but I'm not even tired and this is the first nice…" Her voice trailed off while yawning. Perched on the edge of the bed, she flopped sideways onto the pillow. David took her sandals off before lifting her feet up to tuck her in. "Maybe I am a little bit tired," she mumbled.

"It would be wise for you to rest. Sleep well, *cor meum*. You'll be safe here." He kissed her cheek and tiptoed back out of the room.

Elisabeth smiled, stretched, and sat up before whipping the blanket back off, deciding she wasn't tired after all. Looking down at her filthy hands, she cringed. The condition of her dress was even worse. Suddenly, having a shower, brushing her teeth, and putting on clean clothes seemed the most important thing in the world to do.

She put her shoes back on and reached for the crystal; thoughts of home on her mind.

Home.

Chapter Seventeen

Forgetting she was in the library with Mrs. Waters and David, Elisabeth let out an exaggerated sigh while opening her eyes. "Oh, look, it's the happy couple." Frowning, she rose to her feet, unable to make eye contact. "I am going home now. Goodnight." Still feeling a bit fuzzy, she shifted back and forth to find her balance and then fumbled around the desk.

"Well, that's my cue." Sissi cleared her throat and stood. "I need to tell you something rather important, my dear."

Elisabeth shook her head while trying to hold back tears. "Look, I just wanna go home."

David opened his mouth to say something, but then closed it again and remained silent.

Mrs. Waters took a calming breath. "What I have to tell you is…well, it's a game-changer."

Elisabeth's nails bit into her palms. "A game-changer?" Heat flushed through her body. "Is that all my life is to you? A game? Am I nothing but a pawn in some…some elaborate scheme for immortality and wealth?" With a dramatic sweep of her arms, Elisabeth looked at David and forced a laugh. "And what about *Aquari* here?" The lame attempt at name-calling backfired when he bit his lips to hide a smile instead.

A flush crept across Mrs. Water's cheeks and she gave David an apologetic glance.

When he grinned at his wife and then wiggled his eyebrows, Elisabeth's lungs constricted, making it difficult to breathe. He looked at Mrs. Waters the same way he always looked at her; with complete adoration.

Elisabeth lowered her head, making a beeline for the door, but David reached for her arm to hold her back.

"If I recall correctly, you've had some wine. I can't let you walk home alone."

She lifted her chin, forcing herself to make eye contact with him. "Incredible memory, but I'm fine."

"My dear…" Mrs. Waters removed Elisabeth's blue *palla*. "Accidental or not, how will you explain to your parents the fact that you are intoxicated? How will you explain your swollen, snake-bitten leg? The fact that you are dressed in a *stola* and are a complete mess would be the least of their concerns. Tell you what—I'll throw this in the laundry and you can get washed up here. Heaven knows you'll feel better once you're clean, and if you don't, I certainly will." With a smile and a wink, she excused herself from the room.

Elisabeth's shoulders began to quake and she buried her face in her hands.

David pulled her to his shoulder.

"No, don't touch me." She pushed him away. "Please don't make this harder for me than it is. I know what's coming and it terrifies me. I'm trying desperately not to think about it." Her tone deepened while glaring at him. "Do you want to know an if?"

The color drained from his face.

"If only this had never happened. If only you hadn't manipulated me into this entire mess. If only I could forget you." She gave him a pained stare. "But I can't. I can't because I love Aquarius and I won't let him die the way I think it's going to happen. I don't belong there, but here…you're not mine here." She shook her head in denial. "You're not *my* Aquarius anymore, yet there's this debt hanging over me."

David scrubbed a hand over his face. "Elisabeth, I'm still me."

She struggled not to cry. "I should never have allowed myself to get swept away with the adventure in the first place. I'm an idiot for thinking that I…Why? Why'd you drag me into all of this?"

"I know how this looks, but…" his voice cracked. "It's not what you think."

Elisabeth's head jerked back and her face reddened. "Of course it's what I think. She's your wife!"

"*Cor meum…*"

"You mustn't call me that anymore. I am not your sweetheart here."

"Do you remember when I first met you?"

Her eyes clouded with tears. She sniffled, knowing she'd never forget a single moment they'd spent together. "No, as a matter of fact, I don't." She wiped her nose with the back of her hand before heading toward the door.

"You appeared out of thin air, dressed like nothing I'd ever seen." His voice was quiet. "I knew something wasn't right. I teased you about being from the heavens and kept asking and waiting for you to tell me your secret; your if."

She came to a sudden stop.

"Why did you wait before telling me you were a time traveler? Why did you wait before telling me I never age? *Cor meum,* think about it." His voice choked with emotion.

Elisabeth stared down at the floor, shoulders curled over her chest. "I was trying to protect you. It would have been too much information for you to handle at once."

"Exactly."

Mrs. Waters cleared her throat while walking back into the library and put a comforting arm around Elisabeth. "Come with me. We'll get you all cleaned up."

Elisabeth averted her gaze, knowing David was right. Puzzle pieces she still knew nothing about overwhelmed her. If she wanted answers, the only option was to trust them. She followed the old woman down the corridor and to the doorway of a room with walls painted a classic gray. A bed with an ornate iron canopy dominated the space.

"You can have a shower. Make yourself at home and feel free to use anything you see. It's all there just for you, my dear. If you want to throw your tunic in the hamper when you're finished, I have something for you to wear that I know you'll like a lot better." She flashed a secretive smile and leaned closer to whisper, "And it's a thousand times prettier. Aquarius and I will wait for you in the library."

When Mrs. Waters left, Elisabeth walked around the bed to the door of the ensuite bathroom. She sucked in a quick breath—and with it the wonderful scent of French perfume. An old-fashioned claw tub sat in one corner, with a chandelier hanging over top of it. In another corner was a modern, glass shower stall. Marching toward the white marble vanity, Elisabeth stood on a fluffy bathmat, recoiling when looking in the mirror. "Oh, good grief." She ran fingers beneath sunken eyes, along pale cheekbones. "I look like crap."

She whipped off her clothes, and hopped in the shower, eager to wash all the filth away. While the soap cleansed her, the after-effects of the wine seemed to wash away as well. With a clearer mind, she came to terms with the fact she'd be returning to Ancient Rome, no matter what. The whole purpose for going was to save David's life at some point. She'd never leave him to die. Never.

Wrapped in a soft, white towel, teeth brushed, hair washed, Elisabeth felt like a new person. Mrs. Waters had left a pile of lotions and creams for her to use, forgetting nothing, not even lip balm or an eyelash curler.

"Impressive," she mumbled while slipping into a pink satin robe she'd found hanging on a hook.

After exiting the bathroom, Elisabeth's glance darted to the bed where an ice blue gown had been laid out. She brushed her fingers along the silky fabric and then held the dress up to judge its size before slipping into it. With a smile, Elisabeth stared down at the material, admiring the elegant way it flowed. She pranced toward a full-length mirror to see her reflection. Gold detail at the shoulders pinched the fabric of the sleeveless gown together with a band of the same gold trim around the tailored waist. The perfect size suggested it had been custom-made for her to wear. She took an easy breath, grateful to feel feminine and pretty once again.

With a fluttery feeling in her chest, Elisabeth started back toward the library. Unnoticed, she paused in the hallway, able to observe them for a moment. Mrs. Waters seemed to be searching for something in a book. David fidgeted in a chair, bouncing his knee while staring at the carpet. She smoothed out her dress before tiptoeing into the room.

David's eyes widened as he looked up at her.

His smile took her breath away.

"Elisabeth…" he said with a soft tone.

"Yes, darling?" Mrs. Waters turned around to answer him.

Elisabeth's head flinched back in confusion. David cleared his throat.

"Oh…oh my…" The old woman's voice choked with tears while gazing at the blue gown. "You look so lovely, my dear. Come, sit down." Sissi grabbed a hairbrush, tapping one of the chairs as she stood behind it. "Aquarius, I never realized how pretty…oh, never mind." She let out a shallow sigh

David nodded and bit down on a smile.

With a slight shake of her head, Elisabeth eased into the seat to let Sissi brush her long hair. "All right, what is it you have to tell me? What's this…game-changer?"

"Well, I'm not sure how to start."

"Don't worry," Elisabeth said. "After finding out you two are married, nothing could possibly shock me now."

David shifted in his seat, unable to get comfortable.

Mrs. Waters took a calming breath and then let the words tumble out. "Did-I-ever-tell-you-how-my-parents-met?"

"No—" Elisabeth answered in an uncertain tone.

"It's a really sweet story. You see, my mother was

working as an English tour guide at a palace in Austria and my father ended up on one of her tours."

Elisabeth opened her mouth to say something, but stopped short.

"It was love at first sight." Mrs. Waters pinned up a small braid. "My father always teased and said he was more interested in my mother than the palace."

Elisabeth glanced at David for answers, but he swallowed an obvious lump in his throat and looked away.

The old woman's lost her mind!

Sissi continued to fiddle with Elisabeth's hair. "I was named after a beautiful Bavarian princess, well…an Empress really, who once lived in the palace where they first met."

"Mrs. Waters. I'm afraid you're confused." Her heart raced. "That's how *my* parents met and how I was…" For a split second, everything seemed suspended in time. Elisabeth turned around to stare up at Sissi.

"Say it. Say what you're thinking, my dear."

"Aquarius…?" Her voice rose in pitch. "What is Mrs. Waters talking about?"

"*Cor meum*, think." He cleared his throat and rubbed a hand down his pant leg. "My wife…my wife is a time traveler."

Elisabeth's head jerked back and she stared at the old woman again. "You can time travel too?"

Sissi pinched her lips together to keep from smiling. "What are the odds I'm a time traveler, married to him…" She nodded toward David's direction. "…and also named after Empress Elisabeth? Franz Joseph had a pet name for his beloved wife. Do you remember what he called her?"

Elisabeth's chest tightened while turning away. "Franz Joseph called Empress Elisabeth…" She squeezed her eyes shut, trying to put the pieces together. "He called her Sissi."

"That's right," Mrs. Waters said in a soothing tone. "That's right."

Elisabeth stood up, bringing a shaky hand to her forehead.

"Time travel is an amazing thing, isn't it?" Sissi pointed across the room. "Aquarius, there's a small mirror in that mess somewhere. Would you mind bringing it over here?"

David rubbed the back of his neck and walked over to the desk. Rummaging through the papers, he moved a vase out of the way to reach a silver hand mirror.

Elisabeth became light-headed; staring at the pink rose in the vase he'd pushed aside.

Then we agree you shall always have pink roses.

Her head flinched back. David stole a glance at her as he placed the mirror into her trembling hand.

"Look. Your hair is perfect now. If anyone asks, remember to say you did it yourself." With a light giggle, the old woman walked around to the front of the chair. "Let me hold that for you." She took the mirror from Elisabeth, holding it up beside her own face so they could compare their features side by side.

The shape of their face, their noses, their mouths, even their teeth were identical. Elisabeth's heartbeat raced while staring at the crow's feet surrounding the old woman's beautiful, intelligent eyes. Love and kindness radiated from Mrs. Waters. For the first time ever, Elisabeth noticed her own dark eyes, although older, wiser, looking back at her. Her hand flew to her mouth, staring at the woman for confirmation.

Elisabeth's voice choked with tears. "Oh, my gosh." It felt like her legs would no longer hold her. "I need to sit down again."

David rushed to her side, lowering her onto the sofa before taking a seat beside her. "Are you all right?"

She shook her head. "I'm her?"

He held his breath, nodding.

"I've time-traveled to my own past?" With a pounding heart, she stared up at Sissi.

Mrs. Waters gave Elisabeth an understanding nod. "Didn't I tell you that I have a vested interest in the two of you?" A slow smile appeared. "Believe me, there is no one on Earth who loves you both more than I do."

The room seemed to spin. "So…let me get this straight. You…I came back to my past to set all these events in motion?"

"Well, it's not that simple, really. I did everything I could to help, but the truth is you can go home if you like. You can forget all of this. You still have free will. Time-travel doesn't change that."

Elisabeth's posture stiffened. "How is that possible, if this has all happened before? Aren't you going to tell me not to worry? Tell me that everything works out fine in the end? That he's not going to end up…" She choked on her words. "End up being cooked to death at the foot of an erupting volcano? I'm not stupid. I know how Aquarius is supposed to die."

"You must realize that nothing is set in stone." Mrs. Waters attempted to keep her voice light.

"Just tell me how to avoid his death. Didn't this

already happen to you?"

"No. Not exactly. For whatever reason, this timeline is slightly different. I…I never met my future self."

Elisabeth did a double-take.

"A kind old woman named Hattie Monk taught me Latin. Aquarius had secretly arranged and paid for her to tutor me, much like I have been doing with you." Her voice hitched and she glanced at David who shrugged his shoulders.

Elisabeth shook her head in denial. "I've already screwed something up?"

"Darling, listen," Mrs. Waters continued. "I've never lied to you. I am a…" she pushed back obvious tears, forcing herself to continue. "I am a widow now and…"

Elisabeth grabbed David's hand.

"Don't feel sad. We had a glorious life and grew old together, which is all we ever truly wanted. I hadn't touched the crystal for sixty years, until one day…" Her chin trembled. "I came back. Aquarius is still alive here, waiting for *you*…and to see Mother and Daddy again…? I've missed them all so…much." With a quaking voice, she turned away before losing her composure. "But this time, there was no Hattie Monk to teach you Latin. I don't know why, but Hattie doesn't exist on this timeline. I felt I had no choice but to take matters into my own hands. I stayed and loved you like a granddaughter. You are me after all…well, a version of me." She turned around again, ready to face them. "So you see, nothing is set in stone. This is still your life to live, whichever path you choose. Don't worry about your actions changing my past because I don't think that is…"

Elisabeth cleared her throat and tried to put a coherent sentence together, but something was wrong. Without saying a word, she stood up and stumbled toward the door, trying to catch her breath. She ran along the hall back to the guest suite and dropped to the floor beside the bed, struggling not to lose control.

A moment later, David tiptoed into the room and sat beside her.

No longer able to keep it together, Elisabeth began sobbing, unable to stop. "I don't…I don't…" She gasped for air. "This is too…"

"Shhh. Slow down," David whispered with a soothing voice. "Take deep breaths."

"I don't…" Her chest ached.

"Deep breaths." He stroked her hair. "Shhh."

"I-don't-want-to-go-back-but-I-can't-let-you-die-there."

The room became blurry. Oxygen didn't seem to be filling her lungs.

Elisabeth heard Mrs. Waters' voice and a moment later David was holding a paper bag for her to breathe into.

"Take deep breaths, *cor meum*. Deep breaths."

In and out.

In and out.

In and out.

The noise and movement of the bag seemed hypnotic, and her breathing began to slow down. Falling against David, he wrapped his arms around her and rested his cheek on her head. Elisabeth's heart stopped racing while putting the paper bag aside, no longer needing it. The only thing on her mind was how safe and secure his hug felt.

For several long minutes, neither of them felt the need to fill the silence.

"I'm okay now." Voice cracked with emotion. She wiped tears away and turned to look at him. "Thank you."

With a sympathetic smile, he nodded.

"That's never happened before." A flush crept across her cheeks. "I guess I was wrong when I said nothing could shock me now."

David stood and pulled Elisabeth up. "Well, under the circumstances, anyone…"

"How? How can I be her? Sissi Waters?" She shook her head. "Can you even begin to understand how much I adore her?" Her chin started trembling. "That makes me the…the-vainest-person-in-the-world." Her arms fell limp and tears tumbled.

David clamped his lips together to keep from smiling while handing her a tissue. "Oh *cor meum*, no….it means you are able to see what I see in you."

She wiped her nose. "Yeah. I'm a real prize; a vain coward. I don't feel like I'm Mrs. Waters at all. I've always idolized her."

His lips parted and he looked at Elisabeth with a soft expression. "Never idolize anyone. That's giving your power away. Anything worth admiring in others is found inside of you." David skimmed his fingers along her cheek. "As you now know."

"You sound like Balinus." She took a deep breath, but then looked up at him. "It's Pompeii, isn't it? If I don't go back, you'll die in Pompeii when Vesuvius erupts."

David gave her a pained stare.

"Oh God, I knew it. I knew it." She shook her head. "Balinus told me there's no such thing as a coincidence. I'm not stupid. We're in 79 AD, aren't we? I know where this is going to end up and the thought of you dying there...that's why I'm so scared."

"Elisabeth, you..." His voice broke. "You don't have to..."

Her eyes widened. "Are you kidding me? Of course I have to. I may be terrified of what's coming, but I would never, in a million years, just leave you to die there." Elisabeth's chest caved in. "I love you, Gaius Cornelius Aquarius."

With a slight moan, David turned his face away to hide his emotions and Elisabeth stepped closer, expecting to nestle into a hug. Instead, his body went stiff and he sniffled, desperate to hold back tears. She wrapped her arms around his waist and rested her head against his chest anyhow.

"Aquarius, what have we done?"

"We're realigning the stars ourselves, *cor meum*." His breath hitched. "We're realigning them ourselves."

She squeezed her eyes shut when David's shoulders began to tremble. He struggled to regain his composure and Elisabeth knew if she looked up at him now they'd both break down. "Is this a huge mistake?"

"No," he said with a firmer voice. "And I should know. I've wandered...I've wandered this earth long enough." The cuckoo clock downstairs whistled and he shook his head. "That stupid clock always reminds me of you."

"Stupid? I love that cuckoo clock. Have you ever watched it?"

"I'm afraid so." David sniffled. "That poor couple

only wish to dance, yet they always seem frozen in time, waiting to be reunited. Once an hour they come together for mere seconds. It's depressing." His shoulders slumped. "I should throw it away, but I can't, because it reminds me of you."

"Wait." Elisabeth stepped back. "Is this *your* house?"

He stared down at his hands. "It's ours. Someday."

Elisabeth's eyes filled with tears. "Somehow, you always give me the courage I need. I can do this. All I have to do is keep you away from Pompeii." She took a deep breath and reached for her crystal. "How hard can that be?"

"Wait." He bowed his head but watery eyes glanced up at her. "Stay with me a while longer?"

"Why? What does it matter? Time stands still so it will all be the same to you."

"No…it won't." He reached for her hand. "It won't be the same at all. It will be a different moment for you and I want to share *this* moment." David laced his fingers through Elisabeth's and then lifted her arm. "I don't want to be frozen in time like the man in the cuckoo clock." He placed his other hand on the small of her back and pulled her closer. "I want to dance with you a little longer." His eyes seemed to hold her tighter than his arms as they danced, even though no music played. "Don't go running to him yet," David mumbled when she rested against his shoulder.

Her head jerked back. "Running to who? You?" Her lips clamped together. "Aquarius…" Elisabeth couldn't help giggling. "Oh my gosh…you're jealous?"

With a bemused smile, he raised an eyebrow. "You're one to talk, my dear."

"We're quite the pair, aren't we? I'll be jealous of Mrs. Waters and you can be jealous of my beloved Aquarius."

"Oh…" He let out a shaky laugh. "So he's your *beloved* now, is he?"

With a shy grin, she nodded. "He kind of stole my heart."

David stopped dancing and kissed Elisabeth's hand. "Well, I guess the best thing you can do is let him keep it," he whispered before leading her back to the library.

Mrs. Waters fidgeted with her scarf as they entered the room. "Everything okay?"

"So far," David whispered.

She let out a huge breath. "That's a relief. Now, sit down and let's get right to it."

Elisabeth took a step back. "Whoa…I sound serious."

"You are." David winked and pulled her beside him on the sofa. "So you better have a seat right here next to your beloved."

Elisabeth shook her head, grinning as she sat next to him.

"Make sure you listen to yourself," he said with a smile that didn't reach his eyes. All of a sudden, he was holding the freshly laundered blue *palla*.

She let out an appreciative sigh as he wrapped it around her shoulders.

Mrs. Waters' eyes were bright and glossy. "I'm not a physicist so I won't pretend to understand how time travel works, but here is what I believe has happened to us."

"This sounds like a well-rehearsed speech."

Sissi gave a curt nod. "You better believe it, so pay attention. I want you to think of life as a novel." She reached for a nearby book and held it up. "Between the front and back cover, a story is written. When you read it, there is a beginning, a middle, and an end. That is the illusion of time. In reality, all the parts of the story exist simultaneously. Do you understand so far?"

"I think so. When we go through life, our story flows from beginning to end, but the continuity of it is just an illusion."

"Right. You know that we could spread all the pages of the book out on the table and look at them as a whole. Time itself is just an illusion."

Elisabeth nodded.

"However, the universe is infinite. It's not a single book, it's an entire library." Mrs. Waters bit down on a smile when she glanced at a stack of paper on the desk and hurried to grab hold of it. "Look at all this paper. Every decision you can make, every path you can choose…it's a new piece of paper that gets added to your book. For the most part, you choose which sheets go into your story, but every possible choice and outcome is here." Sissi held up one sheet. "This is the page in which you go back to ancient Rome and try to save David." She grabbed another sheet. "This is when you were bitten by the snake, but died. Oh…let's not use that one in our story." She crumpled it up and tossed it on the floor. "Let's use this sheet instead. This is when Balinus gave you the elixir and you lived. Do you see? Your timeline is your book—your story. All the choices we make, all the thoughts we think, *they* create this timeline and our experience of life. Yet, you have to remember that *all* possibilities exist." Sissi held up another book. "For some reason the crystal enables us to jump to other timelines, to step into another book, so to speak. That's how we ended up in Ancient Rome and Scotland. It might be easier if you think of it, not as time traveling, but shifting to a parallel reality."

Elisabeth exuded calm and focus while trying to follow Mrs. Waters' theory. "So, we ended up in Ancient Rome and began a new timeline in that…parallel reality?"

"Yes." Sissi bit her lip. "A famous scientist once explained it as being like a river. When I…*we*…appeared in ancient Rome to try and change David's future, that original timeline divided into two different rivers. The original one, of course, remains, the one in which he dies in Pompeii, but a new one was formed as well, in which you enter into his life and he survives."

"But what if we end up changing a huge event and with it the course of history?"

"No, no…It's not like that. Everyone thinks that. Remember that all possibilities already exist. It's just another possible scenario, on a seemingly insignificant timeline, within an ever-expanding universe. You can alter the course of history there no more or less than you can here. And, this leads me to our little dilemma."

Elisabeth rubbed her chin. "Dilemma? I'm too lost to even—"

"That's fine. I realize the nature of time travel is confusing. Just know that when I came back here, I…I didn't realize it at the time, but it ended up creating a parallel reality, not exactly like the one I came from."

Elisabeth swallowed the lump in her throat. "You mean because you didn't meet your future self?"

She nodded. "My original timeline continues and I haven't changed anything there. There is no grandfather paradox, nor any paradox. But here, I've unintentionally made a different timeline, so to be perfectly honest…" She lowered her voice. "I am not certain how this is going to turn out for you."

"It doesn't matter." Elisabeth sat up taller and her fists tightened. "I don't care. I don't care because I can do this. I am *going* to do this. All I have to do is keep Aquarius away from Pompeii. It can't be that hard and we've come this far. Get ready to add a new sheet of paper to my story." She stared at David. "The one that tells of how I saved your life."

Mrs. Waters cleared her throat. "That's the perfect way to look at it, the perfect attitude." She paused and started coughing. "Elisabeth, darling, would you mind getting me a glass of water from the kitchen?"

David jumped up. "Let me get it for you."

Elisabeth pulled him back down and stood up herself. "It's all right. I'll get it."

"Cor meum…" his voice cracked. He knew her true intention.

"I'll be right back. I promise."

The color drained from his face and he grabbed her by the waist to pull her closer. "I'm holding you to that promise."

"You know I have to do this."

David didn't seem to have the strength to let her go. He forced a watery smile and nodded before turning his head.

"It will be fine. Really," she whispered.

Once in the hallway, Elisabeth reached for her crystal.

****

Elisabeth flopped back down on the bed and glanced around the room. Funny how the craftsmanship of the furniture and the general attention to detail, found in this Ancient Roman home, seemed more advanced than what you'd find in Castle Ealasaid. The amount of knowledge lost during the Dark Ages must have been astronomical. Although electricity had obviously not been invented yet, Aurelius' home looked as fine as anything built today. With a deep, satisfied breath, she closed her eyes. A newfound confidence pulsed through her and for the first time, Elisabeth felt in control of the situation. Rufus should be a long way from the area by now, all while they passed the time in this luxurious villa. The only thing left for her to do was keep David away from Pompeii, but that should be simple, especially since she planned to tell him about the eruption later this evening. Her muscles relaxed knowing the chances were slim that anything could mess up her plans.

Chapter Eighteen

A loud, obnoxious noise awoke her, as someone marched in the atrium outside of the room, clanging pots and pans. Elisabeth climbed out of bed and crept to the door, almost tripping over David after opening it. She laughed. "Aquarius, what are you doing down there?"

"I was just..." He lifted his head to stare up at her and then sucked in a quick breath. His ears turned red as he scrambled to his feet. "When I came back from the bath you were asleep so I thought I'd wait here for you." David scraped a nervous hand through his damp hair. "Elisabeth, you look..."

"Oh..." A flush flamed across her cheeks while she fidgeted with the fabric of the new dress. "I kind of went home to bathe and change my clothes."

David nodded. "I can see that. By the gods, you are—"

"Oh good, you're awake." As Aurelius poked his head out from the atrium, his eyes widened. "I must say you both clean up rather well." He gave Elisabeth a second glance. "Come quickly, you do not want to miss the magic hour."

Elisabeth raised her eyebrows, glancing at David. "I don't know about you, but I certainly don't want to miss anything called the magic hour." She laughed, grabbed his hand, pulling him to a run. She felt weightless and giddy while leading him back to the gallery surrounding the courtyard.

"Over here," Aurelius called to them from a large open doorway on their left.

Colorful marble decorated the walls and floor of the lavish room that overlooked the *peristyle* while three pillow-laden beds were positioned in a u-shape in the center of the space.

"This is the dining room, isn't it?" Elisabeth whispered as she stared at silver dishes lining a sideboard.

Wide-eyed, David nodded, but he wasn't looking at anything in the room. His gaze wandered beyond it.

Turning to see what had caught his attention, Elisabeth squealed in delight. Aurelius laughed.

"Are you kidding me?" she said to their host.

He gave a humble shrug. "Go, enjoy the magic hour in the outer *peristyle*. I did not want you to miss it."

Speechless, she tiptoed through the doorway and stood at one end of an enormous outdoor courtyard, this one at least four times the size of the inner one. A colonnade surrounded the entire garden and a large rectangular pool ran down the length of the space. Elisabeth glanced at David to see if his reaction was the same as hers.

He let out a long, low whistle.

She walked down the steps. "Have you ever seen anything this beautiful?"

"I have not." David winked at her before turning around, calling out to Aurelius. "Tell me, what is this magic hour you speak of?"

"Well…" He stood overlooking his domain and

took a sip from his goblet. His eyes then wandered up to the sky. "You know when you see something breathtakingly beautiful for the first time; you cannot help but stop and pay attention? You are really *in* the moment?"

David nodded.

"I try to live every day like that and to me, there is nothing more beautiful than twilight. That magical time just before sunset or sunrise is constant, yet how often does one stop to pay attention? It is the perfect reminder to live, to be alive in the moment while you are…well…" He paused and took another sip of his drink. "While you are alive." Aurelius ducked his head, seeming to hide his emotion before sauntering down the steps to join Cato and Balinus, who sat talking on a semi-circular bench, nestled within a boxwood lined alcove.

Elisabeth looked up at the darkening sky, watching it turn shades of fuchsia.

David extended his elbow. "Shall we?"

With her arm through his, he led the way along a path beside the reflecting pool filled with fish. She turned around to glance at Aurelius. With a sad smile, he tipped his head and then said something to Balinus and Cato, who both started laughing.

Elisabeth pointed to the covered walkway that surrounded the courtyard. "Do you want to walk over there?"

Without saying a word, they walked toward the colonnade, watching a slave make his way along the perimeter, lighting all the lanterns. Salmon-pink marble floors stretched as far as the eye could see, and *trompe-l'oeil* paintings decorated the walls. Every other panel had a window framing a view of the lake beyond it.

She leaned into David playfully. "You're so quiet."

"I'm afraid that is your fault." He gave her a sidelong glance. "One look at you tonight has left me speechless."

A flush crept across her cheeks while glancing down at the new gown. "I have to admit I really like this dress. It's twirl-worthy."

He came to a sudden stop and stared at her in confusion.

With an infectious laugh, she gave a quick spin, sending the silky blue fabric spiraling around her. "When I was a little girl, whenever my mother wanted me to wear a dress instead of trousers—"

"Trousers!"

Elisabeth had a bemused smile as they started walking again. "Everyone wears trousers in the future. We are complete barbarians." She giggled.

When David's mouth snapped shut, she gave him a light-hearted nudge.

"As I was saying, when I was a little girl, the first thing I did with any new dress was to see if it was twirl-worthy. If it wasn't, I didn't want to wear it."

His eyes twinkled with mischief. "So, when I was a young boy, learning *useful* skills—"

"Oh, like slinging rocks?"

"Yes, like slinging rocks." David clamped his lips together to keep from smiling. "You were…" He made circles in the air with his index finger. "Twirling?"

"Yep." She laughed, pulling his hand down to stop his teasing. "And having a marvelous time."

He lowered his eyes, chuckling before looking up with a grin.

They reached the far end of the walkway and the setting sun began to glisten on the reflecting pool, giving it the appearance of liquid gold. David sat on a bench while Elisabeth stood staring at the gardens. "I can see why Aurelius calls this the magic hour. It's as beautiful as one of my mother's paintings. My mom is a well-known artist. Did I ever tell you that?"

David pulled her onto his knee, wrapping his arms around her waist. "No."

"My father is a family doctor." Elisabeth's voice became quiet while folding her hands in her lap. "I don't suppose I've really told you anything about myself, have I?"

"Not in so many words, but…" He released an appreciative sigh. "Your mother is an artist; your father is a doctor. They named you after a beautiful princess, yet you carry yourself like a queen. You currently reside in a seaside village in a place called Nova Scotia." He pronounced Nova Scotia slowly, trying to remember the name. "You are…Canadian?"

"Yes." With a grin, she clasped her hands behind his neck.

"You were born approximately two thousand years after me…which does make me older and wiser."

Elisabeth laughed

"You are shy, but brave, kind, and good. You blush when I tell you how lovely you are, and will talk non-stop at times. Your mother is a great cook—she does not serve you rat," he added with a wink. "You love pink roses, something called choco-late, and water with bubbles. You have the warmest eyes, the sweetest smile, and your laughter lights up my entire world."

At a loss for words, Elisabeth openly stared at him

while caressing the back of his neck.

"You are intelligent. I also know you are a student because you have an examination on Tuesday and are worried about it."

Elisabeth groaned. "Calculus. Why'd you have to remind me?"

"How am I doing?"

"Impressive."

He turned his head and stared down at the ground. "Alas, I fear I am forgetting one very important thing." David shot her a sideways glance.

Elisabeth tried not to laugh when he raised a suggestive eyebrow. He then tapped his lips, implying she should kiss him. With a shy smile, she leaned closer, but gave him a blank look instead. "I can't think of a single thing you're forgetting."

With a snort, David wiped at his mouth. "Wait, I recall now." He lowered his voice to a whisper. "You've fallen in love with me."

"Oh, that." Her expression softened. "It seems you've stolen my heart."

He brushed his thumb along her cheek. "Fear not, *cor meum*. I'll keep it safe."

Elisabeth sucked in a quick breath and nodded. "I know."

A silhouette at the far end of the colonnade caught their attention.

"Cato's coming." Elisabeth stood. "And we've totally missed the sunset." She chuckled before planting herself on the bench next to David again. In perfect sync, she rested her head against him as he put his arm around her shoulders.

He hummed while waiting for Cato to reach them.

White flowers scattered amongst the shrubs glowed in the moonlight while countless lanterns illuminated the night. They reflected like a mirror on the pool, twinkling in the darkness like little fireflies. The magic hour had set the stage for this stunning moon garden.

"Aquarius, I wish to speak to you about something rather important." Cato paced.

Elisabeth knew now was the perfect time to warn them both about Pompeii. "So do I, but you go first."

Cato cleared his throat. "I have a great idea. Well, at least I think it to be a great idea. That is…I…" He fidgeted with his hands.

"What is it?" David asked.

"It's just…I…I like it here."

"We all do," Elisabeth said. "What's not to like?"

"Aquarius and I are slaves."

The color drained from her face as she sat up taller. "No, you're not."

Cato gave her an impatient sneer. "Yes, we are. I was born a slave and so was Aquarius."

"I am a freedman," David said through gritted teeth.

"You are naught but an indentured slave now."

David stood, crossing his arms in front of his chest. "What are you saying?"

"Look around you. Aurelius would be a kind and just master. We could live a tolerable life here, perhaps even better than tolerable. I think we should tell Aurelius of our situation, beg him for mercy. Hopefully with Balinus' help, he can be persuaded to purchase us. I am tired of running."

Elisabeth gasped while jumping to her feet. "No! You must trust Aquarius and I—"

"Shut your mouth," Cato hissed. "When I want your opinion I will ask for it. Until then, hold your tongue, you stupid—"

David grabbed Cato's arms, shoving him into the wall. "Do not *ever* speak to her in that manner again. Do I make myself clear?"

"You fool, listen to reason. You mustn't let some stupid girl cloud your judgement."

"You try my patience," David warned. "I will never be a slave again. Do not dare think…I am so close…so close to a life of actual happiness I can taste it." His face turned red. Spittle built up in the corners of his mouth as he whispered frantically, "I swear to the gods, if you so much as mutter a word of this idiotic plan of yours I will never speak to you again. You will be dead to me."

"You know that isn't true," Cato said with a condescending smile. "Your loyalty to those you care about never wavers…brother."

David grabbed Cato by the scruff of the neck. "Do not mistake my kindness for lack of strength. I swear you will be dead to me." His eyes then widened. "Where is Elisabeth's box?"

"What box?"

"You know very well which box."

He pushed David off him and straightened his tunic. "How should I know?"

"You had it last."

Cato's nostrils flared. "As much as you want to, you cannot buy a new life, Aquarius. You had your freedom yet ended up back in the life of slavery to which we were born. Are you so blind? Elisabeth has been trouble from the moment…what is she even doing here?" Cato's eyes widened. "What does she really want? She is no different from the gods and you are naught but a little plaything to her. You are merely a curiosity. How long before she disappears just as quickly as she appeared? I guarantee she will not stay here. Then do you know where you will be? Alone. You will be all alone when she abandons you." Cato's hands clenched and unclenched. "She is ruining your life but you are too blind to see it."

Elisabeth took a deep, pained breath then closed her eyes.

David's mouth went slack. He shuffled back a step before planting his feet in a wide stance. "Control your fear, Cato, before it leads you to actions that will affect all of us. Why must you always be so impulsive?"

"Because of her, we are outlaws. Rufus would have sold us by now and we could be well adjusted in some new life, with a new and perhaps kind master."

"You are the fool. What skills do we have? Look at us. Hard labor in a quarry would have likely been our fate. How many months would we survive there? Three?"

Cato seemed frantic. "All the more reason to try everything possible to persuade Aurelius that we are worth…"

Elisabeth gripped the sides of her head to cover her ears. She could not believe what he was saying.

David moved an inch from Cato's face, jabbing him with his finger while he spoke. "You are a coward. You have always been a coward and you will die a coward. Do not speak to me of this again for I swear to Jupiter, I will…" He raised his clenched fist and then turned and walked away, trying to regain his composure.

Cato angled his body away from them and covered his face with both hands.

"Look…" David rubbed the back of his neck. "Once we settle, we can buy your mother's freedom. I know how much you love her."

"Someone is coming." Elisabeth's eyes clouded with tears. "Cato, please don't say anything to Aurelius. Can we discuss this afterward? Calmly?"

"Aquarius…" Cato stared at the floor with dull lifeless eyes. "I do not wish for you to end up as Orpheus did. There were no happy endings for any mortal who was loved by a god. I realize now it will be no different for you. Remember that." He cleared his throat. "*Cena* is being served. I told them I'd get you." With a bowed head, he turned and made his way back toward the main house.

David scrubbed a hand over his face and then drew Elisabeth into a hug.

"Aquarius, I'd never do anything to hurt you." She suddenly became aware of her own heartbeat while looking up at him.

"I know. I know. Pay no attention to a single word he uttered. I can see…" David swallowed hard. "Cato is observant and notices everything. However, he will often jump to the wrong conclusion."

"Aquarius…?"

"This is not new and is not your fault. This is Cato's…other side. I've lived with it my entire life. He blames you for his troubles this time, but he is just reacting out of fear. Do not worry yourself over him."

It pained her to see him stung by Cato's bitter words. "Aquarius…?"

Still not hearing, David put his hand on the small of Elisabeth's back, ushering her along the empty colonnade, toward the villa. "He will not say anything to Aurelius. Everything will be fine, *cor meum*."

"Aquarius."

"And do not take to heart a single thing he said about you. I swear, the fact that you are even—"

"Aquarius!" Elisabeth planted her feet in place and grabbed his arm. "It's just….I…" She let out a theatrical groan. "Shut up and kiss me." Her cheeks then flushed bright red as she gave him an astonished look before dissolving into a fit of giggles.

David's eyes widened and a slow, lopsided smile spread across his face.

"Oh my gosh, I can't believe I just said that. You were rambling and I was trying to…"

He put a hand behind Elisabeth's head, drawing her closer. "I'm afraid I may begin to ramble more often, love." His playful gaze locked on her for a moment before he kissed her.

Again and then again.

When a slave walked by, Elisabeth pulled away and cleared her throat, unable to remove the silly grin from her face.

David leaned closer. "What is it you wanted to say to Cato and me earlier?" His eyes were bright and glossy.

"It will have to wait until after dinner, speaking of which…" She stepped back and with a grimace, tugged at her hair.

"What is it?"

Her chest caved in and she moaned. "I'm nervous about the dinner."

David lifted his eyebrows.

"What should I do if I don't like what's being served? Nobody seems to mind eating rat around here."

"Dormouse."

She frowned while folding her arms across her chest. "What?"

He leaned closer. "The wealthy prefer to call it a dormouse. Give it a charming name and suddenly, the rodent becomes a delicacy."

Elisabeth's face reddened. "I am not eating a freaking dormouse."

"You can smother it in garum."

"What's that?"

"Fermented fish sauce," he said with a snort.

"Ugh." She swatted at the air. "It's not funny. I don't want to eat here. If the strange customs don't scare me, the things you guys eat sure as heck do. Aurelius will know right away that something is off with me."

He put his arm around her shoulders. "I shall take care of everything. Trust me."

With a heavy groan, Elisabeth stamped her foot before walking again. "I always do, don't I?"

As they climbed the steps and entered the *triclinium,* Aurelius and Balinus already reclined on two of the three dining beds, their left arms propped up on pillows. Cato cleared his throat as he took a linen towel from a slave to dry his hands. He then walked toward the third bed.

"Salve, gentlemen," David said. "Apologies for our tardiness."

"Ah, the young lovers have returned." Balinus grinned as small tables were brought in, covered with tablecloths and followed by trays of unappealing food.

Elisabeth's chest tightened when a boy arrived to wash her hands and feet. She gave him a weak smile before averting her gaze, uncomfortable at being washed by a slave.

David lounged in the middle of the dining bed, reclining on his left side, next to Cato, and patted the spot beside him so Elisabeth knew where to go. She lay down on her stomach, propping a pillow beneath her arms before shooting him a wide-eyed look. His smile said she hadn't made a fool of herself in front of their host, yet.

When Elisabeth pursed her lips to keep from laughing, David edged closer. "Something amuses you?"

"It's just…this seems a rather intimate way to eat," she whispered.

"Intimate you say?" He then wiggled his eyebrows and gave her a peck on the cheek.

Aurelius dipped a piece of bread in oil and chuckled. "Those two are truly in their own little world, aren't they?"

Balinus nodded. "Not unlike when you and Theodora first met, if my memory is correct. And it is."

With a snort, Aurelius popped the bread into his mouth, licked his fingers, and rolled his eyes. "Oh, to be young and in love again."

"Is this Theodora your wife?" David asked as he reached for a large egg.

Aurelius nodded. "Indeed she is, but let us not talk about me tonight. I have been waiting, very impatiently, to hear your tales of adventure. How did you three cross paths with this wise old sage?" he asked, smiling at

Balinus.

"Well." David cleared his throat. "As young men, we…Cato and I, we have always believed it our duty to see the world."

Balinus wiped at his mouth.

"That is very wise." Aurelius nodded. "And you are fortunate to be able to do so."

"While my brother and I…"

"Ah, you two are brothers."

"Indeed, we are. In word and deed, if not in blood." David made firm eye contact with Cato before continuing. "While Cato and I traveled through the lands north of here, we happened to witness the fair Elisabeth being kidnapped by a huge beast of a man."

Aurelius' head jerked back.

"With his wild hair and his evil eyes, this man was bigger than any man we had ever seen. Is that not right, brother?"

Cato nodded in agreement. "We are convinced the man was half beast. You know…like a satyr."

"It is true." David gave a crisp nod. "So ugly was this kidnapper, he appeared to be half man and half goat. Hideous."

"Horrifying," Cato said with a shudder.

Elisabeth turned away to hide her smile.

David sucked in a quick breath. "The vile creature locked Elisabeth in a cage in the back of a wagon."

Aurelius' mouth fell open and he looked at her. "You poor, dear girl."

She stared back at him, blinking her eyes, and at a loss for words. "He, uh, he told me his plan was to keep me, to force me into marriage. He said no one would stop him."

David's smile went stiff as he turned to glance at Elisabeth for a moment. He then cleared his throat and continued. "Cato and I tracked the horrible man-beast, watching and waiting for an opportunity to launch a rescue mission. We knew it was up to us if her life was to be spared. Finally, when the cage door was open for but a brief moment, Cato swept in and rushed Elisabeth to safety while I used my sling to immobilize the man."

"Monster," Cato corrected.

"You are right. He was too hideous to be a man." After pausing to take a drink from a goblet, David continued. "The three of us fled into the night, through the forest, in an attempt to hide Elisabeth from the beast that wanted to make her his bride. Cato made a fire while I hunted for food, trying to feed this fair lady. That is when we found Balinus."

Aurelius shook his head. "Well, what about the pirates? What about the snake bite?" His eyes widened. "You have yet to even mention those events."

Rising to the challenge, David continued. "Well, after several days running from the satyr, we thought we were free. But alas, it was not so. The man-beast chased us through a cave and to the edge of a waterfall, trapping us. When Elisabeth stepped back to hide, she startled a viper asp and it bit her, not once, but twice. Cato fearlessly drew his dagger and battled the monster, while I took on the enormous snake, all on the side of the cliff, mere inches from certain death. Then, believing I was bringing a dying Elisabeth to safety and comfort for her final hours, I carried her right into the camp of a group of barbarians. I unintentionally offered her right up to their leader."

"Pirates," Cato said as he took some seafood off a

platter. "They were blood-thirsty Cilician pirates."

David shook his head in disgust. "Foul, barbaric pirates."

Aurelius let out a long, low whistle. "It is so hard to believe, yet I've seen her snake bite myself."

"Ah-ha, the making of a legend," Balinus said with a chuckle. "Take away a few embellishments and it's surprisingly accurate."

Aurelius leaned in closer. "How many pirates were there?"

"Nine…teen." David cocked his head.

Balinus cleared his throat and confined his laughter to a snort. "Nine."

"Really? I could have sworn…" David scratched his jaw. "Nevertheless, they were so horrible even the man-beast ran away. Cato and I kept guard while Balinus tended to Elisabeth's wounds with his magical red elix—"

"I tended to her wounds and then we rode here to seek refuge," Balinus said with a grin that could not be contained. "Now tell me, Aurelius, how are Theodora and little Aurelia?"

Aurelius' breath hitched, still shocked from their story. "They are both well. Aurelia insisted on having her mother near her. Did you not know she is wed to Polybius' son, Marius, and is with child?" He rounded his hand over his stomach to indicate a large pregnant belly. "I told you she is not so little anymore. The poor girl must be carrying twins," he said with a booming laugh.

"You are going to be a grandfather?" Balinus clapped his hands. "How very, very exciting."

David turned and winked at Elisabeth.

With a radiant glow, all she could do was shake her head while trying not to laugh, knowing he'd kept Aurelius amused so she'd feel less nervous about the dinner.

"They are in Pompeii. You know how much my girls love—"

"Pompeii?" Elisabeth sat up on her knees while looking at him with a grave expression.

Their host nodded and took a sip from his goblet. "I will join them soon, but first I must settle some business matters here."

Elisabeth clenched her fists. "I know this is going to sound strange, perhaps even stranger than the tale Aquarius just told you, but you must get your wife and daughter away from Pompeii as soon as possible."

He wagged a finger at her. "You know something, don't you? Tell me, what information are you privy to? Some political intrigue? I can't promise to believe you after the fanciful tale I just heard," he said with a chuckle.

"I'm, uh...I'm..." She glanced at Balinus for support.

"Elisabeth is somewhat of an...oracle."

"An oracle?" Aurelius let out a belly laugh.

"Aurelius, listen to her." Balinus' tone deepened. "She has previously warned me of her dreams about Pompeii."

Elisabeth nodded. "Yes, I often have dreams, well nightmares really, about a mountain that sits beside Pompeii."

Aurelius sat up. "Vesuvius?"

"Yes. Vesuvius is a volcano."

He stared at her and frowned.

Elisabeth glanced around the room, but nobody seemed to understand what she was speaking of. She tried again, certain she'd used the correct Latin word. "A volcan—"

"Vulcan?" Balinus swallowed a lump in his throat. "It is said that Hercules was fond of Mt. Vesuvius, for supposedly, it is a mountain that can belch fire. Is it a fire mountain?"

"Yes, a fire mountain. Vesuvius is a fire mountain." The Latin name for volcano must not have existed until after the infamous eruption.

Cato's eyes widened. "Vulcan is angry?"

"Who's Vulcan?" she whispered to David.

"The god of fire."

Elisabeth gave an amused snort, realizing the origin of the word volcano was from a Roman god.

"What of these dreams of Pompeii?" Aurelius asked with a quiet voice.

"At the end of the summer, Mt. Vesuvius will erupt...belch out fire, as Balinus put it, and bury the entire city beneath rock and ash. Anyone who remains will die."

David and Cato both turned and gave Elisabeth an incredulous stare.

Aurelius looked back at Balinus while shaking his head. "You, my wisest teacher, you are telling me to believe this?"

"My dear friend, you *must* bring Theodora and Aurelia home at once."

"I swear to you..." Elisabeth closed her eyes while taking a deep breath. "Pompeii as you know it will completely disappear from the face of the earth, but you have the power to save your loved ones."

Aurelius stood up and scratched his neck. "This seems so…implausible…yet…how can I gamble with the lives of my wife and daughter?" He turned to look at his old slave who stood nearby. "Nicea, we leave at dawn for Pompeii."

The slave nodded.

"There is no reason for any of you to leave tomorrow. You must stay on as long as you need." He paused and with a wavering smile looked at Elisabeth. "If—and I pray to Apollo you are incorrect—but if your dream comes to pass, I owe you my deepest apologies for not quite believing you."

An eerie silence filled the room. Elisabeth grabbed a piece of bread to dip in what looked like honey. Her heart was heavy with the knowledge that so many lives would be lost. Even if she shouted what she knew from the rooftops, who would believe her, other than David, Balinus, and Cato? To the rest of the world, she'd be the crazy girl standing on the street corner holding up a sign that read, *Beware for the end is nigh*.

Elisabeth turned away, desperately trying to hide unshed tears. "Will you excuse me?" With a quivering smile, she dropped the bread and bolted out of the room.

Chapter Nineteen

Elisabeth ran down the steps and through the garden. At the far end of the outer courtyard, she stopped, standing with her back to the villa, struggling not to cry. Footsteps hurried toward her. David then hugged her from behind. With his arms wrapped around her chest, she wiped a tear away.

"So many people are going to die, Aquarius."

He gave her a soft kiss on the cheek. "This is what you tried to tell us earlier, isn't it?"

"You must…" Her voice faltered while twisting around to face him. "You must promise me that whatever happens, you won't go anywhere near Pompeii this summer."

His eyes widened and he looked down at her. "Do you honestly believe I would go anywhere near Pompeii? Now? After what you say is to happen?"

"Well, I guess when you put it that way…"

"Everything is going to be fine." He reached for Elisabeth's fingers and led her back toward the villa in silence, stopping in the little boxwood-lined alcove they'd noticed earlier in the evening. David ran a nervous hand through his hair. "Am I…" He cleared his throat. "Am I somehow meant to die in Pompeii?"

Elisabeth's eyebrows drew together. She flopped onto the semi-circular bench, holding her head in her hands. "No."

He let out a huge breath while taking a seat beside her. "That is a relief because you once told me you were here to save my life."

Her head jerked back. "I said that?"

With a thoughtful expression, he nodded.

Elisabeth hesitated before speaking. "You don't die in Pompeii, because…" She stared down at her hands. "I won't let that happen."

With gentle fingers, David tilted her chin to look up at him. "Because you are here to change that." He leaned in closer. "Is that not correct?"

She nodded slowly.

"Then we have nothing to fear."

"You're right." Her voice cracked with emotion. "Just my being here has changed your future. You know to avoid Pompeii now and I already know for a fact you live a very long time."

David paused to examine her. "How do you know that?"

She rubbed her arms, feeling torn at how much to say. "I just know."

With a playful grin, he pulled her into a hug. "I am some great historical hero, aren't I? Admired for generations."

Elisabeth looked up, flashing him a bemused smile. "How'd you guess?"

"It's just a feeling," David said with a wink. "We have nothing to fear, *cor meum*. At times like this…" He yawned while resting his cheek on the top of her head. "…it does seem like you are one with the gods. They too had their favorites amongst men and would warn them of devastating events to come."

She let out a small giggle. "Well, you're definitely

my favorite amongst men." Elisabeth's voice softened. "What did Cato mean when he said he didn't want you to end up like…?" Her eyelids felt heavy. "I don't remember the name but he didn't want you to end up like…"

"Orpheus." David's voice was subdued as he played with her fingers. "Orpheus and Eurydice."

"Who are they?"

"Orpheus was a young mortal man who loved a beautiful nymph named Eurydice. On their wedding night, while dancing in the tall grass, she was bitten by a viper asp and died."

Elisabeth's breath stalled. "You're kidding me?"

He shook his head. "Orpheus, overcome with unbearable grief, traveled to the underworld to bring her back. He crossed the river Styx, which is the boundary between the living and the dead. He made it through the gates of Hell, defeated Cerberus, a giant three-headed dog, and survived all the obstacles in his path. Orpheus finally found himself face to face with Pluto, the god of death, and pleaded with him to let his bride return to the land of the living. Moved by such a great act of love, Pluto relented, on one condition; Orpheus was forbidden from looking back at Eurydice as she followed him out from the bowels of the earth."

Elisabeth rested her palm on his chest. "Sheesh, what a feel good story so far."

With his arm around her, David's thumb stroked her shoulder. "On the journey back, he could hear Eurydice's footsteps behind him. Finally, Orpheus saw the sunlight and was so overcome with joy they made it out, that he turned around to look at his bride…but she had not yet stepped across the threshold from the underworld. In horror, Orpheus lunged for her, grasping nothing but the cold empty air. She'd fallen back into Pluto's domain. In desperation, he tried to follow, but was not allowed back in." David shifted on the garden bench trying to get more comfortable. "In the end, Orpheus wandered the earth broken-hearted, waiting to die so he could be reunited with Eurydice in the afterlife."

Elisabeth's head jerked back. "That's how it ends? Good grief! That's a horrible story." She pressed a palm over her lips to hold back a cry. "Cato was right."

David's eyes widened. "It's just a story, *cor meum*. Cato is not saying…Well, actually, Cato is saying…Cato's an idiot."

She tuned him out, realizing that Cato's warning was more accurate than he could ever imagine. The parallels between Orpheus and David did not go unnoticed. "That's how it ends?" Her posture slumped, feeling guilt-ridden. Here she was sitting with him, hugging him, laughing with him, kissing him, day after day, all the while knowing the more they fell in love, the more she'd be adding to the torment etched into his ageless eyes. Like Orpheus' love for Eurydice, David's love for Elisabeth would send him into his own personal hell. Her fists clenched. She was not innocent Eurydice in this story. She was no different from the manipulative gods who played with the lives of mere mortals.

"What have I done, Aquarius?" she muttered tearfully. "What have I started? I'm a monster, a horrible, evil person."

"Stop." David's tone was sharp.

Elisabeth swallowed a lump in her throat, while

squeezing her eyes shut, surprised she'd been reprimanded.

"I would silence anyone else who spoke of you in that manner."

She looked up at him with watery eyes. "Well then tell me, when one of your gods loved a human, was there *ever* a happy ending? Because it doesn't seem our situation is really that different after all."

David leaned back on the bench, pulling Elisabeth closer. "Will you forget what Cato said about Orpheus? I can see it weighs heavy on your mind." He kissed the top of her head. "Have you heard of Cupid and Psyche?" he murmured.

"Cupid's a chubby flying baby who shoots magic arrows that make people fall in love."

"A chubby flying baby?" David chuckled. "What on earth have you been taught? Cupid is my favorite of the gods: handsome, mighty, benevolent…and somewhat mischievous."

Elisabeth gazed up at him. "Sounds like you."

"If only," he said with a grin. "Now, there once lived a woman of unrivaled beauty named Psyche. As she grew older, the goddess Venus became jealous and ordered her son, Cupid, to shoot one of his arrows to make Psyche fall in love with a horrible beast. However, when Cupid met Psyche he fell in love with her himself, for she was as kind as she was beautiful. He put down his bow, unwilling to obey his mother, which of course made Venus furious.

"Psyche grew older and more attractive, yet her parents could not find her a husband. Fearing she had somehow angered the gods, they visited an oracle who told them that while no man would marry Psyche, they were to bring her to the summit of a nearby mountain, for the gods had decided she was to wed a hideous beast that lived atop it."

"Ahh, Venus' evil plan, right?"

David cleared his throat and continued playing with Elisabeth's fingers.

"Stoic as ever, Psyche was carried to the top of the mountain where she began her new life wed to the creature."

"Poor girl."

"Not quite, for Psyche's new home was a beautiful palace. Everything she could want and desire was at her disposal. However, she was never allowed to see her husband's face. The beast would only come to her at night, in the darkness, so she could not see his hideous features."

Elisabeth's eyes widened.

"He was gentle and kind and showered Psyche with all of his love and affection. Over time she grew to see him with her heart, rather than her eyes, and fell in love with him as much as he was in love with her."

It reminded Elisabeth of Beauty and the Beast. "I like your story much better than Cato's so far," she said with a distant smile.

David skimmed his thumb over hers. "I knew you would."

With a yawn, Elisabeth snuggled closer.

"Psyche and the beast were deeply in love and their marriage, although unconventional, was a happy one. But, as the months passed, Psyche became lonely and asked if her sisters could visit. Her husband reluctantly agreed, but warned not to let them influence her. Of course, he was correct, for when the sisters arrived they were filled with jealousy that she should live like a queen. They convinced Psyche that the beast would kill her in the night, so she must kill him first.

"For days, following her sisters' departure, their words haunted her. Finally, one night, she fooled herself into believing they were correct. While her husband slept in their bed, she crept to his side holding a candle and a dagger, summoning the courage to kill him before he could kill her. Psyche held the light up so she could look upon his hideous features, but instead of being a beast, she saw his beautiful face...for it was Cupid himself."

Elisabeth gasped.

David looked at her with a satisfied smile. "Cupid had wanted her to fall in love with him for who he was, not because he was a mighty, beautiful, and immortal god. Psyche began to weep when she realized her mistake."

Elisabeth sniffled. "You're making me cry."

"As Psyche stood over her husband trembling, wax from the candle spilled onto his arm. In pain, Cupid woke and saw the dagger in her hand. Although she tried to apologize and explain, he flew away in a rage, devastated that his beloved wife had not trusted him. Heartbroken, Psyche left the palace and searched everywhere for him, eventually begging for help from Venus."

"But his mother was jealous of her."

"Yes. Venus pretended to help, by sending Psyche on impossible quests, including traveling to the underworld, like Orpheus had done, crossing the River Styx and getting beyond the giant three-headed dog to retrieve a box of beauty."

"What's a box of beauty?"

His voice rose with dramatic flair. "Exactly."

"Oh, I see."

"Psyche survived every obstacle the jealous goddess put in her path, until Cupid, who had been searching all of the earth for his wife, found her again. Of course, he had long since forgiven her."

Elisabeth placed a hand over her heart and sighed.

"Cupid, unwilling to be parted from his beloved wife ever again, flew her up to the heavens with him and stood before mighty Jupiter, begging him to make Psyche a goddess so they would be equals. Cupid would not give Psyche up."

"Really?" Elisabeth closed her eyes.

"Really," David said softly. "Jupiter granted them permission and Cupid gave Psyche a cup of ambrosia to drink for her to become immortal just like him."

"I love that," she said with a satisfied sigh. Her posture then stiffened while opening her eyes. "Wait a minute…what did Cupid give her to drink?"

"Ambrosia. The nectar of the gods."

She sat upright and looked at him. "What's that?"

"It is the drink which makes the gods immortal. Humans were forbidden from drinking it."

"Why?"

"Because they would become immortal too."

Adrenaline rushed through Elisabeth's body. "They would become immortal too? These gods wanted the rest of the population to remain obedient and not try to be like them?" She gave a slow shake of her head while staring off in a daze. "Knowledge is power, and if you control the knowledge you control the people…" her voice trailed off while reciting what Balinus had told her.

"*Cor meum*, what are you…?"

She pressed her palms to her cheeks. "You know that tablet Balinus gave me?"

He nodded.

Elisabeth looked around the courtyard to make sure they weren't overheard, but the night seemed to belong to them. "Aquarius," she whispered, "the Emerald Tablet that Balinus gave me is the recipe for ambrosia. I am sure of it. Just think…the tablet supposedly came from the gods. On it is written the knowledge of the gods. Although it has been suppressed and hidden throughout the ages, it remains one of the most sought-after treasures in the history of mankind. I know it as the Elixir of Life or the Philosopher's Stone. The medicine that Balinus gave me is what you know of as ambrosia. It's the same thing. It has to be. That's why I didn't die from the snakebite."

David's mouth fell open. "Do you mean to tell me…?"

Wide-eyed, Elisabeth nodded. "Yes!"

"Balinus is a god?"

"Yes! Wait…what? No. Balinus isn't a god. Aren't you listening?"

"Why is he in possession of ambrosia? Sometimes the gods disguised themselves and tried to fit in with humans. It was usually done to seduce a woman though." David's brow wrinkled and he paused as his gaze wandered up and down her silky gown. "You do not think the old man is…"

"Of course not," Elisabeth said with a huff. "What else do you know about this so-called nectar of the gods?"

293

David leaned in closer. "Once, a Greek King named Tantalus was invited by Jupiter to Mount Olympus for dinner. While there, he stole some ambrosia. When his offense was discovered, Tantalus was sent to the underworld, since the gods consider stealing their ambrosia the worst crime imaginable. He was forced, for eternity, to stand in a pool of water beneath a…" He paused and a cheeky grin spread across his face. "I will shut up and kiss you if you find I am rambling, love."

"Aquarius…" She swatted his chest. "Be serious, will you?"

With a groan, his arms fell to his side as he bit down on a smile.

She shook her head, confining her laugh to a snort. "I said be serious. You know that Balinus' elixir is why I didn't die. What if…what if your gods of old weren't gods at all? What if they were as human as you and me? I mean…they looked like humans, they certainly acted like humans. They just had knowledge and technology…probably from the future." Elisabeth swallowed the lump in her throat. "Do you know what a jigsaw puzzle is?"

"No."

"Okay, if I took a painting and cut it all up into little pieces, you'd have no idea what it was. But, if you took all the pieces and figured out how they fit together, then you could see what the painting was a picture of."

David nodded in understanding.

"That's how a jigsaw puzzle works. They are little interlocking pieces that fit together to make a larger picture. I am starting to think that all these random legends and stories: Atlantis, Mythology, the Emerald

Tablet, the Philosopher's Stone, the Elixir of Life, the Ancient Gods, Celtic Fairy Lore, Ambrosia…at first they seem like random pieces, unsolved mysteries of life, but I think…I think maybe they fit together. Maybe they're not random at all. There is a bigger picture here and it's not that we can't put the pieces together; it's more like we don't even know there is a jigsaw puzzle. We don't know they are connected." She squeezed her eyes shut while rubbing the middle of her forehead. "Aquarius, you become immortal. You're…you're like one of the gods. Not me—*you*. I already knew you before I came here." Elisabeth looked up at him with a pensive expression. "I'm sorry I didn't tell you sooner, it's just…"

He grabbed onto her arms. "What do you mean?"

"You're the one who sent me here." Her chest caved in. "I don't even know if or how I'm supposed to tell you that."

His eyes bulged. "You told me this the night you were recovering from the asp bite. You said my name was David Perrier. I thought it was delirium from fever."

Elisabeth's shoulders tensed, and she shook her head. "No. It seems you and I have always known each other. I don't think we've ever really been strangers."

David tipped his head back, turning his face toward the sky, before closing his eyes and covering his mouth.

With a watery gaze, she reached for his arm, wanting to comfort him, yet unsure of what to say.

David looked back down at her, his eyes beaming. He then jumped up and whooped loudly before pulling Elisabeth to her feet. "That is how we do it? For the life of me, of all the scenarios that played out in my mind of how I could keep you by my side, becoming an immortal god was not one of them."

"Aquarius, no…you must promise me that you never do this. I am trying to stop that from happening."

"But why, *cor meum?*" He ran his hands down her arms and then took hold of her fingers. "This is amazing. If you have the recipe for ambrosia, and you and I can become one with the gods, how can that not be the greatest scenario imaginable?"

"Because you will end up like Orpheus if you do. Just promise me you'll never take the elixir to become immortal. I've seen what happens to you. We'll figure this out another way." She paused, pulling back slightly. "Even if I have to stay here."

"Did you just say what I think you said?" His voice was shaky. "You would choose to stay here if it came to that?"

"You're…you're worth fighting for. That's how important it is to me that you do not take the elixir. You have to trust me like I've always trusted you."

David flopped down, pulling her onto his lap. "You say I sent you here?"

Elisabeth snuggled into his hug. "It's a long story."

He tried to suppress a yawn. "I have all the time in the world."

"Just…just don't ever take the elixir to become immortal," she said with a firm voice, deciding to keep the details to herself for now.

David let out a deep breath. "I'd do anything for you."

Chapter Twenty

Someone cleared their throat.

"Oh…" David gave Elisabeth a gentle nudge to wake her and then stood up and straightened his tunic.

Still in the outer *peristyle*, Elisabeth stretched before looking up to see the silhouette of Aurelius standing over her. His hands rested on the edge of the semi-circular bench and his lined face wore its usual bored expression, but something about his demeanor caused her stomach to knot.

"The two of you need to come with me,' he said while clicking his fingernails on the marble.

Elisabeth's gaze flitted around the garden, looking for Cato. Had he spoken to Aurelius after all? She rose to her feet while twisting a lock of hair. "I can't believe we fell asleep out here. I'm…*we're* very sorry about that." With a pounding heart, she tried to play it cool in case she was wrong.

"For the love of Apollo, don't apologize. If I am anything, it is a sentimental old fool." Aurelius focused his gaze elsewhere pretending to ignore them. "This way." He then turned, walking away with a slow, steady gait.

David glanced at Elisabeth and raised his eyebrows as they followed their host through the villa and outside of the compound. The sky was still dark, yet twilight glowed just beneath the horizon.

"Can you believe it?" Elisabeth whispered. "The first night we have the chance to sleep in actual comfy beds we fall asleep outside?"

With a snort, David shook his head.

"When I was your age," Aurelius called back as he led the way along a dim footpath, "Theodora and I used to meet down here almost every—"

"Morning!" a boy of about twelve called out as they reached the water's edge.

"Good morning, Marcus. Catch anything yet?"

The boy fiddled with his fishing line. "Almost a dozen already." He then started dancing in place, causing them all to laugh. "They're jumping into my arms."

"Ha-ha, young Marcus, what did I tell you about the hour before sunrise? I may be old, but I do know a thing or two about catching fish." Aurelius then walked toward a small boat. "Both of you, get in."

Elisabeth gave him a blank look.

Aurelius held the boat steady while chuckling. "Hurry. You can thank me later."

Elisabeth bit her lips to keep from smiling, realizing Cato had kept his word. With a wink, David helped her into the boat before he climbed in and sat across from her. He grabbed hold of the oars and Aurelius jumped in with them, taking a seat beside Elisabeth.

"Can you feel the thickness in the air?" Aurelius asked as David dipped the paddles in and out of the lake, the sound of splashing water somehow melodious at this hour. "I like to believe at twilight a doorway opens and the two worlds briefly meet."

Elisabeth's posture stiffened. "That space between

dreams and reality."

The old man nodded. "The magic hour. Truth be told, it was Balinus whom I first heard call it that."

David continued rowing. "How long have you known Balinus?"

"A long time, close to forty years," Aurelius said with a slight smile. "He is a great man and I'd like to be…" He closed his eyes for a moment. "I'd like to be more like him. Balinus may present himself as a poor wanderer, but the truth is…" He looked down and let out an amused snort. "The truth is he and his brother were raised in incredible luxury and received the best education available. When their parents died, Balinus gave his share of the inheritance to his brother and to poor relatives, keeping only enough to cover his basic needs."

Elisabeth's eyebrows rose.

"That's the kind of man Balinus is. None of these…" Aurelius waved his hand toward his large villa perched on the hillside. "None of these trappings matter to him. Balinus cares nothing of accumulating possessions and believes the more he does for others, the more he has, and the truth is…" With a shy grin, Aurelius cleared his throat. "Have you ever met a happier man?"

Elisabeth shook her head.

"Anyone Balinus considers a friend is luckier because of it."

Rays of sunshine began to form on the horizon. Elisabeth swore she could feel the magic pull of twilight slipping away. "I do feel fortunate to have met the wise old sage."

Aurelius took a deep, satisfied breath and nodded.

"Now, just beyond that mountain, the sun will rise shortly." He stood up, rocking the small boat. "So make a wish. What is it you really want? Quickly, for the gods are listening." He then turned and jumped into the lake.

Elisabeth gave David an incredulous stare and they both laughed.

"Old man, I believe you have taken leave of your senses," David said with a chuckle when Aurelius resurfaced.

"I certainly hope so." He clung onto the stern, rubbed a shivering hand over his face to wipe the water away, and then stared up at the sky with a blank expression. "Alas, sunrises are far too romantic for three. I bid you farewell." He then pushed off and swam away. "I leave for Pompeii within the hour," he called back.

They watched his dark shadow swim with ease toward Nicea, who stood at the bank, holding a blanket and waving a lamp to guide his master's path. Aurelius climbed out, dried himself off, and then turned around to wave goodbye.

Peals of laughter echoed across the lake. "Bye, Aurelius," young Marcus called out.

David let go of the oars while they watched the day break over the mountain. The sun blazed like molten gold, causing the sky to turn a vibrant shade of yellow, which reflected onto the surface of the water.

Elisabeth let out a satisfied sigh and smiled at David.

With a quick breath, he grabbed the oars. "I am a fool. Forgive me, *cor meum*, but if Rufus is anywhere nearby, we…"

A cold chill ran up her spine. "No, you're right. We're sitting ducks out here."

Using long, graceful pulls, he rowed back to their starting point below Aurelius' villa. David jumped out, extended his hand to help Elisabeth, and then pulled the boat onto the bank where they'd found it.

In silence, she led the way back up the dirt path until David grabbed hold of her arm.

Elisabeth spun around. "What?" Her eyes widened as she froze, hearing nothing but a choir of birds and the water lapping against the shore.

David pinched his lips together into a strained smile, which faded quickly when he turned his head to look away.

She stepped closer. "What's wrong?"

With a wrinkled brow, he led her by the hand toward a secluded spot beneath a blossom-covered tree. He flopped down and patted the grass next to him. "Sit."

Elisabeth sat, hugging her knees to her chest. "Did you make a wish like Aurelius said to?" she asked.

He stared straight ahead. "Do you want to know an it?"

"Of course." She playfully fell against him, letting him catch her.

Lowering Elisabeth to the ground, he cradled her head in the crook of his arm, lying on his side next to her. Her skin flushed as David's fingertips traced her collarbone before feeling for the chain of the necklace. "If you asked me to go with you to your time, I would say yes." He gave a gentle tug, pulling the crystal out from beneath the fabric of her dress. "I'd stay there if it meant—"

"Aquarius…" Elisabeth fiddled with the crystal before laying it on her breastbone. "It doesn't work that way."

With a heavy sigh, David rolled onto his back. "This is completely backward. There is nothing keeping me here. I have no family; unless you count Cato." His voice went quiet. "I know you won't stay here. Not forever. Not when you have a home filled with people who love you. How could anyone leave that?" Turning, David offered a long, pained stare before looking away again. "It's not the same for me. You are the only person my heart is tied to, and by the gods, I would rearrange the stars for you if I could."

Elisabeth's chest tightened. "I don't even know how I ended up here. I don't know if I can bring another person with me. I've only ever brought…things." She took a deep breath and paused to stare at the spring blossoms hanging from a branch over her head. Their situation was far more complicated than he could ever imagine. "Aquarius, if it did work, I don't know that you would end up with me at the same point in the future. What if we lost each other forever?" Her voice cracked. She turned onto her side, gazing at his profile.

David stared straight ahead with a stony expression and, for the first time since being here, Elisabeth caught a glimpse of the tormented man he would become.

Her lips parted while watching his jaw clench and unclench. "I can't lose you somewhere in time. I won't risk it," she muttered tearfully.

"We are forgetting another rather important thing."

She fidgeted with her necklace before nodding. "You already exist in my time."

At that moment, Elisabeth realized that bringing Aquarius to the future was not an option, even if she knew how to. As the immortal David Perrier, he had already spent countless lifetimes waiting for her. But, staying here in Ancient Rome with Aquarius meant she'd have to give up everything. *Everything.* She brought a shaky hand to her forehead and let out an uncontrollable whimper. How had this become some bizarre love triangle between David and Aquarius? They were the same person.

David looked at Elisabeth with a pained expression. "Why do I become immortal? What happens to us?"

"I have no idea." She moved closer, nestling into his arms. "You're more a mystery to me there than you are here."

He let out a heavy sigh. "The last thing I want to be is a mystery to you."

Elisabeth exhaled a heavy breath. "I swear, I will find a way to…" Her heart froze and then began to pound when he kissed her neck. "To fix…" Ticklish, she started giggling, unable to stop. "I'll find a way to…to…fix everything." She then squealed with laughter when David tickled her ribs.

He stopped to stare down at her with a soft expression.

"Gaius Cornelius Aquarius," she whispered while trying to catch her breath. "I—"

Leaves began to rustle, sending a chill up Elisabeth's spine.

"Stay down," David whispered. He jumped up, bending his neck forward. "Do you hear that?"

Elisabeth tensed while watching him take cautious

steps toward the footpath.

A child then screamed for help as wild splashing echoed in the air. By the time Elisabeth scrambled to her feet, David was almost at the water's edge.

"It's the kid!" he shouted, before diving into the lake.

When she reached the shore, Elisabeth froze, staring at the boy floating face down in the water. She couldn't stop trembling while watching David swim as fast as he could out to young Marcus.

The ground then seemed to shake when heavy footsteps ran down the path. Elisabeth turned around to see who else was coming to help. Her eyes bulged at the sight of Rufus barreling toward her. She cried out in pain when he dove into her stomach, flipped her over his shoulder like a sack, before racing away from the lake.

"AQUARIUS!"

She heard his voice scream back to her, but couldn't make out what he'd said. David stopped swimming and, for a moment, panicked, torn between rescuing Elisabeth or the boy. After a split-second of conflicting emotions, David went for the boy, struggling to drag him back toward the shore.

When the giant detoured through the trees, Elisabeth lost sight of David. She tried to kick her legs but Rufus held them tight against his chest. When they reached the slave wagon, he dumped Elisabeth to her feet, shoving her against the bars outside of the cage.

With angry tears, she kicked the wheel next to her before letting out a guttural roar. "You are the vilest human being I have ever met!"

He raised Elisabeth's arm, cuffing her wrist to a

waiting shackle. "It's not personal. It's business." Rufus then unsheathed a dagger from his waistband while walking over to the smoldering remains of a campfire. "And you are the bait, my dear." He took a seat on a small wooden stool while stoking the glowing embers with the pointy blade.

"Business? You call this business? You kidnapped me."

"If you are a free woman, you stole my slaves. That makes you a thief in the eyes of the law." Rufus shrugged his shoulders. "But if you are a runaway slave, that makes you a fugitive. Either way, you cannot win."

She clenched her fists as he turned his attention back to the smoldering fire, resting the blade of his dagger against the red hot embers.

"Let me go, Rufus." She trembled all over, feeling powerless and lost. "Please…don't do this. Show some compassion."

His eyes widened. "And who has ever shown compassion to me?"

"Rufus, please…"

"ELISABETH!" David seemed close as he cried out for her.

"Elisabeth!" Young Marcus echoed with an excited voice, clearly joining him in the hunt.

Her eyes went heavenward in thanks, for not only was the boy alive, but David would find her at any moment and put an end to this. She had no doubt he'd drop Rufus with a single shot of his sling.

While licking his lips, Rufus pulled his dagger out of the embers. He then grabbed the stool, marched over, holding the hot blade near her cheek.

With rasping breaths, Elisabeth began blubbering in fear.

"Scream," he whispered, inching the knife closer.

Heat radiated from the metal next to her skin. Tremors rippled through her entire body. Elisabeth let out a primal scream.

"Good girl."

Young Marcus' voice became louder. The tall grass rustled near the wagon. "This way!"

Rufus let out a deep, gratifying sigh before positioning himself behind Elisabeth. With one arm, he lifted her onto his wooden stool. It became obvious his intention was to make her his human shield from David's wrath.

"Aquarius…" Elisabeth muttered tearfully as he and the boy, both dripping wet, stepped into her line of sight.

"A fine drowning act, young man," Rufus said to Marcus as he tossed a handful of coins to him. "A fine job. You're a hero, you know."

Elisabeth's mouth fell open.

"Get out of here, kid, before you get hurt," David hissed. With a wild appearance, he planted his feet wide apart, slapping a rock into his dripping wet sling. "Let her go, Rufus. Make no mistake…" His nostrils flared and the sling gained momentum as he whirled it over his head, splashing droplets of water everywhere. "I *will* kill you this time."

Without another word, young Marcus fled after grabbing his coins.

Rufus clutched Elisabeth tighter, holding the blade near her throat. "Are you confident you will not miss?"

Her eyes bulged while staring at David in terror.

Rufus moved the dagger to her cheek again. "Because it would be a shame to brand your sweetheart's pretty face to let the world know she is a fugitive."

David's neck corded as he continued to whirl his sling. "Put down the knife, Rufus."

"Put down the sling, Aquarius," the giant mocked.

Elisabeth couldn't stop shaking.

"Oh look," Rufus whispered into her ear, "we have some guests." He then tilted his head back.

"Is everything all…?" Balinus' eyes widened when he and Cato stumbled upon the scene. He then froze, placing his hand out to suggest Cato stay back.

"I have no quarrel with you, old man," Rufus said to Balinus. "These are legally my slaves."

Elisabeth held her breath while watching David. He stopped whirling his sling and repositioned it by extending one arm at shoulder height, aiming the rock in front of him. With a slight grimace, he shook his head. Elisabeth could tell he didn't think he could get a clean shot without the risk of hurting her.

"Rufus, put down…" David swore under his breath. "Put down the knife."

The slave dealer waved the dagger in the air before touching it to Elisabeth's forehead. "Make your choice, boy," he said through gritted teeth.

Elisabeth closed her eyes for a moment, drawing in a deep breath when she felt the blade was no longer burning hot.

David gave her a pale, haunted look. "I'm so sorry, *cor meum*." He dropped the rock, shoved the sling into his belt, and held his hands up. "Don't do it, Rufus. Look, you've bested us."

"I've heard that before."

"No tricks this time. Promise me you won't lay a finger on her and you have my word." His voice choked with emotion. "You know yourself you cannot fetch as much money for the girl if she is disfigured and branded."

"Then drop your slings and dagger where you stand."

David unsheathed his dagger, removed numerous slings from his belt, and dropped them to his feet. He reached into his pouch, dropped a handful of rocks and lead bullets to the ground before raising his hands. "I am unarmed."

"You know what to do." Rufus gestured toward the slave wagon. "You too," he said to Cato.

Balinus cleared his throat and then stepped forward. "A wise sage once said—"

"Stay out of it, old man, unless you plan to make a purchase."

Elisabeth's shoulders quaked knowing Balinus had no wealth.

David pulled at his soaking wet collar as he made his way into the cage.

With a grim twist to his mouth, Cato followed.

Side by side, Cato stood at least two inches taller than David and was built like a quarterback, yet he did nothing to help. Elisabeth turned her head, disgusted with Cato's compliance.

"Perhaps this is enough to make a purchase?" Balinus gently bit his lip. "It was suggested I save these for a rainy day."

Elisabeth held still, trying to keep a blank face. Balinus was offering the very coins she'd given to him for helping exchange the ruby.

Rufus sheathed his dagger, unlocking Elisabeth's shackled wrist before dumping her into the cage and locking the door.

She held her breath, grabbing the bars as Rufus walked over to Balinus to count the money.

The slave dealer then burst into laughter, clapping him on the back before storing the footstool away. "Sorry, old man. As fond of you as I am, that is not enough to buy anything I am selling." He climbed onto the bench at the front of his wagon.

"Elisabeth…" Cato said with unnatural stiffness as he put his arms around her neck, pulling her into an awkward hug. "Despite what you may think, I am relieved you are safe."

"Thank you, Cato." Her voice choked on tears while giving him a rigid hug in return.

He then took a step back and stared down at his feet. "Because when Balinus found your necklace on the ground, I thought the worst."

Her head jerked back. She reached for her crystal.

It was gone.

"Balinus…?" she called out to him in an uncertain tone.

The old man rubbed his chest. "Remember, fear is the greatest illusion," he shouted as the wagon drove away.

"Balinus?" Elisabeth's eyes widened. "BALINUS!"

"Perhaps it is for the best," Cato said with a hard smile.

She turned and gave him an incredulous stare, not sure she'd heard correctly, but the smug look on his face told her she had.

"It seems the old man is forcing your hand." Cato swallowed hard. "You don't deserve Aquarius," he then muttered under his breath.

With a guttural roar, she charged toward him. "Why don't you shut your—?"

"Cor meum," David's voice cracked and he held Elisabeth back. "Stop."

Her vision clouded as she shoved David away and began to kick at the door, over and over again, trying to break it open. She no longer cared what happened to anyone. The only thing that mattered was her ability to return home.

"Aquarius!" Rufus shouted back at them. "Control the girl or else I will."

"Elisabeth…Elisabeth…" While kicking and screaming, David pulled her by the waist away from the door and to the back of the slave wagon.

Wide-eyed, she watched Balinus disappear from view before clamping a hand over her mouth, sobbing. She fell to her knees. "He has my necklace."

David knelt and pulled Elisabeth to his shoulder. His voice choked on tears. "I believe we are still at least a day and a night's journey from Rome," he whispered. "We've escaped before, *cor meum.* We'll do it again." He hugged her tighter, running his fingers through her hair. "We'll get out of here. We'll get your crystal back."

"How on earth are we going to do that?" she mumbled.

His hand rested on the back of her head and then his breath seemed to hitch. "It won't be easy to escape from here, love." David quietly exhaled while gazing down at her. "What we are going to need is something to pick the lock." He blinked his eyes playfully then looked away before glancing at her again, this time with a small smile. "Something like…a hair pin."

Elisabeth's mouth fell open when David pulled a bobby pin from her hair that Mrs. Waters had used to hold a small braid in place. "Oh my gosh, I had no—"

He put a finger to his lips to hush her, then sat on the floor of the wagon, pulling her down beside him.

Elisabeth stole a glance at Cato, who sat with his back to them. Over her shoulder, Rufus stared straight ahead at the road. She remained still to let the relief sink in before sagging against David.

"Keep this safe for now," he whispered, handing the bobby pin back to her.

With a curt nod, she pushed it back into her hair.

Chapter Twenty-One

Endless hours passed, and Elisabeth kept envisioning their escape. The plan may not be brilliant, but it was simple. Once the opportunity presented itself, David would use the bobby pin to pick the lock. They'd disappear, backtracking to find Balinus to take back her crystal necklace. So far, neither of them felt confident including Cato in the plan. Elisabeth's stomach hardened every time the scene replayed in her head of Balinus turning his back and walking away from them. How could he betray her like that?

"I wonder who we'll be sold to," Cato said, deciding to speak to them again.

David shook his head while pulling off his belt. "I've told you before, we'll end up in a quarry and dead within three months."

Elisabeth looked at the belt in David's hand then stared at him in awe, realizing it was another sling, hidden in plain sight.

Cato turned his head to gaze off into the distance. "You don't have to be so pessimistic, Aquarius." He leaned back against the bars and crossed his arms over his chest.

David scoffed at him. "Oh, that's rich, coming from you." With a somber expression, he reached into his leather pouch, grabbing the red ribbon he'd plucked from Elisabeth's hair. Using it as a measuring tape, he removed a similar length of fiber from his sling and then set it aside while readjusting his belt around his waist once again.

Elisabeth crept closer, watching him tear the ribbon in half with his hands.

Cato stared at them from a distance. "It truly is the red string, isn't it?" With an unkind smile, he lowered his eyes before glancing back up at David. "Why have the fates always favored you?"

"We make our own fate," David replied while knotting the ribbon and rope fiber together.

Scowling, Cato turned his attention to Elisabeth. "We knew a merchant when we were younger. Domina would purchase expensive fabrics from him. Her favorite was a luxurious cloth called silk. It's made from a vegetable that grows on trees found in the land of Serica."

"Wait—" Elisabeth's brow furrowed while trying not to laugh. "What?"

David nodded in agreement as he fiddled with the ribbon. "It's true. Silk is a vegetable grown by the Seres. They say…" His eyes were dark, serious, as he looked up at her, saying nothing else for several long seconds. That slow, adorable grin then spread across his face and she turned to jelly.

"Oh." With a bemused smile, Elisabeth raised her chin, playfully puckering her lips.

While chuckling, David leaned forward. "Is this like the cuckoo bird?" he whispered.

She nodded before kissing him.

Cato stared down at his hands. "The merchant told us an old legend of how their gods tie an invisible red string to connect two people who are destined to be together. Place, circumstance, even time do not matter. This red string can stretch and tangle, but it can never be broken. Aquarius believed the man, but I never did."

David chuckled. "I always told Cato that someday a girl would appear and I'd know we were connected because I would be able to see the red string attached to her."

"And so I ask," Cato said with a hard expression as he stared at Elisabeth's scarlet ribbon in David's hand. "Why have the fates always favored you? Why is everything so easy for you?"

"The fates favor no man," David insisted. "The red hair ribbon is nothing but—"

"A coincidence." Elisabeth looked down to hide her smile. "It's a sweet legend, however, it's nothing but a coincidence."

Cato crossed both arms over his chest, turning his back to them. "It doesn't seem that way."

Elisabeth gave David a slow, disbelieving shake of her head, then whispered in his ear, "There is no such thing as a coincidence."

A bright smile lit up his entire face as he resumed work on whatever it was he was making.

When the sun began its descent, Elisabeth passed the hairpin to David. He fiddled with it, twisting it this way and that until it resembled a pair of tweezers. She folded her hands on her lap and watched the sun slip beneath the horizon.

At last, Rufus ventured into a small village, stopping the wagon in front of a brick building with large wooden doors thrown wide open.

A thin man, with a gray beard and a bald head, tapped his foot in annoyance. "It's about time."

"I was ambushed by a gang of barbarians."

"Oh, bravo," the man's voice was thick with sarcasm. "I see you managed to escape unscathed, hmm?"

Rufus nodded.

"You were supposed to be here two weeks ago!" he screamed. "Every day this livestock remains is money lost." His voice trailed off as he stormed through the large doorway. "I will not have some giant imbecile…"

Rufus drew in slow, steady breaths and led his oxen into stables attached to someone's large home. A mouse skittered across the floor and Elisabeth wrinkled her nose at the stench of hay and urine. The slave dealer closed and locked the wooden doors that led to the street before following the man into the main house.

David stood and made his way to the door of their prison with Elisabeth close behind.

Cato's brow wrinkled and he scrambled to his feet. "What are you doing, Aquarius?"

"Getting out of here."

"It didn't work out so well the last time." Cato paused to glance over his shoulder when an animal began to shuffle about in one of the dark stalls. "For here we are."

David positioned his arms around the bars. "A temporary setback," he said through clenched teeth as he tried to insert the pin into the lock.

"I can't let you do this," Cato muttered, almost to himself.

Elisabeth shot him an incredulous look.

"Aquarius…this is for your own good." Cato's hands then curled into tight fists. He swung at David, punching him in the side of the face.

With a guttural roar, David whipped around. A red welt was already forming on his cheek. "There's the Cato I know!" He moved toward him, a tight smile frozen on his face. "I am *so* glad Elisabeth sees the kind of person you truly are now."

"And what kind is that?" he asked with an emotion-choked voice.

"A coward. Too scared to live your own life."

Cato gave him a pained stare and stepped back. "You are willing to break the law and become a fugitive? For what? For a girl? I am trying to stop you from making a huge mistake, brother."

David planted his feet wide apart. "If you want to stay that is fine, but this…" He held the hairpin up under Cato's nose. "This is the key to freedom for those not afraid of living." He then glanced toward the entrance to the house when Rufus' voice could be heard again.

Elisabeth's heart pounded as David rushed back to the door. "Hurry, Aquarius."

"I can't let you do this." Cato's lips curled and he lunged forward.

David spun around, but Cato grabbed his tunic at the neck and shoved him into the bars of the cage with such force they both crashed to the floor of the wagon. In the scuffle, the hairpin flew out of David's hands.

Elisabeth's eyes scoured the floorboards and when she saw the bobby pin, she dove for it. Before reaching it, Cato shoved her out of the way, sending her flying into the bars and then to the floor. As she cried out in pain, David jerked his head back in shock. In that split second, Cato snatched the bobby pin and threw it out of the wagon.

Elisabeth's mouth fell open. Their only chance of escape was gone.

Cato rubbed his lips, sat down, and acted like nothing had happened.

"I *hate* you," Elisabeth hissed through clenched teeth as she curled up on the floor and rubbed the goose egg that was forming on the back of her head.

"You don't hate me," Cato said with a bone-chilling voice. "You *fear* me."

A cold shiver ran up Elisabeth's spine.

Rufus returned, tossed some bread and a canteen into their cage, and then disappeared into the building again. He seemed too preoccupied with the angry man to pay them close attention.

David crouched down beside her. "Are you hurt?"

Any bravery Elisabeth had mustered up until this point vanished. She sat up, looking at him with a trembling chin. "What are we going to do?"

"I don't know," he whispered.

"Aquarius, I'm scared."

He pulled her into his arms and leaned back against the bars of the cage. "I won't let anything happen to you, *cor meum*." He then glanced away with a worried look on his face. "Try and get some sleep. I'll think of something."

****

As dawn broke, Rufus returned to the stables with two buckets of water and unlocked the doors to one of the stalls. He barked orders into the darkness and the livestock whispered and coughed.

Elisabeth gasped. "There are people in there?"

"You didn't realize…?" David nodded.

With bulging eyes, Elisabeth shuffled closer to

David and watched the slaves wash themselves. Rufus stood with his arms crossed, waiting for them to finish before they donned clean tunics.

"What's going on?" she asked in an uncertain tone.

"He's attempting to make the goods as appealing as possible."

Elisabeth's stomach clenched. "And we're the goods."

One by one, the other slaves crowded into the wagon.

A young man of middle-eastern descent sat next to Cato; the look of fear on his face undeniable. Two muscular, angry-looking men climbed in next. Elisabeth guessed them to be in their mid-twenties. One blond and the other brunette, they sat and exchanged a few words in a foreign language. The oldest man in the group looked to be in his forties. He had a pallid complexion, wore a reddish-brown turban, and kept his eyes downcast.

A black-skinned man squeezed into their cage next and found a spot on the opposite side of Elisabeth. She winced when the man held his arms out and a little girl curled up in his lap.

A blonde-haired girl of about twelve looked rather composed as she found a spot to sit, followed by a boy about the same age. He sat, glancing about the wagon to take in his surroundings.

Rufus lifted the smallest boy into the cage with them and then locked the door. The kid must have been no more than eight years old, but he stood in the middle of the crowd and crossed his arms, glaring at Rufus, before taking a seat near Cato.

Elisabeth's jaw clenched. She squeezed her eyes

shut as the final leg of their journey began.

David cleared his throat and drew Elisabeth closer.

****

After several hours of bumping along, more and more wagons and pedestrians began to crowd the road. Elisabeth's heart sank, realizing they were on the outskirts of Rome now.

"I've messed everything up." Her voice shook while whispering to him.

He rubbed his nose and then kissed the top of her head as they crossed over a bridge leading toward the city gates. "Give me your arm, *cor meum.*"

Her limbs felt too heavy to lift, but she placed her hand into his waiting palm. Elisabeth then blinked back tears at the sight of a bracelet he'd made from her red hair ribbon and a piece of rope from his sling. Entangled together, they formed a beautiful ornamental knot.

"This is…" David took a shaky breath. "This is a Hercules Love Knot," he whispered into her ear while tying the bracelet around her wrist. "It is the strongest knot you can tie and is a symbol of…" He looked at her with a quivering smile. "Of the unbreakable bond you and I share."

Her voice choked with tears. "Aquarius…" Who'd have thought her feminine hair ribbon, intertwined with rope from his primitive sling, could form something so beautiful and complementary to one another. "They're perfect together."

"They are." He lowered his head and sniffled. "They are." When he looked up at her, his eyes were red. "The Hercules knot is supposed to act as an amulet, to protect you…when I can't."

The sun shone down on David like a spotlight and everyone else in the slave wagon seemed to fade into the distance. Elisabeth pulled him closer, kissing the blue bruise on his cheek from where Cato had punched him. She then curled up into his familiar embrace and hugged him tighter than ever.

David stared straight ahead until he sucked in a quick breath when something caught his attention.

Elisabeth covered her face with her hands after seeing the Coliseum. Wooden scaffolding erected in front of the enormous venue indicated it must be in the final stages of construction.

A few minutes later, the slave wagon came to a stop. Rufus opened the cage, allowing everyone to spill out.

Elisabeth stepped down, staring at the depressing, crowded market they were in; a market selling humans. Some people were skin and bones, most were filthy, hunched over, pitiful looking. Rufus had a gleam in his eyes, proud his slaves were cleaner and healthier than most others for sale. This truly was nothing but business for him.

The smell of vomit, urine, and excrement overwhelmed Elisabeth's senses. Several naked men stood on a revolving podium while people decided which ones to purchase.

Screaming voices in the crowd caught her attention. She scanned the area, looking for the source of the uproar. Across the busy marketplace, she happened to make eye contact with the cause; a middle-aged man desperate to escape from his fate. The man's black hair and alabaster skin reminded Elisabeth of her father. The only thing missing were glasses, which constantly fell down her dad's nose, needing to be pushed back up again.

The man's dash for freedom brought him straight toward Elisabeth, where armed soldiers were on him within seconds. As they beat him, she whimpered, shaking her head in denial, unable to stop imagining it was her father they were beating.

"No...no...no..." Elisabeth gasped for air. Her muscles tightened, ready to run.

"Hey, hey, look at me, *cor meum*. Look at me." David's voice exuded calmness as he held her head in his hands, shielding her from the violent scene next to them. "You don't need to see that, my love."

Wide, terrified eyes stared at David, wishing there was a way to drown out the screams from the torturous beating.

With a watery gaze, David's posture slumped as he wiped a tear from Elisabeth's cheek. He then pulled her into a tight embrace. "Promise me you won't do anything impulsive," he whispered into her ear. "Whatever happens here, I will find you again, *cor meum*. Believe me—I will move heaven and earth to find you again."

A moment later, Rufus pulled David away, grouping his male slaves together. Elisabeth was lined up across from the men, placed next to the little blonde girl, who cried.

Teary-eyed, Elisabeth watched as the doppelganger for her father was dragged away, his body covered in blood and sweat. She then reached over to hold the little girl's hand, attempting to comfort the crying child.

Chapter Twenty-Two

Shoppers stopped to inspect Elisabeth. Their hands wandered everywhere. Her chest hitched, but they'd never break her spirit. Standing tall, head held high, her gaze remained unfocused as people poked and prodded her. Looking over at David would only cause her to burst into tears.

A short, beady-eyed man with a receding hairline picked up Elisabeth's hand. After recoiling at his touch, his grasp tightened painfully. "She is so soft," he said, while petting her arm. A malicious smile then spread across his face. "Have her undress. I like to see what I am buying."

Elisabeth's entire body tensed. A look of defiance blazed in her protruding eyes. She turned, giving Rufus a pained stare. "Please, not him," she whimpered.

"A saucy one?" the man asked.

"Perhaps, but nothing that cannot be broken." Rufus seemed to usher him away. "What exactly are you looking for? Can I interest you in one of my…?"

With trembling hands, Elisabeth let out a huge breath but then froze when the man turned around, wandering back again.

"I am still interested in this one. How much is she?"

Rufus held his hands behind his back. "I'm afraid if you have to ask, she is more than you can afford. This slave is very well educated and—"

"She is? Oh, I see. Well…" He let out a heavy sigh. "Perhaps it is for the best. I fear my wife would divorce me if I brought this one home. Not that *that* would be a bad thing," he added with a cackle.

Rufus nodded and then pointed to another section. "You will find less expensive slaves over there, my friend."

Elisabeth stared at Rufus.

"Do not mistake business motives for compassion," he whispered to her. "I can make a lot more money from you than he could ever afford."

Her stomach clenched at his words.

"Do you rent by the day?" a wrinkled old man with an enormous smile interrupted as he gestured toward Cato and David. "I need some work done. Those boys look strong and healthy."

Rufus shook his head, pointing to a bearded slave dealer on the other side of the market. "That man does."

An older woman, with long gray hair, a heavily-lined face, and thin, straight lips stood with her arms crossed in front of Elisabeth. "Tell me about this one."

"A clean bill of health," Rufus said with a satisfied smile. "All my slaves are healthy and of sound temperament. You will be untroubled by any of my stock. If for some reason one runs away, I personally see to it they are returned to their rightful owner."

Elisabeth knew that was a warning to her, more than a sales pitch to the woman.

"Who did her hair?" The woman touched the small braid that Mrs. Waters had originally pinned up.

"Your hair is perfect now. If anyone asks, remember to say you did it yourself."

323

"I did it myself," Elisabeth whispered.

She gave a curt nod and then addressed Rufus. "I am looking for a new body slave for one of the Vestals."

Elisabeth's heart pounded. *A body slave?*

Rufus licked his lips and smiled. "The Vestal Virgins? Well, I must say, she would be perfect. Look at her; very well kept. She is also intelligent and educated. This slave would serve extremely well."

The woman crossed her arms, pursed her lips, and stared at Elisabeth. "I can pay you three thousand denarii."

He opened his mouth as if to counter the offer, but stopped short. "Sold."

"Good. Deliver her to the House of Vesta at day's end."

Rufus smoothed down his tunic and nodded before turning his attention to other potential patrons.

A wave of nausea washed over Elisabeth.

"Rufus Leptis!" a voice yelled through the crowd.

"Tarquitius! How are you?" Rufus called out as he locked Elisabeth back in the cage with the other slaves he'd already sold.

An older, but handsome man, with bronzed skin and silver hair walked up to him. "What can you show me today? I need more rock cut for Vespasian's arena."

Elisabeth grabbed hold of the bars. *The quarry.*

"See if you like any of these." Rufus walked over to where David and Cato were on display with the other men. He made them all remove their tunics and stand, wearing only their loincloths, so Tarquitius could see if he wished to make a purchase.

A dark-skinned man, wearing a patch over his eye,

stopped in front of Cato.

Elisabeth's bottom lip trembled as Tarquitius from the quarry took a second glance at David. "Please no, please no, please no…" she mumbled repeatedly, wringing her hands.

Rufus pulled Cato forward so the man could take a closer look while Tarquitius examined David in more detail.

At that moment, Cato suddenly lunged for David, punching him in the face.

Elisabeth gasped, hands to her mouth as they fought.

With a harsh roar, David swung at Cato, knocking him to the ground. While straddling him and about to throw punches, Cato flipped him over. The two friends wrestled in the middle of the slave market until they were pried apart.

As Rufus waved the soldiers away, attempting to laugh it off with his potential customers, Elisabeth caught David shoot Cato a glance of hidden thanks.

Cato replied with the slightest nod before his chin trembled and he lowered his head.

"By the gods, I recognize him!" The man with the patch let out a belly laugh before walking over to David. "Speak slave. Are you not the young man who nearly died from fright over a chicken in the arena?"

With a grimace, David swallowed the lump in his throat and stared straight ahead. "I was not afraid. I simply passed out from lack of food."

"I cannot recall the last time I laughed so hard. The crowd loved you." The man turned to Rufus. "I want this one as well."

With a polite smile, Tarquitius nodded. He walked

away from David while Rufus and Patch negotiated before shaking hands.

Elisabeth stumbled back in relief. At least the man who bought them seemed kind.

When Cato and David grabbed their tunics from the ground, Elisabeth rushed to the door of the cage. Instead of being ushered back to the slave wagon, they were led away by their new owner.

"Aquarius?" Elisabeth let out an uncontrollable sob. "Aquarius!"

"*Cor meum!*" He attempted to run to her but winced when he was shackled to Cato instead. "Who bought you?" he screamed over his shoulder as they were marched away. "Who bought you?"

"Vesta! The House of Vesta!" A feeling of dread washed over Elisabeth realizing this was their goodbye. "Don't forget about Pompeii!" she screamed at the top of her lungs as he disappeared around a corner. "Don't forget about Pompeii!" Tears burned behind her eyelids, and she grabbed the bars of the cage for support.

"What's so special about Pompeii?" Rufus grumbled when he returned to the slave wagon.

Elisabeth grabbed his sleeve. "Who bought Aquarius? Where is he going? Are they going to another fullery?"

Rufus pulled himself away from her grip and fidgeted with his keys before answering. "You can thank Cato for saving…no, not saving, for…*prolonging* your sweetheart's life with that little stunt he pulled. It saved Aquarius from the quarry."

"Their fight?"

Rufus cleared his throat and nodded. "I wager it

was all for show."

"Why?"

"Obviously, Cato didn't want to go through gladiator school without his lifelong friend."

Her jaw clenched. "What?"

Rufus flashed a fake smile. "Your beloved Aquarius is going to be a gladiator."

Chapter Twenty-Three

In a daze, Elisabeth stumbled back a step. "You're telling me the wrestling match they had was to attract the attention of someone from a gladiator school?"

Rufus opened the door to the cage, pulled Elisabeth out by the arm, and then locked it again. "It will be faster if we walk."

"Aquarius is…" Her voice choked on tears. "He's as good as dead."

"Three years. If he survives the arena for three years he will have earned his freedom."

Elisabeth's nostrils flared. "What gladiator has ever lived long enough to earn his freedom?"

Rufus pounded his chest. "This one."

She shot him an incredulous look. "You were a gladiator?"

The giant pinched his lips together and remained silent as he led the way through the busy streets, never once loosening his grip on her arm.

Elisabeth's breath hitched. "You were once a slave and now you sell them?"

He made a low growling sound. A warning to drop the subject.

"Is Aquarius even old enough to be a gladiator?"

"The boy is whatever age I say he is."

She fiddled with her bracelet then glanced down, noticing the road was now paved with huge marble slabs. When they passed opulent palaces and temples, Elisabeth knew they were making their way through the Roman forum.

Shortly after turning down a side street, Rufus stopped. As he was about to knock on an unassuming wooden door, it flew open. A heavy-set man, probably around nineteen years old, almost crashed into them. His big, hazel eyes were as warm as the smile plastered across his round face.

"Oh…I am so sorry." With a nervous laugh, he ran a hand through his wavy brown hair. "I'm…" He paused, smiling at Elisabeth. "Oh…are you…are you the new—?"

"I am here to deliver the new body slave," Rufus interrupted.

"Yes, yes." He cleared his throat, stealing another glance at Elisabeth. "Wait here. I will get Gavia," he said, rubbing the back of his neck before he scurried off.

A few minutes later, Gavia, the gray-haired woman who'd purchased Elisabeth, waltzed over. "Very good," she said, looking Elisabeth up and down once again before turning to Rufus. "Follow me."

The man who had crashed into them stepped forward, giving Elisabeth a shy wave. "I guess I can bring you to Claudia?" He looked around, unsure of what to do. "I am Kastor."

Elisabeth held her breath, realizing it might be possible to escape from here at some point. If she could manage to slip out the door, she'd be able to disappear into the busy forum and—

"Me. Kastor," he said again, pointing to himself and then pointing to Elisabeth. "You…?"

"What? Oh...sorry." Her cheeks felt red hot. "I'm Elisabeth."

"Pretty." He shook out his hands. "I mean the name, not you." His hands covered his face. Groaning, he quickly added, "I mean..."

Elisabeth bit her lips to hide a smile. "I know what you meant."

With a shaky laugh, he fidgeted with his tunic, like a big, nervous teddy bear. "You are to be Claudia's new hairdresser?"

Her eyes widened. "Hairdresser?"

"Well, hair, body, all that..." he cleared his throat. "Uh...shall we?" Kastor ushered her along a covered footpath that led away from the tiny side entrance.

Elisabeth looked around. Like Aurelius' villa, it was built around a stunning courtyard. It seemed hard to believe that just beyond these tranquil walls buzzed the chaos of the eternal city.

In the center of the long rectangular *peristyle* were three reflecting pools, each surrounded by white rose bushes. Statues of women edged the entire garden. Elisabeth couldn't help but stare in wonder at this gilded prison.

She followed Kastor beneath the elegant colonnade. He spoke quickly while pointing out various rooms as they neared the far end.

"Kitchen, mill, oven."

They exited the *peristyle,* entering a secluded patio nestled beneath a vine-covered trellis. Comfortable sofas and tables scattered the small courtyard, while urns and potted plants turned it into the perfect garden hideaway.

"Arria," he called to a woman sitting on a pillowed

sofa, looking quite relaxed. "Have you seen Claudia?"

Arria, with salt and pepper hair pulled back in a loose bun, appeared to be in her late thirties. The utilitarian look of her pale red tunic made Elisabeth think the woman was another slave.

"I was going to ask what you're doing over here, but..." she glanced at Elisabeth before winking at Kastor. "I figured it out."

He let out a nervous laugh. "Um, I'd like to introduce you to my future wife."

Arria laughed. "Aww, did you two fall in love between here and the door?"

With a dimpled grin, he nodded. He then coughed, glancing at Elisabeth. "We tease."

Elisabeth smiled, feeling her face heat with embarrassment again.

"Claudia still guards the fire," Arria said, continuing to lounge in comfort. "So the new girl is free for further bonding."

Kastor bit down on a smile and then turned to Elisabeth. "Are you hungry? I'm one of the cooks." He straightened his posture. "I'd be happy to prepare something for you to eat."

"Kas is a fabulous cook," Arria called out. "So don't break his heart, new girl, or we all suffer."

"You can call me Kas, if...if you want." He curled and uncurled his fingers. "All my friends do. Did...did you want something to eat?"

Elisabeth locked her hands together. "Yes. Please. That would be nice, Kas."

"Perfect." He led her out of the courtyard. "Are you from Gaul?"

"Yes," she lied.

Kastor glanced at her, nodding. "I thought so. You look like a Gaul. Are you familiar with the House of Vesta?"

Elisabeth shook her head.

His face seemed to shine. "I can show you the temple first, if you'd like. That's where Claudia is. She's one of the Vestals."

"Vestals?"

"The Vestal Virgins," Kastor explained. "They become the brides of Rome after taking an oath of chastity."

Elisabeth sucked in a quick breath when she realized this palace was nothing but a convent. "Oh."

"The girls are chosen when they are about seven years old and take their vows for thirty years."

At a loss for words, she followed Kastor.

When they exited the courtyard and stood in the forum, Elisabeth's knees nearly buckled. Escaping from here would be possible once she had a plan. Until then, she'd stay here, safe within the walls of this palatial nunnery.

Kastor pointed to a circular building ringed with huge Corinthian columns. "That is the temple of Vesta. The sacred fire that burns inside must never go out."

"Why not?"

"If the fire goes out, Rome will fall."

Elisabeth's mouth fell open. "Are you kidding me?"

Kastor shook his head. "The entire fate of Rome lies in the hands of the Vestal Virgins."

"Has the fire ever gone out?"

He fiddled with his ear. "Of course. The gods are fickle, no? You do *not* want to be here when that happens," he said as they returned to the tranquility behind the palatial walls.

"Why not?"

"If the fire goes out the behavior of the Vestal Virgins is called into question. Especially their..." he paused and cleared his throat. "Their chastity."

Elisabeth gave him a blank look.

"The punishment is death," Kastor said as they entered the courtyard again.

Her eyes widened. "Death?"

"Buried alive." He raked a hand through his hair and led her up a staircase.

From the second-floor balcony of the *peristyle*, Kastor pointed back to the far end of the courtyard. A small vaulted hallway with a tall statue in the center was flanked by six doors, three on each side.

"Those rooms belong to the six active Vestal Virgins." He called out names as he pointed to each door. "Aemillia, Didia, Caecillia, Flavia, Julia, and that last one is Claudia's. She's the newest to tend to the fire, which is why you're here now."

At that moment, six little girls in matching dresses appeared in the corridor below them, skipping along the walkway before disappearing into another room.

"There are eighteen Vestal Virgins here," he explained. "Those little ones spend ten years in training. Then, there are the six active ones who tend to the sacred fire and a variety of other duties."

"And are buried alive if the flame goes out," Elisabeth said, still trying to digest that fact.

Kastor nodded. "When they are finished ten years of active duty, they go on to become tutors to the new ones. After thirty years of service, they retire extremely wealthy and powerful. They can even marry, but of course, they're old women by then."

Elisabeth nodded in understanding. "Is Arria a body slave to one of them?"

"Flavia. They've been together since Flavia's capture ceremony." He glanced back at Elisabeth. "Claudia will not be returning until later, and you must be starving. If you want to come to the kitchen, I have some leftover dorm—"

"Please…" Elisabeth squeezed her eyes shut. "Don't say dormouse."

Kastor froze. "Soup. I meant to say soup," he replied as a bemused grin spread across his face.

With a huge sigh of relief, she offered him a smile. "Thank you."

****

After dinner, Arria brought Elisabeth to the alcove where the Vestal Virgins' rooms were located and handed her two folded utilitarian dresses for work.

"Flavia will soon return. Good night," Arria said while standing in a doorway. "Claudia's room is that one."

Elisabeth opened the heavy wooden door she'd been directed to. Inside, the walls were painted in a deep jewel tone. A wooden bed sat in the middle of the room, topped with luxurious fabrics. Elisabeth groaned, noticing the small pallet at the foot of the bed. It wasn't for a dog, but for a slave. Bedside tables held silver candlesticks along with a variety of expensive-looking trinkets. Elisabeth walked over to inspect a desk pushed against a far wall. Brushes and hair accessories littered the top of it. A little wicker basket held what looked to be hairpins made of bone or something similar.

While examining Claudia's things, the door opened. Elisabeth jumped. She wasn't sure what was more startling, being caught snooping, or the fact that the young priestess was dressed like a bride, complete with veil.

Elisabeth cleared her throat. "Claudia?"

She nodded in reply while fidgeting with a brooch at the breast of her gown.

"Uh..I...I'm Elisabeth. Your new body slave?"

Claudia looked Roman, with a strong nose and dark eyes. She also appeared to be a bit younger than Elisabeth; maybe sixteen. Her posture slumped while letting out a shaky laugh. "I survived my first shift guarding the fire," she said with a child-like voice before parking herself in the chair at the desk. "You may undress me," she said, pointing to her veil. "I want to go to sleep."

"As you wish." Elisabeth stepped forward, knowing she'd have to play along for now in order to stay safe.

Chapter Twenty-Four

With little to do, the days crawled by. It took an hour to make the ceremonial braids for Claudia's hair. After dressing her in the white bridal gown every morning, Elisabeth was often not needed again until the evening, when it was time to undress the Vestal Virgin and brush her hair out.

When Claudia lay in bed each night, Elisabeth would curl up on her own little pallet on the floor. She'd then attempt to hold back tears as all the homesickness and worry would come crashing down like a tidal wave, threatening to drown her. She was desperate to take action, but had yet to come up with an intelligent plan.

One afternoon, Claudia left to tend to the fire. The Vestal Virgins worked in rotating shifts and, therefore, so did Elisabeth. Outside, the clouds rolled in, the sky darkened, and a thunderstorm promised a welcome break from the summer sun. Inside, the smell of something wonderful cooking for dinner filled the palace.

At home, she loved lazy days like this; wrapped up with a good book as it poured rain outside, the scent of a roast in the oven wafting through the house. Elisabeth's heart ached at the thought. Curling up on the little mattress, it didn't take long for the pitter-patter of falling rain to lull her to sleep.

****

With a racing heart, she held back a scream when a hand covered her mouth. Claudia knelt over her, trembling.

As Elisabeth sat up, a crack of lightning made the hair on her arms stand on end. "What's wrong?" she whispered.

"The fire…" Claudia covered her face with her hands. "The fire's gone out."

An explosion of thunder shook the ground. Elisabeth jumped up, muscles tightening as she raced to the door.

While it seemed most of the inhabitants of the House of Vesta took cover indoors from the storm, Elisabeth and Claudia ran through the *peristyle*. Rain pelting into the courtyard blew across the covered walkway, drenching the bottom of Elisabeth's tunic as her bare feet sloshed through the puddles. When they arrived at the temple, instead of a raging fire, only a faint glow of embers remained.

With precise movements, Elisabeth searched the circular room for something to reignite the flame with, but the temple appeared to house nothing except a stone hearth at the foot of a statue of a woman; presumably the goddess Vesta.

"I fell asleep after I swept the temple floor." Claudia weaved in place. "There is nothing here to rekindle it."

Elisabeth charged toward her, tore a piece of fabric from her veil, and placed it in the hot ash.

Sobbing, Claudia dropped to her knees and began praying to Vesta.

"Rip some more of your veil for me," Elisabeth

demanded, still trying to ignite the first piece.

Consumed with grief, Claudia continued crying and praying, but didn't move.

Elisabeth cursed under her breath, tearing some more fabric from Claudia's headdress.

After a few minutes, the embers started to glow brighter. She looked around the temple again and this time found a pile of chopped wood stacked behind a niche. She frowned, knowing smaller sticks were needed, not fire logs.

"I'll be right back." Elisabeth bolted outside and back to Claudia's room.

Once there, she grabbed the little wicker basket from the desk, tossed the hairpins aside, and wrapped it in the fabric of her dress to keep it dry from the rain outside. She then ran through the courtyard, sliding across the wet marble floors, and back into the temple.

Claudia was now pacing.

"Cross your fingers," Elisabeth whispered, placing the wicker basket onto the embers.

They both held their breath, waiting for it to ignite. Within a moment, flames engulfed the basket.

Elisabeth let out a sigh of relief, and her posture slumped. "There. Nobody will ever know."

Flavia waltzed into the temple, attempting to shake the rain off her veil. "Nobody will ever know what?" Her eyes then widened after noticing Elisabeth. "What is your slave doing in here?"

Claudia's face turned ashen, and she wiped puffy eyes with the back of her hand. "I fell asleep. The thunder woke me, but the sacred flame…"

Flavia froze and then lowered her voice. "Go. Make certain your slave is unseen when you leave and speak of this to no one."

****

The next morning, Claudia sat while Elisabeth arranged the ceremonial braids in her hair and attached the headdress.

"How easy your life is," she said with a dejected sigh. "You spend your days brushing my hair and dressing me. Not a single thing to worry about."

Elisabeth half-listened while pinning the braids in place; David haunted her thoughts instead.

"So, why do you still cry yourself to sleep each night? Although you try not to make a sound, I hear you."

Elisabeth paused. "I miss my family, my friends."

Claudia gave an understanding nod. "When I first came here, I too cried myself to sleep. I was six years old when the Pontifex Maximus chose me and I had to leave my—"

Interrupted by a quiet tap on the door, Flavia's head poked into the room. Dressed in a nightgown, she peeked outside toward the courtyard before tiptoeing inside, closing the door behind her. "Does anyone know about yesterday?" she whispered while twisting waist-length brown hair around a finger. Like Claudia, Flavia appeared to be the same age as Elisabeth; perhaps a year or two older.

Claudia shook her head. "Just you and I."

Flavia tiptoed across the room and flopped down on the bed. "What happened? You weren't in some nook with a secret lover, were you?" She flashed a wide grin.

"Don't even say that in jest," Claudia whispered as someone else knocked on the door and then opened it.

The slave, Arria, stood in the threshold with her arms crossed. "Flavia, come. I need to dress you."

Flavia let out an exaggerated sigh and stood up. "Do you want to go to the games later today?" she asked Claudia.

The games? Elisabeth's posture perked up.

"Flavia, no!" Arria clasped her hands together. "You need to bake the *mola salsa*."

"We have time to bake it tomorrow. Today, we go to the circus."

"You mustn't." Arria's eyebrows drew together while marching into the room. "You've already been warned."

Claudia's head jerked back. "Warned?"

"Much ado about nothing. The priests reprimanded me last week."

Arria lowered her voice to a whisper, wagging a finger. "They said you are too vain, you need to refrain from jesting, and you attend too many games."

Flavia rolled her eyes and stomped out of Claudia's room with Arria, the two bickering like mother and daughter rather than slave and master.

****

"Morning, Kas," Elisabeth said as she shuffled into the kitchen a short while later.

The kitchen was tucked in a back corner on the ground level of the palace. A wooden table, acting as a worktop, dominated the center of the space. On a wall opposite the door, a fire blazed in a brick oven beneath a tiled stovetop. Serving bowls and dishes lined a sideboard, and another table held baskets filled with fresh produce. The air smelled of savory herbs and warm bread.

The other slaves ate in their allotted dining space, but Elisabeth didn't feel like being social. She ate all her meals in the kitchen while Kastor kept busy preparing a variety of dishes.

"Elisabeth!" He greeted her the same way every morning. "How are you today?"

She replied with the same melodramatic answer. "I am in the depths of despair."

Kastor looked down to hide a smile.

Elisabeth let out an appreciative sigh while sagging onto a stool. He always had a plate of plain scrambled eggs, bread and honey, along with a bowl of berries, waiting on the center table just for her. "You're too good to me."

With a flushed appearance, he crossed and uncrossed his arms. "Are you…" He cleared his throat. "Are you free for the day now?"

Elisabeth took a bite of the warm bread and nodded. "Claudia won't be back for hours."

He turned his back and she heard the tapping of a spoon as he stirred a pot on the stove. "Do you want to go to the circus with me this afternoon?" he blurted out.

She choked on the bread and coughed.

Kastor dropped his wooden spoon and then fumbled for it again. "We could go to the Circus Maximus. For the next seven days, they're having beast hunts and gladiatorial contests, in addition to the chariot races. It should be quite the spectacle."

Gladiators?

Elisabeth's posture stiffened. "Are we allowed to go?" she asked, fidgeting with her bracelet, needing to feel the rope from David's sling.

"Yes." Kastor turned around, seeming to hold his

breath as he stirred a bowl he now held in his arms. "Yes, of course."

"Then yes!" She swallowed rapidly while nodding. "I'll definitely go to the circus with you."

His eyes widened. The bowl dropped, spilling its contents all over the floor.

With a chuckle, Elisabeth helped him clean the mess.

****

Kastor led the way along the congested streets. Within fifteen minutes, Elisabeth could see the Circus Maximus stretched out in a valley ahead of them. A mammoth oblong structure, bigger than any stadium she'd ever seen, even by today's standards. As she looked up at the statues that filled numerous niches, it appeared to be three times the size of the still unfinished Coliseum. "Do we have to pay?"

He shook his head. "Have you never been to the games before?"

"Once," she said with a sigh. That day seemed like a lifetime ago.

They entered through a large arch, following the thinning crowd up several flights of stairs to a cavernous, but dimly-lit corridor. When Elisabeth stepped out into the already packed spectator stands, trumpets blasted in the distance. She blinked, trying to adjust her eyes to the sunshine while following Kastor to two empty seats.

The crowd cheered at a parade led by two guards on horseback, followed by a bronze statue of a wolf carried on the shoulders of four men. As the music continued, colorfully dressed dancers, huge wooden cages on wheels, shackled prisoners, a flock of ostriches, and a giraffe followed. The spectacle went on and on. When a chariot pulled by four white horses with blue feathers in their manes appeared, the audience went wild.

Kas pulled a square of blue fabric from his belt, waving it over his head while whooping loudly.

The charioteer wore a blue tunic and a bronze helmet with tall blue plumes rising from the top of it. A true showman, he stood on the handles of his chariot, held the reins of the four horses with one hand, waving at the screaming fans with the other. Elisabeth's eyes widened. She leaned in closer to watch the man's blue cape billow dramatically behind him.

Charioteers with horses decked in green, white, red, or blue waved to the audience. They joined the parade around a long, narrow racetrack before disappearing from Elisabeth's view behind obelisks, arches, and statues perched along a stone median running down the center of the track.

The fans cheered and clapped while colorful team flags fluttered in the spectator stands.

"The opening ceremonies are…"

Elisabeth couldn't focus on a single thing Kastor said. All she could think about was David. She stared down at the field with trembling hands. If he was here, how on earth could she find him, let alone help him escape? The situation felt hopeless.

As the morning progressed, elaborate animal hunts took place. Each time a man came out; Elisabeth held her breath, desperate to get a closer look. Seated at the top of the stadium, they were so far away from the action. The nosebleed section her dad would have called it.

By lunch time, there was still no sign of either David or Cato.

"I cannot wait for the races later," Kastor said as the field filled with dozens of men. "But, the convicts are here now." He cheered when they began butchering one another.

Elisabeth trembled with worry watching the men. She studied the way they moved; praying David wasn't amongst them.

What if she was too late?

What if he was already dead?

Whipped into a frenzy, the crowd stood, cheering. Elisabeth crumpled to her seat, shaking her head in denial, unable to watch another minute of it. This was David's life now.

"Elisabeth?" Kastor gently pulled her up and away from their seats.

Once in the shadowy corridor, her gaze lowered. "You were looking forward to the chariot races. I'm really sorry for ruining—"

"Believe me, you didn't ruin anything," he said in a soothing voice. "I've known many women…" A flush crept across his cheeks. "I don't mean I've *known* many women…I meant…"

Elisabeth smiled through tears. "You're the cook in a palace of females. I know what you meant."

He let out a shaky laugh. "Some women are more…more delicate than others. That's not a bad thing."

She gave him a pained stare. "My two friends have just been sold to a gladiator school."

"Did…?" Kastor's voice rose in surprise as he led Elisabeth down a flight of stairs. "Did you see them today?"

"No." Elisabeth shook her head. "I didn't."

He lightly stroked her arm. "Maybe I can help. Come with me."

She walked with him along a corridor. They stopped at a locked metal gate that led into a backstage area; far grander than where she'd first met Cato and Aquarius. A cobbled ramp descended into the bowels of the venue. Elisabeth could make out muffled noises from beyond: horses neighing, men arguing and shouting, lions roaring. The distinct trumpet of an elephant was heard.

"Get Severus," Kastor called out to a man behind the gate who carried a water bucket.

He pointed a long, crooked finger down the corridor. "Severus!"

A skinny fellow with long legs seemed to glide up the ramp to the locked gate. "Kas! What are you doing down here?" he asked with a huge gummy smile.

"I know you tend to the chariots, "Kastor whispered to him. "But do you know of any new gladiators?"

Severus pressed his lips together. "When were they bought?"

"A little over a month ago," Elisabeth said.

"They wouldn't have been in today's show yet," he said with a curt nod. "They are probably in training still."

Her heart skipped a beat. "So, they aren't just sent out to be killed?"

"By the gods, no," Severus said with a snort. "The *lanista* is not going to waste all that money. No, they'll spend weeks in training and be taught to put on a good performance. I don't recall any newcomers, though. You certain they're *here*?"

Elisabeth swallowed the lump in her throat. "No, I'm not."

His brow furrowed. "What are their names?"

"Aquarius and Cato."

"Kerza! You know of two *novicus,* Aquarius and Cato?" he asked the man with the bucket.

The man shook his head and kept walking.

Severus cupped his elbow with one hand, tapping his lips with the other. "Did you see who purchased them?"

"Yes. A black man with an eye patch."

With a smile, he held his arms out wide, relieved to have solved the puzzle. "Your friends aren't here. I know who you mean, though. I don't remember his name but…"

Elisabeth gently bit her lip.

"He runs a traveling gladiator troupe."

Her shoulders dropped. "A *traveling* gladiator troupe?"

"Your friends could be anywhere by now," Kastor said with a deep sigh.

She did a double-take. "Anywhere here, in Rome?"

Severus shook his head. "Anywhere in the Empire."

Terror held her hostage for a split second. "Thank you." She then stumbled for the exit, eyes clouding with tears.

Kastor jogged to catch up and then walked beside her in silence, twisting his hands together.

She clutched her belly as it dawned on her where to find Aquarius. If he was in a traveling gladiator troupe, he was going to Pompeii. With a deep breath, she forced a watery smile. "Sorry. It's just—"

Kastor shook his head. "No reason to apologize. I completely understand. I…I'll take you back to the house now, if you like."

Elisabeth gave him a small nod, biting down on a smile as a plan took shape. Tomorrow, she'd wake, braid Claudia's hair and dress her. She'd have breakfast with Kastor, making sure to act like nothing was any different. Then, she'd slip out the door, disappear in the crowded Forum, and find her way to the city gate. Once there, the long trek south to Pompeii would begin. Chances are her absence would be unnoticed until later that night, but by then, she'd be miles—

"So…" Kastor interrupted her thoughts. "Tell me of these friends of yours. Which one have you…"

Elisabeth steadied him as he stumbled over a curb. "Careful."

His ears turned red. "Which one have you tied the knot with?"

She jerked her head back. "Tied the knot? I haven't tied the knot with anyone."

"Oh, I…I assumed…" With a blank expression, Kastor pointed to the lover's knot on her wrist. "I noticed that today and…"

She stared down at David's sling entwined with her hair ribbon and then confined a small laugh to a snort. *Tied the knot.* "It's a token of friendship. From Aquarius."

"And…and what of your friend Cato?"

"I hesitate to use the term friend." She let out a heavy sigh. "I think he hates me. And to be perfectly honest, I'm not fond of him either."

Kastor lifted his eyebrow. "You are not wed to the one with whom you've tied the knot, and are not fond of your friend."

Elisabeth gave him a playful nudge. "Well, when you put it that way…" They both started laughing. At that moment, an old man crossed the street ahead of them. "Excuse me, Kas." Her voice trembled while running after the man. "Balinus! Balinus!"

Balinus said he was en route to Rome to visit Vespasian, the emperor himself. Elisabeth took a deep breath, realizing not only did she now know where to find David, but her crystal was also within reach.

After grabbing hold of his arm, the old man turned around.

It wasn't Balinus.

Elisabeth's shoulders dropped. "I'm sorry, I…I thought you were someone else." Blinking back tears, she walked back to Kastor. "Where does Vespasian live?"

He pointed across from the Circus Maximus to a huge palace. "Right there."

Elisabeth rubbed the back of her neck. If she ran away, heading south to Pompeii, before Mt. Vesuvius erupted, she might be able to save David. But, waiting here in Rome, in the safety of the house of Vesta, she had a much greater chance of finding Balinus. He had her crystal, and that was the only way home.

Cato was right.

She had a choice.

Love versus fear.

Elisabeth swallowed the lump in her throat. The old man may think he'd forced her hand, but leaving David to die in Pompeii was never an option.

Chapter Twenty-Five

Returning from the games, Claudia was already in her room, pacing back and forth while blubbering to herself.

"Claudia…? What's wrong?"

With bulging eyes, the girl turned around to face Elisabeth. "Did you speak to anyone of what happened the other night?"

"Of course not." Elisabeth felt the color drain from her face. "Why?"

"Flavia and I…" Her voice choked with tears. "Flavia and I have been suspended from our duties."

"What!" Elisabeth gasped. "Why? I swear, I didn't say anything."

Claudia's chest caved in. "Do you recall yesterday's storm?"

"Yes…?"

"The daughter of a knight was riding on horseback. She…she was struck and killed by a bolt of lightning."

"That's terrible, but what does it have to do with you?"

Claudia took a deep breath and closed her eyes. "The bolt of lightning left the girl naked."

"Obviously, it burnt her clothing…"

"They say it's an omen. For this to happen to an innocent girl, the Vestal Virgins must not be pleasing Vesta."

Elisabeth's voice rose in pitch. "They can't think that had anything to do with you?"

"They're putting me on trial." She brought a shaky hand to her forehead. "They say I have been unchaste."

Elisabeth grabbed Claudia's arm. "This is ridiculous! Clearly they can see that."

"They're going to kill me." Both hands rushed to cover her mouth.

"No, no, everything will be fine." Elisabeth pulled Claudia into a hug. "You've done nothing wrong."

Claudia took a deep, pained breath and then threw herself onto the bed. "But the flame did go out. Perhaps I *have* angered the gods."

Elisabeth sat on the edge of the bed and rubbed Claudia's back. "You haven't done anything wrong."

Still dressed in ceremonial clothing, the girl curled up in a ball and cried herself to sleep.

With a sinking feeling in her stomach, Elisabeth crumpled onto the little pallet on the floor and tossed and turned all night. Was she cold-hearted enough to run away in the morning without saying a word to defend an innocent person?

Claudia could be buried alive.

****

She woke later than intended the next morning and found Claudia gone. Elisabeth sprinted out of the room and pounded on Flavia's door.

Flavia cracked it open, just enough to poke her head out.

"Have you seen Claudia? She isn't in her room and…" Elisabeth clutched at her throat when she noticed Flavia's puffy red eyes. "What's wrong?"

With a pained stare, she opened the door enough to

show Arria lying on the bed; the slave's back bloody and raw from the lashes of a whip.

Elisabeth gasped. "Who did that to her?"

"The priests." Flavia sobbed. "Emperor Vespasian is dead." Her hands trembled, and she shut the door again.

A cold chill ran up Elisabeth's spine as she returned to Claudia's room. If the Vestal Virgins were being blamed for the death of a young girl who was hit by lightning, the Emperor's death so soon afterward had obviously been considered their fault as well, but why was Arria, a slave, the one being whipped?

Elisabeth let out a huge breath when Claudia tiptoed through the door a moment later. "The priests..." Claudia rocked back and forth. "The priests know I let the flame go out."

"How?"

"Flavia told them." She wept into her hands. "They accused her of being unchaste with a slave...one of the cooks...and they beat Arria."

"Wait..." Elisabeth clutched her stomach. "One of the cooks?"

"There has been gossip lately of a budding romance in the kitchen between one of the cooks and a girl. I've heard the rumors too. Everyone has. At first, the priests accused Flavia of being the girl, but when Arria told them it was you—"

"Please don't tell me the cook's name is Kastor. Oh...please don't say it's Kastor."

Claudia nodded. "Yes. Kastor was nowhere to be found yesterday afternoon and now the priests are saying that he and I were..."

Elisabeth's eyes widened. "Yesterday afternoon?

Kastor was with me yesterday afternoon. We spent the day at the games and…"

Claudia's shoulders slumped. "Are you in love with the cook?"

"What? No." Elisabeth's breath burst in and out. "Of course not. But he's…" Fidgeting with her bracelet, her heart ached for David. "He's my friend. Kastor is the only friend I have here."

"You're…you're being called as a witness later today to give testimony. They think Flavia and Arria are lying." Claudia began sobbing. "I am so sorry."

Elisabeth's hands clenched and unclenched. "No, don't be sorry. I am happy to testify for you. I will tell them the truth. That Kastor was with me at the games and not with you. I will defend you and tell them how devoted you are to your duties and how…" Elisabeth rubbed at her arms. "I can't stand by and allow you…a sweet, innocent girl…to be put on trial for something so stupid."

"Elisabeth, do you not understand what this means for you?"

"For me?" She thought of the whip marks across Arria's back. "No. What?" Her lips and chin began to tremble, realizing the answer.

Claudia took a step back. "A slave's testimony can only be allowed if it has come through torture."

Elisabeth's hands flew to her mouth. "You're telling me I'm about to be tortured…?"

Claudia nodded. "As my slave, your loyalty to me is unquestionable. They know that."

"I have to get out of here," Elisabeth said with feverish eyes. "We…we have to get out of here. We have to escape."

Claudia answered with a small shake of her head. "I must stay and accept my lot."

"No…you can't!"

"I must confess to letting the fire go out and face the consequences. It was my failure and mine alone. Clearly, I have offended Vesta."

"Claudia." Elisabeth gave her an incredulous look. "You must leave here. Come with me and—"

"Where would I go?" she said with a bitter smile. "I am as recognizable as the Imperial family. Besides, I cannot hide from the gods." Head held high, she walked closer to Elisabeth. "You've been a loyal slave." Her voice broke. "I'm sorry we weren't together longer." She then reached up and touched Elisabeth's arm. "With just the touch of my hand, I once had the power to free a slave or release a condemned man. I'm afraid I no longer have that power. They will be here for you soon," Claudia warned before tiptoeing out of the room, shutting the door behind her.

****

As Elisabeth rushed to grab her blue gown from a basket beside the little pallet, she bumped into the nightstand, knocking one of the silver candlesticks over. She grabbed it and then the one on the other table. With no idea how long it would take to get to Pompeii, she figured the silver could be sold in order to buy supplies. Hands trembling, Elisabeth wrapped the candlesticks in the gown, attempting to hide them in the basket.

Taking a deep breath, she opened the door and stood in the little alcove. The *peristyle* ahead was empty, but she had to head to the kitchen to warn Kastor first. He needed to leave with her this very minute, before he too was tortured.

Elisabeth! How are you today? He would say to her.

In the depths of despair, would be the reply.

"Where's Kas?" Elisabeth asked Iris, an auburn-haired woman who seemed hard at work in the kitchen. She'd seen her before, but they'd never spoken.

"I'm not sure." Iris looked up, rubbing an eyebrow. "He was called away last night but has yet to return."

A wave of coldness washed over her. "Oh…" Elisabeth forced a watery smile into place. With shaky hands, she dropped some fruit into the basket in an attempt to cover the dress and candlesticks within it. "I'm supposed to get some food for Claudia and Flavia."

"Do you know what's going on?" Iris whispered, helping to load up the basket with food.

Elisabeth swallowed hard and watched the exit. "What do you mean?"

"Here, I just took this one out of the oven." She added a round loaf of bread to the hamper and then lowered her voice. "There's been a lot of unusual activity today."

While Iris turned to grab a chunk of cheese, Elisabeth slipped a sharp knife in with the rest of the spoils. "Really? I haven't noticed anything." She needed to get out of here. *Now*. "If you see Kas, tell him I was looking for him?" Elisabeth hurried toward the door.

"Wait."

She squeezed her eyes shut and then turned around, hands gripping the basket.

"Take some of this. It's good."

"Thanks." She grabbed the wedge of cheese and then dashed out of the kitchen.

Standing in the wide-open *peristyle*, Elisabeth still had to make it to the other end of the palace, toward the temple, before she'd be out in the Forum.

With an empty feeling in the pit of her stomach, she started down the long colonnade, praying to escape before the priests sent the guards to collect her. Sweat beaded on her forehead as she crept along.

Halfway there.

Her feet seemed to drag while forcing herself not to run.

Two soldiers advanced from another entrance and headed toward the alcove. Her heartbeat thrashed in her ears as they pounded on the door and burst into Claudia's room.

She then heard footsteps behind her. Getting closer. Now running.

Her chin trembled. She stumbled over her own feet while glancing behind.

A man grabbed hold of her arm and Elisabeth gasped.

"Sorry," he said with a laugh as he made his way around her.

"Found you!" several childish voices sang out and then four of the youngest Vestal Virgins giggled and ran after the man, buzzing past Elisabeth in the process.

Her chest hitched when she reached the end of the *peristyle* and turned around to look at the House of Vesta one last time.

As the soldiers stormed out of Claudia's room, Elisabeth stepped out of the colonnade, sprinting down the footpath that led to the Temple and the Forum.

With shaking hands, she reached for the door handle.

Chapter Twenty-Six

She drew in a deep breath and marched past the temple, attempting to disappear into the crowd, heading toward the opposite end of the Forum. An excited mob crowded together. Elisabeth tried to fight her way through the chaos but recoiled when realizing they were gathered to watch a man tied to a post, being whipped to death on the steps of one of the majestic buildings.

With blood splattered everywhere, the executioner threw down his whip, wrapping his hands around the criminal's throat.

Elisabeth squeezed her eyes shut and turned away.

"Serves him right for coupling with a Vestal Virgin," a man beside her said to his friend.

She froze.

"Serves them both right for putting Rome in jeopardy. Heard he was a cook at the palace. Guess he liked things spicy." With a snort, he elbowed the man next to him. "The sun's strong. Won't take long for his carcass to rot."

"Throw him in the Tiber!" a woman yelled. "I can't stand the smell," she added quietly.

Elisabeth stifled a scream, watching in horror as the executioner untied the man's body from the post. His lifeless head sagged forward, hiding his face, but she recognized Kastor's wavy hair, now slick with blood and sweat. When his body was tossed unceremoniously down the marble stairs, the crowd dispersed.

A wave of nausea washed over her.

Elisabeth rocked back and forth, staring at Kastor's blood-soaked corpse laying twisted at the foot of the stairs, his neck bent at a grotesque angle. She felt light-headed and couldn't breathe, but ran to him and fell to her knees, knocking the basket of food over in the process.

An uncontrollable sob escaped. Elisabeth straightened Kastor's head before reaching for his hand. "Kas, oh my God. What have they done to you?"

With a quivering chin, she thought back to his adorable awkwardness around her; the way he'd stumble over his words and drop things. She could still see his beaming face when walking into the kitchen every morning, a special breakfast prepared just for her. He treated her like the queen of the manor rather than another slave.

While weeping over his body, someone tiptoed closer and began to pick up the spilled food, returning everything to her basket.

"I'm so sorry for your loss," Balinus whispered.

Elisabeth shook her head and let out a sigh of relief at his familiar voice. "He was my friend," she said with a quaking voice. "And he didn't deserve this, Balinus. He didn't deserve to die like this." She then lowered her voice. "Please, bring him back? Give him some of your elixir?"

Balinus' shoulders drooped and he crouched down beside her. "My dear girl," he whispered, "the elixir only works if there is still life in the body."

Elisabeth gave the old man a pained stare and lifted

Kastor's hand, desperate to feel for a pulse. She muttered anxiously to herself, putting an ear to his heart, praying for even the faintest rise and fall of his chest.

Kastor was gone.

"He didn't…" Elisabeth sobbed. "He didn't deserve to die like this, Balinus. We can't leave him here to rot. He needs a proper burial. He needs…" Elisabeth looked up and her eyes bulged.

Gavia, the woman who had purchased her, wandered through the crowd with two soldiers.

Balinus glanced over his shoulder and then, with an understanding nod, grabbed Elisabeth's basket. Linking his arm through hers, he pulled her up, and led her away. The old man's arm, strong and steady, kept her from running away in a panic and drawing attention to herself. He weaved his way through the labyrinth of streets and before long, Gavia and the soldiers were nowhere to be seen.

"You have something of mine," Elisabeth said with a monotone voice.

Balinus' head flinched back slightly. "I do?"

"Was this some sort of stupid game to teach me something? You've forced my hand. I choose love. No matter what, I am going to find Aquarius."

His eyebrows squished together. "My dear girl, I have no idea what you are speaking of."

"Come on, Balinus," she moaned. "You took my crystal."

"Oh, alrighty then. If you say so."

Elisabeth scratched her temple. "Cato said—"

"Ahh, Cato said." Balinus shook his head. "Well, I promise you, I do not have, nor have I ever had, your crystal."

"But, Cato said you were forcing me to decide between Aquarius…"

The old man looked at her with a sad smile. "Does that sound like me?"

"No," Elisabeth whispered while bowing her head, trying to put the pieces together. "But it does sound like Cato." She gasped, realizing where the crystal was. "Just before he told me you found it, he grabbed my neck and yanked me into that stupid hug. That wasn't a moment of kindness. That was him pulling a sleight of hand trick. That means…" Her voice choked with tears. "Cato had my necklace the entire time we were in the slave wagon."

"I worry about Cato," Balinus said with a wrinkled brow.

"Why? He's an…" Elisabeth stopped to clear her throat. "I'm far more worried about Aquarius. They've been sold to a gladiator school. I need to get to Pompeii as soon as possible."

Balinus did a double-take. "Gladiator school?" His walk seemed to slow. "I will take you to Pompeii myself. We'll leave tomorrow at first light."

Elisabeth gave him an incredulous look. "Tomorrow? I'm leaving right now. And there's no way you're coming with me to Pompeii."

"May I point out that it is a long journey and you need to prepare for it? Do you even know how to get there on your own?"

Her brow furrowed. "I'll figure it out."

"A wise sage once said, 'Nature does not hurry; yet everything is accomplished.'"

"What are you saying?"

"Oh, I think you know what I'm saying."

Elisabeth let out a heavy sigh. "Fine. But you're not staying."

Balinus led the way along side streets and knocked on a door next to a bakery with a red and white awning hanging over it.

"Thank you, Nikola," he said to a quiet man with a wide nose and short dark hair who answered with a warm smile.

Nikola bowed his head and then left them alone.

Although far less grand than Aurelius' villa, the layout inside was similar. A small atrium, with an *impluvium* that collected rainwater, sat in the center of the space, with rooms opening off of it. Straight ahead was a small outdoor *peristyle* that held a pretty garden with a water fountain in the center.

"This is my brother's property," Balinus said as he guided Elisabeth toward an alcove off the courtyard where three chaise-lounges were positioned around a low table. "But he prefers our ancestral home, so it is empty, except for Nikola and his wife, the caretakers. I came here after Vespasian's death yesterday." With a heavy sigh, Balinus put Elisabeth's basket down on the table. "The man in the forum…?"

"Kastor." She sniffled after saying his name. "And he was completely innocent."

"How did you come to know him?"

"Rufus sold me to the House of Vesta." Elisabeth shuffled over to a chaise lounge and sat down, resting her head in her hands. "Kastor was another slave and my only friend there. He helped me find out what happened to Aquarius and Cato." She looked up, giving Balinus a pained stare. "I thought I'd be safe there until

I figured out a plan; to get Aquarius, to get my crystal. Everything seemed fine in the beginning, but the temple is in chaos right now."

The old man tilted his head to the side.

"The priests are blaming everything bad that has happened lately in Rome on the Vestal Virgins; on Claudia in particular, even though she's done nothing wrong. They lied and accused her of being unchaste. They say she was with Kastor when he was with me at the arena looking for Aquarius."

Balinus dropped his chin to his chest. "It appears Kastor was offered as a human sacrifice in order to appease the gods."

"It's madness." Her voice choked with tears.

The old man walked closer and rubbed her back. "I need to take care of something right now, but you will be safe here. Rest, for you'll need your strength for our journey."

****

After several hours, she heard the front door open and ran to greet Balinus. Her head jerked back at the sight of the old man, sweating and covered in dirt. "Is everything all right?"

"Yes." He stared at Elisabeth with a thoughtful expression. "I removed your friend's body from the Forum and gave him a proper burial."

She sucked in a quick breath. "You did?" With an emotion-choked voice, she hugged him. "Thank you, Balinus. Thank you."

"Yes, well…" He gave her an awkward pat on the back. "I'm afraid I have bad news about Claudia."

Elisabeth's chin started to tremble and she turned away.

Chapter Twenty-Seven

The next morning, Elisabeth grabbed her basket before rushing out of the bedroom she'd spent the night in. The sun had risen and it promised to be another scorching hot day. A back door thrown wide open led her to Balinus.

"Good-morning-and-how-are-you?" The old man called out from the quiet street as he loaded a donkey with provisions. "Did you sleep well?"

Elisabeth pressed fingers to her smiling lips. "Thank you. Yes. Here…" She handed him the contents of the basket. "I have some cheese, bread, and fruit we can eat along the way. Plus, some silver we can sell. And I know it's silly, but I want to bring this," she said while holding up the blue gown.

Balinus gave a crisp nod, adding her provisions to bags already tied around the donkey. "Alrighty then. We should arrive in Pompeii in about ten days."

She jerked her head back. "Ten days?"

The old man whistled while he handed Elisabeth a canteen of water and nodded.

She prayed that was enough time. "When we get to Pompeii, I want you to promise me you won't come into the city. You will turn around and leave."

He flashed a knowing grin.

"Balinus…I'm serious."

"Ready?" He locked the house and led the donkey

away.

"Ready as I'll ever be." She stepped in line beside the old man. "I'm glad you found me in the forum yesterday," Elisabeth said with a sigh.

"I was searching for you."

Her mouth fell open. "You were?"

"Is that so hard to believe? You're a young girl, alone in a strange land." He gave her a knowing look as they turned onto a main street. "I knew Rufus would sell you in Rome and I also knew you'd never stay put wherever you were sold. If I didn't find you here, I was certain your path would lead to Pompeii. Speaking of Pompeii, how did you discover that's where Aquarius and Cato are?"

"I didn't. After listening to a certain wise old sage for so long, I realized I already knew."

"Well done, my dear." Balinus had a gleam in his eye. "The student is quick to learn."

"Well, there's no such thing as a coincidence, right?"

The old man replied with a satisfied smile.

****

They led the donkey along the busy roads and headed toward the city gates. As the streets became more and more congested, Balinus seemed jumpy and unusually quiet.

"Is something wrong?"

"Yes. These crowds…" The old man rubbed the back of his neck. "It appears these crowds are here to attend Claudia's funeral."

"Claudia's…" Elisabeth stared ahead, realizing they were in the midst of the huge funeral procession. Both hands then rushed to cover her mouth.

"We don't have to be here," he said in a soothing voice. "You have to realize that—"

"No…it's all right. I'd like to say goodbye to Claudia. We were…friends, in a way."

"In that case, you do not want to be recognized." Balinus stopped the donkey, reached into one of the packs, and pulled out her blue *palla*. "I forgot I had this. It was left behind at Aurelius'."

Her eyes filled with tears while taking the *palla* from him and burying her face in the soft fabric. It reminded her of David.

"Thank you." With an achy chest, she wore it like a headscarf in an attempt to disguise herself should anyone from the house of Vesta recognize her.

It wasn't until they passed through the city gates that she caught a glimpse of Claudia. Laid out in a ceremonial white gown, four slaves carried the priestess on a bed-like stretcher to her final resting place. Elisabeth sniffed and wiped her nose, but then her eyes narrowed, trying to understand why Claudia's hands and feet were bound. With a gasp, she grabbed onto Balinus' arm, realizing what she was looking at.

Claudia wasn't dead yet.

Elisabeth began to tremble all over. "They're burying her alive."

With a grim twist to his mouth, Balinus nodded.

The huge procession came to a stop in an open field, beyond the city wall where a pile of dirt sat next to a freshly dug grave.

The priests untied Claudia's hands and feet and lowered a ladder into the hole.

Elisabeth winced when Claudia rose from the stretcher and then positioned herself at the top of the ladder. When her dress stuck on the first rung, the priest reached out to help her, but she stared at him with dull eyes and waved him away instead, refusing to touch his extended hand. Untangling her gown, she then continued down the ladder to her death chamber.

Elisabeth's chest caved in when Claudia disappeared from sight and she struggled to hold back tears.

A high priest chanted prayers.

The ladder was lifted away and slaves quickly shoveled the dirt back in place, hiding any sign of what had just happened.

"I can't…" She struggled to catch her breath while walking away. "I can't watch this."

"This way," Balinus whispered, leading her away from the field, toward a paved road.

As they marched for hours, Rome faded into the distance before vanishing along the horizon. Elisabeth wiped sweat from her brow and adjusted the *palla*, thankful for the protection it gave from the blazing sun.

"I'll never complain about being cold again." She stared at her feet as they trudged along before looking at Balinus with puffy red eyes. "There was no way we could have saved Claudia, was there?"

"None at all," Balinus said with a deep sigh.

****

The hot days seemed endless as they continued hiking south to Pompeii. Punch-drunk with exhaustion, she couldn't help but snort at the predicament she found herself in. Dressed like a character straight out of a bible story, with a knife tied to her leg for protection, Elisabeth journeyed with an ancient philosopher across the rugged backcountry of the Roman Empire and straight toward a town about to be annihilated by a volcanic eruption. All to save the life of a cheeky slave she'd found it impossible not to fall for. Elisabeth forced a watery smile into place and patted the donkey walking next to her. Looking at the love knot tied to her wrist, she held her breath, thinking of David.

"You better still be alive," she mumbled to herself.

Chapter Twenty-Eight

The old man was correct. It took ten nights to reach Pompeii. Because they'd avoided the cities and lived off the land, the silver candlesticks did not need to be sold. Elisabeth's eyes widened as they walked up a steep road and through a narrow pedestrian gate into the city. Ahead of her, slightly to the right, a lush mountain loomed over Pompeii like a sleeping giant.

Elisabeth stopped walking and extended her hand to Balinus in a formal farewell. "Thank you for bringing me here."

The old man snorted and kept walking.

"Hey!" She jogged to catch up to him. "You promised you'd leave once we got here."

"Although you insisted," he said with a curt nod, "I did not make any such promise."

"Balinus, do you see that mountain over there? Any day now it's going to rain fire and brimstone on this city and kill anyone and anything in its path. You cannot stay in Pompeii or any of the towns nearby."

Balinus cleared his throat. "I am aware of that, but I fear Aurelius still remains with both his family and that of Julius Polybius'."

Elisabeth held her stomach. "You don't think he left?"

With a furrowed brow, he shook his head. "Not if I know Aurelius."

"Oh, crap." She let out a long, low sigh and followed the old man.

They walked down what appeared to be a main street and Elisabeth's stomach growled as the smell of yeasty bread drifted in the air. A dog slurped from a bowl of water on the ground outside of a restaurant and people around them stopped to chat with one another. After about eight blocks, Balinus stopped and knocked on a large wooden door before he unloaded their bags from the donkey.

"Let's hope I am wrong this time," he said with a shaky voice as he threw the packs onto his back.

Elisabeth twisted the palla in her hand, hoping Aurelius had taken his family and left.

A tall slave answered the door. With a hint of a smile, he ushered them inside. "I will get the master."

They waited in a spacious two-story foyer with walls made of white rock slabs above a decorative black trim. Straight ahead, a single step led up to an atrium littered with ladders and buckets. The plain plaster walls suggested it was in the middle of a renovation. Beyond that was another doorway and sheer curtains blowing on a breeze.

A thin man with graying-blond hair waltzed across the atrium and hopped playfully down the step. As he held his arms out, his blue eyes sparkled and his lips pursed into an amused smile. "Balinus."

"Polybius!"

Three young boys ran through the front door, almost knocking over a ladder as they tore through the atrium before disappearing around a corner. Next, a little blonde girl in a long pink dress came running from the back of the house and through the atrium toward the front door, wailing at the top of her lungs.

"Papa!"

Polybius rolled his eyes and swept the little girl into his arms. "Were your brothers teasing you again, *lumen meum*?"

"Yes." Wide-eyed, the little girl sniffled while glancing from Elisabeth to Balinus. A second later, she jumped out of her father's arms and ran back after the boys. "I told Papa on you!"

Elisabeth couldn't help chuckling.

"Good to see you, old friend." Polybius pulled Balinus into a hug. "And this must be the girl bitten by the viper. I heard quite the tale from Aurelius," he said with a small laugh. He then turned around and shouted, "Aurelius!"

Elisabeth's heart sank and Balinus' shoulders dropped, but then he propped them up again. "Yes, this young lady is Elisabeth. Think of her as…as my adopted kin."

She blushed and looked at him with a soft expression.

"I thought I smelled something," Aurelius said with a grin as he poked his head out from around the corner.

"Father!" With a hearty laugh, a young lady tucked a lock of shiny blonde hair behind her ear and then gave him a playful smack.

Elisabeth grabbed Balinus' arm. "You get them to leave and I will find Aquarius," she whispered in his ear. "As soon as you see any activity from that mountain, you walk away from this city and do not stop."

Balinus looked down at his feet and nodded before

looking up again with a warm smile. "Aurelia, my goodness, I haven't laid eyes on you since you were knee high."

"I am a bit taller." She chuckled, smoothing her dress over a pregnant belly. "And a lot rounder." Aurelia smiled and stole a glance at Elisabeth.

"Well, you've grown into a beautiful young woman," Balinus said.

"She certainly has." Aurelius linked his arm through his daughter's as they strolled closer. "Thank the gods she looks like me and not her mother." His droopy eyes rolled up to the ceiling as he bit down on a smile.

Aurelia shot her father a bemused grin.

"Come inside, come inside," Polybius insisted and motioned a slave over to collect Balinus' bags.

Aurelia blinked while staring at Elisabeth and then her lips slightly parted. "Are you the one who survived the deadly snake bite?"

"Indeed she is." Aurelius laughed. "And I think you two girls will get along very…" His voice trailed off as he wandered away with Balinus and Polybius.

Aurelia's arms flew up in excitement. "I want to hear all about your tales of adventure. And romance," she added with a wink. "You don't look anything like I pictured."

Elisabeth cringed when looking down at the filthy tunic she'd spent ten days traveling in. "I'd do anything for a bath and a change of clothes, but I haven't time. There's someone I need to find right away."

Aurelia lowered her voice and wiggled both eyebrows. "Who-do-you-have-to-find?"

"A certain gladiator."

"By Jupiter…" Aurelia bounced from foot to foot. "It's one of the men who rescued you from the satyr, isn't it?" She sucked in a quick breath. "Please don't say it's Celadus the Thracian. My friends and I have loved him since—"

"His name is Aquarius." Elisabeth made her way to the door, determined to search every last inch of this city for him.

"Wait, wait, wait." Aurelia waved her arms. "I am going to help you. Just give me a minute to grab some things."

Grateful to have help, Elisabeth bit her lips to keep from smiling.

Aurelia returned a few minutes later, supporting her pregnant belly with one hand while handing a young slave girl a basket. "You'll be happy to know there is a banquet tonight and all the gladiators will be in attendance." She flashed a cheeky grin before stepping out of the house.

Elisabeth's mouth fell open. "Really?"

"Really."

Her heart raced at the thought of seeing David again in a few hours. She followed Aurelia along the street, no longer caring where they went. It had been at least two months since she and David had been sold into slavery and separated—and since Cato stole the necklace, trapping her here.

Tonight she'd fix everything.

Elisabeth wanted to twirl with happiness and break into song. Rejuvenated with hope, she glanced behind and gave the slave girl who followed them a wave. About eight years old, with sun-kissed golden-brown hair tied up off her neck, she stared back with wide brown eyes.

"I don't think you'll have any trouble finding your sweetheart tonight," Aurelia said as they used stepping stones at the intersection to cross the street.

Elisabeth did a double-take, noticing a sewer grate at the curb.

"But, I should warn you the women will be falling all over themselves in front of the gladiators...especially the Thracian, so..." She gave Elisabeth a conspiratorial wink. "You cannot go looking like that. We're going to the baths."

Elisabeth opened and then closed her mouth. While staring at Mt. Vesuvius ahead of her, it pretended to look like any other peaceful mountain nestled between the city and the sea. Her brows pulled together, thinking back to the details of the story she'd read to Mrs. Waters. They'll have an hour or two to get out of Pompeii once the eruption begins at about noon.

Noon.

With a slow smile, Elisabeth realized it wasn't happening today.

She looked down at the filthy dress she'd spent almost two weeks traveling in. "All right. Let's go."

****

After they paid an entrance fee for the baths, Aurelia ushered Elisabeth into a change room. Filled with chatty, laughing women of all ages, the large, airy space had vaulted ceilings and walls decorated with elaborate mosaics and paintings.

"Here." Aurelia handed her an herbal scented sheet and undressed. "For some reason, they're having problems with the fountains." She hung her dress on a hook after placing sandals in a cubby. "Some of the springs have dried up, but at least the pools are still in operation."

"Really?" Fear enveloped Elisabeth with the knowledge it was the awakening volcano that caused the springs around it to run dry. She undressed and wrapped the sheet around her chest. "I've heard it said that Vesuvius is a fire mountain. That could be a sign that it's—"

"A fire mountain?" Aurelia laughed. "I don't believe that for one minute." She then whispered something to the little slave girl, who took the basket and ran off.

The sound of gentle splashing made Elisabeth smile as they walked past a series of spa-like pools filled with female bathers. Aurelia stopped where a small group of slaves gathered around a table of scented oils and lotions. She dropped her sheet and a woman began to rub oil into her skin like one would use soap.

Elisabeth swallowed the lump in her throat, trying to position herself behind a potted tree. "When in Rome…" she mumbled before dropping her sheet as well. She took deep breaths, drinking in the soft, warm fragrance of the luxurious oil.

After the slave scraped her skin with a metal utensil, Elisabeth entered a pool lined with intricate mosaic tiles. The water soothed tired muscles and she closed her eyes, imagining this was a hotel spa a million miles away rather than a Roman bath house in Pompeii. She listened to the soft murmurs of Aurelia and the other ladies laughing and gossiping, not realizing how much she'd needed to rest and recharge. It felt like food for the soul.

"Guess what I have?" Aurelia said with a sing-song

voice once they returned to the change room after bathing and having their hair done. She then motioned to her slave.

Elisabeth's posture picked up while grabbing her filthy tunic from the hook, wishing she'd brought the other dress to wear. "I have no idea."

The little girl walked over with a blue gown draped across her arms.

"Recognize anything? They've cleaned it for you."

Elisabeth tossed the work tunic onto the bench as her eyes widened. "Oh my goodness." She adjusted the sheet around herself and whispered a thank you to the child before taking the dress from her. "Did you get this from Balinus?"

Aurelia nodded and let out a deep, gratifying sigh. "I think of everything. Now, do everyone a favor and throw that ugly tunic away, will you?" She grabbed the utilitarian uniform from the bench.

"Shouldn't I give it to a slave or something?" Elisabeth asked while stepping into the beautiful dress Mrs. Waters had given to her. With a slow disbelieving shake of her head, she reminded herself that *she* was Mrs. Waters.

Aurelia crunched the tunic into a ball and threw it across the room. "Believe me, even the slaves don't want this one."

****

By dinner time, the oppressive heat subsided. Activity on the streets outside began to pick up and the two families continued to lounge about, as if on island time, while children scampered around the house.

"Can we go to the banquet now?" Elisabeth's palms were sweaty as she whispered to Balinus.

"I do not know, can we?"

She covered her face and then peaked. "I mean, is it time?"

Balinus stood and extended his elbow. "I will return shortly, gentlemen," he said to Aurelius and Polybius. "I am going to escort Elisabeth to the gladiator banquet to find—"

"Whatever happened to that boy, Aquarius?" Aurelius paused to examine her. "I thought for sure you two—"

"That is exactly who I'm looking for," Elisabeth said with a sigh.

Aurelius sat up straighter. "That boy is a gladiator now? What on earth…?"

"It's a long story," Balinus said with a grave expression.

"Well I for one want to hear it. I am coming with you."

With a furrowed brow, Aurelia stood up. "Wait for me. I'd like to come too."

"Greetings." A handsome young man with curly blond hair walked into the *peristyle* followed by two elegant middle-aged women, obviously his mother and mother-in-law. The man made his way toward Aurelia. "Where is everyone going?"

She leaned against him with a silly grin. "To the gladiator banquet."

"Oh…no-no-no," He chuckled and kissed her forehead. "I'm not letting my beautiful wife anywhere near Celadus the Thracian."

"But, Marius, he's the delight of all the young girls," she teased.

"Which is exactly why I insist on going with you,"

Marius said with a wide-eyed look that made Aurelia break into a fit of giggles.

"Theodora and I will remain and leave the men and the young ladies to the gladiators," one of the mothers said.

Containing anxiety building up, Elisabeth shook her hands while turning to Balinus. "I don't know what I'm going to do if Aquarius isn't there."

The old man stopped and held both her hands in his. "Take a deep breath, my dear."

Elisabeth took a shaky breath.

"A wise sage once said, 'To the mind that is still, the whole universe surrenders.'"

She turned away to gather her thoughts and then looked back at him with teary eyes. "If I stop all the worrying and clear my mind of all the questions, it will be easier to receive the answers and know what to do?"

With a smile, he tapped her nose and nodded.

She linked her arm through his and followed Aurelia and the men out the door.

Chapter Twenty-Nine

Ahead of her, the sidewalks were lined with people, young and old, and in the distance, music played. As the volume increased, she realized the performers were moving closer. Elisabeth's party came to a stop where crowds lined both sides of the street.

The musicians turned a corner and came into view. Dressed in a colorful array of tunics, they marched while making their noise. It wasn't pretty. One man blew into that horrible sounding aulos; one played on a little guitar. Others clanged drums while accompanied by flutes—or something like that.

She then saw the parade of gladiators and her heart stopped. A sea of tanned physiques, dressed in muddy shades of mustard, sienna and brown, they marched in two straight lines, without armor, toward their banquet.

As the spectators crammed together, Elisabeth craned her neck to get a better view; Aurelia winked and discreetly fanned herself, trying to be funny. Her eyes then widened, touching her stomach before reaching for Marius.

With a pasted-on smile, Elisabeth crossed and uncrossed her arms, scanning the parade for David while people bumped into her.

"BARCA!" A man shouted out and the crowd cheered.

The shuffle of feet grew louder as the gladiators marched closer.

Elisabeth swallowed hard.

"I love you, Lugo!" a woman's high-pitched voice yelled out and the crowd started laughing.

The cheers around Elisabeth became louder as the gladiators filed past the spectators.

"Marius and I are taking Aurelia home," Aurelius shouted in Balinus' ear.

Balinus nodded in understanding and Elisabeth's brow wrinkled. "Is she all right?"

"Just overheated and in need of rest." Aurelius then followed his daughter and son-in-law away from the crowd.

Elisabeth turned back to the gladiators and wanted to crumple to the floor when she finally saw David.

Marching beside Cato, they both looked different somehow. On a physical level, their muscles were more sculpted than before, but it was deeper than that. Cato seemed ice cold as he stared straight ahead, and gone was any hint of playfulness on David's face.

Elisabeth's hand covered her mouth as her eyes filled with tears. David caught the movement and looked her way. His own eyes widened, locking on hers. And then he was gone.

Balinus gently squeezed Elisabeth's shoulder.

"CELADUS!"

The crowd went wild when they saw the last gladiator. Dressed in a leather kilt and wearing a collar with shoulder pads, he followed the parade on a chariot led by two horses; one black, the other white. With short dark hair and a stubble beard, Celadus the Thracian held the reins with one hand and waved to the crowd with the other, like a total rock star.

The gladiators disappeared through a tall doorway and most of the crowd followed.

Elisabeth turned to Balinus. "You need to go back and do everything to make Aurelius and his family leave. I will take care of Aquarius and Cato."

With unnatural stillness, the old man nodded. "Would you remember how to find my brother's house in Rome?"

"I think so. The bakery beside it has that red and white awning."

"Meet me there so I know you've all survived."

While nodding, her nostrils flared. "And if Aurelius and his family are too stubborn to leave…" She gave him a pained stare and wiped a stray tear away at the thought. "Promise me you'll still go. When that mountain starts to erupt, promise me you will leave, even if it's by yourself. Promise me."

With a strained smile, the old man pulled Elisabeth into a hug. "I promise. Now go. Rescue your boy," he whispered to her.

Elisabeth watched Balinus turn and walk back down the street toward Polybius' house. Her heart broke wondering if she'd ever see him again.

Clutching at her stomach, she followed the crowd past the now-empty chariot and through wooden doors flanked by armed guards. The dark-skinned man with the eye patch who'd bought David and Cato lingered near the entrance. As Elisabeth wandered into a courtyard, chickens roamed the stone floors, pecking at hay strewn about. In the center, wooden tables and stools were set for the massive feast. Garlands of shiny green leaves hung from the walls and a pig roasted on a fire pit at the back of the premises, far too close to a wooden staircase. She glanced at the top of the stairs and watched as another guard walked through a door that looked ready to fall off its hinges.

Celadus and some of the gladiators were already seated at the center tables, digging into the food. Most of the people from the street stood around watching and talking about them, placing bets on tomorrow's games. Young ladies huddled in corners, pointing and giggling, while a few older women were brazen enough to walk closer and whisper God-knows-what into gladiators' ears. Elisabeth scanned the tables and saw Cato. After catching his eye, his face stretched into a snarl before he averted his gaze.

She swallowed the lump in her throat and continued to search for David, wondering where he went.

A gladiator with blond hair walked past Elisabeth and then stopped, looking at her sideways with an intimidating stare, not once blinking.

Her eyes widened and she froze, unable to speak.

"Are you looking for someone?" he asked in a gravelly voice.

She replied with a quick nod.

"Then, I'm right here." With a wink, he leaned in closer and began to twirl a lock of her hair around his fingers while flashing the smallest of smirks. "Don't worry, I won't bite."

"Hands off this one, Soran," David said as he swooped in and grabbed Elisabeth around the waist into a bear hug, lifting her feet off the floor. "This one's all mine."

She gasped, throwing her arms around him.

He let out a small, nervous laugh and they openly stared at each other for a moment before David touched his forehead to hers. Overcome with relief, she burrowed against his neck and broke down crying.

While still holding Elisabeth, he marched through the crowd to a corner of the courtyard before lowering her feet to the ground again.

"No." Her arms locked. "I don't want to let go of you yet," she whispered into his neck, which was now wet from her tears.

David hugged Elisabeth even tighter and kissed her head. When finally wiping her eyes and looking up at him, he held the sides of her face in his hands. His small, sad smile was capable of melting hearts. "I cannot believe you are here."

"I did it." Elisabeth let out a shaky laugh as a feeling of breathlessness washed over her. "I found you." With a grin that could not be contained, she bounced onto tiptoes and smothered his face with playful kisses while he chuckled. She then pulled away and pursed her lips, failing miserably in an attempt not to smile.

David's feverish eyes searched Elisabeth's, causing her heart to pound. With a disbelieving shake of the head, he then pushed her up against the wall and pressed his lips to hers.

She would have kissed him forever, but a loaf of bread bounced off his shoulder.

Then another.

And another.

As the gladiators at the tables became rowdier, they started to shout vulgar suggestions across the room for David.

He ignored the jibes as Elisabeth looked up at him "We have to get out of Pompeii," she whispered. "Tonight."

With a heavy sigh, he turned and leaned against the wall himself, pulling Elisabeth's back against him and wrapping his arms around her chest so they could both survey the huge space. "It won't be possible tonight," he whispered in her ear. "The crowds of people and the armed guards are both here to prevent that from happening."

Her head drooped while sagging against him. "What are we going to do? We're running out of time."

She felt David's body stiffen. "Maybe you could rent Cato and I."

Elisabeth turned around to look at him. "What do you mean?"

"Last week, a wealthy Patrician placed a bet on me in the arena."

"You've…you've already fought in the arena?"

David pulled her closer. "I'm fine, *cor meum,*" he whispered while rubbing her back. "After I won, the Patrician gave me a generous tip." When reaching for his money pouch, Elisabeth noticed he wore a wide leather belt now instead of a sling. His shoulders dropped after counting the money. "Never mind," he said with a sad smile.

"What was your plan?"

"Well, Celadus is often called away to…"—he paused, trying to find the right word—"to *appointments* with wealthy women. The Thracian doesn't arrive back at the barracks until a few hours later, and sometimes, not until the next morning."

Elisabeth's eyebrows squished together.

"Appointments? What kind of appointments?"

With a knowing look, he reached for her fingers.

"Oh," she said in an uncertain tone and then her eyes widened. "OH!"

David lowered his head and chuckled to himself before looking up with a grin. "You're adorable." He then lifted her hand to kiss it.

"Well…" Feeling her cheeks flush, she cleared her throat. "How much would an *appointment* with you cost?"

When David clamped his lips together and tried not to laugh, she gave him a playful pinch.

"I wouldn't be as expensive as the Thracian, but…then again, you'd have to request both Cato and I."

"I'm staying at a house nearby." Elisabeth's breath hitched. "I could send for you and Cato after the banquet tonight and then we could get out of Pompeii."

"But Cato and I are still new…" His forehead wrinkled. "They'll be guards stationed outside the doors."

She wrapped her arms around his waist. "We'll figure something out."

"If only we had one of your jewels to pay the *lanista*. I have no idea what Cato did with your box, but if I—"

"Aquarius," she said with a grin. "I have two—rather large—silver candlesticks in my possession that I can sell."

With a slow, disbelieving shake of his head, a smile spread across David's face and Elisabeth giggled while they stared at each other.

"Then, that's our plan," he said. "Bring the silver

to the barracks after the feast tonight and request a private audience with Cato and I for your...party."

She released an appreciative sigh and leaned against him while observing the banquet. When Cato stood and slammed his fists into the table, she looked up at David. "Balinus didn't take my crystal. It was Cato," she said with a gentle tone. "We have to get it back from him."

David's mouth fell open as he stared at her.

"He tricked us. It was a sleight of hand trick and he blamed the old man. I traveled here from Rome *with* Balinus."

"Aquarius, come eat something," Cato muttered as he walked up to David, avoiding eye contact with Elisabeth. "You need your strength for the arena tomorrow."

David's nostrils flared as he pushed Elisabeth safely behind him.

Cato's face turned ashen and he swallowed hard. "What is wrong, brother?"

"Brother?" He grabbed the neck of Cato's tunic into his fists. "Do not ever call me brother again." David's muscles twitched beneath his skin as he hissed at him. "You deceived me."

A hush fell over the banquet and people started to point in their direction.

"Wh...what are you talking about?"

"Do not lie to me, Cato," he whispered through clenched teeth as a crowd gathered around. "Was it not enough to steal *my* freedom? When you took Elisabeth's necklace, you not only took her freedom, you took her entire world." He released his grip on Cato and shoved him hard while taking an intimidating step

385

forward. "What in the name of Jupiter were you thinking?"

The gladiators at the table, drunk from wine, heckled and egged them on.

Cato stumbled back. "I was trying to help you. If I forced her to choose between you and her home, you'd have seen that…" His arms hung limp at his sides. "I did it for you, Aquarius." Cato looked past David and then his posture stiffened as he glared at Elisabeth. "It didn't go as anticipated."

David turned his back to Cato and squeezed his eyes shut. His neck corded and he planted his feet wide apart.

"I wish I'd just killed her instead," Cato whispered in a scathing tone.

Elisabeth's head jerked back.

David whipped around and lunged for Cato, grabbing him by the throat, forcing him to his knees. "Have you gone mad?" His choke-hold tightened and Cato gasped for air, but didn't fight back. "If you *ever* lay a finger…"

The gladiators broke out into wild laughter as the closest guard raced toward them.

"You…" David's lips pulled back, baring his teeth. "You are dead to me," he whispered before letting go of Cato.

"All right, save it for the arena, you two," the guard said while shaking his head and pushing them apart.

At that moment, Cato reached over, unsheathed the guard's sword, and knocked David out of the way. With an ugly laugh, he held it up to Elisabeth's throat and backed her into the wall. "It would be so easy…"

Her legs wanted to crumple beneath her, but the

blade under her chin forced her to remain upright.

Out of the corner of her eye, she saw David instinctively reach for his belt before realizing he wasn't carrying a sling.

Cato's bloodshot eyes glared at Elisabeth as he took a small step closer. "Every time I look at your face, I am reminded of everything I lost: my mother, my brother, my—"

"Drop your sword, gladiator!" Patch screamed as more of the guards raced toward him.

"Aquarius!" Blowing a wolf-whistle to get David's attention, Soran tossed him a carving knife from a table overflowing with food. It landed on the ground at his feet.

"The day you arrived..." Cato let out an odd, high-pitched laugh as he kept his focus on Elisabeth. "The day you arrived we mistook for a blessing, but..."

David crouched low, reached for the knife, and aimed.

Elisabeth squeezed her eyes shut as her pulse raced.

"You're naught but a curse," Cato said through clenched teeth. "A plague on—" He then let out an ear-piercing roar, stumbled to the side, and dropped the sword.

Cato's eyes watered and David tackled him to the ground, his fists flying until four guards pulled them apart.

"Back to the barracks for both of them," the man with the patch yelled.

As a slave wrapped Cato's bleeding leg with a napkin, Elisabeth could see it was a deep gash from being grazed, rather than a stab wound.

She rocked back and forth as David was shackled.

With the show now over, the festivities and noise level returned to normal.

"Wait," Elisabeth said to Patch as he marched past her. "I'd like a private audience with that one." She stopped wringing her hands to point at David. "He just saved my life. I…I can pay you…"

Patch shook his head and kept walking. "These two need to cool off tonight. There's a lot of money riding on tomorrow's games," he called back over his shoulder.

David frowned, lowering his chin as he was led to the exit. He then turned around and stared at Elisabeth with bulging eyes.

She felt the color drain from her face when she saw what he saw.

Patch stood in the doorway, talking to Rufus.

With rasping breaths, Elisabeth slipped behind a pillar to hide, realizing Rufus was here to return her to the House of Vesta in Rome.

"What's so special about Pompeii?" he'd asked in the marketplace after David had been sold. The slave dealer knew exactly who and where she'd run to.

Her hands curled into tight fists as her eyes scanned the room, looking for another exit.

Soran stood up, walking toward her with a set jaw.

Elisabeth swallowed hard, avoiding eye contact with the gladiator.

His confident stride didn't slow as he drew nearer. "Walk with me," he whispered in an intimidating voice as he put his arm around her shoulders. "Aquarius is my friend."

She gave him a wide-eyed look.

"Told you I won't bite," he said in a more easy-going manner.

Soran moved stealthily, shielding Elisabeth from Rufus' view with his own body as the slave dealer wandered the premises. The gladiator weaved through the crowd, leading the way to the opposite side of the courtyard and then to the exit.

Elisabeth placed a hand on her heart and looked up at him. "Thank you," she whispered.

He gave a small nod of his head before she slipped out the door.

Small pieces of white marble embedded in the road reflected both moonlight and lamplight, illuminating the streets. Elisabeth held her breath while knocking on Polybius' door a few minutes later, not sure if anyone had remained behind in Pompeii to answer it.

She cursed under her breath when it flew open and she was greeted by one of the young boys. He looked at her wide-eyed before running off, crashing into Balinus on his way out of the foyer.

"They haven't left yet?"

The old man shook his head and sighed. "Apparently they'll believe it when they see it."

She rubbed both hands over her face and let out a dramatic groan.

Balinus wrinkled his brow. "What of Aquarius and Cato?"

Elisabeth's gaze flitted around the room while struggling to hold back tears. "Aquarius and I have a plan, but he must first survive the arena tomorrow."

The old man looked at her with a thoughtful expression.

She brought a shaky hand to her forehead. "Will you tell everyone I had a headache and went to bed?"

"Of course," he said with a gentle tone. "Of course."

Chapter Thirty

Elisabeth tugged at her bottom lip while pacing in the empty peristyle the next morning, waiting for the others. Aurelia's little slave rushed along the colonnade. With trembling hands, she stopped the child. "What's your name?"

The little girl's eyebrows rose when looking up. "Larisa."

Elisabeth crouched down in front of her. "Do you want to know a secret, Larisa?"

She nodded slowly.

"I hunt giants."

Larisa's lips parted.

"Do you see Mt. Vesuvius, over there?" She pointed up over the colonnade toward the mountain. "There's a giant sleeping inside of it."

The little girl jerked her head back.

"Now, I want you to listen to me very carefully. That sleeping giant is starting to wake up after a *really* long nap. He's going to be grumpy and throw rocks out of it. When that starts to happen, I want you to run out of Pompeii and go as far away as possible. You do not want to be here when that giant comes down the mountain and into Pompeii, do you?"

The color drained from Larisa's face. "No."

"Even if adults tell you to stay inside, or that the gods are angry, I want you to run as fast as you can.

Don't stop and don't try to hide. Remember, other people are not giant hunters like I am. Right?"

Larisa nodded.

"So, even though you might be scared, that's all right. You're only scared because you're being super brave. When he starts to wake up, you run away from here and do not stop for two whole days. Can you promise me you'll do that?"

"I promise," she said in a quiet voice.

"Good girl," Elisabeth whispered as the others started to come out of their rooms, dressed and ready for the games.

Larisa's eyes widened and then she hurried off to complete whatever task she'd been sent to do.

Elisabeth made her way down the crowded streets toward the amphitheater with the two families. Not a fan of the sport, Balinus opted to stay behind.

When they turned a corner, Aurelia adjusted her lavender *palla*. "Finally, some shade." The hem of her violet dress fluttered in front of her, thanks to a breeze off the bay. She and Marius walked ahead of their parents, arm in arm, down a bustling tree-lined promenade. Edged with colorful wooden stalls, shopkeepers called out to fans en route to the games, enticing them to buy souvenirs and edible goodies.

Elisabeth glanced behind at the volcano. It still looked like a lush, green mountain. However, she knew it was just a matter of time before it exploded with a force more powerful than a thousand nuclear bombs.

The amphitheater loomed ahead of her; thick stone walls challenging Mt. Vesuvius to a battle of their own. Heavy rope extended from winches on the ground up to wooden masts that lined the upper rim of the building.

Elisabeth realized it supported an awning that provided shade for the fans inside the venue.

She followed her party up an external staircase crammed shoulder to shoulder with people. Sketches of gladiators lined the walls and the crowd moved into an arched corridor where light streamed through doorways leading to the stands.

Elisabeth walked out of the passage and stood overlooking the beautiful arena. Attached to ropes and brackets, a grayish-beige awning covered the spectator stands, while the circular opening in the center allowed sunlight to dramatically illuminate the field. Large square windows encircled the top of the amphitheater wall, allowing light to flood in.

She followed the others down to their seats. Although it held tens of thousands of spectators and was decorated with colorful frescos, the stadium itself dwarfed in size and grandeur compared to both the Circus Maximus and, no doubt, the Coliseum in Rome. She took a seat next to Aurelius and surveyed the excited crowd. Men laughed while drinking from large goblets, vendors climbed up and down the stairs selling refreshments, and women fanned themselves to keep cool. If you put the people in modern clothes this might have been a baseball game rather than a gladiatorial contest.

Music began and the audience cheered. Elisabeth clasped her hands in her lap, trying to stop them from trembling.

Six armed guards, wearing red tunics and metal helmets, marched out of a grand entryway that led to the sandy arena floor. Two stopped to flank the entrance, spears upright beside them, while the others led the procession of gladiators clockwise around the ring, accompanied by fanfare trumpets.

Carrying their helmets and weapons, the gladiators were on parade for the fans.

"Lugo!" someone screamed and the cheers grew louder.

Elisabeth's hands flew to her chest when she saw David.

Unlike most of the others, he carried neither a helmet nor shield. Dressed in a skirted loincloth with a wide leather belt and sandals, his only protective armor was a metal shoulder guard that extended down one arm. In one hand he held a dagger and in the other, a length of rope.

Aurelius pointed at David and then looked at Elisabeth with a wrinkled brow. "By the gods, that…that *laquearius* is Aquarius, is he not?"

She clutched her stomach. "It is."

"Well…" He swallowed a lump in his throat and leaned closer. "I'm sure he will come out of this unharmed." His wavering smile was meant to reassure. "Gods willing."

Elisabeth held her breath and nodded.

Two of the guards leading the parade stopped at another entrance on the opposite end of the arena, while the gladiators continued to loop around back to where they started.

She recognized Soran. He carried a bronze helmet decorated with bright feathers, followed by Cato who wore a protective breastplate.

About forty gladiators marched around the circular arena before disappearing through the grand entryway again.

The crowd started chanting.

"CEL-A-DUS!"

"CEL-A-DUS!"

At last, the Thracian stepped out into the spotlight. He carried his helmet and a huge rectangular shield in one hand while waving his sword in the air at his fans with the other. As he strutted around the arena, Elisabeth's eyes filled with tears at the memory of the hilarious way David had charmed the crowd the first day she'd arrived here in Ancient Rome: flirting with the ladies, flexing imaginary muscles, and running a mock victory lap… all before fainting.

That day was a lifetime ago.

With a now empty arena floor in front of them, the spectators hooted and hollered, calling for the games to commence. The fanfare began again and the crowd cheered even louder as a gladiator stepped out of the darkness and stood in the archway. Although his face was hidden behind a bronze helmet decorated with bright feathers, as he lumbered his way to the center, Elisabeth lowered her head.

It was Soran.

Bare-chested and dressed in a loin cloth, he stood in the arena and with a roar, thrust his spear into the air. He raised his small round shield over his head while turning to let the screaming audience admire him. Unlike David, he wore heavy armor on one arm and both of his legs. Soran made a dramatic lunge with his sharp lance, the musicians keeping time with his movements.

Elisabeth held her breath as she glanced back to the entrance.

A shadow lurked in the doorway.

Her mouth went dry. David walked out.

He planted his feet wide and exaggeratedly cracked his neck, tilting it left and right to appear intimidating. David then pointed his dagger toward the crowd while holding the rope in his other hand. He turned in a circle for the cheering spectators and then thrust his hips and chest out with both arms up in the air, whipping the crowd into a frenzy.

The hair lifted on the back of Elisabeth's neck.

Four more gladiators made dramatic entrances and then all six saluted a man sitting in an ornate, covered section of the stands.

When music signaled the start of the games, the gladiators ran and charged one another. Swords, shields, and a trident clashed and David, the least protected, stepped back to put distance between himself and the more heavily armed gladiators.

Soran gave chase. Elisabeth couldn't look away as David sheathed his dagger and draped the rope between his hands. From where she watched, it looked like the two ends were each tied in a knot.

David spun the lasso to the left and right of him, faster and faster until it created a buzzing sound that filled the arena. He then snapped it against the ground for dramatic effect as two other gladiators fought nearby, their wide swords clashing over and over again.

The crowd cheered. Soran spread his legs wide and raised his spear.

Like the crack of a whip, David aimed for Soran's bare chest. The gladiator blocked with his shield; lunged with his lance.

David pulled back and whirled the rope in front of him so quickly, it created a protective wall. Unable to attack, Soran retreated and Elisabeth let out a huge breath. David stepped away, draping the cord between his hands while calculating the next move.

She looked away for a moment to watch two other gladiators. One wore a full-faced helmet and the other she recognized as Lugo from the opening parade. The one with the helmet stalked closer and Lugo lunged with his sword but missed.

The crowd let out a collective gasp.

Helmet leaned in. He punched Lugo across the face with the hilt of his sword and then kneed him in the stomach before karate-chopping his upper back.

Lugo fell to his knees.

"Get up, Lugo!" someone in the stands yelled.

"GET UP!"

Fans screamed and booed as Helmet grabbed a chunk of Lugo's hair and ran with him, bashing his head into the wall of the spectator stands.

Helmet held his arms up in triumph as Lugo lay face down on the ground. He then delivered a brutal kick to Lugo's stomach.

Helmet retrieved his nearby shield, banging his sword against it, taunting the crowd. While the spectators jeered and hissed, he walked back to Lugo, placed a foot on his shoulder, and stood with his arms in the air, victorious.

The manic crowd jumped to their feet; some cheering, most booing.

Helmet picked Lugo up by the scruff of the neck. With a sword to his throat, he dragged him to the center of the field toward the man in the gilded section.

"Lugo, you idiot!" a man screamed at the top of his lungs.

Elisabeth gasped, turning her attention back to David as he pummeled Soran's exposed shoulder and bare torso with the ends of the rope. Left. Right. Left. Right. Left. Right. He whipped over and over again until Soran stumbled back.

Elisabeth didn't blink her eyes for fear of missing a single move.

David spun the lasso over his head like one of his slings, holding the two ends in his hand.

Neither gladiator looked away from the other.

Soran charged and David snapped one end of the rope. The knotted end wrapped around Soran's spear. With a quick, hard tug, David sent the spear crashing to the ground.

The crowd roared in approval and Elisabeth held her breath.

Two men carrying a stretcher dashed across the field and over to Lugo. They lifted his body from the blood-stained sand and carried him to the doorway opposite the one the gladiators had entered.

As Soran dove for his spear, David ran at him, kicking the shield out of his other hand.

The shield rolled across the sand.

Elisabeth's hands covered her mouth.

Because David wasn't in heavy armor, it allowed him to move around quickly. He was far more nimble than Soran, but had no room for error.

Soran gripped his spear in one hand and David kicked the shield further away. When the gladiator charged at David, he whipped his rope. This time, Soran grabbed the end with his free hand.

Elisabeth froze, rooted to the spot.

A hush fell over the arena as the two faced one

another, each holding an end of David's rope while the other three gladiators battled on the opposite side of the pitch.

Soran positioned his spear in front of him. David widened his stance.

Instead of stepping back so he wasn't impaled, David grabbed an arm's length section of the rope, moving closer. Soran thrust forward to stab him, pulled back, and thrust again.

David flinched as he stepped to the side; the rope now positioned between him and the spear. He moved one hand up and the other down, knotting the lance in his rope.

Elisabeth let out a slight moan and the crowd whooped and cheered.

David landed a powerful kick into his opponent's gut. When Soran dropped to his knees, David flung the rope around his head, pulling the hand holding the spear along with it.

Elisabeth recognized the move from the brawl at Severina's. "Come on, Aquarius…" she mumbled.

With a final loop of the rope, David now had a noose around Soran's neck. He pulled the spear out of his tied hand and flipped him onto his back.

With one foot on Soran's stomach, David held the spear in the air with one hand and placed his other hand near his hip. He then looked up at the man in the gilded section for permission to finish the job.

"*Iugula! Iugula!*" the crowd screamed. "Kill him! Kill him!"

Elisabeth's heartbeat slowed. Soran didn't deserve to die any more than David did.

As the man in charge paused, exciting the crowd

even more, rolling thunder filled the air, and the earth beneath the arena bounced.

"EARTHQUAKE!"

Screaming people ran in all directions.

The ground continued to tremble and shake. Inner walls of the amphitheater crashed down around Elisabeth. Several of the tall wooden masts that held the awning smashed down into the crowd, bringing ropes, beams, and the billowy fabric with it.

She coughed while waving the dust and debris away, glancing up at Mt. Vesuvius, clearly visible thanks to the collapsed awning. Although expecting it, nothing could have prepared Elisabeth for the sight of the eruption. She curled both arms over her head protectively as the top of the mountain exploded, sending a mushroom cloud the size of a nuclear bomb blasting toward the heavens. A moment later, the sound followed, shaking her to the core as the air rippled around her.

She looked back at the center of the arena and gasped.

David, with his arm wrapped around Soran's neck for support, hobbled across the sand while holding his side.

Blood trickled with each step he took.

Chapter Thirty-One

People screamed, running toward the exits. A few stood in awe, staring at the volcano with no understanding of what they had witnessed. The smoke kept climbing, higher and higher into the sky.

"Elisabeth…" Aurelius had a dazed look on his face as his hand slowly covered his mouth. "It's happening, just like you said."

"Now do you believe me?" Her nostrils flared and she grabbed his arm. "You need to get everyone out of Pompeii as fast as you can!"

Aurelius' posture slumped. He turned away and his droopy eyes filled with tears as he reached for his wife.

The crowd pushed and shoved their way up, creating a stampede, but Elisabeth scrambled down the stands, over the seats, heading in the opposite direction.

When she reached the front row, she climbed over the wall and dropped onto the field, running toward the opening the gladiators had used.

Hundreds of others began to do the same thing; jumping down and running in the same direction, causing the doorway to bottleneck.

"Get up," she muttered anxiously while pulling a frail old man to his feet as the stampede continued around them.

Trying to stay outside of the wave of people to avoid being trampled, Elisabeth weaseled her way toward the huge doorway and hugged the wall, making her way through.

She cried out in pain when her toes smashed into a bench. With no room to move, she hopped up and sprinted along it, running her hand beside the stone wall to keep her balance. Straight ahead, bright light from the exit filled a short, steep tunnel. To her immediate left and right, a dark service corridor led to the gladiator cells.

Elisabeth jumped off the bench, making a right-hand turn, away from the panicked crowd as they raced toward metal gates thrown wide open.

"Aquarius!" she shouted while running along a curved passage. "Aquarius!"

Soran poked his head out into the corridor. "Over here."

With wobbly legs, she ran as fast as she could, sliding across the dirt floor while trying to stop at the doorway.

Elisabeth stumbled into a room reminiscent of a castle dungeon, with the added luxury of a lion's head waterspout mounted on the wall over a stone fountain.

David sat on the dusty ground with his legs stretched in front of him. "*Cor meum…*" He then leaned his head back and grimaced.

Elisabeth dropped to his side struggling to catch her breath. Next to them, a heavy stand holding a collection of swords, spears, and a trident, rattled together as the ground trembled again, followed by crashing sounds from the spectator stands above them. "Are you all right?"

He nodded while moving blood-soaked fingers away from his side to inspect the wound.

"No." Cato took a swig from a jug as his arm draped over the handle of a wooden hand truck. "He's not."

Elisabeth jerked her head back. She hadn't noticed him in the shadows.

"We need to…" Soran paused as his eyes darted across the top of a large wooden crate used as a table to hold medical supplies. "We need to bandage him up."

Cato handed the jug to David. "Drink some. It'll dull the pain."

"Gladly." With watery eyes, he gulped it down.

Still in his leg armor, Soran lumbered back carrying a bowl of water and a sponge along with a wad of linen cloth.

"I'll do it." Elisabeth grabbed the sponge and David squeezed his eyes shut. She gently washed the blood away and then took the jug of wine from him. "I need to disinfect it."

David's breaths sawed in and out as the alcohol stung his flesh. "Couldn't you just kiss it better, love?" he said through clenched teeth.

"Are you able to stand up so I can bandage you?"

David's legs shook as she helped him to his feet. He leaned back against the wall, staring at Elisabeth with a melancholy look. Garbed in the skirted loincloth and a metal arm guard, his state of undress caused her cheeks to flush.

"Press this tight," she said while holding a folded piece of fabric against the wound.

David held it and suddenly became still, watching Elisabeth's trembling fingers as she unfastened a strap on his bare chest. She pulled the armor off, dropped it on the floor, and wrapped the bandage around his waist.

When she looked at him with watery eyes, his brow wrinkled.

"We need to get out of here."

He held her shaky hand in his and glared at Cato. "Where's the necklace you stole from Elisabeth?" David grabbed his rope and hobbled a step away from the wall.

"Wait a minute." Soran's eyes widened. "Not only did you pull a sword on your best friend's girl, you stole her jewelry too?" He let out a long, low whistle. "I never trusted that guy," he muttered to Elisabeth as he removed his leg armor.

"Unfortunately, I did." With a heavy sigh, she watched David fiddle with his rope, loosening the fibers in the center to make it into a sling before tucking it into his wide leather belt.

Cato bowed his head as Elisabeth grabbed David's arm, pulling it around her shoulders to support his weight and stop him from walking on his own.

"Her necklace, it's…" Cato hesitated. "It's back at the barracks. We'll never make it there in time."

Elisabeth tried to blink away tears before looking up at David. "It's all right*."* She forced a watery smile. "Right now, the only thing that matters is getting out of Pompeii."

"Should we not head back to the barracks with the others?" Soran asked.

"No, we're leaving Pompeii." Cato brushed Soran aside and walked toward the door. "Trust us on this one."

David softly shook his head. "I'm taking Elisabeth to the barracks."

Cato scrubbed a hand over his face and groaned.

"Do you realize what you're saying?"

"Of course I do!" he shouted.

"Aquarius…" Elisabeth gave him a pained stare, knowing he planned to retrieve her crystal to send her safely home. "We're closer to the city gate than we are to the barracks. You know anyone who stays in Pompeii will die."

He rubbed a hand through his hair as he studied her.

"Well…" Soran's eyes widened. "No piece of jewelry is that valuable. If staying means we die, I vote for leaving." Ignoring Cato, he tossed David a sword, grabbed two for himself, and led them down the dark corridor.

When they reached the gladiator entrance, where the stampede of people had passed through, Elisabeth froze and stared out at the empty arena, now littered with debris that had crashed onto the floor of the ring.

She stepped out of the doorway and covered her head as small stones rained down. The cloud of dark ash from Mt. Vesuvius had crept toward Pompeii, plunging it into darkness.

"By the gods…" David's voice trailed off as he held one of the white pebbles in his hand. "They're light, like pumice."

Elisabeth's eyes clouded with tears. She walked further out onto the arena floor, shuffling her feet through ash and stones. Animals howled in the distance and people screamed in hysteria. A thunderous rumble from Vesuvius filled every cell in her body. She squeezed her eyes shut and listened to popping noises. Breaking pottery?

The falling pumice would pile atop the terracotta

roof tiles throughout the city and Elisabeth knew it was only a matter of time before they collapsed under the added weight, trapping the people seeking shelter inside their homes.

A large black rock sped to the ground like a meteor, smashing at her feet. As she jumped and let out a sharp cry, David yanked her off the field, pulling her back into the corridor.

"I'm all right." She let out a shaky laugh.

David cursed under his breath, sheathed his sword, and pulled her to his chest. "That could have killed you," he whispered.

"I know." Elisabeth's voice hitched and she could feel his heart pound as fast as hers. "I know."

"Um…" Soran cleared his throat. "That giant of a man Elisabeth was hiding from last night?"

David's head jerked back. "Rufus?"

"He's right behind you."

Elisabeth's eyes widened as the slave trader came barreling down the exit tunnel with six of the guards, wearing their blood red tunics and bronze helmets.

"We need to get out of here," Cato said with a shrill voice.

"Stop! That slave is stolen property," Rufus screamed.

Soran jerked his head back and a wide grin spread across his face as he stared at Elisabeth. "You're a runaway slave?"

"Depends who you ask," she called out as David grabbed her hand and limped back onto the arena floor.

"I love it," Soran said with a chuckle.

David grunted in pain while leading them across the field to the opposite archway.

As Rufus and the guards gave chase, two more appeared ahead, blocking the way out.

They were surrounded.

"If we give you the slave, will you let us go?" Cato yelled. "We're on our way to the barracks and have done no wrong."

David squeezed Elisabeth's hand tighter.

"Of course." Rufus walked closer as the falling pebbles rained down on everyone, pinging on the helmets the guards wore. "I'm here to return the girl to Rome. Do I need remind you it is the law?"

When David moaned and doubled over, Elisabeth gasped at the sight of his blood-soaked bandage. She wrapped her arms around him protectively.

"She's not worth it, Aquarius," Cato hissed as his hands clenched and unclenched. He jumped when a heavy rock smashed into the ground beside him. "We're outnumbered and surrounded. Give her to Rufus so we can escape from Pompeii before you bleed to death."

Soran spun around and punched Cato in the face.

Elisabeth jerked her head back, giving the blond gladiator an incredulous look as Cato stumbled back, covering his nose with both hands.

"Sorry," Soran said with a scowl. "But I *really* don't like that guy." He then crisscrossed his arms and simultaneously unsheathed his two swords. "Let's go!" With a guttural roar, Soran went on the attack, clashing blades with several guards at once.

David slapped a heavy rock into his sling, wincing while he spun it over his head.

"Aquarius, look out!" Elisabeth screamed as a guard tried to attack from behind with a sword in one hand and a dagger in the other.

Whirling the sling over his head, David turned around and released one end. She heard a rock clank against metal a millisecond before the dagger dropped from the guard's hand.

Although his sling no longer had a rock in it, David kept spinning the rope above him while glaring at his assailant.

With a roar, the guard raised his sword, charging.

David whipped the rope and the knotted end wrapped around the man's hand. He then flung his arm down, which lowered the man's sword hand as well. David took a step closer, quickly rotating his wrist, winding the rope around the blade. He now had some control of his opponent's weapon, but the two were an arm's length apart.

With the sword pointed straight out, the guard lunged again.

David stepped to the side, punched the rope in his hand toward the ground, forcing the sword and the man down with it. He then unsheathed his dagger, plunging it into the guard's back.

Elisabeth turned away just as Soran cut down another guard. He grinned and flipped one of his swords in the air before going after Rufus.

Even Cato, in his desperation to get out of Pompeii, had drawn his sword. He held it up for protection as he stepped back.

Lightning near Mt. Vesuvius flashed in the sky and David looked ready to collapse as he unleashed rocks and pieces of debris from his sling, over and over again.

Elisabeth curled both arms over her head. Her gaze concentrated on the now unguarded gladiator entrance and an idea came to her. The sound of metal clashing against metal continued and she bolted to the entranceway, running through the storm of ash and pumice, and back into the service tunnel.

Reaching the room she'd found them in earlier, Elisabeth sprinted to the wooden crate and swept the medical supplies off the top with her arms. She then tried to push the enormous box out the door.

Her heart raced, knowing she didn't have the strength to bring it back to the field.

She muttered anxiously, looking around the space. When Elisabeth spotted the wooden hand truck Cato had been leaning on earlier, she let out a huge breath and wheeled it over to the crate. She tipped the box forward to slide the platform underneath, before wheeling it down the passageway, across the uneven dirt floor.

Out of breath, Elisabeth arrived at the entrance to the field and moved the crate onto the sand until it became stuck in the ash and pumice.

"Let them go!" she screamed while climbing atop the crate, flinching when a huge rock crashed in front of her, just missing the box.

David's head jerked back, but then a slow smile formed on his face when he realized her plan. "Do it, *cor meum*. Release the lion!" He bent down to pick up a large rock. "I'd rather be torn to shreds by—"

"What the…?" Soran stared at David with bulging eyes. "Are you both completely mad?"

Elisabeth moved her hand to the latch and Soran held his stomach.

"No…no…" Rufus screamed as the remaining guards bolted for the exits and fled the arena. "It's a ruse. Come back!"

The men in red ran for their lives as she undid the latch.

She couldn't help but grin when the wooden door fell open and Soran raised his sword, ready to fight the lion.

He shook his head and closed his eyes, realizing the crate was empty. "You son of a donkey," he said with a shaky laugh when Elisabeth jumped down and raced toward them.

While Soran and Cato pulled David's arms over their shoulders to support him, Rufus stalked toward Elisabeth. With his mottled skin and extended sword, she no longer saw the ruthless businessman. She now stood face to face with the gladiator who'd survived three years in the arena and earned his freedom.

She turned to run but stumbled over debris. The giant grabbed her hair, yanking her against him. Elisabeth squeezed her eyes shut as pebbles rained down on her face.

"You are the property of the house of Vesta." Rufus moved her into a chokehold and held his sword in front of him. "Stand down and return to your barracks. By law, this slave needs to come with me."

David's neck corded. He shoved Cato and Soran off him and slapped a rock into his rope. His lips pulled back, baring his teeth, and he whirled the sling beside him before releasing one end.

The rock nicked the side of Rufus' head.

When the slave dealer roared, stumbling back, Elisabeth broke free.

David spun the sling over his head, faster and faster. As Rufus lunged with his sword, he whipped the lasso toward the giant's leg. The knot wrapped around Rufus's ankle. With a sharp tug, he sent the giant crashing to the ground. He then unsheathed his sword—his face and neck bright red as he barreled toward Rufus with a battle cry.

Elisabeth gasped when David raised his arms, running his blade down through the slave dealer's chest.

He pulled the sword out and swayed back and forth while glaring at Rufus' body on the ground. With angry tears, David dropped the bloody gladius at his feet.

"Can you not see what she has done to you, Aquarius?" Cato gave him a pained stare. "She's turned you—of all people—first into a fugitive, and now into a cold-hearted killer. Rufus Leptis was obeying the law. She is the one who—"

"Shut up, Cato," Soran warned. "He's a gladiator now."

With an arrogant laugh, Cato motioned toward the empty stands. "Then where is the audience?"

David's breathing was noisy. He yanked Elisabeth into his arms, burying his face in her neck. "*Cor meum*, you'd never be free here...as long as...Rufus..." His back arched. David turned away, his legs buckled, and he collapsed into a heap on the ground.

"Aquarius!" Elisabeth dropped to her knees beside him. "Oh God, Aquarius, don't die. Please don't die." Her voice choked with tears as she looked up at Soran. "I think he's going into shock. He's lost too much blood."

Soran pushed past Cato and lifted Aquarius, carrying him into a corridor, away from the falling debris.

When they lay David down, his eyes fluttered open.

Cato paced back and forth while pinching his bottom lip.

"Soran…" David panted. "Take Elisabeth with you…leave Pompeii." He squeezed his eyes shut and winced in pain. "Keep her safe."

"Aquarius, no. Don't you dare talk like that." Elisabeth brushed tears away and shook her head as she crumpled over him. "I am not…I am not leaving you here. We're getting out of this together." Her chest tightened, knowing even if they managed to get out of Pompeii, David would likely die from the stab wound while on the road.

"I don't really fancy your girl, Aquarius," Soran said while removing a torch from the wall. "So why don't you rest for a while. That way, you can bring her yourself and I'm not stuck…" His voice trailed off when he neared the other end of the short exit tunnel and held the torch up, casting a glow onto the street outside as it continued to rain stones.

Elisabeth stroked the hair off David's brow. His skin felt cool and clammy. As he stared at her with glassy eyes, her breath hitched. "I know what to do!"

"Go." His voice was barely a whisper. "It's too late for me, *cor meum*."

"No." Her eyes widened. "I have to find Balinus. I have to get his medicine for you."

Cato stopped mid-stride. "The old man is here?"

She prayed he hadn't left yet. "I'll be gone a half-hour, at the most."

With a quiet moan, David's eyes rolled back in his head.

"No…no…" Sobbing, she slumped over him, tears streaming down her cheeks. Elisabeth wrapped her arms around him and rested her head on his chest. She could feel the faint beating of his heart. "I'm going to bring you ambrosia," she whispered with an emotion-choked voice. "You're going to live forever, like one of the gods. I *do* want you to become immortal. You have to because…because I can't let you go, Aquarius." She sat up, wiped her eyes, and looked at Cato with a pained stare. "Don't let him die while I'm gone. I am begging you. There has to be a breath of life in him for the elixir to work."

Wide-eyed, Cato nodded his head.

With poor balance, Elisabeth stood and took a deep breath. "Come on, Soran. I'm getting some medicine for Aquarius and you're leaving Pompeii." She ran to the exit and put her arms protectively around her head as she stepped outside.

Chapter Thirty-Two

A block away from the arena, Elisabeth stopped to orient herself. She continued to hold her arms over her head to stop the little stones from hitting her face.

"I know where we are. The city gate is right there." As she pointed to the right, her shoulders slumped when she saw how gridlocked the huge stone archway was. "Thank you for your help." Her voice choked with emotion and she didn't know whether to hug Soran or shake his hand, so she awkwardly patted his arm before turning left and fighting her way down the sidewalk. Polybius' house was eight blocks away. Or was it ten? She'd counted when they first arrived in Pompeii, but now she couldn't remember.

The streets were in mayhem as a wall of people tried to make their way to the city gate, shielding themselves from the storm of pebbles. Holding back a scream when she almost tripped over the body of a dead woman, Elisabeth jumped down from the sidewalk and onto the road, forcing her way through the crowd.

"When you get through the gate, do not stop walking for at least a day and a night," she shouted back at Soran as he continued to follow her. "And just so you know, you're going the wrong way."

A large black rock crashed to the ground beside her.

Soran jumped in front of Elisabeth, moving the

torch to his other hand. "Look, it's my fault Aquarius—"

She screamed when another rock smashed next to her and then cursed under her breath wishing Soran would leave before he was killed. "It's not your fault. Nobody blames you."

They both glanced up when they heard the creaking of beams and then exchanged a wide-eyed look. Elisabeth swallowed her fear and pressed on. Polybius' house had to be close.

Ahead of her, the silhouette of a little girl stood in the middle of the sidewalk, frozen as people pushed past her.

Elisabeth gasped and ran closer. "Larisa?"

As she scooped the little slave girl into her arms, a heavy rock plunged to the earth at a deadly speed, landing in the spot she'd been standing.

Elisabeth's breath hitched and she gave Larisa a tight hug, trying not to cry herself. "You're so brave." She then glanced at Soran, shaking her head in denial as tears blurred her vision. "I'm not leaving her here."

With a dejected sigh, the gladiator reached over and traded the torch for Larisa, shielding her small head from the falling stones. "Don't worry. I won't bite."

The little girl's eyes bulged as she stared at him.

"It's all right," Elisabeth said with a soothing voice. "Soran is a giant hunter too."

With a nervous laugh, he nodded. "You're safe now, kid."

"Elisabeth!" she heard a familiar voice call out.

She held the torch higher, trying to see him through the dusty darkness and falling debris.

"Elisabeth!" Balinus ran toward her from the

direction of Polybius' house.

She let out a huge sigh of relief. "Oh, thank God. Where are the others?"

With a long exhale, he shook his head. "I tried, but they feel it wiser to seek shelter."

Elisabeth jerked her head back. Her shoulders dropped and she gave him a small nod knowing there wasn't enough time to save everyone. "Aquarius needs your help." Wrong or right, David was her first priority, and he was slowly bleeding to death.

Balinus took the torch from Elisabeth's shaking hand. "Let me hold that for you."

"Look out!" someone in the crowd behind them yelled. "THE ROOF!"

The top of a building ahead started to creak and moan. When Elisabeth covered her head and turned to shield herself, she spotted a chained dog, whimpering as it cowered in a doorway nearby.

The people directly beneath the building screamed in terror, pushing and shoving to get out of the way.

With a horrifying rumble, the entire top of the building collapsed. Bricks, wooden beams, and clay roof tiles crashed down into the street, burying part of the crowd beneath it and forming a barricade along this main road.

A woman beside them wailed.

Elisabeth coughed, waved the dust away, and rushed to unchain the dog. Her heart raced when she saw a pair of legs sticking out from the bottom of the rubble, but she climbed up over the debris, trying not to think of the dead bodies beneath it.

The little stones continued to fall, sounding like hail on the roof tops, and the dog raced past her, instinctively heading in the right direction.

"Quick, give me Larisa," she said while holding her hands out once she'd reached the other side.

With the little girl clutching him tightly, Soran climbed to the middle of the rubble and adjusted his footing.

Elisabeth glanced across the street at a young family trying to make it over the mountain of debris as well. A father stood at the top, extending his hand to help his young son over it. He reached for his daughter's hand next and gave her a reassuring smile.

"It's all right. Papa won't let anything happen to you, darling."

As the mother gave the little girl a gentle nudge, a huge rock freefalling from the sky smashed into the father's head.

Elisabeth struggled to catch her breath when the father dropped dead where he'd been standing.

The wife stood frozen in shock while the children became hysterical.

"Papa! Papa!"

The wave of people kept moving and the wife and children were swept away, lost somewhere in the crowd.

With a dazed look, Soran passed Larisa to Elisabeth, then turned around to help Balinus over the barricade before climbing down himself. "Well, you're certainly a brave girl," the gladiator said with his gravelly voice when Larisa jumped back into his arms.

The city gate was straight ahead. She stopped and grabbed the old man's arm. "Aquarius is at the amphitheater, but you have to get her out of here now. Take Soran with you. I'll be right behind with Aquarius and Cato."

The old man glanced at Larisa. "The poor child is terrified." He looked back and nodded. "We'll give her a head start."

"Balinus…" Elisabeth's voice started to quake. "Aquarius was stabbed in the arena. He…he's not going to survive."

Before she could beg, the old man pulled the elixir of life out of his robe and handed it to her. "I trust only you with it," he whispered. "Remember, just the smallest amount."

Elisabeth teared up and hugged him as the little stones bounced off her head and shoulders. "I'll see you soon." She then sniffled and rubbed Larisa's back while looking at Soran. "Cato and I will be right behind you with Aquarius. Get as far away from Pompeii as possible."

Soran leaned closer, wearing his intense stare. "You are a bossy little thing."

She felt her cheeks flush. "Sorry, but—"

He held his hand up to hush her. "And I can see why Aquarius is crazy about you. Go. I'll protect the old man and the kid. Feel free to leave Cato behind," he added with a wink before flashing the tiny slave in his arms a reassuring smile. "The old man and I have a little girl to rescue from a giant."

****

Elisabeth's hands trembled as she made her way back to the arena and through the arched entrance. Her heart pounded, echoing in her ears when she spotted David lying motionless at the other end of the short tunnel.

Cato paced back and forth.

"Aquarius…?" Was she too late?

When David's eyes flickered open she raced toward him.

Cato stepped forward, blocking her. "Where are the others?"

"They're at the gate. I have the elixir and…" She flinched, turning around as the ceiling over the doorway creaked.

"The ambrosia…" Cato said through clenched teeth. "Give me the ambrosia."

Elisabeth cleared her throat and moved her hand behind her back. "Ambrosia?"

"Why did you tell Aquarius you want him to live forever, like one of the gods?" He grabbed her arm and his voice deepened. "What game are you playing?"

With a grunt, David pushed himself up to a sitting position and leaned against the wall. "Back off, Cato…"

"Aquarius…" Elisabeth's chest hitched knowing he needed to remain calm. "Be still. Everything is all right," she said in a reassuring voice.

"It also turns lead into gold, doesn't it?" Cato's grip tightened. "I heard you say as much to Balinus after he gave you the tablet, but I never realized…"

His voice droned on as she stared at the face she'd once considered handsome. The chipped tooth that reminded her of a big dumb jock now made him look like a madman.

Still dressed for the arena, Cato let go of her arm, reached behind his breastplate, and pulled out Elisabeth's crystal necklace.

She gasped and lunged for it, but he shoved her back.

"I am going to prove to you, Aquarius, that I was right all along. There is no happy ending for any mortal who was loved by a god and it is no different for you."

Elisabeth's nostrils flared. David tried to pull himself up.

Cato stepped closer, dangling the necklace, still blocking her from reaching David. "The elixir or the crystal, which do you choose?"

"Aquarius needs the elixir right now!" Her stomach was in knots. "Will you give it to him if I choose my necklace?"

Cato palmed her crystal and stared at the floor. "No." He looked up, pursing his lips. "Why should I? We must live—or die—by our choices. Leaving him here will be the most painful thing I have ever done, but I am already dead to him. Our friendship is dead. I see that now."

Elisabeth clenched her teeth. "That's not fair, Cato—"

"Life's unfair. Make your choice."

"If I choose the elixir, I save David's life; *if* we make it out of Pompeii." Her hands went limp. "But I'll be trapped forever in this timeline."

"*Cor meum…*"

Her chin trembled and she couldn't look at David. "If I take my crystal, I can return home, but I'm leaving him to die. Either way, I choose, I can't win."

The creaking from the ceiling increased. A chunk of plaster fell to the floor.

"I'm sorry. I'm so sorry, Aquarius." Elisabeth's voice quaked and she averted her eyes. "I choose my home and family. I choose my crystal."

Cato let out a quick, disgusted snort. "I told you

you're naught but a plaything to her."

When he grabbed the elixir of life, Elisabeth snatched her crystal from his outstretched palm. She drew a deep breath through her nose and briefly closed her eyes before fastening the chain around her neck.

"Perhaps you were right, Aquarius." Cato stared at the philosopher's stone in his hand and then took several steps toward the doorway when the beams overhead groaned. More dust and plaster fell from the ceiling. "Perhaps we do make our own fate." He looked at David with a grave expression. "I am sorry it came to this, brother, but I warned she would eventually—"

At that moment, the wooden beams and bricks crashed down in front of Cato, trapping David and Elisabeth inside the arena.

When the dust settled, Cato's voice, devoid of emotion, could be heard from the other side of the barricade. "Goodbye, brother."

David winced.

Elisabeth ran to him and lowered his head back down. "He's gone. Everything's going to be all right now."

"You made the right choice, *cor meum*," he said with shuddering breaths.

"Of course I made the right choice." She brushed the hair off his forehead. "I bested him—as you would say."

David's eyes widened.

"Aquarius, you're…" Her voice shook and she pursed her lips to keep from crying. "You're my best friend in the entire world. I'd never leave you to die. Never."

"My Elisabeth," he mumbled.

"Always."

She wiped a stray tear away and reached for her crystal.

****

Elisabeth stood in the upstairs hallway. When she raced back into the study, Mrs. Waters continued coughing.

"Oh never mind. I'll get my own glass of water," the old woman said as she waltzed out of the room.

Elisabeth crossed and uncrossed her arms. "Please, please tell me you have some of the elixir here. I need it—for you."

David's head jerked back and he hurried to the desk. "The stab wound?"

"Yes."

"Is everything okay?"

"No." She leaned across the desk, grabbed his face in her hands, and kissed him. "But I freaking adore you."

He bit down on a smile while handing her a vial from the drawer. "Do you have a safe place for this?"

She glanced down at her gown and shook her head.

David reached into the drawer, switched the top of the vial for one with a chain, and then placed it over her head like a necklace. "Remember, just the—"

"Just the smallest amount, I know."

"Elisabeth…" His eyes turned dark and serious. "There is enough here to keep a man alive for centuries."

Her eyes narrowed in confusion before shuffling back a step. "I understand," she said with a too quiet voice.

"No, I don't think you do," he muttered tearfully to

himself.

"Hey, you and I…" Elisabeth pushed her shoulders back as she stared at him. "We're going to get through this."

She then reached for her crystal.

****

David's breathing was shallow and his eyes lifeless. She put a tiny bit of the red powder onto her fingertip and placed it under his tongue.

"Now, we wait for the elixir to kick in," Elisabeth said, mostly to herself as he slipped into unconsciousness again. She leaned back against the wall, stretching her legs out.

After a while, she curled up on the floor next to him and nervously brushed the hair off his brow, over and over again, trying to ignore the nightmarish sounds from outside. Rocks crashed into the stands above them, people screamed in terror, dogs howled, and buildings crumbled down. She understood why Pompeiians sought refuge inside their homes. It felt safer than being on the streets.

It must have been two hours before David moved his hand. She reached for it, running her thumb across his.

At one point, Elisabeth dashed back to the medical room in search of more cloth and a jug of water for her parched throat. She returned and changed the blood-soaked bandage. The powerful elixir worked fast for the stab wound appeared to be healing.

David's breathing began to deepen.

Finally, his eyes fluttered open.

"Well, hello again," she said with a slow smile and handed him a cup of water.

423

His eyes narrowed in confusion as he glanced around the corridor. With a gasp, he sat up. "We need to get out of here, *cor meum*."

"No kidding," she said with a shaky laugh while helping him to his feet.

Chapter Thirty-Three

"What do you think?" Elisabeth asked as they stood hand in hand at the gladiator's entrance to the arena floor. A small fire burned in one section, and rocks and stones continued to rain down. "It'll be faster."

With the closest exit to the street blocked by the collapsed roof, they needed to find another way out of the amphitheater.

David's brows pulled in as he glanced left and right down the curved corridors. "We don't know if they've caved in further along." He cleared his throat and turned to look at Elisabeth. "I think we should go for it."

"Me too." She swallowed hard as deadly rocks crashed down nearby. "Ready?"

He nodded, squeezing her hand tighter. "I won't let go of you."

They sprinted across the arena floor, slowed by the accumulation of pumice. As black rocks smashed with more and more frequency all around them, Elisabeth noticed the sounds of screaming from outside the walls of the amphitheater had stopped. Anyone who intended to flee the city had already left.

When they were more than halfway across, the ground started to tremble and bounce.

"Earthquake!" David yelled.

Elisabeth lost her balance and as David helped her up, more of the stadium crumbled down, this time blocking the doorway they were heading toward.

A new, thunderous explosion roared from the volcano.

They turned around. Missing sections of the upper spectator stands gave them a perfect view of Vesuvius.

It now spewed fire.

With rasping breaths, Elisabeth watched part of the miles-high cloud of ash collapse over the volcano, triggering a massive avalanche. Smoke and debris swirled and churned, gaining momentum as it plunged down the left side of the mountain.

David covered her protectively. "What's happening?" he screamed.

"Go back! Go back!" she shouted, pulling him toward the doorway they'd just left.

Once inside, David scooped Elisabeth into his arms as she sobbed; positive she'd just witnessed the pyroclastic surge that wiped out the nearby city of Herculaneum. The next surge—in a few hours—would finish Pompeii.

Clutching her upper arms, David pushed Elisabeth back. "You have to go home, *cor meum.*"

"No." She swiped at her tears. "I am not giving up."

"Yes. You have to." His raised voice was shaky. "Go home, Elisabeth."

"No! I am not leaving you here."

"Yes." His hands trembled as he yanked the necklace out of her dress, forcing the crystal into her palm.

"I am not leaving you here, Aquarius," she said

through clenched teeth and tears. "This is my decision, not yours."

"Look…" David's eyes were watery. "I'll find a way out of the city, but this is worse than anything I ever imagined."

She stared straight ahead at the barricade from the collapsed roof before glancing outside. The arena floor continued to pile with debris as thunder rolled, lightning cracked, and deadly rocks smashed into the amphitheater.

The gladiator tunnels were the only possible escape route. If she could get to the opposite exit, they might be able to make their way to the city gate. Her muscles tightened. She let go of her crystal and bolted down the dark corridor to her left, knowing David would follow.

"Elisabeth!" His tone deepened. "Elisabeth!"

As the ceiling creaked and moaned, she sprinted down the curved passage. Her breath burst in and out and she ran past the room they'd been in earlier.

"What are you doing?" David yelled with an emotion-choked voice as he chased after her.

When the corridor began to curve back, she held her breath, hoping the cave-in didn't extend to the exit, but when a barrier loomed ahead of her, she saw she'd been wrong. The entire section had tumbled down, trapping them inside the arena.

Her chest hitched and she spun around, running full speed at David as he hobbled toward her with a wrinkled brow. She threw herself into his arms. "I'm sorry…I'm so sorry." Her chin trembled. "There's no way out."

"Go home, *cor meum*." David's voice quaked as he held her tight. "Please, go home."

427

"Stop telling me to go home because I'm not leaving you here to die, Aquarius." She pulled back and ran her hands over his face and neck, needing to touch him as he moved his head closer to hers. "I can't leave you here." She pressed her lips to his. "We'll find another way out."

"You're so stubborn," he said between panicked kisses. "You're *so* stubborn."

Elisabeth leaned her forehead against his and took a deep breath. "We're in this together." The rope tucked into his belt caught her eye. She then grabbed his hand, pulling him to a run. "I've got an idea."

Chapter Thirty-Four

The wall that encircled the arena floor was taller than they were—to keep both gladiators and wild animals inside—but David managed to leap onto a pile of debris and pull himself over. He flung his arms over the ledge, lifting Elisabeth.

They made their way through layers of rubble and pumice.

David quickened the pace. "Come on."

All the exits from the seats seemed to lead to the same blocked tunnel. Time and options were both running out. They climbed higher and higher.

At the top of the spectator stands, David stared up at the rim and at the wooden masts high above them. "I think your plan might work," he said.

"There—" Elisabeth found a spot where thick rope from the awning hung down.

David raced toward it and gave the rope a tug to test its strength. "Can you climb the wall?"

Elisabeth's head jerked back. "Are you kidding me? I'll never be able—"

"I'm teasing, *cor meum,*" he said with a small smile as he tied the rope around her body like a harness. His breath burst in and out. "I'll pull you up." He then grabbed the rope and, hand over hand, climbed to the parapet of the amphitheater. Working quickly, he knelt on the brick rim and hauled her up as fast as he could.

When Elisabeth reached the top, she untied herself and whimpered while crawling on her hands and knees, too terrified to stand up. The ominous rumble from Vesuvius continued as gray smoke billowed from the volcano. From this height, she could see most of the rooftops had collapsed and the entire city was covered in ash like a blanket of snow. In the distance, a building crashed down. Elisabeth shook uncontrollably. It felt like they were the only two people left alive on Earth.

When David found a section of rope still attached to a winch on the ground, he looped his sling around it. "It's now or never, love," he said with a shaky voice, waving her over.

"Oh, God…" Elisabeth swallowed the lump in her throat, took a deep breath, and sprang into his waiting arm. She clung to David for dear life.

He wrapped his fist around the sling tighter and stepped off the top rim of the amphitheater. The steep incline of the rope sent them speeding toward the ground, but the piles of pumice helped soften the crash landing.

With a shaky laugh, Elisabeth helped David to his feet. "Are you alright?"

"Come here." He let out a huge breath, grabbed her into a hug, and kissed the top of her head. "I am now."

Hand in hand, they raced toward the city gate. They needed to get as far away from this god-forsaken city as fast as possible.

Chapter Thirty-Five

Elisabeth's eyes burned. Across the countryside, David led the way to safety, keeping the volcano behind them as they trudged along. Thunder rolled and the unending storm of pumice continued to rain down on them.

She shook her head in denial when dawn broke along the horizon.

"Come on!" David tried in desperation to quicken the pace.

Moments later, a new and spectacular explosion erupted from Vesuvius.

"Aquarius—" Elisabeth gave him a pale, haunted look.

They both knew it was too late.

The earth shook and Elisabeth lost her balance. She sprang back to her feet as the avalanche of ash barreled its way down the mountainside, this time heading straight toward them.

"No….Oh, God, no…" Elisabeth pinched her lips together. Although she tried not to cry, tears streamed down her cheeks. Fear knotted the pit of her stomach.

David's eyes watered as he clutched her against him.

"Aquarius…" The back of Elisabeth's throat ached from holding back her sobs.

He fished the crystal necklace out of her dress,

wrapping her fingers around it. "How about…" His voice broke. "How about a goodbye kiss then, love?"

As the tidal wave of black ash sped toward them, she pulled back and started crying, no longer able to keep it in. "What do I do? What do I do?" Her hands trembled as she yanked the crystal necklace over her head.

David glared at her. "*Cor meum!* Go home!*"* he yelled.

"Come with me." With the crystal in her palm, she extended her hand. "I don't know if it will work, but we have to try," she shouted over the thundering noise.

The surge—as tall and wide as the Manhattan skyline—sped toward them, burying everything in its path.

David took a deep breath, wrapped his arm around her waist, and pulled her tight. Palm to palm, with the crystal in both their hands, they looked like the tiny dancing couple in the cuckoo clock. Elisabeth buried her face in his chest and squeezed her eyes shut.

"A wise sage once said," David whispered in a soothing voice. "'Loving someone deeply gives you courage, while…'"

The world around her turned to darkness and she was falling. Falling.

Chapter Thirty-Six

Before Elisabeth opened her eyes, she knew it hadn't worked.

Her arms were empty.

She dropped the crystal and the elixir to the floor, covering her face with both hands. "No….no….no…"

As David walked around the desk toward Elisabeth, her head fell back. She gasped for air, trying to get enough oxygen into her lungs.

"Cor meum…"

"It didn't work." Elisabeth's shoulders quaked as she shuffled toward him. "It didn't work." She wrapped her arms around David's waist, buried her face in the crook of his neck, and broke into sobs.

"I'm right here." His voice choked with tears as he held her tight, stroking her hair. "I'm right here."

"It's-not-the-same," she whimpered.

She felt his shoulders drop. "Elisabeth, I'm…still…me," he said with an emotion-choked voice.

Her chest tightened. She pulled away, giving him a pained stare.

When he lowered his head and closed his eyes, she pressed a palm to her lips to hold back a cry.

No matter how you looked at it, the boy she'd fallen in love with was dead.

Gaius Cornelius Aquarius died outside of Pompeii.

Memories attacked her: Aquarius plucking the red ribbon from her hair, Aquarius trying to suppress his cheeky grin when she pretended to be the fortune-teller. Elisabeth crumpled to the floor as thoughts kept pouring in. They tortured her now. She rocked back and forth while wringing her hands.

"*Cor meum…*" David's voice was soothing as he pulled her to her feet. "It did work."

She held her breath while looking up at him. "What?"

"You saved my life." He tucked a strand of hair behind her ear. "I didn't die in Pompeii."

Her eyes clouded with tears and she shook her head. "No. I couldn't save you. Not this time. I know because there'd be two of you with me right now and there's just…" she waved a dismissive hand and her lip started quivering again. "There's just you."

He squinted his eyes, trying to stifle a grin. "So, you're upset because you don't get two of me?"

Elisabeth smiled through her tears and gave David a half-hearted swat. "You know what I mean." Her voice broke again. "The pyroclastic—"

"The pyroclastic surge came." He wrapped his arm around her waist and pulled her against him. "We joined hands," he said while entwining his fingers with hers. "And we both lived."

Elisabeth's head flinched back. "Then, where are you?" She squeezed her eyes shut, realizing the answer. "I've lost you. I've lost you somewhere in time, haven't I?"

"Well now, I wouldn't say that, exactly," Mrs. Waters said as she strolled back into the room. "You just haven't figured out how to use the crystal yet. How to *steer* for lack of a better word."

Elisabeth sniffled and pulled away from David. "Care to enlighten me?"

"It's exactly what you think."

She swiped her tears away. "Exactly what I think?"

The old woman tapped her temple and smiled. "Think about it."

"I have no idea!"

"No, I mean it literally. It's exactly what you think."

"What I think?" Elisabeth's eyes narrowed. "My thoughts control it?"

"Your thoughts control everything. All energy vibrates and your thoughts are a measurable energy. Where do you think a thought goes after you've thunk it?" she asked with a wink. "The crystal is just a conductor of that energy. It amplifies and focuses it, but once you're on that new timeline—"

"Aquarius is alive?" With wobbly legs, she scooped her crystal up from the floor. "I have to find him." She turned to David. "Where are you? How did you get there?"

He looked at her with a soft expression as she held the necklace in her fingers. "Now that, my dear, is the million dollar question."

"Wait...wait...wait," Mrs. Waters shouted. "How's your French?"

Elisabeth took a step back. "I'm still top of my class."

"Excellent." The old woman grabbed a magazine from the desk and handed it to her. "Take this with you."

David snorted and exchanged a knowing look with Mrs. Waters. "Seriously?"

"Why not?" Sissi's eyes twinkled with mischief. "Might as well keep the legend alive."

Chapter Thirty-Seven

Elisabeth opened her eyes and let out a sigh of relief to find she was no longer in Pompeii. A moonbeam from an open window illuminated a cold, shadowy bedroom. The floors, walls, and furniture were all made from the same dark wood and someone sleeping in a chunky canopy bed turned over, pulling the blanket up.

With a quick breath, she eyed the exit ahead of her. Elisabeth clutched the glossy magazine in her hand and tiptoed toward the door.

The floor creaked beneath her weight.

"Who's there?" a man's voice asked in a bastardized form of French.

Elisabeth froze.

The person sat up. "*L'ange*". His voice filled with wonder. "*Es-tu un ange?*"

Angel. Are you an angel?

Elisabeth looked down at her blue gown bathed in the moonlight. She swallowed the lump in her throat and spoke in French. "*Oui, je suis ton ange.*" Yes. I am your angel. With a sing-song voice she turned and extended her hand, offering the magazine to the man in the bed. "*C'est un rêve.* This is a dream…so look upon this book for but a moment. Although you will not understand a single thing in it—"

"Elisabeth…?" With a giggle, the man, dressed in a

shapeless white nightshirt, crept out from beneath the covers.

Elisabeth's mouth fell open. "Balinus?"

He put a finger to his lips. "Let's not wake the wife."

Her head jerked back. "The wife?" she whispered.

In silence, Balinus ushered her out of his bed chamber, quietly shutting the door behind him.

"Oh, my word…" Elisabeth gave a slow, disbelieving shake of her head,

With a wide grin, the old man led her downstairs from the loft-like balcony, into a spacious great hall with a soaring two-story high ceiling.

He grabbed a candlestick from a dining table, lighting it from the smoldering embers of a campfire in the middle of the room. "My dear, girl. I cannot believe you are here." Balinus brought a shaky hand to his forehead while staring at her Roman gown. "You…you just left Pompeii, didn't you?" He put the flickering candle on the table.

Her breath burst in and out as she nodded.

"Nicolas?" a woman's voice called out from the bedroom upstairs.

"Everything is fine, my dear," he called back.

Elisabeth gave him a blank look. "You're married?"

"At last," the old man said with an adorable smile.

She raised her eyebrows. "Wow."

"Perenelle is a lovely—"

"Where's Aquarius?"

He did a double-take. "Aquarius?"

Elisabeth squeezed her eyes shut. "He's not with you?"

Balinus gave a slow shake of his head. "I've seen neither the boy, nor you, for over a thousand years."

"Wait." She shuffled back a step. "What?"

The old man rubbed his chin while studying her.

"You haven't seen me in over a thousand years?" Her brows squished together and then she looked at him with an incredulous stare. "You've been using the elixir of life, haven't you?"

Balinus' gaze darted upstairs for a moment before nodding.

"I've *just* come from Pompeii." Elisabeth's trembling hands fidgeted with the glossy magazine and then her posture slumped. "Thank God you're alive." With a shaky laugh, she reached over, hugging him tight. "Please tell me Soran and Larisa made it safely out of Pompeii."

"Soran and Larisa?" His eyes brightened at their memory. "Yes. They did. We traveled together. All the way to what was once Tyana, my hometown. Soran began a brand new life there." With a grin, Balinus leaned in closer. "As a free man. A…a baker if I recall correctly."

"A baker?" Elisabeth pressed fingers to her smiling lips. "Really?"

He let out a shallow sigh. "That gladiator became a baker and raised Larisa as his daughter."

Elisabeth covered her mouth to stop from squealing. "I can't believe it," she whispered.

"Oh…how that girl loved her Papa," he said with a deep, satisfied breath.

"Oh my gosh." Elisabeth's voice choked with tears. "Finally, some good news."

Balinus turned, giving her a sidelong glance.

"What of Aquarius and Cato?"

"I have no idea what happened to Cato." Hands clenched at the thought of him, she began pacing. "He stole your elixir and left Aquarius for dead in the arena. I hope a huge rock fell from the sky, smashed into his skull and…" She paused, clearing her throat when the old man's eyes widened. "It's Aquarius I'm searching for."

His head jerked back. "What…? Here?"

"He has to be somewhere around here, Balinus." With a furrowed brow, Elisabeth rushed toward what she assumed was the front door.

"Elisabeth…?"

"I've lost him, Balinus. I've lost him somewhere in time." She slapped the magazine into the old man's hand, and threw open a large wooden door, before stepping out onto the moonlit dirt road.

To the left and right of her, half-timbered houses, looking like something out of a fairy-tale, lined either side of the street. "Aquarius!" she yelled while running. "Aquarius!" A choir of chirping crickets seemed to be calling out for David as well.

Ahead of her, an imposing silhouette stepped out of the shadows, walking to the middle of the street.

She slowed to a jog while trembling all over.

Legs planted wide apart, the silhouette stood watching Elisabeth for a moment, before walking, then running toward her.

With a shaky laugh, she raced straight toward the dark shadow and jumped into his arms. "Aquarius…"

Wrapped in his bear hug, David spun Elisabeth around, sending her blue gown twirling around her. *"Cor meum."* With a smile that could not be contained, he slipped his hand behind her knees, scooping her off the ground. "You never kissed me good-bye, love."

With a quivering smile, she touched his face. "It'll never happen again." Her lips met his, blending into a tender kiss—which became two and three and then four.

David put Elisabeth down while taking a deep breath. He stood before her still dressed for the arena. "This is not your time, is it?"

She bit her lip and wrapped her arms around his waist. "No."

"I thought not. It's…it's nothing like you described." He put his arm around her shoulders as they walked back through Balinus' sleepy little village. "I didn't…" His voice quaked. "I didn't think I'd ever see you again." He sucked in a quick breath before kissing the top of her head.

Elisabeth gazed up at him. "I'll always find you," she whispered.

"Aquarius?" Balinus squealed with delight and stepped out of his doorway.

David's eyes widened.

Elisabeth smiled at him. "I was as surprised as you are," she said with a giggle.

Balinus pulled them both into a hug. "Welcome to the fourteenth century my friends," he whispered.

"Nicolas?" his wife called from the doorway with an uncertain tone. "What's going on?" she asked in French. The old woman's head jerked back when she looked at the skirted loincloth David was dressed in.

Balinus answered in Latin. "Perenelle, may I introduce you to my nephew from Rome, Aqu—"

"David." He cleared his throat while smiling at

Balinus' wife. "David Perrier."

The old man's eyes widened. He then nodded his head, pretending he wasn't surprised at all.

With a warm smile on her face, Perenelle stepped closer. "Nicolas Flamel," she pretended to scold her husband, "you never told me what a handsome nephew we have."

Elisabeth's mouth fell open. She stared at Balinus while Perenelle pulled David into a hug. "Nicolas Flamel?"

He tilted his head back and forth before nodding. "The name had a nice ring to it," he whispered.

"You don't know the half of it," she muttered before turning her attention to Perenelle, who was coming at her with outstretched arms.

"And you must be…?"

"I'm Elisabeth," she said as Mrs. Flamel pulled her into a hug.

"Come inside. Come inside. You must be weary and famished from your travels." Perenelle's eyes widened while staring at David's loincloth again. "And cold," she added while rubbing the back of her neck.

Elisabeth reached for David's hand, and with a slow, disbelieving shake of her head, followed *Nicolas Flamel* back into his house.

Author's Note

In 1975, beneath the ash that buried the city of Pompeii, the remains of twelve people were discovered in a house owned by a man named Julius Polybius. Among the victims were six adults, four children—and a heavily pregnant woman estimated to be about eighteen years old.

Research into alchemy will always lead you to Nicolas Flamel. Flamel lived in 14th century Paris and one of his houses, built for the homeless, still stands today, making it the oldest stone house in the city. Legend says he dreamed of an angel who handed him a book of strange pictures, which eventually led him on a quest to discover the secret of how to make the Philosopher's Stone. In the late 1300's, he became inexplicably wealthy and donated much of his money to those less fortunate. Upon Flamel's death in 1418, following that of his wife Perenelle's, he left everything he owned to a nephew named…Perrier.

Nothing at all is known of this mysterious man.

Nicolas Flamel's passing was always questioned, for he was reportedly spotted several times after his death, including at a Paris opera house, in the 18th century.

A word about the author…

An adventurer at heart, Tammy has explored ruins in Rome, Pompeii, and Istanbul (Constantinople) with historians and archaeologists.

She's slept in the tower of a 15th century castle in Scotland, climbed down the cramped tunnels of Egyptian pyramids, scaled the Sydney Harbour Bridge, sailed on a tiny raft down the Yulong River in rural China, dined at a Bedouin camp in the Arabian Desert, and escaped from head-hunters in the South Pacific.

I suppose one could say her own childhood wish of time traveling adventures came true…in a roundabout way.

http://www.tammylowe.com

Thank you for purchasing
this publication of The Wild Rose Press, Inc.

For questions or more information
contact us at
info@thewildrosepress.com.

The Wild Rose Press, Inc.
www.thewildrosepress.com

www.ingramcontent.com/pod-product-compliance
Lightning Source LLC
Chambersburg PA
CBHW070307040726
47501CB00018B/231